The
Sisters

Claire Douglas is a former journalist, writing features for women's magazines and national newspapers, but she'd dreamed of being a novelist since the age of seven. She finally got her wish after winning the *Marie Claire* Debut Novel Award, with her debut novel, *The Sisters*. More recently, *The Couple at No. 9* was a Kindle number one bestseller, *The Girls Who Disappeared* was a *Sunday Times* number one bestseller, and her latest novel, *The Woman Who Lied*, was a Richard & Judy Summer Bookclub pick. She has sold nearly 1.5 million copies of her books.

Claire lives in Bath with her husband and two children.

@DougieClaire
@clairedouglasauthor
/clairedouglasauthor

Also by Claire Douglas

The
Sisters

Claire Douglas

HarperCollins*Publishers*

HarperCollins*Publishers* Ltd
1 London Bridge Street
London SE1 9GF

HarperCollins*Publishers* Ltd
Macken House, 39/40 Mayor Street Upper,
Dublin 1, D01 C9W8

www.harpercollins.co.uk

First published by HarperCollins*Publishers* 2015
This edition published 2024
21

Chapter illustrations © Nicolette Caven 2015

A catalogue record for this book is available from the British Library

ISBN: 978-0-00-759441-2

Typeset in Sabon LT Std by Palimpsest Book Production Ltd,
Falkirk, Stirlingshire

Printed and bound in the UK using 100% Renewable
Electricity by CPI Group (UK) Ltd

In memory of my brother, David,
and for my sister, Sam

I would like more sisters, that the taking out of one, might not leave such stillness.

Emily Dickinson

. . . we're twins, and so we love each other more than other people . . .

Louisa May Alcott, *Little Men*

Chapter One

I see her everywhere.

She's in the window of the Italian restaurant on the corner of my street. She has a glass of wine in her hand, something sparkly like Prosecco, and her head is thrown back in laughter, her blonde bob cupping her heart-shaped face, her emerald eyes crinkling.

She's trying to cross the road, chewing her bottom lip in concentration as she waits patiently for a pause in the traffic, her trusty brown satchel swinging from the crook of her arm.

She's running for a bus in black sandals and skinny jeans, wire-framed glasses pushed back on to bedhead hair.

And each time I see her I begin to rush towards her, arm automatically rising to attract her attention. Because in that fraction of a second I forget everything. In that small sliver of time she's still alive. And then the memory washes over me in a tsunami of emotion so I'm engulfed by it. The realization that it's not her, that it can never be her.

Lucy is everywhere and she is nowhere. That's the reality of it.

I will never see her again.

Today, a bustling Friday early evening, she's standing outside Bath Spa train station handing out flyers.

I catch sight of her as I'm sipping my cappuccino in the café opposite, and even through the rain-spattered window the resemblance to Lucy makes me do a double take. The same petite frame swamped in a scarlet raincoat, pale shoulder-length hair and the too-large mouth that always gave the impression of jollity even when she was anything but happy. She's holding a spotty umbrella to protect herself from another impromptu spring shower and her smile never fades, not even when she's ignored by busy shoppers and hostile commuters, or when a passing bendy-bus sends a mini tidal wave in her direction, splashing her bare legs and her dainty leopard-print pumps.

My stomach tightens when a phalanx of businessmen in suits obscure my view for a few long seconds before they move, as one entity, into the train station. The relief is palpable when I see she hasn't been washed away by the throng but is still standing in the exact same spot, proffering her leaflets to disinterested passers-by. She's rummaging in an oversized velvet bag while trying to balance the handle of her umbrella in the nook of her arm and I can tell by the hint of weariness behind her cheery smile that it won't be long before she calls it a day.

I can't let her go. Gulping back the rest of my coffee and burning the roof of my mouth in the process, I'm out the door and into the rain while shouldering on my parka. I zip it up hurriedly, pull the hood over my hair to guard against the inevitable frizziness and cross the road. As I edge closer I can see there is only a slight resemblance to my sister. This woman's hair is more auburn than blonde, her eyes a clear Acacia honey, her nose a small upturned ski-slope with a smattering of freckles. And she looks older too, maybe early thirties. But she's as beautiful as Lucy.

'Hello,' she smiles, and I realize I'm standing right next to her and that I'm staring. But she doesn't look perturbed. She must be used to people gawping at her. If anything, she looks relieved that someone has bothered to stop.

'Hi,' I manage as she hands me the leaflet, limp from the rain. I accept it and my eyes scan it quickly. I take in the bright print, the words 'Bear Flat Artists' and 'Open Studio' and raise my eyes at her questioningly.

'I'm an artist,' she explains. By the two red spots that appear at the apples of her cheeks I can tell she's new to this, that she's not qualified yet to be calling herself an artist and that she's probably a mature student. She tells me she has a studio in her house and she's opening it up to the public as part of the Bear Flat Artists weekend. 'I make and sell jewellery, but there will be others showing their paintings, or photographs. If you're interested in coming along then you're most welcome.'

Now that I'm closer to her I can see she is wearing two different types of coloured earrings in her ears and I wonder if she's done it on purpose, or if she absent-mindedly put them on this morning without noticing that they don't match. I admire that about her, Lucy would have too. Lucy was the type of person who didn't care if her lipstick was a different shade from her top or her bag matched her shoes. If she saw something she liked she wore it regardless.

She notices me assessing her earlobes. 'I made them myself,' she says, fingering the left one, the yellow one, delicate and daisy-shaped, self-consciously. 'I'm Beatrice, by the way.'

'I'm Abi. Abi Cavendish.' I wait for a reaction. It's almost imperceptible but I'm sure I see a flash of recognition in her eyes at the mention of my name, which I know isn't down to reading my by-line. Then I tell myself I'm being paranoid; it's still something I'm working on with my psychologist, Janice. Even if Beatrice had read the newspaper reports or watched any of the news coverage about Lucy at the time, she wouldn't necessarily remember, it was nearly eighteen months ago. Another story, another girl. I should know, I used to write about such things on a daily basis. Now I'm on the other side. I am the news.

Beatrice smiles and I try to push thoughts of my sister from my mind as I turn the leaflet over, pretending to consider such an event while the rain hammers on to Beatrice's umbrella and on to the back of my coat with a rhythmic thud thud.

'Sorry it's so soggy. Not a good idea to be dishing out flyers in the rain, is it?' She doesn't wait for me to answer. 'You don't have to buy anything, you can come along and browse, bring some friends.' Her voice is silky, as sunny as her smile. She has a hint of an accent that I can't quite place. Somewhere up north, maybe Scottish. I've never been very good at placing accents.

'I'm fairly new to Bath so I don't know many people.' The words pop out of my mouth before I've even considered saying them.

'Well, now you know me,' she says kindly. 'Come along, I can introduce you to some new people. They're an interesting bunch.'

She leans closer to me in a conspiratorial whisper, 'And if nothing else it's a great way to have a nose at other people's houses.' She laughs.

Her laugh is high and tinkly. It's exactly like Lucy's and I'm sold.

As I meander back through the cobbled side streets I can't stop my lips curling up at the memory of her smile, her warmth. I already know I'll be stopping by her house tomorrow.

It doesn't take me long to reach my one-bedroom flat.

It's in a handsome Georgian building in a cramped side road off the Circus that's lined with cars parked bumper to bumper. I let myself into the shabby hallway with its grey threadbare carpet and salmon-pink woodchip walls, pausing to peel a brown envelope from the sole of one of my Converse trainers. I look down to see several letters scattered in the hallway and pick them up hopefully when I see they're addressed to me. They have muddy footprints decorating the front where my neighbours have trodden over them to get to their flat without bothering to pick them up. I flick through them and my heart sinks a little; all bills. Nobody writes letters any more and certainly not to me. Upstairs, in a box on top of my wardrobe I have a stash of letters, notes, museum stubs and other ephemera that was Lucy's. Rescued from her room after she died. We both kept all our correspondence from over a decade ago when we were at different universities, before we could afford computers and laptops, before we even knew how to email.

I push past the mountain bikes that belong to the sporty couple who live in the basement flat, cursing as my ankle scrapes on one of the pedals, and climb the stairs to the top floor. I'm still clutching the leaflet which has started to disintegrate from the rain.

I unlock my front door and step into the hallway, which is much smarter than the cluttered communal entrance downstairs. I'm only renting it but the landlord decorated the walls a pale French grey and installed an antique oak effect wooden floor before I moved in. Then

Mum promptly turned up and swiftly dressed the place with rugs, throws and framed photographs to make the flat look more 'homely', to give the only child she has left a reason to live.

As I hang up my wet coat my heart sinks when I notice my mobile phone on the black veneered sideboard. I pick it up with dread, hoping that I don't have any missed calls, but there are ten. *Ten.* I scroll through the list. Most are from Mum but a couple are from Nia too, along with messages asking me to give them a call, their voices laced with barely disguised panic. I've only been gone two hours but I know they think I've tried to do away with myself. It's been nearly a year since I ended up in *that place* – I still can't bear to think of it – but they still believe I'm unstable, psychologically weak, that I shouldn't be left on my own for too long. I pull the sleeves of my jumper over my wrists, subconsciously hiding the silvery scars that will never fade.

The flat is steeped in dark shadows although it's only a little after five. Outside it looks as if a giant dirty grey sheet has been thrown over Bath. I switch a lamp on in the living room, instantly warmed by the bright orange glow, and sink on to the sofa, putting off ringing my parents. I'll have to do it soon otherwise Dad will speed over here in his acid-green Mazda on the pretence that he's 'just passing' when he actually wants to check that I'm not lying unconscious on my bed surrounded by empty bottles of pills.

My mobile punctuates my thoughts with a tinny

rendition of 'Waterloo Sunset' by The Kinks and I drop it in shock and watch, bewildered, as it body-pops across the floor. Panic rises. I didn't catch the name flashing up on my phone. I don't know who's calling me. My heart starts to race and I feel the familiar clammy palms, the churning in my stomach, my throat constricting. *Calm down, remember your breathing exercises. It must be someone you know. That song means something to you.* 'Waterloo Sunset'. *London. Nia.* Of course.

I almost want to laugh in relief. It's Nia calling. Only Nia. My heart slows and I bend over to pick up my phone. By now the music has stopped and Nia's name flashes up under missed calls.

'For Christ's sake, Abi, you had me worried. I've been trying to get hold of you for hours,' she snaps when I call her back.

'I've only been gone for two and I forgot my phone.'

'What have you been doing?' I detect the thread of doubt in her voice, as though she suspects I've been preparing to hang myself in the woods or stick my head in the gas oven. 'Have you got no work on?'

I suppress a sigh. Work used to be commissioning editor on a glossy magazine. Now it's the odd bit of freelance when I'm up to it, or usually when I'm running low on cash. I know if I'm not careful I'll lose all my contacts. I've only got a handful of loyal ones left, which isn't surprising after everything that's happened over the last year or so.

'Miranda says there isn't much work around at the

moment,' I lie. Miranda, my old boss, is one of the loyal ones. I toss the leaflet I'm still holding in the direction of the coffee table; it misses and, weighed down by the rain, sinks to the floor. It's unreadable now, turned into papier-mâché, but I've made a photocopy of it with my retina. I kick off my trainers then put my feet up on to the velvety cushions and stare out of the sash window over the rooftops of Bath, trying to pick out the spire of the Abbey among the mellow brick. The rain abruptly halts and the sun struggles to reveal itself from behind a black cloud.

Her voice softens. 'Are you okay, Abs? You're living by yourself now in a place you barely know and . . .'

'Mum and Dad live four miles away.' I force a laugh but the irony isn't lost on me. I'd been desperate at eighteen to go to university to escape my parents and the small town of Farnham in Surrey where we lived. And now look at me. Nearly thirty years of age and I've followed them, like a stalker, to this new city where they've come in a bid to try and rebuild their fractured lives. Not much chance of that with me hanging around, reminding them of what they've lost.

I can't bring myself to tell Nia about Beatrice. Not yet. Not after last time. She'll only worry.

'I'm honestly fine, Nia. I was walking around Bath and then it began to rain so I went for a coffee. Don't worry about me. I love it here. Bath's peaceful.' *Unlike my mind,* I add silently.

'Peaceful?' she scoffs. 'I thought it was full of tourists.'

'Only in the summer. I mean, it's busy, but not as frenetic as London.'

She falls silent and there it is. All that's unspoken between us, wrapped up in one word. London. I know she's thinking about it. How can she not? It's all I think about when I speak to her. That cramped Victorian terrace that the three of us shared. That last night. Lucy's final hours.

'I miss you.' Her voice sounds small, comfortingly familiar with its soft Welsh lilt. For a second I close my eyes and imagine how my life used to be; the hustle and bustle of London, the job that I had loved, the array of glittering parties and glamorous events thanks to Nia working in fashion PR, Lucy and Luke, Callum . . .

But looking back before that night is as if I'm looking back at someone else's life, it's so different to the one I lead now.

'I miss you too,' I squeak, then I force myself to make my voice sound cheerful. 'How is it, living in Muswell Hill? Anything like Balham?'

'Different, and yet the same. You know what I mean,' she sighs. I know exactly what she means. 'Abs, I've got to tell you something. I've been worrying about it for ages. I'm still not sure if you should know.'

'Okay . . .' I feel a sense of unease.

'It's Callum. He's been in touch.'

I wait for the panic to descend upon me. But nothing, apart from a slight fluttery sensation behind my belly button. Is that what the antidepressants have done to me? Dulled the sensations, the memory of him? I try to conjure up an image of his six-foot-two-inch frame, his almost-black hair, his heavily lashed blue eyes, those tight jeans and leather jacket. I loved him, I remind myself. But he too is wrapped up in the memories of that night. He's been sullied for ever, as has everything else.

'What did he want?' I'm trying to sound nonchalant but I know Nia won't be fooled. She's my best friend and she was there, she knows how much he meant to me.

'He asked me for your number. He wants to talk.'

'Shit, Nia,' I gasp, taking ragged breaths. 'Did you give it to him? Does he know where I live? If he knows, he'll tell Luke. You promised me that you wouldn't tell them where I've moved to. You promised.' My voice is rising as I think of Luke's face the last time I saw him, frozen in grief as he told me calmly that he would never forgive me for Lucy's death. His words, along with his detachment, were as painful as the blade I took to my wrists.

'Abi, calm down,' she urges. 'I haven't told him anything. I don't even think Callum lives with Luke any more.'

'I'm sorry,' I gulp, making an effort to suppress my anxiety, my fear. 'I can't speak to him. I can't. Ever again . . .'

'It's okay, Abi. Don't worry. I haven't told him anything about you. I have his number, if you ever decide that you're ready to speak to him . . .' she trails off.

I stay silent, knowing I'll never be ready. Because to speak to him would mean revisiting the night I killed my sister.

Chapter Two

Beatrice's house stands on the left-hand side of a tree-lined cul-de-sac. Huge Georgian terraces that reach up to the cloudless sky in all their Bath stone, five-storeyed glory stand proudly on both sides of the road, and where the street widens, there are gated tennis courts, presumably for the private use of the residents.

The sun is at last blazing as if in celebration of the first day of the May bank holiday weekend and I can hear the buzz of a lawnmower in the distance, the yappy bark of a dog. I shrug off my leather jacket, bundling it up and cramming it under my arm as I hover on the pavement outside the address in Pope's Avenue that I've memorized from Beatrice's leaflet. A white Fiat 500 with two parallel stripes in green and red is parked on the road in front of the wrought-iron gate. Large stone steps lead up to a wide royal-blue door with the number nineteen etched in the glass of the fanlight above. Can this be the right place? It all seems too monied, too posh. It's certainly not the student digs I'd been expecting.

Before I can talk myself into leaving I'm pushing open the gate and walking up the short black-and-white-tiled pathway, past a fat ginger cat cleaning itself on the manicured lawn. I hesitate, my throat dry, before pulling back the old-fashioned brass doorbell. A wave of nausea washes over me as the ding-dong of the bell reverberates behind that ornate door that any minute will open on to the next stage of my life.

I wait, heart thumping. Then I hear the dull thud of footsteps and the door is thrown back to reveal Beatrice, a huge grin on her face. She's barefoot with black nail varnish decorating her toes; a wispy charcoal dress falls to her knees in sharp contrast to a pretty silver pendant which hangs between her two small breasts. A delicate tattoo of a flower weaves its way around her ankle like a vine.

'I'm so glad you're here.' She looks genuinely pleased to see me. 'Come in.' She guides me into a long wide hallway with creamy flagstones that match the outside of the house and I take in the elaborate coloured chandelier that hangs from the ceiling, the coat stand that looks as if it might buckle under the weight of all the coats hanging off it, the daisy-shaped fairy lights that weave along the balustrade of the stairs leading to a higher floor, the daisy-shaped rugs (she must have a thing about daisies) and the old-fashioned school-type radiator that's been painted pink. The house smells of Parma violets mixed with a faint whiff of cigarette smoke.

'Wow,' I can't help but say as my eyes sweep the hallway. A vase of fresh daisies sits on an antique console table next to a small glass ashtray which is overflowing with bunches of keys. The leopard-print pumps she wore yesterday sit neatly next to the radiator. 'This place is amazing. Whose is it?'

She looks at me in astonishment for a second, before emitting her already familiar tinkly laugh. 'It's mine, of course. Well, mine and Ben's. Come on, everyone's downstairs.' She leaves the door on the latch, so that she doesn't have to keep answering it, she explains. Not that she wants to take it for granted that people will come. 'It's my first open studio,' she says. 'There are quite a lot of us in this street who are opening their houses up this weekend and a few in other streets, so all in all it should generate some interest.' She seems jittery, excited, pink-cheeked and almost skips down the hallway. I follow, wanting to know who this Ben person is that she mentioned. If she's married it might change things.

We pass two big reception rooms, one with a paint-splattered canvas propped on to a large easel and the other with a strange smooth white sculpture that resembles Cerberus, the Greek mythical three-headed dog. It gives me the creeps.

The flagstone staircase curves down into a big square basement kitchen with hand-painted chunky units in a dove grey. The worktops are pale marble with a darker

15

vein snaking through it that reminds me of a Stilton. A wooden table dominates the room where two young girls and one man sit drinking and chatting. A broad-shouldered plump woman with nose piercings and frizzy dyed-black hair pulled back so tightly that her eyebrows arch up in surprise, stands at an old Aga nursing a cup of something hot, judging by the steam coming off it. When she notices me hovering behind Beatrice she smiles warmly, flashing a gold tooth. 'Hi, I'm Pam,' she says in a thick West Country accent. 'Are you Beatrice's sister? You're like two peas in a pod.'

Beatrice laughs a little too loudly. 'I haven't got a sister,' she says, before turning to me. 'I've always wanted one though,' and a lump forms in my throat when I think of Lucy, and I know that my instincts are right about Beatrice.

She places an arm over my shoulder protectively. 'Everyone, this is Abi. She's our first . . . what would you call it? Potential client?' Beatrice raises an eyebrow questioningly. I'm aware of all these pairs of eyes on me and it makes me want to run straight back to the security of my little flat. I'm not used to meeting new people, not any more. I spend my life – my new life – keeping my head down and my emotions in check, and here I am in this massive, funkily decorated house with strangers.

'You've come to see our art?' says Pam. 'That's splendid. It's probably obvious we haven't done this before?' She laughs, it's loud and booming and I warm to her straight away.

I stand mutely. When did I become inept at making

small talk? Although I know the answer. Lucy was always the gregarious one out of the two of us. Beatrice squeezes my shoulder as if she can read my thoughts and I'm grateful to her. I know she understands me already.

'Pam paints amazing pictures and she lives in one of the attic rooms,' says Beatrice. Taking her arm away from my shoulder she turns to indicate the pretty girl with a bleached blonde pixie cut perched at the table. 'And this is Cass, she's a fantastic photographer. She lives here too and sitting next to her is Jodie. She's a sculptor.' I nod at Cass, and then at Jodie, who looks not much older than Cass, with mousy brown hair, striking blue eyes and a sulky mouth. I imagine she's responsible for the three-headed monstrosity upstairs.

Beatrice leaves my side to skip over to the only man in the kitchen, the man I've been trying to avoid looking at even though I've sensed his eyes on me since I walked into the room. He stands up as she approaches, lanky but substantially built. 'And this is my Ben,' she says, wrapping her arms around his waist. She only comes up to his shoulder. He looks a similar age to Beatrice, with a freckled face, hazel eyes and tousled sandy-coloured hair. With a jolt of realization I note that he's handsome. Not my usual type but good looking nonetheless. He's dressed in smart indigo jeans and a white Ralph Lauren polo shirt. I glance at his left hand to see if they're married and for some inexplicable reason I'm relieved when I see the absence of a ring. I can't quite fathom why this pleases me so much or if it's her or him that I want to be single.

To my annoyance I blush. 'Hi,' I say shyly, thinking they make an attractive couple. 'Are you an artist too?'

His eyes scan my face and I get the sense that he's trying to place me, that I remind him of someone. 'Definitely not. Some people might say I'm a piss artist, but I don't think that counts,' he grins. He has a soft Scottish accent, more pronounced than Beatrice's. He sounds like David Tennant.

Beatrice prods him in the side. 'Ben,' she admonishes, 'don't put yourself down. My brother's the clever one, he's into computers,' she explains, glancing at him fondly. Brother. Of course. Now that she's said it I can see the resemblance: the identical smattering of freckles over a ski-slope nose and full mouth. Only their eyes are different. She disentangles herself from him almost reluctantly and claps her hands. 'Right, come on, everyone, let's get to our stations. Abi, why don't you come with me – I could do with an honest opinion on how I've set everything up. Is that okay?'

I nod, flattered to be asked, and we all troop after her as though we are her obsequious maids. As I'm following the others up the stairs, I turn to glance behind me. Ben is still standing in the middle of the kitchen. My eyes meet his and I quickly turn away and run up the remainder of the steps, my cheeks hot.

'I haven't got a studio at the moment,' says Beatrice as she ushers me into her bedroom, propping open the door with a floral cloth door-stop. Pam, Jodie and Cass have disappeared into their own rooms to begin setting up, although I can't imagine that Jodie will be selling the three-headed sculpture that I saw downstairs any time soon.

Beatrice's room is huge with its high ceilings and intricate coving. It could belong to a movie star from the 1940s; a velvet buttoned headboard in sable, pale silk sheets and walls the colour of plaster. My feet sink into a champagne-coloured carpet. By the sash windows Beatrice has set up a French-style dressing table with sparkly stud earrings carefully laid out on midnight blue velvet and it has the effect of stars twinkling in the night sky. Behind the earrings is a stand in the shape of a tree. Silver necklaces dangle enticingly from its branches.

'Wow,' I say, going over to the jewellery. 'Did you make all of these? They're brilliant.'

'Thank you,' she says shyly. She's standing behind me so I can't see her face, but by the tone of her voice I imagine she's blushing at my compliment, and I find it endearing that she doesn't know how talented she is.

And then I see it, hanging from one of the branches. A short silver chain with raised daisies intricately arranged in the shape of a letter A. My heart flutters. That necklace is meant for me, I'm sure of it. It's as if Beatrice somehow knew a girl would come into her life with this very initial. I reach over and touch it, running my fingers over the daisies.

'Do you like it?' Beatrice is so close her breath brushes the back of my neck.

19

Claire Douglas

'I love it. How much is it?'

She steps in front of me and lifts the necklace from the stand, draping it over the palm of her hand. She holds it out towards me. 'Here, I want you to have it.'

'I couldn't . . .' I begin, but she hushes me, tells me to turn around so that I can try the necklace on. I lift my hair away from my neck to allow her to place the chain around my throat. Her fingers are cool against my skin.

'There,' she says, her hands on my shoulders, gently steering me so that I'm facing her. 'Perfect.'

'Please let me pay you for it,' I say, uncomfortable with her generosity.

She waves her hand dismissively. 'Call it a thank you for helping me out this afternoon.' She wrinkles her nose in concern. 'You will stay and help, won't you?'

I touch the necklace at my throat. 'How can I resist now?' I joke, not wanting her to know that it was always my intention to stay. And that I would have done so for free.

The afternoon flies by as a steady stream of people trickle into Beatrice's room to view her jewellery. Some are time wasters who have come purely to nose around Beatrice's lovely home, a few are on the way down from the attic rooms after buying one of Cass's photographs, or Pam's paintings. We quickly fall into our roles, Beatrice as the sales person, me as the cashier, and in spite of how busy it gets I find that I'm enjoying myself. Beatrice interacts with everyone with such confidence and aplomb that I can't help but admire her. I'm disappointed when Pam pops her head around the door at seven to ask if they should call it a day.

'Definitely, I'm exhausted,' says Beatrice as she flops on to her bed. Pam rolls her eyes good-naturedly and I can hear her heavy footsteps as she disappears off down the corridor. 'Well, that was good fun. You will stay for a glass of wine?' Beatrice asks me. 'I think we need to celebrate.'

'I'd love to,' I say, although I would prefer to stay up here with her. We've had such a lovely afternoon, the two of us and I've enjoyed her company more than I thought possible. We were a team and I don't want it to end. If we go downstairs I would have to make small talk with the others. I'd have to share Beatrice. I feel slightly deflated as I help her pack the few items of jewellery she has left into their respective boxes.

'I wonder what Ben's been doing all afternoon?' she muses as she forces the lid shut on a bangle. 'I think he wanted to steer clear of the whole thing.' She gives a small sharp laugh but I sense her disappointment that Ben didn't come up to see how she was getting on.

'Is he older than you?' I say as I hand her a pair of earrings.

She takes the earrings from me and shoves them in a drawer. 'Only by a couple of minutes. We're twins.'

I'm aware of the blood draining from my face. *Twins.*
Beatrice pauses. 'Are you okay, Abi? You've gone pale.'
I clear my throat. 'It's . . . well, I'm also a twin. Was

21

a twin. Am a twin.' I'm rambling because I hate telling people about Lucy. I hate the way they look at me, with a mixture of pity and embarrassment, terrified that I might dissolve into tears. Inevitably there is an awkward silence, then they turn away to glance at their shoes, or at their hands, anywhere but at me, while mumbling how sorry they are before they change the subject, leaving me worrying if I've made a massive faux pas by mentioning my dead sister. Some of my old friends have avoided me since Lucy died. Nia assures me it's because they don't know what to say to me, but why can't they understand that saying something, anything, is better than not acknowledging it at all?

I hold my breath, expecting something similar from Beatrice. But she stops what she's doing and looks me directly in the eye. 'What happened?' she asks, and I can tell she genuinely wants to know. She's not pushing me away, afraid of my grief. She's not embarrassed by it. She's facing it head on. I'm so relieved that she's not like everyone else that I want to hug her.

'She . . . she died.' Tears cloud my vision. *And it was my fault,* I want to add. But I don't. If she knew the truth about me it would ruin everything.

'Abi, I'm so sorry,' she says and she places a hand on my arm. 'Do you want to talk about it?'

I pause, knowing I can't talk about Lucy. What is there to say? That she was my identical twin sister, that I loved her more than anyone else in the world, that she was the other part of me, my other half, my better half, and that without her I am lost, in limbo, that it doesn't seem right being alive without her, that it's my fault and that I can never forgive myself even if the courts of law did exonerate me. I shake my head.

'I understand,' she says, her voice gentle. 'Our parents died when Ben and I were small but I still find it hard to talk about it, even after all this time. I don't think you ever get over losing a loved one.'

And in that moment I sense it, the bond between us; formed over a shared grief and the special relationship that can only be understood by twins.

By midnight I've lost count of the amount of champagne I've consumed to stem my nerves and give me the confidence to talk to all of Beatrice's friends. I excuse myself from her gathering and lock myself in the downstairs loo, afraid I'm going to be sick. I should have eaten more. I lean over the sink and take deep breaths until the nausea subsides. I need to go home, I think as I splash cold water on my face and assess myself in the glass of the bathroom cabinet. As always, I jolt at my reflection; at the dark circles under my eyes, the blonde hair that has long grown out of its neat bob, the too-big mouth that always gives the impression of jollity even when I'm anything but happy.

I see Lucy everywhere, but never more than when I look in the mirror.

Chapter Three

The front door slams. Beatrice moves to her bedroom window just in time to see two dark figures weaving out of the front gate and towards the bus stop at the end of the road. They're giggling, stumbling, quite obviously a little drunk. He has his arms about her slim waist as if to keep her from folding in on herself and their pose reminds her of a puppet-master holding up his marionette.

They pass a streetlamp, thrusting them into the spotlight and her stomach falls when she realizes it's Ben. And Abi.

The number fourteen bus trundles past her window like a lethargic old man, the brakes squeaking against the still-hot tarmac as it halts. Beatrice watches as Abi disappears on to it, watches as Ben continues to wave even after the bus has rounded the corner out of sight. It's too dark to see the expression on her brother's face, but she can imagine it. The twinkle in his hazel eyes, the crooked smile on his full lips. It's the look of a man who's been stupefied, it's a look she's only ever seen on his face once before.

And as he turns slowly, reluctantly back towards the house, she knows – in that special way that only a twin can – that this is the start of something.

Beatrice thrusts the curtains together so vigorously that they continue to swing even when she turns away from them to pace the room. She refrains from switching the light on, preferring to listen out for the telltale sounds of the key in the lock, the clip-clop of Ben's Chelsea boots on the flagstone hallway, the thud as he climbs the stairs two at a time to her room. Why does the realization that her brother might have found someone he likes make her want to cry?

He flings open the door, flooding the bedroom with light from the landing.

'Why are you in the dark, you mad cow?' he laughs, flicking the switch.

She shrugs and perches at her dressing table. Ben sits heavily on her double bed, the mattress sighs under his weight. 'Cass and Jodie have gone out and Pam has fallen asleep at her easel again. So, how do you think it went?' He seems genuinely concerned for her, which tugs at her heart.

'Okay, I guess.' She pulls the earrings from her ears. 'I sold some pieces of jewellery. I gave Abi a necklace.' She watches Ben's expression carefully in the mirror, looking for signs. She notices the shy smile at the mention of Abi's name, then his eyes meet hers and the smile snaps off his face.

He frowns. 'Are you okay, Bea?'

'I saw you with Abi.' She knows she shouldn't but she can't help it. 'You fancy her, don't you? That wasn't in the plan, Ben.'

'Plan?' A pulse throbs in Ben's jaw and Beatrice knows she's made him angry. 'There is no plan. We all spent some time together, got a little drunk, had a laugh, and then I walked her to the bus stop. Not much to tell.'

'You know what I mean. You have to be careful. You know what she's been through.'

'She's a big girl.' Ben lays back on the bed with his hands behind his head, staring at the ceiling. She notices he still has his boots on and this irritates her.

'I'm supposed to be the one helping her,' she snaps. 'And I don't think getting emotionally involved is good for her at the moment.'

'Whatever, Bea. You've obviously decided she's another one of your projects.'

'Projects?' she says querulously. 'This is more than a coincidence, Ben . . . It's a sign.'

'I know, you've already said.' Ben sits up again and sighs. 'Look, I've had a lot to drink. I'm going to bed.' He gets up and leaves the room, letting the door slam behind him.

Beatrice stares at herself in the mirror. She refuses to cry. Instead she swipes at her eyes with a cotton pad doused in oily make-up remover, then cleanses her face and throat in rhythmic strokes.

She'd known as soon as she met Abi who she was. Those big green eyes had tugged at her memory before she even had the chance to reveal her name. But the name had cemented it, of course. Abi Cavendish. The Cavendish twins. Their delicate heart-shaped faces had peered endearingly out of the newspaper reports at the time, unknowing of the future that lay ahead for them. She'd got home yesterday – was it only yesterday? – and retrieved the newspaper cutting hidden between her bras and knickers in her underwear drawer and shown it to Ben, prodding it with an excitable finger, telling him that it must mean something. Didn't he see, she urged, didn't he see that this was fate? She'd cut that piece out of the paper over a year ago, and now, nearly a year to the day, she meets the very girl from the story. She told him that if Abi turned up for the open studio then it was a sign that this was the woman that Beatrice was meant to help.

And she did turn up. See, Ben? Fate.

Beatrice swipes angrily at her face with her cotton pad. No, she mustn't obsess. Today has been a good day, a success. Not only has she taken the first steps to becoming a bona fide artist but she has Abi in her life.

She knows she's done something terrible, unforgivable. But by helping Abi she can begin to put things right. She can Be A Good Person. Karma.

She has to do whatever she can to ensure that this time Ben doesn't stand in her way.

Chapter Four

Returning to my cold, empty flat after the warmth, noise and babble of Beatrice's vibrant house makes me feel like a dog that's been banished from its family home to a kennel in the garden.

The silence bears down on me oppressively, reminding me that I do live on my own, that there is no Nia clattering around the kitchen making endless cups of tea, or Lucy curled up on the sofa tapping away at her laptop. Even though they've never lived with me here, in this flat, I still can't get used to being without them, still expect to see the ghosts of them around every corner. It's one of the reasons I left London.

I switch on the lamp and when I cross the living room to close the curtains I catch sight of something, *someone*, on the street below. My heart quickens. A man is standing by the front gate, I can barely make out his silhouette against the inky night. He has his collar turned up, a cigarette hanging moodily from his lips; the detail of his face is unclear, shadowy, a pencil drawing where his features have been rubbed out, but the shape of his head, the lanky figure, is so familiar I instantly know it's Luke. It's Luke and he's found me. I fumble for my mobile that's in the pocket of the jacket I'm still wearing, desperately scrolling for my parents' number with trembling fingers. Then he looks up at my window, his eyes briefly meeting mine and I freeze. I watch, my mobile still in my hand, as he flicks his cigarette to the kerb and saunters down our garden path to ring the bell of the flat below. It's not Luke, of course it's not Luke. Nia would never break her promise to me. But it's an unpleasant reminder that I'm not the only one who can't forgive myself for what happened that Halloween night over eighteen months ago.

I sprint around the flat in a sudden frenzy of drawing curtains and switching on lights. When my heart finally slows and my breathing returns to normal I settle on the sofa with a cup of coffee and call Mum. I need to hear a comforting voice after the fright I've had.

She sounds husky, as if I've awoken her from sleep and I realize it is past midnight. 'Abi? Are you okay?' I imagine her sitting up in bed in her flannel pyjamas, her heart racing, expecting to hear me in tears, so I quickly explain that nothing is wrong. And then, without thinking, I tell her about Beatrice. I mentally slap myself when I hear the apprehension in her voice as she answers, 'This isn't the same as before is it, love?'

29

'Of course it's not,' I snap, my cheeks burning when I think about Alicia.

She hesitates and I can tell that there is a lot more she wants to say, but my mother has always been a great believer in thinking before speaking. Instead she says how wonderful it is that I've found a friend, that I'm beginning to settle in Bath. Then she reminds me, as she always does, that I need to keep seeing Janice, that I mustn't forget to take my antidepressants, that I have to do all I can to make sure I don't end up in *that place again* – she lowers her voice when she says this last bit, in case the neighbours can hear through the walls that her daughter has been in a mental institution.

When she eventually rings off I sit with the phone in my lap. I'm consumed with an urgency I've not felt for a long time when I think of tonight, of Beatrice. The dancing in her living room after all her potential 'clients' had gone home, her cool, arty friends, the wine we drank so we were floppy and silly and finding everything hilarious, and then afterwards when the lights went down and we all slumped on to Beatrice's velvet sofa, me squashed in between her and Ben so that each of my thighs touched one of theirs; believing for the first time in ages, that I belonged.

I touch the necklace at my throat, the necklace that Beatrice has made with her own two hands. She's the one, surely? Even our names merge with each other – Abi and Bea – Abea. Does she sense it too? This connection, this certainty that we are supposed to meet?

Then the darkness washes over me, dousing my joy. I don't deserve to be happy. Guilt. Such a pointless emotion, Janice constantly tells me that, yet I am consumed by it tonight. *You were found not guilty, Abi.* I can almost hear Lucy's soft voice, her breath against my ear, as if she's curled up on the sofa next to me, and then to my surprise, my own, deeper voice, coming out of nowhere, bounding off the walls of my tiny flat so that it startles me: 'I'm so sorry, Luce. I'm so sorry. Please forgive me.'

Two days pass without a word from her. Two days holed up in my flat with the rain drumming on the skylights in the roof, the fluke hot weather of Saturday a distant dream. Mum rings and invites me over, but I decline, telling her I've got some work to catch up on, when in reality the thought of spending the bank holiday with my parents but without Lucy makes the grief bubble back up to a dangerous level. Our family resembles a table with a leg missing; incomplete, forever ruined.

I know it's not healthy for me to be on my own for too long, it gives me more time to obsess, to think about Lucy, to remember her last night; the panic, the fear. It comes back to me in moments when I least expect it, when I'm lying in bed on the edge of sleep, or when I'm perusing Lucy's page on Facebook, re-reading the condolences from her three hundred-plus Facebook friends. I can suddenly smell the wet grass mixed with the smoke from the engine, see the blood caked on Lucy's head, her beautiful but eerily still face as Luke cradles her in

31

his arms, hear Callum shouting desperately into a mobile phone for an ambulance, feel the touch of Nia's comforting hand on my shoulder as I crouch by the tree, the bark rough against my back, the metallic taste of blood on my lips and bile in the back of my throat as she whispers over and over again that Lucy's going to be okay, in a futile attempt to reassure me, or herself. And the rain, so much rain, coming down in sheets so that our clothes clung to our bodies; coming down like tears.

To vanquish the relentless, soul-destroying thoughts, I try to remember Beatrice's soft Scottish accent, the hurried excitable way she talks, her warmth, her humour. I'm still unsure if she knows about what I've done – a quick Google search would reveal everything. Is that the reason she hasn't got in touch? Who wants to be friends with someone who's killed her own twin sister?

I have a connection with Beatrice, even more than I first thought. Not only is she a twin too, she's lost someone close to her, she understands me. Now that I've found her I know that I can't let her go.

It's still raining when I turn up at her door clutching an umbrella and cradling a bunch of large white daisies. I pull the bell and wait, jumping back off the stone step in alarm when a brown spider with yellow flecks drops in front of my face then desperately clambers its way back up its own silvery thread to the fanlight above.

There's no answer so I wait a few more seconds before

stepping forward to pull the bell again. When nobody comes to the door, I lean over the iron railings and peer into the ground-floor window where, apart from an easel and a couple of bookshelves crammed with irregular-sized, glossy hardbacks, it's empty. I'm about to reluctantly leave when my eye catches a flash of something at the window of the basement, what I remember as being the kitchen. It's fleeting, a blur of hair and clothes, but it makes me uneasy and the familiar paranoia creeps over me, causing sweat to pool in my armpits. I know with a certainty that I didn't feel this morning that I'm not wanted. Am I making a nuisance of myself, as I did once before with Alicia? The feelings I'd thought I'd long since buried of that time – before I was sectioned, when I thought in my grief-addled mind that Alicia was some kind of soul mate – resurface, making me nauseous. Could I have got Beatrice so very wrong like I did with her?

Before Lucy died, I was fun, hard-working, popular within my group of friends. Now look at me. I've become the sort of person that others try to avoid, to hide from. My eyes sting with humiliated tears, blurring my vision as I stumble back down the tiled pathway towards the bus stop, the daisies wilting in my arms.

The voice is almost lost in the wind but I can just make out someone calling my name. I turn and there she is, standing in her doorway in her bare feet, toenails bruised with black nail varnish, wearing a blue spotty vintage tea-dress underneath a chunky cardigan, waving frantically at me and smiling. Relief surges through me

33

and all the old doubts crawl back into the recesses of my mind where they belong as I trot towards her.

'I'm sorry,' she says as I get nearer. 'I was on the phone, talking to a client, oh I'm so thrilled to be saying that. I've actually got a client. I wasn't going to answer the door until I saw it was you. Come in, come in.' She's talking in her usual fast, excited manner and I can't stop grinning.

I cross the threshold into the hallway, breathing in the familiar Parma violet smell I already love so much and handing her the now crumpled-looking daisies. Confusion alters her features for a moment so she appears older, sharper. 'Are they for me?' she frowns. When I nod self-consciously, explaining that they're a thank you for the necklace, she takes them from me and smiles shyly, her face softening again. 'Thanks, Abi. But you didn't have to. I wanted to give you the necklace. You did me a huge favour on Saturday. Do you want a cup of tea?'

I tell her that I'd love one. Dumping my wet umbrella on the doormat, I nudge off my trainers, relieved that I remembered to put matching socks on this morning, and follow Beatrice through the hallway, the flagstones warm under my feet – of course, she would have underfloor heating – and down the stairs to the basement kitchen. 'I love your house,' I say as I admire, yet again, the high ceilings and intricate coving, the Bath stone floors and Farrow and Ball painted walls. Considering it's full of young people, the house is surprisingly tidy.

By now we've reached the kitchen and I shrug off my

wet coat and hang it on the back of the chair to dry
before taking a seat at the wooden table and it's as though
I've come home. A fluffy ginger cat with a squashed face
is curled up asleep on the antique-looking armchair in
the corner. Beatrice follows my gaze and informs me the
cat, a Persian called Sebby, is hers. Lucy loved cats too.

'He's getting old now,' she says fondly. 'He mainly
likes to snooze.'

The house is quieter than it was on Saturday, with the
dripping of rain on an outside drain the only sound to
be heard, and I hope that it's only the two of us here. I
didn't notice the little white Fiat with its red-and-green
stripe parked outside. Ben told me the other night that
the car was his and I recall making a joke about why a
tall man would want to drive such a small car.

I watch as Beatrice busily runs the taps of her deep
Belfast sink to fill a vase and then plunges the flowers
into it. 'These are lovely, thanks, Abi,' she says as she
arranges the flowers. I notice some of the daisies have
drooped over the side of the vase. 'That's kind of you to
say you love this house. I think it's quite special, but
maybe that's because of the people who live in it with
me.' She turns to me and flashes one of her amazing
smiles and a lump forms in my throat when I think of
my empty flat.

'It's a huge house,' I say. How can an artist and someone
who works in IT afford a pad as luxurious as this?

'It is. Too big for me and Ben. So it's nice that we've
got the others living here too, although Jodie is moving

on.' An emotion I can't quite read passes fleetingly over her face like a searchlight. I play with the necklace at my throat, waiting for her to elaborate. She looks as if she's about to say something further then appears to change her mind. 'Let me put the kettle on,' she says instead. 'It's a pitiful day and it was so sunny at the weekend. Honestly, this weather.'

'Is Ben at work?' I ask. Her narrow back stiffens slightly at the mention of his name. I watch as she pours boiling water into two cups, pressing the teabags against the side with her spoon, her fair hair falling in her face, and I find myself longing to go over to her, to push her silky hair back behind her ear so that it's no longer in her eyes.

'Yes. He only works contract.' Her voice sounds falsely jovial and it occurs to me that perhaps they've had a row. 'I don't completely understand what he does, but I do know it involves computers.' She laughs as she hands me the mug of tea and pulls out a chair opposite me and sits down. 'What about you, Abi? You said on Saturday you were a journalist?' Even when sitting, Beatrice seems to ooze energy; her legs jiggle under the table, her elegant fingers tap the side of her white bone china mug. She takes an apple from the bowl of fruit in the middle of the table and indicates I do the same. I murmur my thanks and choose a dark-red juicy plum, but when I take a bite it is hard and sour.

'I used to work for the features pages for one of the nationals, in London,' I say through a mouthful of plum which I manage to swallow with difficulty. 'That was before I got my dream job on a glossy magazine. But I've done my fair share of news too. I used to work at a press agency and spent a lot of time hanging around the houses of famous people or public figures. We call it door-stepping, although some might call it stalking.' I laugh to show I'm joking but Beatrice smiles seraphically and I wonder what she's thinking. She takes a bite of her apple and chews it slowly, thoughtfully. 'But now I freelance and things are a bit slow,' I add hurriedly, wanting her to forget the stalker comment.

'Is money a problem?' She looks at me with concern and my cheeks burn. Judging by her lovely expensive-looking clothes and this beautiful house, money isn't a problem for Beatrice. I don't want her to think that's the reason I want to be her friend.

'No,' I lie. 'My parents have said they will help out if I need it. And I can always go and live with them if I can't afford to pay rent any more.'

'I've had an excellent idea,' she almost shouts, her eyes bright and her cheeks pink. 'Why don't you move in here?'

'Here?' I'm so shocked that I can barely form the words and almost choke on a piece of hard plum. Of course, there is nothing I'd want more than to move in with her, to be with her all the time.

'Oh, it's perfect,' she says, jumping up and dropping her apple in her exhilaration. I watch as it rolls across the table, falling off the end on to the tiled floor. Beatrice ignores it and stares at me, an intensity that I haven't seen before in her eyes. 'I was so upset when Jodie said she wanted to move out. But it's fate, it's so you can move in here with us. I should have thought of it before. Durrr!' She actually slaps her own forehead with her hand and pulls a silly face, making me giggle. Her enthusiasm is infectious and the thought of moving into this stunning house, living with people again rather than rattling around my empty flat makes me want to bounce happily around the kitchen. 'Why don't you come and view the room now? I think Jodie's gone out. Oh, it will be such fun if you move in.'

'But . . .' This is all going too fast and my heart begins to race. I'm not sure if I can do this, if I can start living a normal life again rather than my current hermit existence.

'There are no buts, Abi. We got on so well on Saturday. I was so nervous about the showing, but you made it such fun. You'll come to love the other girls. Pam is larger than life and such a laugh, and Cass is a sweetheart . . .' She holds out her hand. 'Come on.' She smiles. Her eyes are wide with excitement, making her look even more beautiful. I think of how great it would be, living with Beatrice and not being alone any more; it would be like having a sister again, and I can't stop the smile spreading across my face.

'You're right,' I say as I take her outstretched hand, allowing her to pull me gently to my feet. 'It will be perfect.' And I follow her out of the kitchen, leaving the sour plum on the table behind me.

Beatrice's bare feet make a slapping sound on the stone steps as we climb the winding staircase and I touch one of the daisy-shaped coloured lights that have been wound around the banister, excitement building at the thought that soon this beautiful house could be my home. The heady scent of Parma violets hits me again and I'm aware it's coming from Beatrice. It must be her perfume or the washing powder she uses for her laundry. Either way, it's intoxicating.

When we reach the first floor I can't resist poking my head around the door of the huge sitting room that runs the length of the house, remembering from Saturday the velvet squashy sofas, the artefacts that Beatrice has collected from her travels to places such as India, Burma and Vietnam, the French doors leading out to a large terrace overlooking the garden. I remember the frisson of exhilaration I felt, wedged between Ben and Beatrice on one of those sofas, wine glasses in hand, chatting away as though the three of us had known each other for years.

Beatrice stops halfway up the next flight of stairs and turns in my direction with a questioning rise of her finely arched eyebrow.

'I'm only being nosey,' I admit as she continues up the stairs. I fall in behind her. 'And remembering Saturday night.'

Claire Douglas

She laughs her endearing tinkly laugh. 'It was a great night – and there will be many more like it if you move in. Jodie's room is up here, next to mine. And Ben's room is opposite, next door to the bathroom. Then, upstairs we have two more bedrooms, the attic rooms, which Cass and Pam use. They have their own bathroom, thankfully, as usually one of them is ensconced in there, dyeing their hair. I expect you remember all this anyway, at the open studio event the other day.'

I nod, not wanting her to know how accurately I've memorized the layout of her house; then she really would think I was a stalker. We reach the landing, pausing outside one of the first doors we come to. It's painted in a creamy white with a solid brass knob for a door handle. There's no lock. Beatrice raps her knuckles gently against it. When there is no answer, she pushes the door. It opens with a lingering creak.

The room is so at odds with the rest of the house that it's as if I've been teleported into a student bedsit. It smells of unwashed bedding and dirty clothes mixed with something acrid, chemical. I give a little start. Jodie is lying on the single bed that's been pushed up against the wall to make way for two more ugly sculptures. She has huge earphones clamped on either side of her head, her eyes are closed and she's quietly mouthing the lyrics of the song that she's listening to. I can't quite make it out, but it sounds slow and angsty. I survey the large room with its indigo walls blu-tacked with many posters of gothic bands from the early 1980s, the high ceilings and marble fireplace, and try to imagine it as my bedroom. Two sash windows that are nearly the height of the wall face on to the street below and the identical five-storeyed houses opposite. A silver birch in the front garden bends and stretches in the wind, its leaves casting dappled shadows on the grubby-looking carpet.

Jodie's eyes snap open and she pulls the headphones from her ears.

'Sorry, Jodie, I did knock,' says Beatrice, not looking particularly contrite.

Jodie sits up and swings her legs over the side of the bed, glaring at us sullenly. She's wearing a huge black T-shirt with a silhouette of Robert Smith on the front which makes her look about twelve. Her legs are pale, her calves adorned with so many moles they remind me of a child's dot-to-dot drawing.

'Do you remember Abi?' says Beatrice. Jodie nods gruffly as I say hello, her bright blue eyes surveying me so intently it's as though she can read my thoughts, that she knows all about me. My heart skitters and I mentally recall Janice's words, the mantra she taught me to calm myself when I sense a panic attack coming on.

Jodie turns to Beatrice, her little face pinched into a frown. 'I only told you I was moving out yesterday and already you've found a taker for my room.' She gets up and steps into a pair of grey skinny jeans that are in a coil by her bed.

'It wasn't planned, Jodie. It only occurred to me a few minutes ago when I was chatting with Abi downstairs,' says Beatrice casually, as she walks over to one of the gargoyle-esque sculptures. I might not know much about art but surely anyone can see her sculptures are hideous.

'Is she an artist?' she says, as if I'm not even in the room. When Beatrice shakes her head, Jodie's frown deepens. 'I thought you only let artists live here?' I can sense the animosity emanating out of every pore in Jodie's body. I stand awkwardly by the door, feeling like an intruder. Beatrice opens her mouth to reply but Jodie cuts her off with a shrug. 'Whatever. It's none of my business any more. I'll leave you to it.'

As she stalks towards me I instinctively breathe in, but instead of walking past me to go out the door, she stops so that her face is inches from mine. 'For some reason, she desperately wants you here,' she says in a low voice. I glance to where Beatrice is standing on the other side of the room, examining the sculpture, running her hands over its beaky nose and making appreciative noises, much to my surprise. My eyes flick back to Jodie as she continues, coldly: 'I'd watch my back if I were you.' And then she storms off, leaving me staring after her in bewilderment.

Chapter Five

Beatrice perches on her new antique leather sofa, watching as the hands of the reproduction 1950s clock on the mantelpiece move around to five thirty, its every tick pulsating through her fraught body. Any minute now, she thinks, he will be home. Her heart gives a flutter of anticipation when she hears the key in the lock, the slam of the front door, his boots on the stone tiles, his soft Scottish burr calling her name, and she tries to second-guess how angry he will be when he finds out what she's done.

'I'm in here,' she calls back.

He pokes his head around the door and frowns when he notices that Jodie's three-headed sculpture has been replaced by an unfamiliar leather sofa and a large mahogany desk.

'Where's Jodie?' He comes into the room, dumping

his laptop bag by the wall. Beatrice glares at it pointedly, concerned that the ugly black bag will mark her freshly painted lime-green walls. 'And what have you done to this room?'

Beatrice swallows. 'I've repainted it.'

'In a day?'

She shrugs. 'It didn't take long.' She decides he doesn't need to know about the decorator she paid to help her out. Her knees jiggle and she pulls the skirt of her cotton dress over them in a bid to still them. 'And Jodie's gone.'

Ben shakes his head as if struggling to process what his sister is telling him. He ignores his bag and Beatrice bites back the stirrings of irritation. 'Jodie's gone? Gone where?'

'Back to her parents' house.' Beatrice makes an effort to keep her voice even; she knows it unnerves Ben when she becomes too animated, and she can't reveal to him how excited she is. 'Her dad came to pick her up this morning. Thankfully, she's taken those sculptures with her. They took up too much room. And now I can have this as my studio instead of using my bedroom.'

Ben glances around the room as if he is expecting Jodie to be hiding behind the long drapes that frame the French windows. He runs a hand over the prickly stubble that's beginning to show on his chin. 'I don't understand. Why has she left so suddenly? She's said nothing to me.'

Beatrice gives him a long, scrutinizing gaze, then says cuttingly, 'You know why she left.' It gives her pleasure to note the way his hand moves to loosen his striped tie, as if it's choking him, the beads of sweat that bubble around his hairline. He pales, causing his freckles to look more prominent.

'Because of what she overheard?'

She nods. 'It was careless of you, Ben. And you're never normally so careless.'

He paces the room and groans. 'I know. I'm so fucking angry with myself.'

She winces at his display of frustration. 'Anyway,' she says, in an effort to placate him. 'Luckily, no harm done. Although she says you told her to leave.'

He stops pacing and stares at her, his hazel eyes wide. 'Of course I didn't,' he bursts out. 'Why would she say that? And why hasn't she spoken to me about it?'

Beatrice shrugs. She's enervated by the whole experience. She's past caring about Jodie.

'And where has this come from?' he says, walking across the oiled wooden floorboards to stand next to the sofa. He runs his hand along its curved back. 'This must have cost a bomb.'

'That's what the Trust is for,' she says. 'I ordered it last week. I was always going to ask Jodie to move out of this room anyway. It wasn't fair that she'd taken this over as well as the bedroom upstairs. She wasn't paying any rent.'

'You never asked her for any rent,' he says.

'It's not about that,' she snaps. 'We don't need the money.'

Ben takes a seat next to her on the sofa and places a

soothing hand on her bare arm. Even though his fingers are warm, the gesture makes her come out in goosebumps. 'Bea, what you're doing is great.'

She turns to him, suspecting sarcasm but his hazel eyes are full of admiration and she's overcome with love for him. *Oh, Ben, I'm doing all this for you,* she wants to tell him, but knows she can't. He won't understand, not yet.

She takes his hand. 'What *we're* doing, Ben. We're in this together, remember?'

They sit in companionable silence and Beatrice thinks that maybe she won't tell him about Abi yet, that it will only spoil this precious, rare moment when it's the two of them, alone. He moves his hand from her arm and snakes it around her shoulder, pulling her to him, and she sighs contentedly as she leans against him. He's still *my Ben,* she thinks. *My twin.*

And then he has to go and ruin it all by asking the inevitable question.

'What are you going to do with Jodie's room?'

Beatrice detaches herself from his embrace and moves over to the fireplace. She kneels down in front of it, the draught from the chimney blowing against her bare legs and methodically, and for no reason other than to stall Ben, she places a log from the nearby bucket on to the cold grate, trying to remember the last time they lit a fire in this room.

She hasn't mentioned to Ben about Abi turning up unannounced two days ago, clutching those pathetic daisies, a sad, haunted expression in her big green eyes. She had stood by the gate, soaking wet and tiny in her oversized parka, looking so frangible that Beatrice's heart had gone out to her. What she felt for Abi, in that moment, was almost maternal. She wanted to fold her in her arms and tell her that everything was going to be okay, that she, Beatrice, was here to help her.

Ben won't understand, she thinks as she carefully lays another log in the grate, playing for time before answering her brother's question. Because she knows that any burgeoning feelings Ben might have for Abi will have to be quashed and she's not sure how he will react. They have an unwritten rule, no romances between housemates. He plays it down, of course, but she saw the look he gave Abi at the open studio, the way he made a beeline for her at the party afterwards. She understands exactly why he's attracted to her. Vulnerable, a little shy, slim and fair-haired. Abi's completely his type.

'Shall we get someone else to move in?' he says, cutting into the silence impatiently.

She stands up, rubbing her knees, and faces Ben, wanting, needing, to see his expression, but before she even opens her mouth his face falls as what she's planned finally dawns on him. *Oh, Ben, you know me so well,* she thinks.

'You've already asked Abi to move in, haven't you?' His eyes are hard, sharp. A hunted animal.

I'm sorry, Ben.

'You didn't even bother to ask me. It's my house too.'

She can't help but feel a flicker of remorse as he gets up wordlessly from the sofa and leaves the room, the door banging closed behind him.

Chapter Six

Monty's house, or rather, his mansion with its gabled roof and turrets, sits grandly at the top of a steep hill overlooking Bath. A crescent moon floats above the chimney and I think how eerie the house looks in the fading light, how gothic. I'm almost expecting to see bats swarming around one of the towers. It gives me an unwelcome flashback to Halloween, to that night over eighteen months ago, to that fateful party we attended, the argument that resulted in us all leaving earlier than planned.

Beatrice sidles out of the taxi, elegant in her black shorts and opaque tights that show off her long, shapely legs. I follow her as we pick our way over the gravelled driveway. The cacophony of voices, clinking of glasses and the beat of some dance tune floats through the open windows, alerting us that the party is already in full swing.

'Are you okay, Abi?' asks Beatrice as she stops to extricate her stiletto heel from the gravel, leaning on me for support. 'I imagine these things are hard for you.'

Beatrice hasn't asked me any more about Lucy, which I'm relieved about. That way I don't have to lie to her. Would she still want to hang around with me if she knew about Alicia and how I ended up in a psychiatric hospital after Lucy's death? I pull the sleeves of my blouse further over my wrists to hide the evidence of my downward spiral.

'I'm fine,' I lie. I'd been so flattered when Beatrice rang me up and asked me to Monty's party. Not only does she want me to be a housemate, but she's invited me to be part of her group of friends too, to be part of her life. All the same, my anxiety levels are high this evening, despite the antidepressants.

'Isn't this place amazing?' she says, in an effort to lighten the mood, linking her arm through mine. 'Monty is minted. Ha, Minted Monty, that's what we should call him.' She laughs at her own, rather feeble joke while my heart pounds uncomfortably in my chest.

Beatrice told me she'd met Paul Montgomery, or Monty for short, after he'd given a talk while she was studying for her MA at the university, and they had become 'great friends' apparently. 'He's gay and very flamboyant,' she says. 'And quite a successful artist. His parties are legendary.'

I take a deep breath before we push our way through the heavy front door and the heat hits me like an invisible wall. I find it hard to swallow, my tongue sticking to the dry roof of my mouth. There are people everywhere, clusters of them on the landing, milling about the hallway, languishing against door frames with easy smiles, glasses of bubbly in their hands. Waiters dressed in black and white manoeuvre expertly through the crowds, refilling glasses surreptitiously and handing out hors d'oeuvres from silver trays. The music pulsates in my ears, making my heart beat even faster, my pulse pounding painfully in my throat. I always knew this was going to be difficult, the first party without Lucy.

I suddenly glimpse her amongst the knots of people gathered on the sweeping staircase, a floaty scarf around her long neck, her familiar encouraging smile playing on her too-large mouth, but when I blink again she's gone. Beatrice glances at me, mouthing if I'm okay and when I nod she squeezes my hand reassuringly, telling me I'm doing fine and to stay close to her. I follow her swishy bob, my hand gripping hers as we snake our way through the hordes of jostling bodies, in the same way I used to follow my sister whenever we went to parties or clubs.

It was always Lucy and Abi Cavendish and never the other way around. She was two minutes older than me, my better half, the brighter, shinier, more intelligent twin. I was the runt of the litter. As my mum was always so fond of telling us, as a baby I was the sickly one who suffered from acid reflux, whereas Lucy thrived, consuming all the milk and solids that she could get her chubby little mitts on. In the faded photographs taken with Dad's instant Polaroid camera from the mid-1980s, square-shaped and yellowing, the corners curled with age, Lucy and I sit together on a sheepskin rug in front of a stone fireplace or on a picnic blanket on the lawn of our garden, two almost identical toddlers dressed in matching clothes, her pudgy-thighed and cute and me, her stunted skinny twin, Lucy's distorted mirror image.

Even at school she made friends easier than I did; she had a natural, breezy way about her, whereas I was too intense. When she suggested we join in with the other girls in the playground I would stick out my lower lip and shake my head, which infuriated her. She was a social butterfly and I was clipping her wings. I wanted her all to myself, as if I somehow knew, even then, that the time we had together would be short, finite. When Lucy did play Hide and Seek or Tag with the other kids, I would drift around the playground by myself, inventing stories in my head of the great adventures we would have, just the two of us.

It was only at university that I stepped out of Lucy's shadow. I had no choice. With her brains she was always going to be accepted at a red-brick, Russell Group university; my parents wanted her to be a doctor, and she didn't disappoint them. I, on the other hand, only ever aspired to the local poly, although I think I surprised everyone, myself included, when I got into Cardiff to study journalism.

Lucy would have walked into this party with her head held high, as if she belonged in this world of wealth and art and I would have followed, her confidence rubbing off on me like body glitter.

'Beatrice, my pretty darling,' booms a loud voice and a big bear of a man with a frizzy beard, who looks to be at least fifty years old, parts the crowd. 'I'm so glad you could make it.' He's wearing a dazzling print shirt that's open at the neck and strains over his ample stomach. They busily air-kiss each other and then turn to me. 'So, this is Abi,' he says, his chocolate brown eyes meeting mine. 'I've heard a lot about you. I'm Monty.' He gives my hand a hearty shake. 'Come and get a drink.'

They walk off together, leaving me trailing behind them. I can see the strap of a blood-red bra poking out of Beatrice's black vest top and cutting into the flesh of her shoulder. I can't quite catch what they are saying above the boom of the music.

We reach a huge, high-ceilinged drawing room with white walls, the coving and Georgian shutters painted a lead grey. Monty thrusts a glass of something orange into my hand and then resumes his conversation with Beatrice and I'm hit with a twinge of jealousy that he's taking up so much of her time. I take a gulp of my cocktail; it's so strong the alcohol burns the back of my throat, coating my anxiety, and before I know it I've finished the glass and taken another one from the tray of a passing waiter. I feel light-headed as my eyes sweep the room, noticing the many gilt-framed oil paintings of scantily clad, angelic-faced men and women, almost like modern versions of Botticelli, that adorn the walls. I recognize the paintings as being Monty's own work. Beatrice had shoved a leaflet from his most recent exhibition under my nose while we were in the taxi on the way here. His paintings aren't to my taste.

I catch snippets of conversations about artists I've never heard of or books I've never read, and I'm reminded of the parties in London that I attended with Nia and Lucy. They were similar to this; glossy, monied people, effortlessly cool and confident. But I didn't mind that I never quite fitted in, because I had Nia and Lucy, and we usually only went along for a laugh and a free goody bag.

A cluster of thirty-somethings are dancing rather self-consciously in the corner to Happy Mondays. I turn my attention back to Beatrice, relieved when I see Monty drifting away from her to talk to an elegant woman in her mid-sixties. Beatrice raises her eyebrows at me and wrinkles her nose. 'Is that woman wearing a real fur stole?' she giggles. 'Look, it's even got a head.' She seems to find this hilarious and I stare at her, perplexed; how many cocktails has she been plied with? 'Come on, let's go and explore,' she says. 'I've always wanted to have a nose around Monty's place.' She takes my hand and we make our way through the different rooms, all as huge and elaborate as the drawing room and filled with people drinking cocktails or champagne. It's like being in a Stephen Poliakoff film. My heart pounds in my chest. Not with the usual anxiety but with a growing sense of exhilaration at being so near to Beatrice. Her confidence, her joy, is infectious. When I'm with her I experience that heady rush of adrenalin at being around someone who I admire so much. She makes me believe that I can do anything, be anyone.

Giggling and clutching each other, we stumble across a small music room and dump our now-empty cocktail glasses on top of a glossy cream piano. 'At last,' sighs Beatrice as she leaps on to a Chesterfield leather sofa, dangling her long legs over the arm. 'A room with nobody in it. There's too many people at this party. And my feet are killing me.'

To emphasize this point she kicks off her high heels and stretches her toes, webbed like a duck's in her opaque tights. I plonk myself next to her, grateful for a break from the relentless music and chatter and noise that accompanied us around every room as if we were being chased by a swarm of bees. The lighting is dim and I'm flattered that Beatrice is comfortable enough with me to lean back against me. I breathe in her smell; her perfume, the apple shampoo from her hair. We sit this way for a while in companionable silence. Me, upright against the stiff back of the Chesterfield, with Beatrice using my lap for a pillow, her legs stretched out so that she takes up most of the sofa.

Without consciously thinking about it, I reach out and gingerly brush her fair hair back from her face. It's so fine, the skin of her forehead as soft as velvet. Her eyes are closed and at my touch she exhales contentedly. And as I stare down at her beautiful face, so similar to Lucy's yet so different, my feelings for her merge like the paints on a palette until they become murky, unclear. On one hand she's becoming a friend, a sister . . . and yet, just out of reach, a shadow in my peripheral vision, I'm experiencing another, unfamiliar feeling. I lean over her, studying her delicate features. Her eyes are still closed, her long lashes casting shadows on her smooth cheeks and I suddenly long to kiss the freckles that fan across her nose, to touch the clavicle in her throat. I imagine kissing a girl would be softer, sweeter somehow. I lean over her, my mouth hovering above hers and time seems to slow down.

As if reading my thoughts, Beatrice opens her eyes and lifts her head from my lap in one swift movement and I shrink back against the sofa, my face burning at what I was almost compelled to do. What was I thinking? Those two cocktails have obviously gone to my head. I don't fancy Beatrice. The feelings I have for her are confused in my mind, that's all. *I admire you, Beatrice,* I want to yell. *You remind me of Lucy. You're the sort of person I wish I could be and you're so beautiful. Reminiscent of a sculpture, a piece of art.* But the words won't come, it's as if my brain has been stuffed with cotton wool, and I can only stare at her as she swings her legs from the arm of the sofa, bending forward to pull on her heels.

If Beatrice suspects the internal struggle I'm having with my emotions, if she knows I was moments away from kissing her, from making the biggest fool of myself, she doesn't let on. Instead she jumps up and offers her hand to me. 'Come on,' she says, her usual bright bubbly self. 'Let's go and dance.'

I take her hand and follow her humbly from the room.

The mood has changed when we re-enter the drawing room. Someone has dimmed the lighting and a monotonous house tune that is devoid of a chorus or verse is thumping away. Monty is swaying in the middle of the floor with a drink in his hand and his eyes closed.

I open my mouth to comment when I see a girl I recognize weaving her way through the sweating, heaving crowd towards us. She's wearing a cute babydoll dress that suits her petite figure and her bleach-blonde pixie crop has been gelled off her face. Her large dark eyes are entirely focused on Beatrice. 'I've been looking for you everywhere,' she says querulously when she reaches us. Her voice is thin and reedy. And then it hits me who she is: Cass, the photographer who lives with Beatrice.

'Cass, you remember Abi?' Beatrice says. 'She's going to be our new housemate.'

Cass drags her eyes reluctantly from Beatrice to murmur a hello before turning her gaze back to her. 'I need to talk to you,' she says.

'Okay,' says Beatrice, taking her hand, as she did with me half an hour earlier. 'I'll be back soon,' she says, flashing me an apologetic smile and I have no choice but to watch as they walk hand in hand further into the room and I can't help the white-hot flame of hurt that flickers in the pit of my stomach.

I consider calling a taxi and leaving. I'm humiliated by what happened with Beatrice in the music room, and now I've been jettisoned for Cass. There is no reason for me to stay. I hover in the doorway self-consciously and I'm about to make a run for it when I spot a familiar face in the crowd by the large bay window. He's dancing with two guys and a girl I've never met and he doesn't notice me at first. I watch as he moves his body with the confidence of someone who knows they can dance. A waiter breezes past and I take another cocktail from his silver tray and sip it while staring at Ben; at his long legs encased in dark indigo jeans, at the crisp white shirt that's open exactly the right amount to show off his tanned neck and contrasts with his expensive fitted char-coal blazer. I'd forgotten how attractive, how sexy, Beatrice's twin brother is.

Then, as if he's sensed me assessing him, he lifts his hazel eyes in my direction and he grins at me and I draw breath. He is extremely good looking. He stops dancing and we drift towards each other like two magnets and I'm unable to stop the smile spreading across my face. He's so tall, taller than I remember, his sandy hair longer and more tousled, and before I know it we're face to face. I suddenly have the urge to throw myself into his arms, to nuzzle against his chest, inhaling his lemony scent. He's so different to Callum, the eternal student with his scruffy trainers and mussed-up hair. Ben seems more sophisticated, more grown-up somehow, even though at thirty-two they are the same age.

I process Ben's full sensual mouth, his freckles scattered across the bridge of his straight nose. They belong to him but they are part of Beatrice's beautiful face too and it suddenly occurs to me, in that moment, that some of Ben's attraction is that he's *her* brother, her *twin*. He's the male version of her.

'Abi,' he says, his lips twisted in a smirk. 'Fancy seeing you here.'

'Hi, Ben,' I say shyly. 'I came with Beatrice.'

'Of course you did.' He's smiling but I notice a coldness to his tone and his eyes flicker to where Beatrice is standing with Cass. She turns in our direction, a scowl decorating her pretty face and it has the same effect on me as a child's scribble would have on a famous painting.

'Have you two had a row?' I ask, shocked at the animosity I detect in Beatrice's eyes. Or was that aimed at me?

'You could say that,' murmurs Ben, much to my relief. Ben doesn't take his eyes off Beatrice. It's almost as if they're having a staring-out contest, maybe a game from their childhood and I'm frozen out, invisible, it's the two of them, always the two of them. How can there be room for a third? I realize I'm holding my breath, waiting.

Then his gaze snaps back to meet mine and I exhale, grateful that I've got his attention again. 'I'm desperate for a cigarette,' he says. 'Do you want to join me in the garden?'

I follow him back through the chequered-tiled hallway, edging past a group of lads hanging out in the kitchen and dump my half-empty glass on the worktop before stepping into a large garden. It's a fresh spring night and I wrap my arms around my thin blouse, wishing I had brought a coat but relieved that at least I'm wearing jeans and not the one skirt that I possess.

'Here, have this, you look freezing,' he says, inching off his blazer and placing it over my shoulders. The light from the kitchen casts a glow over us and I can see the outline of his slim body through the cotton fabric of his shirt. He huddles nearer to me, cupping his hands around his lighter as he sparks up his cigarette, the tip crackling and glowing as he takes a puff and then offers the packet to me. I haven't smoked in a long time, but I take one gratefully, thankful that I have a use for my hands. He lights it for me and I inhale deeply, instantly calmer as the nicotine travels to my lungs. *Oh, I've missed this.*

'So,' he says, exhaling puffs of smoke that disappear into the dark night. 'I hear we're going to be housemates.'

I stamp my feet against the cold and nod. 'Not until mid-June. I've got to give my landlord a month's notice on my flat.' I take another drag on my cigarette.

'It's a shame you're moving in,' he says, a shy smile on his lips. I stare at him mutely, disappointment coursing through me that Ben doesn't want me to move in. Have I offended him in some way? We seemed to get on well at the party on the night of the open studio.

'We have a house rule, you see,' he says gravely. 'No romances between housemates. Beatrice is very particular about it.'

My face flames and I try and hide it by blowing on my hands theatrically even though it's not that cold.

'And I was hoping that maybe you would come out for a drink with me sometime? But I'm not sure that would go down too well, now that you're going to be moving in.' He regards me intently over the tip of his cigarette.

I'm speechless. He's attracted to me, I can hardly believe it. He flicks his cigarette butt into the flower bed where it glows orange against the brown soil before slowly burning out.

'Well, I'm not a housemate yet,' I say shyly.

'That is true.'

We stare at each other and I wonder if he's going to kiss me; my heart bangs against my chest at this unexpected turn of events.

'So you will come out for a drink with me?' His voice is hopeful, his pupils dark as he inches closer.

'I will,' I almost whisper, without breaking eye contact. We stand together for a few moments, neither of us speaking. *Come on, kiss me*, I think.

A far-off peal of laughter breaks the moment and he moves away from me slightly to retrieve his mobile from the back pocket of his jeans. When he asks me for my mobile number, I reel it off to him and he taps it into his phone. Then he rings my mobile so his number is stored on my phone as well.

'No excuses, no saying you've lost my number,' he jokes. 'The joys of modern technology.'

I laugh, knowing I'd never have the nerve to ring him unless he called me first. I'm about to open my mouth to say something when I notice Ben stiffen. His eyes shift away from me to look at someone or something over my shoulder. I turn and see Beatrice standing in the doorway, her long fingers toying with the stem of a champagne glass, staring at us thoughtfully. Cass is nowhere to be seen. She smiles but it doesn't quite reach her eyes and I can tell she's annoyed about something. 'There you are,' she says. 'I was wondering where you'd got to.' I'm unsure if she's talking to me or Ben.

'I'm having a cigarette,' says Ben.

'Oh, Ben, you're so naughty,' she laughs, although I'm not sure she's really amused. She steps on to the patio and stands next to her brother, holding out the palm of her hand and batting her eyelashes at him. Ben sighs and rolls his eyes at me in mock annoyance then rummages in his pocket for his cigarette packet, taps one out on to his hand and places it between her lips where he dutifully lights it. 'I shouldn't,' she says to nobody in particular, snaking her arm around his waist while his languishes over her shoulder and I'm envious of their closeness.

She takes a few heavy puffs. 'Pam and Cass are here too, somewhere,' she says, turning towards Ben and avoiding meeting my eyes. I feel a stab of panic at the thought that I'm being slighted by her. Since she's come outside she hasn't glanced my way once. What if she suspects that I was tempted to kiss her earlier and no longer wants to be friends with me, regrets asking me to move in? I couldn't bear to be cast aside now, not after everything. I don't want to go back to my own, lonely life, rattling around that flat, terrified every time the sun goes down because I'll be alone with my thoughts. I want to move in with her, be part of her life. 'They're having a great time,' she continues, still not looking at me, 'although Pam's a little drunk and flirting with Monty. She's convinced she can turn him.'

I laugh as if this is the funniest thing I've heard in ages. Beatrice turns to me and flashes me a puzzled smile. 'Are you okay, Abi?'

'Actually, I've got a headache coming on.' I urgently need to get away from this party, from this situation. 'I think I'll go home.'

Ben's hazel eyes fill with concern. 'Do you want me to see you home?'

'*I* will see her home.' She shoots Ben a warning look and uncoils herself from him. 'Come on, Abi. I'll call a taxi.' She puts an arm around my shoulder and steers me back into the house, away from the garden and away from her twin brother.

Chapter Seven

It's the second Saturday in June when I finally move in. The sky is a cloudless powder blue and as we drive by the tennis courts I notice a couple of teenage girls in short swishy skirts, showing off tanned, lean legs, rackets insouciantly slung over their shoulders as they chat by the net, and I feel it, the unfamiliar stirrings of excitement at the thought that this is my new life. A new me. For once I am optimistic about the future, hopeful that maybe I can have a semblance of a life without Lucy.

'Nice part of town,' says Dad. He reverses his Mazda in between two parked cars to the right of Beatrice's house. *My house.* I peer out the window and with a twinge of disappointment I see no sign of Ben's little Fiat. Dad switches off the engine and points to number nineteen. 'Is that it?' When I nod he lets out a low whistle of approval. 'You've done all right for yourself.' He chuckles. 'And you don't even have to pay rent.'

'I'm not sure about that,' I admit. 'Mum said I should insist.'

Dad shrugs, then tells me, as he always does, that my mum is probably right, before climbing down on to the kerb. I snatch my mobile phone from the dashboard and follow him around to the back of the car as he opens the boot, revealing my life packed up in an array of cardboard boxes and black bags. He turns to me and my heart pangs at the concerned look in his sea-green eyes. 'Are you sure about this, sweetheart? You can always come and live with us if you don't want to be on your own. Your mum was never happy about you moving into that flat by yourself, and after everything . . .' He clears his throat, but when he speaks again his voice is gruffer. 'Anyway, you don't really know much about these people, do you?'

His concern brings a lump to my throat. A stranger wouldn't be able to see it – his grief – but I can. He wears it like a heavy trench coat, one that he refuses to remove so that he's buckling underneath its weight. It's evident in the greying of his dark eyebrows, the hollowness of his once-rounded face, in the new lines etched into his sallow skin, and I think, *I've caused this*. For a man of nearly six foot two, he seems diminished, shrunken, older.

'I want to move in here, Dad,' I say. If only he knew how much. 'Beatrice has become a friend, she understands me.'

Dad opens his mouth to reply but is interrupted by shrieks as Beatrice and Cass bound out of the house and towards us with Pam ambling after them, grinning good-naturedly.

Since Monty's party I've only seen Bea a handful of times; the vintage fair a couple of weeks ago where she bought two expensive tea-dresses, a trendy bar in the centre of Bath one evening and last Saturday she asked me to accompany her to a showing of one of her favourite artists at the Holburne Museum. Afterwards we met up with Pam and Cass for afternoon tea in the café down-stairs. The day was pleasant enough, I enjoyed the company of the other girls, even if Pam did monopolize me, regaling me with tales of her past, living with a nudist painter, and I tried to concentrate on what she was saying, but it was difficult with Beatrice and Cass murmuring to each other in the corner, the usual pained expression on Cass's pretty elfin face, making me curious as to what they were talking about. I haven't seen Ben since Monty's party. He never did call to arrange to take me out for a drink, and maybe, on reflection, that's for the best. I can't deny that there is an attraction between us, but it's prob-ably not a good idea to get romantically involved with a housemate, particularly Beatrice's twin brother. I sense that she's quite over protective, maybe a little possessive of him.

'Abi,' shrieks Beatrice, throwing her arms around my neck as if she's known me for years. 'Happy Moving In Day!' She laughs her familiar tinkly laugh. Then she unlinks her arms from me and turns to Dad to introduce herself, and I'm amused to see the flush of pink staining his rough skin as she bends in to kiss him on the cheek, informing him how happy she is to finally meet him.

She indicates the mobile in my hand. 'Let's do a selfie. We need to commemorate this day,' she says, pressing her head against mine so that we are cheek to cheek, shoulder to shoulder.

I stretch my arm out, trying to aim the phone so that it captures both our faces and press click. I take half a dozen photos before we look through them, laughing at our cross eyes and silly expressions.

'I could have taken a photo of the two of you, if you'd wanted.' I turn to see Cass standing a little way behind us, the toes of her sandals on the edge of the pavement, her hands behind her back. She's blushing as she says this, but there is something else in her expression, a tinge of petulance, like a child who feels left out because her best friend is giving someone else some attention. I smile warmly at her, but she doesn't meet my eyes.

We each grab a box from the back of the car, and I show Dad into the house and watch, amused, as his eyes widen in surprise as he surveys the vast hallway and the large high-ceilinged rooms that run off of it. I follow his gaze, half-hoping that Ben will be in one of the rooms.

Beatrice comes up behind me hugging one of my boxes, small and oblong, the one that contains Lucy's old letters. I have the sudden urge to snatch it from her. She tells me casually, as if she's read my mind, that Ben had to be called in to work. 'He said to tell you he's sorry he isn't able to help,' she pants, scuttling past me and up the stairs. I trudge behind her despondently, grappling with my own box and wondering if Ben is trying to avoid me.

It takes most of the afternoon to unload the boxes from the car and heave them up the two flights of stairs to my new bedroom, which has been stripped bare of Josie's belongings leaving a narrow single bed, with an iron frame and a sagging mattress that has been pushed up against the wall facing the sash windows. Next to it there is a rickety pine chest of drawers and a bedside cabinet. The indigo walls are marked where Jodie has ripped down her posters, leaving little holes of crumbling plaster where the blu-tac has been. The once champagne-coloured carpet is murky with the tread of numerous footsteps and there's a dubious stain in the shape of a large moth by the built-in wardrobe. My excitement at moving in with Beatrice, at being part of her life at last, is dampened by the state of this bedroom. Apart from its size, the room reminds me of the one I shared with Nia during our student days in halls. The prickles of regret creep over me when I think of my tidy little flat in the centre of town, with its freshly painted walls and wooden floors. I drop the box at my feet and throw open one of the sash windows, taking in lungfuls of fresh air, hoping to dispel the stale smell of Jodie.

'I'll help you paint it.' I hear Beatrice's soft Scottish voice behind me. I turn to see her standing in the doorway, surveying the room, her ski-slope nose wrinkled in disapproval. Her cat, Sebby, weaves himself in and out of her legs. She looks fresh and pretty in her vintage tea-dress, even after lugging boxes all afternoon, whereas my jeans are sticking to my legs and there is a grey stain on my white T-shirt. 'I'm not happy with the way Jodie kept it. I asked her to put mats down when she was working on her sculptures, but she's got no respect for other people's things.'

I can't help but agree and I make a silent vow to look after this room so that it fits in with this beautiful, eclectic house. I glance up at the intricate coving around the high ceilings; a cobweb hangs from a corner, shimmying in the breeze from the open window, and I know with a fresh coat of paint and the carpet cleaned I can make this room my own.

Despite Dad's earlier reservations, I can tell by the slight blush that travels up his neck, the chuckle that emerges from his throat every time Beatrice addresses him, that he's as taken with her as I am. And when he says goodbye a few hours later, he tells me, 'I think you'll be happy here, sweetheart,' and envelops me in a hug. 'It will put your mother's mind at rest at any rate.'

I watch as he strides on his long legs to the car, his tall frame bending almost in half as he gets behind the wheel, and I wave as he pulls away from the kerb and rounds the corner, out of sight. In the distance I hear the scream of an ambulance, the shrill noise at odds with the blue skies, the perfect summer day, and it sends goosebumps all over my body as I imagine the life that hangs in the balance, the family that could be torn apart. I will never be able to hear the sound of an ambulance again without thinking of the night my twin sister died.

We sit around the table drinking wine, our plates empty, relaxed and enjoying each other's company. Pam is in the middle of telling us about bumping into her ex-boyfriend at Monty's party with his attractive, and much younger, girlfriend when Ben walks in and for some reason we all stop talking. The air crackles with tension.

His hair is slightly dishevelled from the humid June day and he's wearing a crisp linen shirt, open at the collar, revealing a tanned neck which I have sudden visions of kissing and I'm shocked at the impact he has on me.

Beatrice pushes back her chair and gets up from the table. 'Ben,' she seems surprised to see him, as if she's forgotten he lives here too. 'There's some lasagne left over.' She goes to the Aga, donning a pair of Emma Bridgewater oven gloves, and carefully lifts out a plate from its innards as if conducting an operation. She places it on the table next to Cass. From the corner of my eye I can see that Ben has taken the seat opposite me and alongside Cass, but I keep my eyes firmly fixed on the burnt curl of pasta left on my empty plate.

'I don't know if you've forgotten, Ben, but Abi moved

in today,' says Beatrice, as she takes her place at the head of the table.

'I haven't forgotten.'

I look up into Ben's hazel eyes, flecked with gold, his familiar crooked smile tugging at his lips and a bolt of desire, so strong and unexpected, shoots through me, causing my cheeks to burn and giving me away. I pull my gaze from his reluctantly and glance towards Beatrice, who is staring at us intently, eyes narrowed, her pale fingers almost merging with the porcelain cup that she's gripping.

And for some reason I can't yet fathom, a sweat breaks out all over my body.

I'm sitting on the edge of my newly made bed later that evening. My room is still in disarray, boxes, some empty, some still full, are stacked around me, the chest of drawers yawns open, revealing the clothes that I'd crammed in there earlier, a pile of books leans against the skirting board, threatening to topple over at any moment. I pick up the framed photograph of me and Lucy that I've unpacked and placed on the table next to my bed. We both look tanned, our arms around each other's neck, grinning into the camera. It was taken while on holiday in Portugal with Callum and Luke, the summer before she died. We had come from the beach and, as we sat on the wall waiting for Luke to return with ice-creams, Callum, ever the photographer, decided to take a few snaps with his camera. Both Lucy and I have, or should

I say *had*, the same photo by our beds. I wonder idly what happened to hers. Did Mum take it when she came to pack up her room, a job I was too distraught to do so I let my poor grief-stricken mother do it instead? The guilt still gnaws at me. I put the photograph down.

The sky is hazy, shot through with violet and orange, the sun about to go out of sight behind the row of houses opposite. An evening breeze filters through the opening in the sash window, bringing with it the aroma of cut grass and bonfires. I close my eyes and inhale deeply, breathing in the smell of summer. *I'm here, I'm actually here at last*. And, when I think about it, getting here has been easier than I ever thought possible. I've managed to become part of her life within six short weeks.

There is a soft knock on my half-opened bedroom door. My eyes ping open and I see a long denim-clad leg, a linen sleeve. I jump off the bed eagerly, causing the mattress to groan in protest.

'Hi,' says Ben sheepishly. 'Can I come in?'

I shrug. 'If you want.'

'I'm sorry I didn't call you, but it's difficult with Bea. Her rules, you know.'

'That's okay, it probably wasn't a good idea anyway,' I say nonchalantly.

The echoes of chatter, Pam's raucous laugh and the clink of cutlery tell me that the others are still in the kitchen and I push the door closed on the darkening hallway with my foot.

I turn to face him, noticing his downcast expression at my words.

'That's a shame,' he says. 'Because I've not been able to stop thinking about you since the party.'

'Really?' I'm annoyed at how eager I sound.

He takes my hand. We are inches away from each other, his eyes are dark and intense in the half light and my heart hammers and I'm trembling with nerves. I don't know who makes the first move, but we are suddenly kissing, his hands in my hair, mine stroking the warm soft skin of his back under his shirt. I've not felt so much desire since Callum. I press my body up against his, so that we're as close as we can be with clothes on. His erection presses into my abdomen, his teeth nip my lips. I don't know how long we kiss for, but I'm conscious that the room has darkened. Then he stops abruptly, pushing me gently away so that I almost stumble on one of my boxes.

'I'm sorry,' he says, running his hands through his hair. 'I don't know what came over me.'

I frown, confused. 'Ben, it's fine. I wanted you to kiss me. I'm glad you did.'

I watch as he walks over to the window, his face like parchment from the light of the moon that filters through the open curtains. Something is clearly troubling him.

'Beatrice has warned me off you,' he says eventually.

'What?' I'm shocked. Why would Beatrice do that? Am I not good enough for her twin brother? 'Why?' For the first time, I'm furious with her.

'Because of your sister, your twin. She told me that she died. I'm so sorry to hear that, Abi.'

I swallow a lump that's formed in my throat. 'Thanks.' I pause, something doesn't add up. I walk over to where he stands by the window. 'But why would that make her warn you off me?'

He turns to face me. 'She thinks you're vulnerable after everything that's happened to you.'

I frown, oscillating between feeling flattered that Beatrice cares enough to worry about me and angry that she's poking her nose into something that is none of her business. 'She doesn't know what happened to me.'

'No, I know,' he says, too quickly. 'But she knows you've been through a lot. Call it woman's intuition, I don't know.'

'I'm old enough to make my own decisions,' I snap.

'That's what I told her,' he murmurs. He grabs me by the waist and pulls me towards him, encircling me in his arms. He lowers his head and I shut my eyes expectantly, wanting, needing to be close to him.

We are about to kiss again when the creak of the door makes us spring apart. I'm sure my expression can't hide my guilt as Beatrice stands there, a shadowy figure in the doorway. 'I thought you might both be in here. Why is it so dark?' She switches the main light on and I blink with the assault on my eyes, little black patches swimming in my vision.

'I'm unpacking, Ben was helping.' I indicate the boxes

stacked behind me, the nearly empty one by my bed. I know I don't sound very convincing.

'Oh, I'll give you a hand,' she says. 'Ben, be a darling and bring up some wine.' Ben scuttles from the room obediently and I notice that his shirt is hanging out of his jeans. He throws me a rueful smile as he leaves and I can't help but grin back.

I half-expect her to question me about Ben, to tell me she knows there's something between us, but she doesn't. Instead she goes to the small oblong box she carried for me earlier, the one that contains Lucy's letters. It's perched on the top of two larger boxes and I hold my breath as she picks it up, silently willing her to leave it alone. *Don't you know how precious that is?* I want to wail. But she's like a magpie with a new shiny trinket. She swivels on her heels towards me, the box in her upturned hands as if it's an offering, a sacrificial lamb.

'This one's been damaged,' she says innocently, and then I notice that the box is squashed and the brown tape holding the two flaps together, its lid, has come apart so the top is gaping open, revealing a hint of the coloured envelopes beneath. Frowning, I take the box from her.

'I'll go and see where Ben's got to with that wine,' she says, brushing past me, a look I can't read in her eyes. When she's gone I slump on to my sagging mattress, the box on my lap. Peeling back the flap of cardboard I take out the stack of pastel-coloured envelopes bound with an elastic band, and idly flick through them. Then, with a spark of realization and dawning horror, I go through them again, carefully counting them, knowing there should be twenty-seven, but even though I leaf through them five times, each time more frenzied, desperate, I can only count twenty-six. A letter is missing. My heart thuds in my chest, bile scratching the back of my throat. One of my precious letters is missing, the only tangible thing I have left of my twin, the only way I still get to hear her voice. It's missing and I know that only Beatrice could have taken it.

The lasagne from dinner curdles uncomfortably in my stomach. Why would she do this to me?

I remember how Beatrice acted in the garden at Monty's party, her calm nonchalance when she saw me with Ben, the way she stared at us both at the table tonight during dinner, and I'm suddenly painfully aware why she would do such a thing.

Beatrice suspects that I fancy Ben and this is her way of punishing me.

I'm bent double, trying to breathe deeply, my chest tight, my head swimming, and I don't hear Beatrice walking back into the room until she's standing over me with a glass of red wine in each hand.

'Are you okay?' she asks, handing me one of the wine glasses, which I take and place on the chest of drawers next to me. There's something tucked under her arm, a flash of coloured paper. She seems to notice the shocked expression that must be evident on my face and follows my line of vision.

'Oh, I think this belongs to you, it has your name on the envelope. I found it on the stairs. It probably fell out of the box when I carried it up earlier.' She smiles at me serenely, retrieving Lucy's letter from under her armpit, and I take it with a trembling hand, confusion clouding my thoughts. Surely I would have noticed the pastel-pink envelope against the cream flagstones? I've been up and down this staircase enough times since she carried the box for me.

'Come on,' she says cheerfully, seeming not to notice my anguish. 'Let's get some of these boxes unpacked. Ben won't be able to help after all, I'm afraid. Monty's popped over and taken him out for a drink.'

Why doesn't this surprise me?

I replace Lucy's precious letter back into the bundle with the others and when Beatrice's back is turned and she's engrossed in sorting through my clothes, I reach up and shove the box on top of the wardrobe, away from her prying eyes.

Chapter Eight

Beatrice hates lies, despises the havoc, the pain that they invariably cause. She remembers only too well the impact, the devastation that ensues when the truth is finally revealed; it is all still fresh in her mind. And now, the all too familiar feelings of betrayal have resurfaced. Why can't she stop thinking about *him*?

She rolls over on to her back, kicking the quilt to the bottom of the bed. The room is musty even though the window is ajar, her legs are slick with sweat, her nightdress sticking to her body like a second skin. She turns on her side, a shaft of light evident underneath her closed bedroom door. Who is still awake at this late hour? Is Abi having trouble sleeping in her new home? Or Ben, unable to relax knowing the object of his affection is across the corridor? She sighs, sitting up and switching on her bedside lamp and reaching for her phone to see the time. It's gone 1 a.m. It's no use, how is she supposed to sleep, knowing that Abi is next door with only a wall between them, with only a landing separating her from her twin brother?

Of course she knows it's only a matter of time before they get together. She can see the attraction between them, as if they have their very own forcefield. It was obvious at Monty's party; did they think she was blind, not to see the way they were looking at each other in the garden that night? She had never even considered asking Abi to Monty's party, but Abi had left numerous messages on her mobile, wanting to know if they could meet up before she moved in. Beatrice had begun to feel harried and in the end invited her mainly to appease her.

Even her stupid house rules will be powerless to stop them, she thinks. She won't be able to keep them apart for much longer and she's naïve to think otherwise. Unless . . .

She swings her legs out of bed and goes to her dressing table, gently touching the jewellery that she's laid out between her face creams and make-up, calming down, as she always does at the thought of her new, burgeoning business. At last she's found something that she's good at, something that helps make up for all the pain in her past. *Oh, Abi*, she thinks as she touches a silver daisy-chained bracelet interlaced with sapphires, the piece of jewellery she's most proud of creating, *we've got more in common than you could possibly know.*

Sitting at her dressing table she opens one of the

drawers and retrieves a ripped-out page from a news-paper, creased and dog-eared and already beginning to turn to the colour of milky tea. She places it on her lap, smoothing it flat in a futile attempt to iron out the lines where it has been repeatedly folded, and reads the article for the hundredth time.

Identical Twin Not Guilty of
Causing Sister's Death by Careless Driving

A WOMAN who killed her identical twin sister in a crash on the A31 near Guildford, Surrey, has been found not guilty of death by careless driving, a court heard.

A jury of seven women and five men took less than an hour to return the not guilty verdict on Abigail Cavendish, 28, from Balham, South London at Southwark Crown Court yesterday.

Ms Cavendish, her twin sister Lucy, who was a front seat passenger, and three others were travelling home from a Halloween party on 31 October last year when her Audi A3 came off the road in torrential rain and turned over into a ditch. A breathalyser test taken at the scene showed that the accused was not over the legal drink-drive limit.

The prosecution had claimed Ms Cavendish was driving too fast in the rain and hadn't been concentrating on the notoriously dangerous road. A statement from a passenger, a Mr Luke Munroe, the deceased's boyfriend, stated that an ongoing argument had clouded Ms Cavendish's judgement on the night in question, causing her to drive erratically.

Judge Ruth Millstow, QC, told the court that Lucy Cavendish's death was the result of a tragic accident brought on by severe weather conditions.

Beatrice peers at the accompanying photograph, at the twin sisters' happy, smiling faces, mirror images of one another. She would never be able to tell them apart if she had seen them both together. The photograph looks as if it was taken on a holiday, a palm tree frozen midsway in the background, the twins tanned and blonde, the shoe-string straps of a vest or a dress evident in the head-and-shoulders shot.

Beatrice had been on the tube, visiting a friend in Islington, when she saw the piece in the local free newspaper that someone had left discarded on the seat next to her. She had flicked through it idly, barely paying attention to the depressing stories about knifed youths or grannies robbed in broad daylight, until the photograph had caught her eye. The sisters, blonde, slim, with heart-shaped faces and full mouths, could be related to her, so similar were their looks. And when she noticed the headline she felt a rush of empathy. Twins – like her and Ben – and as she read on she actually gasped out loud as her eyes alighted on Luke's name. Her stomach contracted painfully. Would she ever escape her past?

Luke had been the dead sister's boyfriend. He had obviously chosen someone who resembled her. Was the universe trying to tell her something?

She'd tucked the newspaper into her bag, had come home and carefully cut the piece out, knowing that one day it would come in handy.

She surveys herself in the mirror: her pale hair, slightly slick with sweat, her too-pink cheeks in the soft glow of her lamp. It doesn't matter how she feels about what might be taking place under her very nose, about the way they are trying to keep her in the dark, laughing at her behind her back. It is her duty to help Abi, she must remember that, even if Ben seems happy to forget it.

You're not the only one who can't forgive yourself, Abi.

Beatrice carefully refolds the newspaper article neatly into quarters and slips it back into her drawer. And as she gets back into bed and settles underneath the sheets, she knows she has to intervene. Before it's too late.

Chapter Nine

It takes me a few seconds to register that I'm at Beatrice's house when I open my eyes the next morning. The tinny sound of a radio playing floats up from somewhere within the bowels of the house and the sun's rays filter through the gap in Jodie's threadbare navy-blue curtains, creating oblong reflections on the ceiling. I gaze up at the shifting patterns, unsure of what to do, how to act, now that I'm finally here. It's been so long since I've lived with people my own age, my peers, that I'm immobilized with a kind of stage fright.

I wince with embarrassment when I remember last night and my overreaction to Lucy's lost letter. I had been so convinced that Beatrice had taken it, to punish me for the growing feelings she must know I have for Ben, that I could hardly concentrate on a word she was saying as she helped me unpack afterwards. If she noticed my odd behaviour, she did a good job of pretending otherwise as she sipped her red wine and exclaimed about the state of my wardrobe and how we had to go shopping for some new clothes. 'You've got nothing but ripped jeans, holey jumpers and baggy T-shirts, Abi.' When she finally left me alone to go to bed, throwing me a concerned look over her shoulder as she closed the door behind her, I slumped in the middle of the bedroom, hugging my knees, surrounded by a fortress of empty cardboard boxes. Sweat bubbled above my eyebrows and top lip, my heart racing so much that I began to think I might die. In the end I was so petrified I dialled Janice's number, even though it was past midnight.

She talked me down, assuring me it was only another panic attack, reminding me of all the coping mechanisms she had taught me. 'Believing that Beatrice would steal Lucy's letter is your way of punishing yourself because you're happy,' she explained in her usual calm, logical way, her soothing voice coating my frayed nerves like antiseptic cream on a graze. 'And you feel guilty for being happy. It's called survivors' guilt, Abi. We've talked about this before, remember? It's a symptom of your post-traumatic stress disorder. Don't let these destructive thoughts ruin your friendships.'

I know now, in the cold light of day, that Beatrice isn't cruel, that she wouldn't deliberately try and hurt me. She would surely know how important those letters are to me. I've got a bond with Beatrice, she's been amazing, allowing me to become part of her life. It is as if she knew, even at our first meeting, how much I needed her friendship. I have to trust her; that was Janice's advice last night. I have to allow myself to get close to people and allow them to get to know me.

My mobile buzzes on my bedside cabinet and I shuffle to the edge of the bed, turning on to my front to reach out and retrieve it, pleased when I see it is a text from Nia asking how I am, and my heart sinks when I remember that I haven't told her about my new living arrangements, knowing she will be sceptical and worried for me. I sit up, resting my head against the uncomfortable iron headboard, bunching the duvet up around my armpits as I dutifully reply, telling her I'm fine and will ring her in a few days. Putting off the inevitable.

Wrapping myself in my grey velour dressing gown I scurry to the vast bathroom across the hall, relieved when I don't bump into Beatrice or her brother before I've had a chance to clean my teeth and wash my face. The utilitarian white tiles are cold against the soles of my feet and I stare at my bleary-eyed reflection in the large mirror, wiping away the remnants of last night's mascara from under my eyelashes, assessing the all too familiar gauntness of my face, of *her* face. I drag a brush through my blonde hair, noticing my widening parting and the hint of pink scalp beneath, the side effects of stress and the prescription drugs I wash down my throat every day.

I make my way down the many flights of stairs and my disappointment grows with each step when I fail to bump into Beatrice or her brother. Apart from the lachrymose tones that I recognize as Lana Del Ray's, growing louder as I descend, the house is quiet. It sounds as if the music is coming from the kitchen and I hope that Beatrice or Ben is there waiting for me.

When I get to the hallway and pass the reception room that used to house Jodie's three-headed sculpture, a flash of colour makes me stop and double back on myself. Popping my head around the door I'm surprised to see that the walls have been painted an acid lime green that perfectly contrasts with the bright white ceiling and coving and, instead of Jodie's sculpture dominating the room, in its place is a huge leather sofa and a desk. Before I know what I'm doing I push the door open further. It's a stunning room with doors that lead out on to a long and neatly manicured rear garden. I go to the desk that's been pushed up by the wall. Some of Beatrice's earrings and necklaces have been laid out as if on display in a boutique and my eye catches a familiar yellow, daisy-shaped earring and I pick it up, recalling that it was the one she wore when we first met. I hold it in the palm of my hand, marvelling at the way she has designed the flower, so intricate, so delicate. I fold my fingers around it and close my eyes, letting the memory of the first time I saw her linger like the unforgettable lyrics of a love song, and I fight the sudden urge, *the sudden need*, to put it in the pocket of my dressing gown. I touch the necklace at my throat, the one I never take off, reminding myself I have a little piece of Beatrice already, and I place the yellow earring back on to the top of the wooden desk where I found it. Then I notice the bracelet. It's stunning, interspersed with sapphires, but a few of the stones are missing, as if she hasn't quite finished it yet. As I leave the room I think how lucky Beatrice is to have all this: the house, the money, the talent, and most importantly, her twin.

The music gets louder – Lana Del Ray has been replaced by the Arctic Monkeys – as I round the stairs to the kitchen and when I get to the bottom step I jolt in surprise. I'd been expecting, hoping, that one of them would be here, waiting for me. But the only person in the room is a short, rotund woman with a greying blonde bob whom I don't recognize. She seems oblivious to me as she leans over the table so that her large, heavy breasts, encased in a floral apron, are almost touching the wood as she quickly, and quite aggressively, kneads dough.

A glance at the kitchen clock tells me it's just gone ten. I clear my throat to announce my presence and the woman looks up. Her eyes are small and dark, two currants in her rounded fleshy face, which is the colour of the dough that she is vigorously kneading.

She swivels on chubby ankles to turn down the Roberts radio that sits on the worktop behind her and her small eyes sweep over me, no doubt taking in my state of undress. 'Ah, another one,' she says in a thick accent that I guess has its origins somewhere in Eastern Europe, although I can't be sure. 'You are like little stray dogs,' she says, not unkindly. 'Pretty little stray dogs. You girls, you come and stay a while and then you go, never to be seen again . . .' She shakes her head as if she's trying to displace the memories of these 'girls'.

I want to tell her I'm not planning on going anywhere and to ask her who the hell she is anyway, and why is she making what I assume is bread in Beatrice's kitchen. (I can't help but think of the house as Beatrice's even though I know it belongs to Ben as well.)

'I'm Abi,' I say as I shuffle towards the table, the tiles sticky under my feet, pulling my dressing gown around me and suppressing a shiver. The large sash window is open and, although the day is warm, the kitchen is cold due to its basement location, deprived of the sun that blazes outside.

She smiles enigmatically but doesn't offer her name. Who are you? I want to shout, and what are you doing here?

'Where are the others?' I ask instead.

'Ah, the others,' she replies as she digs her elbows vigorously into the dough. 'They are out playing tennis.'

I feel a stab of hurt that they would go off and play tennis without asking me.

She goes to the Aga and, kneeling in front of it, places the bread tin carefully in one of its four compartments. 'Shall I make you a coffee?' She stands up, wiping her hands on the skirt of her apron. I nod gratefully, muttering my thanks, making sure I take a seat opposite the entrance to the kitchen so that I can see them as soon as they return from their game of tennis. I listen as she chatters over a different, more upbeat song on the radio, while fiddling with the coffee machine's intricate workings. She tells me her name is Eva, she's from Poland and she's been a housekeeper for Beatrice and Ben for six years, ever since they moved to Bath.

'The poor lambs,' she says conspiratorially, as she hands me my coffee cup with surprisingly tiny delicate hands for such a large lady. 'They were so in need of mothering when I met them. They lost their parents you know, a long time ago.'

I take a sip of my coffee as a surge of anticipation rushes through me that, at last, I might get to find out more about them.

Eva takes a seat next to me and launches into a story of when she first came to work for them. Although her words are heavily accented so that I sometimes miss exactly what she's saying, I can tell by the relish with which she talks that this woman likes to gossip, and I think that this could work to my advantage.

'I'm local so I don't need to live in,' she explains. 'But I try to come over every day and make them a meal that they can cook up later or freeze.' So, the delicious lasagne that we had for dinner last night was one of Eva's offerings. 'I also do a bit of cleaning for them,' she continues. 'Ben particularly likes things tidy. They have a gardener as well. They do need looking after.'

They're thirty-two years old, I want to shout. *They're hardly children*. But I stay silent, not wanting to interrupt her flow. She pauses and glances at me quickly, and I can see that she's assessing whether she can trust me. She obviously thinks she can as she goes on: 'When Beatrice first moved to Bath she seemed very fragile, she would keep bursting into tears, telling me she didn't know what to do – about what, I never found out. She never told me what happened before moving here, but I got the impression she was running away from something, or someone. This house was in total – how do you say it? – total disrepair?' I nod encouragingly. 'She threw herself into doing it up. Spent a year having it modernized – it must have cost her a fortune. Then Ben moved in too and she seemed happier, more secure.'

I'm intrigued to find out who, or what, Beatrice was running from. I find the fact that she has a history that I know nothing about disconcerting. I want to know everything about her, otherwise it makes us little more than strangers. I take a sip of the coffee, savouring its bitter taste. 'How did their parents die?'

'I think it was a car accident.' Another coincidence, another thing we have in common. 'The twins were babies, maybe toddlers, I can't remember exactly.' She frowns. 'They were brought up by their grandparents and, from what I understand, they were very wealthy. When they died, their money was put in trust for when the twins turned twenty-five.'

So that's where all their money has come from. That's how they can afford this magnificent house and why they don't need to charge any rent.

I think of the three-bedroom semi on a small housing

estate in Farnham, Surrey where Lucy and I grew up. It wasn't a bad place to live, our parents always kept it clean, tidy and cosy and we knew no different, it was our home, but it was worlds away from a house such as this. I imagine Beatrice and Ben as children, the orphan twins, running through large draughty rooms of their grandparents' rambling mansion with extensive gardens and a sweeping driveway, a completely different type of estate to the one where we spent our childhood.

Eva takes a noisy slurp of her coffee. 'Now that their grandparents have died they've only got each other.'

'At least they've got each other,' I say, thinking of Lucy.

She nods in agreement, licking froth from her top lip with the tip of her tongue. 'Yes, but it means they are very protective of one another, of course.' She regards me over the rim of her cup. 'They won't let anything, or anyone come between them.' Her words sound like a warning.

The patter of footsteps on stone and raised jovial voices prevent her from saying anything further. My heart quickens as Beatrice skips down the stairs carrying her tennis racket, followed closely by Cass, Pam and Ben. She's flushed, a white tennis skirt skimming the top of her tanned thighs. I try to catch her eye but she doesn't look in my direction.

'Bread smells yummy, Eva,' she says, as if I'm not even here. 'We've had a good game, haven't we, Ben?' She reaches up and pulls the front of his cap down so that it covers his eyes and he protests good-naturedly. I look at him, willing him to acknowledge me, relieved when he catches my eye and flashes me one of his lopsided smiles. He's wearing khaki shorts that come down to his knees and I'm pleasantly surprised by his muscular calves.

'Morning, Abi.' He moves away from his sister and much to my delight slides into the chair next to me. The sun has brought out the freckles across his nose and he looks tanned and healthy in a white Fred Perry. I resist the urge to touch him. He cheekily asks Eva to make him a cup of coffee and after a bit of banter about her not being his personal slave she gets up and goes to the coffee machine. I can tell by the way her face lights up when she jokes with him, her accent thickening so I can barely understand her, that she would do anything for him.

Now that we're all in the kitchen it seems smaller, claustrophobic, and I'm glad of the slight breeze from the open window. Pam stands next to the Aga, exclaiming excitedly about the bread that we can now all smell and Cass joins us at the table. Beatrice languishes in an old velvet chair in the corner, her legs swinging over the arm, chattering away about their tennis match, making me wish I'd been included. I feel exposed, still sitting in my nightwear when everyone else is dressed and has evidently been up for hours. Even though Beatrice is her usual bubbly self as she recounts the tennis match that she and Ben won, the disagreement with one of the teenage girls from the house next door who wanted to use the courts, she avoids looking in my direction, does nothing to acknowledge me at all, and I sense that I've upset her somehow and now she's freezing me out. A coldness creeps down my spine and I involuntarily shudder and glance at Ben, suppressing my hurt.

'Are you okay?' he mouths, leaning forward. Cass has taken the seat to my left, but she's staring into space with a glazed look in her eye. I've hardly ever heard the girl speak, except to Beatrice.

'I'm fine.' I smile shyly, playing with my empty coffee cup, my tummy rumbling from lack of food.

Beatrice is now chatting to Cass, who goes to sit beside her on the armchair. It's too small for both of them and Cass is practically on Beatrice's lap, their legs intertwined. Nauseous, I force myself to look away. Ben's knee touches mine under the table, sending shockwaves through me so that everyone else in the room is momentarily forgotten.

'Hey, guys.' Beatrice's clear voice reverberates around the kitchen so that we all turn to look at her and Cass squashed together in the armchair. They're both wearing identical trainers. Dunlop Green Flash. I've always wanted a pair.

'Shall we have a get together tonight? To celebrate Abi moving in?' She turns to me at last. 'What do you think, Abi? Would you mind?' She looks at me expectantly; any animosity that I think I perceived earlier has vanished from her beautiful honey-coloured eyes, replaced by a shining hopefulness.

When I mumble my agreement she squeals and leaps

out of the chair. 'Yay! It will be fun,' she says, running behind me and wrapping her arms around my neck so that our heads are touching, her pale hair brushing my cheek. She smells salty and sweet at the same time and I can't help but giggle at her enthusiasm, knowing by now that she will find any excuse to hold a party, relieved at her warmth and I realize with a sickening clarity, that I would do anything to prevent myself from being left out in the cold again.

Chapter Ten

No sooner have I eaten my breakfast – poached egg on toast rustled up by Eva, because, according to her, I need fattening up – than Beatrice frogmarches me up to her bedroom.

'I hope I don't offend you, darling, but you're in dire need of some new clothes,' she says as I shadow her up the winding staircase. 'But until we go shopping you can borrow some of mine.' She ushers me through her bedroom door and I step into her room, remembering with a pang of longing the open studio, my excitement at helping her out, her generosity with the necklace.

'Here we are,' she says, throwing wide the doors of a large ivory armoire, revealing a row of colourful skirts, silk dresses and pretty blouses, some of which are still wrapped in Cellophane. She's got more clothes than Lucy, Nia and I had altogether.

I stand by her dressing table, playing with the necklace at my throat as Beatrice ums and ahs and flicks through dress after dress. 'This will look fab on you, and this . . . ooh, definitely this one,' she says, pulling dresses, skirts and blouses off their respective hangers and throwing them on to her bed. 'Have a look through that little lot, I think we're about the same size. Although,' she turns and surveys me, wrinkling up her cute ski-slope nose – something I've noticed she does often, 'you are a bit thinner than me.'

'I never used to be,' I mutter as I go to the bed and pick up a green-and-white dress with capped sleeves, letting the soft silk run through my hands.

Beatrice touches my shoulder lightly. 'I'm sorry, Abi, I didn't mean anything by it.' She notices the dress in my hands. 'This would look fabulous on you. It's Alice Temperley, isn't it beautiful? And this one . . .' She picks up a navy-blue dress with cream pleats. 'This would definitely suit you.'

'Oh, Beatrice, I don't know if I can borrow these things. These dresses are lovely.' *And expensive.*

'Don't be silly, I insist,' she says, moving away from me and handing me a 1950s-style full skirt and white blouse. 'Here, try on these as well. It's too hot for jeans at the moment anyway, what with this heatwave.' To emphasize her point she pulls her tennis skirt down her thighs and whips off her T-shirt so that she's standing in a pretty white bra and knickers. Her body is petite and toned with pale freckles on her shoulders and chest. I avert my eyes, assessing the pearl pink nail varnish that I painted on my toes months ago, which has now chipped away so that hardly any remains. My cheeks are burning. When I believe it is safe enough to look up again, she's thrown on a wispy cotton dress with shoe-string straps, her décolletage glistening with sweat. The room seems hot and oppressive and I long to shrug off my dressing gown, to let it pool around my feet, but I don't have the confidence to stand here in my underwear.

'Ben's so lucky,' she says, 'having a balcony in his bedroom. Sometimes I think I made a mistake, letting him have that room. And it looks out over the garden, whereas this has a view of the street. But this room is bigger, I suppose.' She surveys the room, wrinkling up her nose as if deciding whether she has, indeed, made the right choice. Then she carefully drapes the rest of the clothes I'm allowed to borrow over my arms, so that it looks as if I'm carrying a fallen maiden, and I think how these clothes aren't really me. I'm usually more comfortable in jeans and T-shirts, not floating around in designer togs. Lucy was always the more glamorous one out of the two of us. On our shopping trips she would hunt for vintage finds in backwater second-hand shops, whereas I preferred to head straight for Gap. A lump forms in my throat that she's not here with me, picking her way through these dresses, exclaiming over the fabric. Her style was so similar to Beatrice's. I know my sister would have looked fantastic in all of these clothes.

'You remind me of her so much,' I find myself saying.

Beatrice pauses, a cotton blouse in her hand. 'Do you mean Lucy?' It's almost a whisper and I nod, unable to speak. 'I take that as the highest compliment.'

It's only when I'm back in my room and tugging the Alice Temperley dress over my head that it hits me. I've never told either Beatrice or Ben my sister's name.

How do you know she was called Lucy?

Beatrice's friends are supposed to be coming over at seven, but when I walk into the drawing room at five past, it's empty. The French doors leading on to the terrace are open and the sun streams in, bleaching the wooden floorboards. The white embroidered voile that Beatrice picked up 'for a bargain, darling' in India flutters in the gentle breeze and from somewhere I can smell the distinct aroma of cigarette smoke.

I make my way around the room, picking up, examining, then replacing a wooden Buddha, a Ming vase, a framed photograph of a young couple with arms wrapped around each other that I take to be their parents, and all the while I try to quash the disconcerting sensation that sits heavily in the pit of my stomach.

Beatrice said my sister's name, she must have googled me.

She obviously knows a lot more about me than she's let on; Ben, too, probably. I'm suddenly hot with shame that they know I caused Lucy's death. How can Ben even bear to look at me, let alone kiss me? How can Beatrice invite me to live in this house? I gaze into the faces of the young couple in the photograph. They look to be in their early twenties, in their first flush of love as they laze against the trunk of a huge oak tree. The woman wears flared jeans and a cheesecloth top and has the same honey-coloured eyes and ski-slope nose as her daughter. The man, with his feather cut and sideburns, is gazing at her adoringly, and he's the image of Ben. They died too, just like Lucy, the difference being that Beatrice and Ben have nothing to reproach themselves for.

'Our parents.' Beatrice's voice makes me jump and I turn to see her waft through the open doors. She's changed again and is now wearing a floaty calf-length cream dress that makes her look ethereal. She must have been out on the terrace this whole time. I grip the photograph, paralysed, as if I've been caught with the crown jewels.

'I wasn't prying,' I stammer.

Beatrice shakes her head. 'Don't be silly.' She takes the photograph from my hands, softly stroking the glass frame with her thumb. She smells of cigarettes. 'Her name was Daisy. I've always thought that was such a pretty name. I wish I could remember her – well, both of them – but we were so young when they died.'

I realize that this daisy-themed house and the jewellery she designs is Beatrice's homage to a mother she hardly knew. I take a deep breath. I need to say it, to clear the air. 'You know, don't you? About how my twin, Lucy, died?'

She stiffens and slowly replaces the photograph on the

mantelpiece before turning to look at me. 'Oh, Abi.' She takes my hand and leads me to one of the sofas. 'I remember reading it in the newspaper, that's all. It resonated with me because I'm a twin too. I wasn't prying either.'

It sounds plausible, and I recall detecting a flash of recognition in her eyes that first day we met, when I mentioned my name. Cavendish isn't a surname you hear every day, it probably is the sort of name that would stick in someone's mind. It doesn't mean she's been researching me.

'So you know I killed her?' I fold my hands in the silk lap of the green tea-dress, unable to meet her gaze.

'You didn't kill her, Abi.'

'The car accident was my fault.' A sob bubbles in my throat, nausea overwhelming me when I think of that night and all that happened afterwards. 'I was driving. It was my fault.'

'It was an accident. *An accident*. The weather was bad, it was dark, it could have happened to anyone. Please . . . you have to stop this.'

'I don't think that I can,' I say, tears threatening. 'I don't think I'm ever going to be able to stop punishing myself.'

'Would Lucy want you to do this to yourself?' she says, her voice sharp, and when I look up I see a glint of anger in her eyes. 'Because I know that if it was me, if Ben had caused my death by accident, I wouldn't want him to go on punishing himself for the rest of his life.'

She takes my hand and squeezes it, and in a softer voice she adds, 'I would want him to be happy, Abi. I would want him to live.'

I respect her opinion the most; after all, she can understand, being a twin herself. But she doesn't know the full story and, thankfully, that is something only the five of us who were in the car that night could ever know.

I'm sitting alone on the sofa when Ben walks in holding a glass of red wine. Beatrice has disappeared to the kitchen with Cass to fetch some wine bottles and glasses. The sun is still burning bright in the sky and the smell of cut grass floats in through the open windows and, after the stifling heat of the day, a welcome breeze.

Ben frowns when he notices me sitting alone, an expression I can't read on his face, almost as if he's seen a ghost. His eyes run over the Alice Temperley dress I'm wearing. 'Is that yours?' he says as he takes a seat next to me. He's sitting so close that his bare knee touches mine. I pull the green silk further down my thighs self-consciously.

'It's Beatrice's. I don't have any summer clothes with me, I wasn't expecting this heatwave.' I laugh in an effort to dispel the tension that emanates from him and it puzzles me. Why would Ben care what I'm wearing?

He turns to me with an urgency that surprises me. 'I hope you don't mind me saying this – and don't get me wrong, I love my sister – but please, Abi, don't let her turn you into her clone.'

My cheeks grow hot. 'I'm only borrowing some clothes, Ben. It's no big deal.'

He looks as if he wants to say more, but takes a sip of his wine instead. I fiddle with my hands in my lap, apprehensive about meeting more people that I don't know. It seems both Beatrice, and Ben, have a wide group of friends. I envy them that.

Ben grabs my fidgeting hands to still them. 'It will be fun, Abi. Don't worry so much,' he says reassuringly, as if reading my mind.

I open my mouth to reply but I don't get the chance as I'm interrupted by a loud, brash voice and Monty appears in the doorway, blocking the light from the hall. One friendly face, at least. He has a bottle of red wine in his huge paw which he places on the walnut coffee table.

'Monty!' Ben gets up and smacks the larger man on the back, guiding him into the room where he pours his bulk into one of Beatrice's elegant Louis XIV chairs. Ben sits back down next to me, his knee brushing mine, sending little shockwaves through my body.

'Thanks for last night, Ben old man,' says Monty, then he turns to me. 'I needed some advice about my computer and there's no one better at technology than Ben here.'

Ben shakes his head modestly. 'You're a technophobe, Monty.'

The doorbell downstairs reverberates through the house and minutes later Beatrice appears, clutching some glasses with one hand and a bottle of wine in the other. Three men and two women follow her into the room.

'Abi, this is Grace and Archie,' she says placing the glasses and wine next to the bottle that Monty brought over. The girl is small, dark, and pretty while the man is stocky with a crop of red hair and freckles. Ben leaps up from the sofa to greet Archie and he and Monty stand around chatting while Grace perches awkwardly on the sofa.

'And this is Maria, Edward, and Niall.' Maria, who looks to be in her late forties with thick dark expressive eyebrows and a Roman nose is resplendent in a voluminous kaftan. Edward and Niall look about my age, but while Edward is short, mousy and nondescript, I can't take my eyes off Niall. He's almost as tall as Ben with a similarly wiry, firm body but instead of Ben's fair hair, Niall has mussed-up dark locks that curl around his ears and to the collar of his black leather jacket; an acoustic guitar hangs on a strap across his body. His skin is the colour of warm toffee, and he has large almond-shaped brown eyes. Dark flecks of stubble dot his chin and upper lip and, although I usually detest facial hair on men, it suits him. His scruffy demeanour reminds me a little of Callum.

Beatrice positions Niall next to me and sits herself on the opposite sofa between Maria and Grace, while Edward joins the men. Monty seems to know them all quite well, although I don't recall seeing any of these people at his party last month.

Wine is passed around while Niall busily rolls a spliff. I sit quietly, sipping my wine while surveying the room.

Niall, to my right, has hardly said two words to me and I suspect he's already stoned. Ben is still standing with Monty, Archie and Edward by the French doors, a cigarette between his long fingers, and Beatrice is nattering away with the two women opposite me. She makes no effort to draw me into the conversation. I'm the only one who notices Cass slink into the room like a nervous greyhound, all big eyes and long limbs, her gaze intently fixed on Beatrice as she places some more wine glasses on the coffee table, along with a bottle of Sauvignon Blanc. I catch her eye and smile encouragingly but she turns away and perches on the edge of the Louis XIV style chair next to Beatrice.

When Beatrice realizes that Cass has arrived she reaches across Grace to give her knee a reassuring squeeze before resuming her conversation. There is something familiar and caring about the gesture. Inclusive. And I suddenly feel left out, sitting by a mute Niall. The women are all laughing at something Beatrice is saying, their faces turned to her adoringly; even the older, frumpy Maria seems enraptured. What is it about her? Her voice is clear and soft and almost hypnotic. I glance across at Ben, hoping to catch his eye, but he has his back to me, the striped shirt he's wearing accentuating his broad shoulders.

As Monty's booming voice reverberates around the room, the sweet scent of marijuana tickles my nostrils and I ask Niall if I can have a drag. *Why not?* I think as I lean back against the velvet sofa and inhale deeply.

I haven't smoked weed since I was at university with Nia, but it beats sitting here not being able to chat with Beatrice. Niall suddenly seems a lot more interesting, and the two of us sit giggling and smoking alone on the sofa. Every now and again I notice Beatrice look up from her conversation to glance over at us, an impassive expression on her face.

Later, as the sun goes down and the others have either gone home or to bed, I find myself alone with Beatrice. The room has darkened and Beatrice closes the French doors and flits about the room, lighting the candles on the mantelpiece.

'Did you enjoy meeting everyone?' she asks as she flops on to the sofa next to me. 'They're a great bunch.' When I don't answer, she turns to me, concerned. 'Didn't you have a good time? Is it about Lucy? If you want to talk—'

'I've got my counsellor for that,' I snap, my jealousy of earlier still niggling at me. I want to hurt her, push her out. Even as I do it, I know I'm not being fair.

Her eyes widen in shock and an injured expression flashes across her face. Instantly, I'm remorseful. 'I'm sorry,' I say. 'I'm just tired, I didn't mean to snap.' And before I know it I'm opening up to her about seeing my counsellor, the post-traumatic stress disorder, my problems with paranoia, although I omit the details about Alicia and all that came afterwards.

'Oh, Abi,' she says when I've finished. 'Thank you for telling me. And I'm here for you, if you ever want to talk. You know, I've had my own problems – nothing like yours, admittedly, but I had a kind of breakdown. I was . . .' she pauses as she rests her head against the soft cushions, her eyes appearing even larger in the candlelight. 'I was extremely hurt by someone I loved.' She tells me of her first year at university when she met the man she thought she'd be with for ever, how devastated she was when it all ended. How she couldn't cope emotionally. 'I had to leave Exeter, I couldn't be anywhere near him afterwards, it was too painful to see him. So I went travelling.'

'You went to Exeter University?'

She frowns as if irritated that I've interrupted her flow, her tale of lost love and broken hearts. 'Yes, why? Did you?'

'No, but a friend of mine did,' I say, thinking of Luke. He wasn't going out with Lucy then, of course, they didn't meet until a couple of years after. But I remember the conversations we all had about our student days, sitting around our favourite table in our local pub, desperate to outdo one another with tales of debauched parties and recreational drugs. Luke always had what he thought was a funny anecdote about Exeter and Lucy would tease him that the place was his first love.

Beatrice is staring at me, her face serious. 'Abi? I said, what friend?'

'Only someone from my past. I don't see him any more.' I can't bring myself to explain; it is too painful to remember how it all was. Before.

'Oh, that type of friend.' She laughs, almost as if she's relieved. I can't be bothered to correct her. I lay my head next to hers, the way I used to do with Lucy. We're silent for a while, then her eyes snap open and she lifts her head from the cushion, staring at me, excitement bright in her eyes. 'What did you think about Niall?' Her eyes are shining, hopeful.

'Very handsome.' I give her a conspiratorial smile, but she frowns.

'Oh, he is, isn't he?' She leans forward to retrieve her wine glass from the coffee table and takes a sip. Her hair falls in her face, hiding her expression, as she says, matter-of-factly, 'As soon as I saw him I thought he'd be perfect. For you.'

When I'm certain Beatrice is safely ensconced in her own bedroom I go to him.

He's lying on his side in bed with his legs pulled up to his bare chest, a stripy cotton sheet draped over him. The doors to his balcony are ajar so that a thin voile curtain ripples in the slight breeze. The light from the moon illuminates his face, his long eyelashes casting shadows on his cheeks and I have a sudden urge to bend down and kiss him where the freckles cross his nose. He's so like his sister. His eyes slowly flicker open, aware that he's being watched. 'Bea?' his voice is thick with sleep.

'It's me, Abi,' I hiss.

He blinks as if his eyes are adjusting to the dark. 'What's going on?'

'That's what I want to know.' I kneel down so that my face is inches away from his and I can smell the red wine and cigarettes on his breath.

He frowns. 'What do you mean?'

'Beatrice is trying to set me up with Niall,' I say in a loud whisper, fuelled by the four glasses of wine I drank earlier. 'If you feel anything for me at all, we have to tell her. It's not fair.'

A slow smile spreads across his face and he reaches out and gently brushes my hair from my face. 'Okay, so let's tell her.' Then he throws aside his duvet, revealing his long tanned legs. He's only wearing his boxer shorts. I crawl in beside him as he pulls the cool sheet over us, cocooning us from the outside world, and curl myself into him, relishing the warmth of his skin, the soft fuzz of his chest against my cheek. In his arms I can believe that nothing bad will ever happen again.

And as his mouth finds mine he unzips the back of Beatrice's dress, and wiggling out of it I discard it on the floor where it lies in a crumpled heap, forgotten.

Chapter Eleven

Their favourite bench has been pelted with huge white dollops of bird droppings and Beatrice can't help but see it as a bad omen as she reaches out to touch its arm, the wood warm under her fingers from the sun that continues to beat down relentlessly. She is unable to stop the tears spilling out from under her lashes. Maybe if she gives in and cries, gets it over with, she can begin to get on with her life, can begin to forget.

She angrily wipes away her tears with the back of her hand, and clutching her flip-flops in the other hand, she moves away from the bench towards the edge of the hill, the grass coarse and prickly beneath her bare feet. She could be Gulliver up here, gazing down on the city sprawling beneath her; her very own Lilliput. She can make out the many arches and four turrets of the Abbey to her left and, a little further behind, the curve of the

Royal Crescent. A dog yaps behind her and she can hear the shrieks of children in the nearby playground.

Beatrice realizes she should be happy for her brother; she *is* happy for him. It's been two weeks since Abi moved in and suspecting, *knowing*, she's with Ben only serves to remind her how alone she is. She always thought she would be married by now, maybe with a baby on the way. But meeting *him* changed the course of her life, like a train forced to make a detour along another track to a different town, so that she's lost, unable to get back on the right track to where her destination should be. And here she is, thirty-two years old, with no lover, no marriage and definitely no babies. She thought moving to Bath would help, a fresh start, but *he's* here with her, always with her, in her head, in her heart. Wherever she goes, *he* will always follow. For the rest of her life. It's been thirteen years, she thinks. Over a decade since her heart was not just broken but crushed, so why can't she get over it? Ben doesn't understand; she knows he's been in love before and got hurt, but he was able to let go of his pain and move forward. *Why can't I?*

Ben. She thinks of her brother's kind hazel eyes, his ski-slope nose. She can't lose him. He's the only family she's got left. By opening her house to other artistic types she feels less alone, part of something, a community, but they aren't true family, they aren't blood. Only Ben shares her genes, her DNA.

I can't lose you, Ben. I need you.

A hand on her shoulder makes her jump and she turns

110

to see Ben standing behind her and she's in shock for a moment, as if it's not really him but a mirage caused by standing in the sun for too long.

'I knew I'd find you here.' He holds up a striped plastic carrier bag. 'I've bought some drinks. It seems our bench has been used as a toilet though.' He wrinkles up his nose in disgust and she laughs, relieved that he's here next to her. They sit in companionable silence under a cedar tree, shaded by the canopy of velvet leaves, watching scantily dressed young couples sprawled on towels; the men in shorts, their chests bare, the girls in bikini tops that leave little to the imagination. A large group of women are picnicking with their toddlers and gossiping under a neighbouring oak.

'Are you okay, Bea?' he asks, as he hands her a can of Pimms, which she takes and guzzles gratefully. 'You seem a bit melancholy.'

Anger surges through her along with the alcohol. 'What do you expect when you're constantly lying to me?'

The sun has brought out the freckles on his face so that he looks tanned and healthy, and he runs a hand through his hair, something he always does when he's anxious. She can tell that he's inwardly debating whether to continue lying to her and she wants to warn him that it's very important what he decides to say next. It could mean the end of everything.

'You're talking about Abi, aren't you?'

She's relieved that he's decided to be honest with her.

'You've been sneaking around behind my back for the last few weeks. But what hurts the most is why you didn't just tell me?'

He has the grace to look ashamed. 'I'm sorry, Bea. I didn't know how to explain it to you. Abi wanted me to tell you. She felt so awkward about it. She thinks a lot of you. And, well, I know you don't agree with romances between housemates.'

She places the can next to her on the ground. 'You've broken the rules, but it's not only that,' she says, without looking at him. She pulls a dandelion up by its root and begins to methodically pick off its petals. 'I care about Abi, but she's incredibly fucked up.' She twists her body around so that she's facing him. 'You do know that, don't you? You've seen the newspaper article about Lucy. Abi blames herself for her death. She sees a psychiatrist and she told me herself she suffers from paranoid delusions and survivor's guilt. She's fragile, probably not the best person to start a relationship with. And she thinks I haven't noticed those scars on her wrists. Well, I have, Ben. Haven't you?'

He nods, slowly. 'I did suspect,' he admits.

'She hasn't said, but I bet she's been on a psych ward. Be careful, that's all I'm saying.'

Ben pauses, as if weighing up whether to be honest with her. 'I do like her a lot. I've not felt this way—'

She doesn't want to hear it. She throws the dandelion, now bald without its petals, on to the ground. 'I understand,' she interrupts, trying to keep her voice even. They

112

sit for a while, watching a group of teenagers playing football. 'Do you think we should be honest with her? About the past, about what we did?'

Ben gapes at her as if he doesn't know who she is, his face turning crimson. 'You're fucking joking,' he splutters. 'We said we would never tell anyone, ever.' He downs the rest of his Pimms and crushes the can in his fist.

'Abi's different. You said so yourself. You want to lie to her?'

'We've done something awful, Bea,' he says in a low voice. 'Abi would never look at me in the same way again. Or you. You would ruin everything. Is that what you want?'

She tuts. 'No, of course not.'

'Abi would never understand, and she definitely wouldn't forgive it.' He emits a manic bark of laughter. 'Our lives would be ruined. We'd have to move away again. We've made a life here now.' His face darkens. 'You can't tell anyone. Ever.'

The Pimms swirls around in her empty stomach, making her nauseous. 'I know. But I feel so guilty, Ben.' She takes his hand as they sit in silence, staring out over the rooftops of Bath. Bile rises in her throat at the thought, but she's compelled to ask, 'Are you sleeping with her?'

He drops her hand as if it's diseased. 'I'm not answering that.'

She blinks back the sting of tears. Fury builds in her

113

chest. 'You make me so fucking cross,' she hisses. 'I told you that it wasn't a good idea to get involved with her. She's my friend, I'm the one who found her. I'm the one who's supposed to be helping her, and you're going to ruin it, the same way you ruin everything . . .' She can hear her voice rising. The women sitting under the neighbouring tree turn to look at her, clutching their toddlers to them as if she might be some drunk, some threat.

Ben grabs her hand and squeezes it hard. 'Stop it,' he urges. 'People are looking.'

'You don't care about my feelings at all, do you? It's bad enough that you've decided to begin a relationship with her regardless of the house rules,' she cries, her anger cancelling out any embarrassment. 'When we moved in together we agreed that we would respect each other . . . we said . . .' She pauses, takes a deep breath.

'I know what we said, Bea.' His face is sweaty, panicked.

'Then why are you shagging her, Ben? Under my roof, in my house—'

'Don't be so melodramatic, for fuck's sake,' he spits, making her flinch. 'And it's *our* house, Bea. Our house.'

'Whatever.' She's crying now, knows she's making a scene. Several other people have turned to look at them and one of the teenagers calls over to ask if Beatrice is all right.

'She's fine,' Ben snaps, standing up and pulling her to her feet. 'Come on, we better go.'

Beatrice thrusts her toes back into her flip-flops and

follows Ben as he stalks down the hill, the plastic bag filled with their empty cans swinging from his arm. She wonders if she's said too much, gone too far? She has to run to catch up with him, but he doesn't stop until he's halfway down the road and by the time she's reached him she's panting and out of breath. She grabs his arm and he spins around to face her, his eyes hard.

'What the fuck is the matter with you, Bea?'

She hangs her head, surprised by his sudden burst of anger. 'I'm sorry.'

'And you can hardly talk. What about Niall?'

She freezes. 'Niall? Nothing is going on with Niall. He's a friend, that's all. And he doesn't live with us.'

He glares at her disbelievingly. Then sighs, shaking his head and she can tell his anger is dissipating like air being slowly squeezed from a balloon. But when she makes a move to take his arm, he shrugs her off.

'What's the matter?' she asks, hurt swelling behind her eyes at his rebuke. 'I'm sorry I caused a scene.' She knows how he hates to row in public, hates attracting attention.

'It's not that.'

'Then what?' She takes a tissue from her pocket and blows her nose.

He hesitates. 'Abi means a lot to me, you know.'

A chill creeps around the back of her neck, despite the heat. 'What are you saying?'

'I want to give things a go properly with Abi. And I want you to take us seriously and stop this jealousy,

Bea. I know it's hard for you, you've always been the most important woman in my life. I get that. But I don't see why Abi can't be my girlfriend and your friend. We don't have to bicker over her.'

'I don't think it's the right time for her to be getting into a relationship,' she says weakly. 'I thought that if I could help her then it would make everything else okay, somehow.'

'Not this karma shit again, Bea?' He sighs. 'Nothing is going to make up for the past, for what we did. You know that, right?'

Her head is spinning and she leans against the wall of someone's front garden for support. How can she explain it to him so that he understands? She's losing control, over him, over their life. She was only trying to help Abi, but instead it's all been thrown back in her face. She closes her eyes and massages her temples. She needs to think, to figure things out in her head. When she opens her eyes again, Ben is watching her very intently, a guarded expression on his face. Her gaze falls to his Armani shorts, his cherry-red Ralph Lauren polo shirt and finally to the very expensive and brand-new Tom Ford sunglasses that are perched on top of his sandy hair. Even working in IT he doesn't earn that much money, and she knows that to get through to him she has to hit him below the belt, to where it hurts.

I hold the power, Ben. I could ruin everything for you.

'Nice sunglasses,' she says pointedly, and by the blush

that creeps up his throat she can tell he understands exactly what she's implying. He's always been the clever one, after all. When she offers her arm this time he doesn't brush her away but takes it and they slowly make their way down the hill towards home, in silence.

Chapter Twelve

The country is in the grip of a heatwave, the likes of which we haven't seen for seven years apparently, and our days are spent languishing under the trees in Beatrice's garden, playing tennis or sunbathing in Alexandra Park with the city of Bath spread out like a model village beneath us. We pack picnics, consisting mostly of cigarettes and wine, and sit for hours, chatting until the sun turns into a burnt-orange ball and goes down over the city. Sometimes, usually when Beatrice is working on her jewellery, Ben and I manage to steal off by ourselves to the botanical gardens, where we kiss, hidden by huge flowering shrubs with exotic names. Occasionally we talk about Lucy and I find myself opening up about her, my guilt, and he assures me, as his sister has before him, that it was an accident. When I tell him I can never forgive myself, he stares at me with a faraway look in his eye, as if he's not seeing me at all but is trapped in a memory of his own. 'I know how you feel,' he says eventually, as if snapping out of a trance. He tells me a bit about growing up in Scotland, but when I begin asking him questions about his mum and dad and his grandparents, automatically reverting to journalist mode, he clams up and changes the subject, and I sense that, even after all these years, it's still painful for him. Will there ever be a time when I will be able to talk about Lucy without that familiar pressure in my chest as if I'm being sat on by a sumo wrestler, without having to fight back tears?

Ben has turned down two contract offers in the past few weeks. 'I'm not going to work in this heat,' he says, and it's as though I'm a student again with no job to go to and no responsibilities, although I know it can't go on. I've eaten into the last of my savings and I can't keep living off of Beatrice's generosity.

One morning I find Niall asleep on one of the sofas, his mouth open and snoring gently, his guitar carefully propped up at his feet, surrounded by wine bottles and ashtrays filled with cigarette butts, but most surprisingly of all, I find Beatrice wrapped around him, her long tanned legs intertwined with his, her head on his chest. They are both fully dressed.

A fortnight after I move in, I'm in the kitchen emptying the washing machine of the few clothes that I possess, plus the dresses that Beatrice let me borrow, into a plastic laundry basket. It took me weeks to identify the Parma violet scent that I detected on Beatrice and in this house when I first visited. I eventually tracked it down to their detergent. I bury my face in my wet clothes, inhaling the wonderful smell that I love so much; it's the scent of this house, the scent of them. I fold the clothes up and make myself a coffee using the posh coffee machine, thinking how at home I am, when Ben clatters down the stairs, a concerned frown on his face.

'Has Bea gone out?' he asks, as I spoon frothy milk into my cup. For some reason the shortening of her name sends a spark of irritation through me.

'She said she was going for a walk, to clear her head.'

'When was this?' He stands over me, silently demanding a quick answer.

I shrug. 'I don't know, about ten minutes ago. Do you want to—?'

Before I can finish my sentence he turns and runs back up the stairs, two at a time. I follow him, mug in hand, and catch him as he rushes out of the ornate front door, bumping into Cass on her way in. He mumbles an apology but continues down the garden path without a backward glance.

'What's the hurry?' she says, a bemused look on her face, her bleach-blonde crop dishevelled. Standing there in the doorway, wearing a striped Breton T-shirt and black shorts, she reminds me of an actress from a 1960s French New Wave film and, with a twinge of envy, I think how beautiful and young she is. She can't be older than about twenty-two. She's holding a can of something chemical in one hand and a wedge of glossy A4 sheets in the other and, as she walks further into the hallway, she kicks the door closed behind her. I stand staring at her mutely. Out of everyone I've met through Beatrice, Cass makes me feel the most uncomfortable and I can't put my finger on why this is. Perhaps because she's so quiet, only ever having in-depth conversations with Beatrice, following her around like a dainty poodle. Maybe because she's self-assured in a way I never was when I was her age. But she's a complete enigma to me. I don't think the two of us have had a proper conversation in the short time I've known her.

'I've just made a coffee, if you want one,' I say, lifting up my mug in an effort to break the uncomfortable silence. It's the one Beatrice normally drinks from. White bone china with a black line drawing of a bird with its wings spread.

She glances at the cup, brow furrowed, and then at me. 'No thanks,' she says coolly. 'I've got to develop some photographs.'

'You have your own darkroom?' I'm impressed. I don't know much about photography but did dabble with it as part of my media studies A-level.

'Beatrice had one installed for me in what was once the en suite. It's tiny, but it serves its purpose.' She blushes as if she's said too much, and, clutching the paper to her chest, hurries up the winding staircase, leaving me standing in the hallway alone wondering what sort of photographs she takes and whether she's at college or university.

I follow her up the stairs, and as she continues up to her attic room, I head into the drawing room to sit on the terrace that overlooks the long and neatly manicured garden. If I look up I can see a terrace above me, but smaller, more of a Juliet balcony, which I know to be Ben's room. It's another hot, airless day and I'm grateful that Beatrice let me borrow so many of her lovely clothes, although Ben keeps on at me to buy some of my own.

I'm reclining on one of the wooden sun-loungers when my mobile phone buzzes in the pocket of my skirt. Nia's name flashes up on the screen and I contemplate not answering it. How am I going to explain to her all that's happened in the last few weeks without causing her to worry? But if I don't speak to her, she will assume the worst. After everything I put her through that day, over a year ago, when she found me semi-conscious in the bath with blood oozing out of my freshly slit wrists, I know I owe it to her to be honest.

'Nia, hi,' I say brightly. My jovial voice sounds fake even to my own ears and perspiration prickles my armpits, only partly caused by the heat. I rest my coffee cup on the arm of the recliner.

'What's going on, Abs?' I can hear the hum of cars in the background, the beep of a horn, the faint indecipherable chatter of voices, the clinking of a spoon against china. I imagine her sitting outside a café somewhere in Muswell Hill, a part of London I'm not familiar with, which is probably her reason for choosing to move there. I imagine her toying with her coffee, skimming the froth off her cappuccino with a spoon and licking it in the way she always does, her dark hair falling around her pale face, her brown eyes serious. 'You haven't spoken to me for weeks, I only get the odd text telling me you're okay. And are you? Are you okay?'

The way I feel about her over-protectiveness flows and ebbs like the sea lapping at the shoreline. Most of the time I understand it's because she's got my best interests at heart, that she cares about me, that she doesn't want a repeat performance of what happened before, but occasionally I find it stifling. Doesn't she understand that, much as I love her, speaking to her reminds me of my old life, which makes the yearning to turn the clock back so intense that it's as if I've received a physical blow?

'I'm okay, honestly, Nia. I've been busy, that's all . . . I . . .'

'Have you been working?' I can hear the hope in her voice, she knows how much my job meant to me before Lucy died.

'Not exactly. I've . . . well, I've met someone. He's lovely, I know you'll think he's great. And his sister, Beatrice. She reminds me so much of Lucy, she . . .'

'Oh, Abi,' she says and I can sense the panic in her voice. 'This isn't Alicia all over again, is it?'

My cheeks flame with indignation. 'It's not like that at all. Beatrice has become a good friend. In fact, I'm living with her, and him. His name's Ben Price. They're twins, can you believe it? They've got this amazing house and she doesn't even charge me rent, instead we all put some money in a kitty to buy food and they have a housekeeper who comes in and cooks for us.'

There is a long, loaded silence on the end of the phone and, for a moment, I think she's hung up on me, something that Nia has never done. In all the years we've been friends we've taken pains to avoid a serious argument, in the way some people avoid meat or dairy products. There might have been times when we've been tempted, but we've always fought the urge rather than each other. I'd known she would disapprove of this though, which is why I've been putting off telling her about it. I touch the necklace at my throat, running my fingers over the letter A. How I can convince her that living here is good for me?

'Nia? Are you still there?'

'Of course.'

'Please try to understand.' I tell her about meeting Beatrice that rainy day at the end of April, how we became friends and how through her I met Ben and came to move in.

'And it's not like Alicia?' she repeats.

I assure her that it's totally different. I hope I've managed to sound convincing.

'It all seems rather quick. And what about your job?' she ploughs on. 'You loved being a journalist, Abi. And now what? You just live off this *Beatrice*,' she spits out her name as if it tastes nasty and I grip my phone, fighting the urge to cry.

'It's harder than I thought, freelancing . . .'

'Have you even tried?'

'Who are you? My mum?' I snap.

I can hear Nia taking a deep breath, in an effort to suppress all she wants to say. My hand trembles as I hold my mobile to my ear. I can hear laughter in the background, the scraping of a metal chair on tarmac. Tears threaten. Why can't she try and see things from my point of view? 'Look, Nia,' I say, in an effort to placate her. 'Why don't you come and visit? You haven't been to Bath for ages. I would love you to meet them, to get to know them a bit. Then you'll understand.'

'Understand what, Abi?'

'How important they are to me . . .' I pause. 'Nia, I was in a bad place when I met Beatrice that day. Yes, I was better than I was, but I still wasn't good. And I was lonely, living in that flat by myself.'

'I live by myself.'

'I know. But, Nia, you're not listening . . .' I hesitate, but she doesn't interject so I continue. 'I feel that Beatrice and Ben, well . . .' I swallow a lump that's formed in my throat. 'They've saved me somehow.'

'Oh, Abi,' she says, and I can hear the desperation in her voice. 'You have to stop looking for someone else to save you. Only you can do that for yourself.'

Despite her disapproval, Nia agrees to come and visit around my birthday in a few weeks' time. As I hang up, I'm hopeful that we are back on an even keel, an argument narrowly avoided.

I'm fed up with waiting for Beatrice and Ben to get back from wherever it is they've gone, so I take the bus into the centre and, as I wander around the side streets, the conversation with Nia plays on my mind. I know she's right, I shouldn't be living off Beatrice, I should be trying to freelance. I've wanted to be a journalist since I was eleven years old, am I really going to throw all my hard work away? I've been living in a bubble these last few weeks and I know that it can't continue. I make a resolution to myself that tomorrow I will call my contacts, even the ones who I've felt have been less than supportive since the court case.

I turn down Northumberland Passage, grateful for the break in relentless sunshine due to the shade from the narrowness of the buildings that rear up on either side of me. The street is rammed with people; swarming outside the stall that sells oilcloth bags; peering through the shop windows at trinkets, or ornaments, or children's clothes; perched at bistro tables, nursing a latte or cappuccino. The smell of cheese pasties permeates the air.

I meander along the lane, taking in the atmosphere, pausing when I come to a little vintage shop that sells the type of dresses that Beatrice wears. Naturally, I'm compelled to go inside. It's empty apart from the assistant perched behind a Victorian-type counter, talking in bored tones into an old-fashioned phone. I flick through the dresses; there is everything from a 1980s ballgown to a 1920s flapper dress. And then I see it, and my heart quickens. It's a crinoline tea-dress from the 1940s, maroon

126

with tiny white swallows, a Peter Pan collar and cap sleeves. It's exactly the kind of dress Beatrice wears. I snatch it from the hanger, letting the material run through my fingers, and I can't contain my thrill when I see that it's my size. It's expensive, and I can't afford it, yet I buy it anyway.

I'm crossing the square in front of the Roman Baths, clutching my new dress in its brown paper bag, when I hear someone calling out Beatrice's name. A large woman in a colourful printed kaftan is hurrying towards me, a wide smile on her mouth, her hand raised, but as she gets closer I notice the flicker of doubt in her eyes, her features rearranged into a frown. 'Oh, I'm sorry . . . I thought . . .' Her hands flap around her dark hair, suddenly awkward. She composes herself. 'I thought you were Beatrice. It's Abi, isn't it? We met about two weeks ago at Bea's house. It's Maria,' she clarifies when I stare at her blankly. Of course, one of Beatrice's friends. We make stilted small talk for a couple of minutes before she makes her excuses and heads back towards the Abbey. I watch her go, bemused that she would think I was Beatrice, probably because I'm wearing her green Alice Temperley dress. Nevertheless, I'm flattered to be mistaken for her.

I can hear faint chatter coming from the kitchen when I get back to the house. Beatrice and Ben are huddled at the wooden table, deep in conversation, but when I walk in they fall silent.

'You're home,' Beatrice says flatly, lifting her eyes to

me. They are red and puffy as if she's been crying. Ben pulls back his chair and goes to the coffee machine. 'It's too hot for coffee,' she says when Ben offers her one. She begins picking at some nonexistent scab on her smooth, tanned arm.

My stomach clenches as I take the seat opposite her, dropping the bag containing my new dress at my feet. I can tell by the hostility emanating from Beatrice that Ben has finally admitted to her that we're seeing each other. I'm suddenly aware that was why he rushed out earlier, to catch up with his sister. I wish he had included me. That we could have told Beatrice together, put up a united front. I feel excluded, pushed out, and it pisses me off.

'So,' she says when Ben sits back down, sliding a coffee in my direction. 'Ben's told me about the two of you.'

'I've gathered,' I want to say, but I keep quiet.

'You didn't have to hide it from me,' she says coldly. 'I thought you were my friend, Abi.'

'I am your friend, you know I am. I . . . we didn't know what to tell you. We weren't sure what was going on ourselves at first . . .' I splutter, trying to suppress the swell of indignation that I'm having to explain myself while Ben sits there silently.

She assesses us both, her pupils flicking from me to Ben and back to me again. And then she grabs one of our hands in each of hers. 'I'm pleased for you both, of course I am,' she says, as if to reinforce this fact to herself. 'But please don't lie to me again. I've had a lifetime of lies.' She glances pointedly at Ben, but he keeps his gaze firmly fixed on a knot of wood on the oak table.

I open my mouth to explain that I've been haranguing Ben to tell her since I moved in, that it was his decision not to, but instead I close my mouth and hang my head and dutifully apologize, relieved that at least she knows now. No more secrets.

Dinner is a rather subdued affair. Beatrice doesn't say much while pushing her chicken salad around her plate with a fork. Cass, as usual, is morose and Ben and I sit side by side, as if we are two chastised children. Only Pam natters away in her warm West Country accent.

Later I go to find Ben in his bedroom. The sun has gone down and the balcony doors are propped open with a large Egyptian cat carved out of a sleek black stone, an expensive artefact – so he informed me once – that he picked up on his travels. The air is still, the voile curtains hardly moving in the nonexistent breeze. Ben has stripped down to his boxer shorts and lies on top of his sheets with his eyes closed. His bedroom, as always, is meticulously tidy and minimalist. I notice what looks like a satellite dish with wooden legs in the corner of the room. It's huge and futuristic with a Scandinavian elegance. I remember him showing it to me in the window of Bang and Olufsen, bending my ear about what an amazing sound it produces, how it would be great for parties. It cost a small fortune. I can't believe he went out and spent all that money on it.

Ben opens his eyes when he sees me. I go to him, kissing him passionately, wanting him more than ever. I pull away to step out of my dress, hurriedly unclasping my bra and letting it fall to the floor.

'What are you doing?'

'I'm taking off my clothes, what are you doing?' I climb into bed and sidle up to him again, inching his boxer shorts over his hips, 'Here, I can help.' He grabs my hands. At first I think he's fooling around, that this is a new game, but when I turn to look at him in the semi-darkness I can just make out the disgust distorting his features.

'Stop it, Abi,' he says, shifting away from me and pulling his boxers back up. 'Can you put something on?'

In anger I whip the sheet from under him and wrap it around me, shocked at his rejection as I scramble from his bed. 'What do you mean?' I can hardly bring myself to say it but the words come out in a rush, 'What's the matter, don't you fancy me any more?'

The moonlight from the window illuminates him as he sits in the middle of the bed, his legs pulled up to his chin. I long to go to him, to put my arms around him, to kiss his neck, his chest, but it's as though I don't know him any more. If there was one thing I was certain of, it was Ben's feelings for me.

'Oh, Abi,' his voice catches. My chest is heavy. 'Of course I do. Only, I don't think we should be having sex.'

'But why not? What's going on?'

His eyes are dark and intense. 'It's Bea. She's funny about us sleeping together.'

130

I laugh. Surely he's joking. 'Why would she care?'

'It's not particularly respectful, is it? Would you want to sleep with me if we were staying with your parents?'

I consider this. 'Well, no, but that's different. We live here, Ben.'

He sighs. 'Look. We've already flouted her house rules. I don't want to piss her off even more. You're the first girlfriend I've had in years. I think she's a bit threatened by you. She's always been possessive. It's only ever been her and me, Abi. Let her get used to us being together first. She'll come around to the idea.'

'What about what I want? Doesn't that come into it? Do I always have to bow down to what darling Bea wants?' I'm so angry I have to bite the inside of my lip to stop myself saying something I will regret.

'It's not like that. Come on, Abi. Be reasonable. Surely you can see her side of it? I'm the only family she's got. She's a bit possessive, that's all. And it is gross to think your sibling is having sex in the room next door.'

'So I'm the one being unreasonable?' Hot angry tears spring to my eyes as I gather up my clothes. 'I want to sleep alone tonight,' I say, throwing the sheet back at him. It lands on his lap but he doesn't touch it, as if it's been contaminated by my nakedness. 'Maybe you should talk to Beatrice instead. It's obvious you only care about her feelings.'

It's not until I'm back in my own bed, wrapped in the duvet which smells of Ben, that I allow myself to cry.

Chapter Thirteen

The weather breaks.

I'm awake most of the night, listening to the rain drumming on the roof tiles, hoping Ben is also tossing and turning in his room across the landing. For the last two weeks I've spent most nights curled up against his chest, only sneaking out in the early hours of the morning so that Beatrice didn't catch us. I pull the quilt over my head to block out the shards of light from the streetlamp that filter through the thin fabric of Jodie's horrible blue curtains. Maybe this is what I deserve, I think. Beatrice has been good to me, inviting me to move in here, being a friend when I needed one so badly, and I've repaid her by shagging her twin brother behind her back.

Ben's hazel eyes haunt me. I see them every time I close my eyes. Deep pools of honey flecked with green. How could I have resisted him? *Even for you, Beatrice.*

I am engulfed by a loneliness so intense I feel as though I'm suffocating.

It's times such as this when I miss you, Lucy. I miss you so much. If only I could talk to you now, what would you advise me to do? Losing you has killed a part of me, so that I'm no longer a whole person. I don't know how to live without you, Lucy. I don't know how to be me, without you.

I long to sink into nothingness, the release of not having to think any more, of not having to be me, and my mind wanders to that dark night in Balham, when I was determined to end it all. I was in a bad place, I know that now, just as I know that I would never do anything like it again. But how living hurts sometimes, as much as the incisions I made in my wrists; the scars a constant reminder of my guilt, my grief.

I must eventually fall asleep because it's starting to get light when the creak of a door wakes me, the heavy tread of footsteps cuts across the darkness and I sense him climbing into my bed, the mattress dipping with his weight as he wraps his arms around me, pulling me close, his familiar lemony scent evident as he nuzzles into my neck. 'I'm sorry,' he whispers, his breath hot against my ear. I feel safe, enveloped by him, and I slip back into unconsciousness, hoping that everything will be okay after all.

He's gone when I wake up and if it wasn't for the smell of his aftershave on my pillow, I would doubt he was ever here at all.

I pull aside the curtains, the fabric thin and slightly sticky under my grasp. The sky is a smoke grey, the streets drenched and shiny from last night's downpour and I experience a sudden pang of loss; for the end of the heatwave. For Ben.

I'm about to turn away from the window when I hear the clunk of the wrought-iron gate, the blip of a car unlocking, and I glimpse Ben, smartly dressed in a suit and tie, folding his lanky body into his Fiat. I remember him telling me he had a new contract, some company in Swindon. As I watch him drive out of the street I wonder if I am being unreasonable. Beatrice is possessive of Ben, but surely that's understandable after the childhood they've had, with no mum and dad and, by the sound of it, grandparents who were wealthy but disinterested.

I move away from the window to gather up my shampoos and body wash. I take a shower, energized as the water sluices over my body. I'm disappointed that it's too cold to wear the new tea-dress I bought yesterday. Instead I pull on a pair of faded skinny jeans and a long sleeved T-shirt, feeling like me again. The heat of the last few weeks has been so intense, so relentless, that I'm almost glad of the rain, the drop in temperature. I think of Beatrice's clothes hanging in a brightly coloured row in my wardrobe. Perhaps it's time to return them, to stop pretending to be something that I'm so obviously not.

Beatrice and Cass are perched next to each other at the kitchen table, their heads so close together that they are almost touching, poring over a sheaf of shiny black-and-white photographs. They barely glance up as I wander in.

'Morning,' I say, clicking the kettle on. The kitchen is dark despite the glow from the overhead light. Every now and again I hear the swoosh of car tyres slicing through puddles on the wet road above our heads.

'All right,' mumbles Beatrice without looking up.

'What are you doing?' I pull out a chair and take a seat opposite them.

'This one is fab,' says Beatrice, turning to Cass and ignoring me. My body tenses. 'I love the way the light falls on to the bracelet. It actually looks as if the jewels are sparkling.' Blood pounds in my ears and I feel the familiar tightness across my chest. *You're being paranoid, Abi. They aren't ignoring you.*

'I agree.' Cass is dewy-eyed and flushed. 'What about this one?'

'Are these your photographs?' I direct my question at Cass. She raises her eyes to me and inclines her head ever so slightly in answer. I'm assuming it's a nod. Beatrice continues to stare at the print.

I get up and make myself a cup of tea without offering them one, then stick two pieces of bread in the toaster. My cheeks are hot as I butter the toast, listening to them exclaiming over one photograph and how the light falls on to another. Is that what Cass was developing yesterday, and, if so, why is she taking photos of Beatrice's jewellery?

'Wow, you look beautiful in this one,' says Cass. I can

135

hear the admiration in her voice. I glance over at the photo. It's a head-and-shoulders shot of a woman with light hair and a heart-shaped face. It's Beatrice, but at a glance it could be Lucy. Or me. It looks as though she's naked except for a necklace at her throat, silver interspersed with emeralds. Cass has managed to capture her almond-shaped eyes, her ski-slope nose and full mouth in a way that is flattering and the effect is stunning. Her freckles are just about noticeable across the bridge of her nose and she looks fresh-faced and natural, much younger than her thirty-two years.

My heart pulls and I swallow back tears as Beatrice laughs, reminding me, as always, of Lucy. I take a bite of my toast and, leaning against the marble worktop, I watch as they continue to discuss websites, clients and commissions.

'Ben's already designed a brilliant website; once we've added these photos to it we can "go live" as he would say. A family collaboration.' She exchanges a fond look with Cass.

I clear my throat. 'If you want I could write something for your website . . .' I begin. But Beatrice waves her hand at me without looking up.

'Thanks, but that won't be necessary.'

Cass says something in an indecipherable whisper and then Beatrice lets out her familiar tinkly laugh. This time her laugh unnerves me and I know that she's punishing me again. Always punishing me because Ben and I care about each other, and I realize, as I survey her with her swishy hair and perfect clothes, that she doesn't compare to my sister at all. Lucy was warm, kind and inclusive, whereas hidden behind their shared bubbly personalities there is something controlling about Beatrice, as if she deliberately enjoys tempting me into the sunshine merely in order to push me into the shade.

My appetite has suddenly diminished. Without saying a word I leave my toast and mug on the worktop and walk out of the room.

I take the bus into town and spend over an hour in a paint shop that stocks brands such as Little Greene and Farrow and Ball, deliberating over their array of colours with unusual names. My bedroom in Balham was an eau-de-nil green, Nia's was yellow, and Lucy's was duck-egg blue, so I steer clear of anything that resembles those colours so that I'm not reminded of my old life. In the end I choose a pale mauve, the colour of a Dolly Mixture sweet. Something new, fresh, with no memories associated with it.

I sit on the bus with my tin of paint, roller and brushes at my feet, the posh cardboard bag the assistant put them in is wet and breaking up at the edges. An old woman who smells of wet dog is squashed between me and the window. She keeps nodding off and then waking up with a jolt and then falling asleep again, her chin to her chest, her head bobbing to the side so that it's nearly on my shoulder. Outside, people are scurrying about with umbrellas and raincoats – the opposite of yesterday when it was so hot that everywhere you looked someone was baring more flesh than is flattering. How is it possible that one day temperatures are edging thirty degrees when the next day it's cold, blowy and feels like we've all gone back in time to the spring?

As the bus wheezes up the Wellsway and stops for a breather at the traffic lights in the high street, the blur of familiar platinum blonde hair catches my eye and I see Cass coming out of the deli. She's linking arms with a girl with dark hair that I vaguely recognize. Of course, it's Jodie. I didn't know they kept in touch, always assuming that Jodie left under a bit of a cloud, although Beatrice has never confided in me about it. The bus moves on to the next stop and I clamber off, bag under my arm. I look around for them but they've disappeared.

The house is silent and empty as I turn the key in the lock and it hits me how big, how lonely it is when it's not full of people, music, parties, wine. Shadows play in the corners of the ceiling like ghosts chasing each other, and I hurry up the two flights of stairs, a shiver running down my back.

I push open my bedroom door and drop the tins of paint at my feet. Someone has been in my room. In my bed. The duvet, that I had meticulously straightened that morning, is rumpled and bunched together. Frowning, I edge closer and my mouth goes dry when I see something nestled within the folds of the fabric. Something dead and bloodied and smelling. I gasp. A bird. Headless. Its brown feathers matted with blood.

I scream and stumble backwards, trembling all over. Who would have put something so disgusting, so horrible, on my bed?

'Are you okay?' I jump and spin round. Beatrice looms in the doorway, dressed in a long black dress, and for a moment, in my frazzled state, she resembles a spectre of doom. She glances past me and to the bed. 'Oh, that's Sebby I expect, bringing you a present.'

'W—what?' I thought she was out. Yet she was here all the time. Was she waiting for me to find this? Hoping to freak me out? Is it some sort of punishment, some omen for ensnaring her brother? I long to tell her she shouldn't have bothered. He's already rejected me. Chosen her needs over my own.

'Sebby. My cat,' she clarifies, walking further into the room. 'He does this a lot. Do you want me to help you change the bed?'

I nod, unable to speak. My tongue is suddenly too thick for my throat. I watch in silence as she carefully rolls down the duvet cover so that the dead bird doesn't fall on to the carpet. 'It's ruined now, I'm afraid. I've got a spare one you can have though.'

'Thanks,' I mutter. And then she's gone, taking the soiled duvet cover and the bird's corpse with her.

By the time Ben gets home late that evening, I've finished painting the bedroom and stand back to admire my handiwork. The new mauve walls clash with the garish green bed linen I've borrowed from Beatrice. 'It's a spare one of Pam's, but she won't mind,' she said as she handed me the duvet cover earlier.

I hear his heavy tread on the stone staircase, sense him pausing outside my bedroom as if contemplating whether he's welcome, and then the creak of the door.

'Wow, you've done well, Abi.'

I shrug, roller in hand. I don't know whether to shout at him or kiss him.

The sky darkens and I can hear a growl of thunder in the distance.

'I think we need to talk,' he says. He's still wearing his suit and his hair has been flattened by the rain. His white shirt brings out his tan and I'm not sure if it's because his body is now out of bounds, but I desire him more than ever.

'I don't know if there's anything to discuss,' I say, placing the roller back into the tray. 'Anyway, I have to wash my hands and face. I've got paint everywhere.'

I make to leave the room but he grabs me around the waist. He's holding me so tightly that I'm winded. 'Please, Abi. I can't lose you.' Pain flickers in his eyes and a lump forms in my throat. 'I know it sounds silly, and I know we haven't been together that long, but I'm falling for you.'

Tears prick the back of my eyelids. 'Ben . . .' but my resistance fails as his mouth finds mine and he kisses me urgently.

Reluctantly I pull away from him, knowing it can't lead anywhere.

'Let's go out for something to eat. To talk. Just the two of us,' he says.

My stomach rumbles. I've not eaten since breakfast, so I agree.

After I've showered the paint out of my hair and changed into clean clothes, we walk to the pub around the corner, away from Beatrice and away from that house. We order at the bar and then find a seat at a wooden table at the back. A candle flickers between us and I think how I miss being on my own with him, away from his twin sister.

He reaches across the table and takes my hand. 'I'm so sorry about last night, springing it on you in that way. I'm sure when she gets used to the idea of the two of us, things will be different.'

'I found a dead bird in my bed today. It had no head,' I blurt out. I'm pleased to note the shock on his face.

'What happened?'

I shrug. 'How should I know? Beatrice said it was her cat.'

'Sebby?' He laughs. 'How weird. Beatrice always jokes that Sebby is missing the mice-chasing gene. That he couldn't catch and eat anything, even if it was right under his nose.'

'So you're saying he's never done this before?' My scalp tightens, my appetite diminishing.

'He's definitely not done that before. How disgusting. Must have given you a fright.'

'It did,' I admit, and then I say lightly, 'I hope it wasn't Beatrice's way of trying to warn me off you.'

Irritation passes across his face. 'She wouldn't do that,' he says, too quickly.

'I'm joking, Ben.' Although I'm not.

We stare at each other for a while. The silence between us is thick, brooding, like the air before a thunderstorm.

The waiter appears with our food. Ben starts tucking into his steak as soon as his plate is placed in front of him, mumbling through a mouthful of meat that he is starving. A group of men are gathered at the bar, drinking and laughing. The noise is abrasive and makes me flinch. One of the men, youngish with a sharp jaw, meets my eye and winks. I look away, blushing. I take a slug of water. 'I don't think Beatrice will ever accept our relationship,' I say, replacing my glass on to the table. 'I'm not sure if it's because I was her friend first, or because she doesn't want to be knocked off her perch.'

A flush appears at his throat and inches up his neck. 'She's fine about it. Happy for us, actually.'

I know he's lying.

I stare back at him until he looks away and resumes eating his steak.

'She didn't seem that happy with me today,' I say as I toy with the salmon. 'She practically ignored me this morning when she was with Cass. And then the bird thing.'

A pulse thumps in Ben's jaw, his mouth set hard. He doesn't look at me. 'She's a bit hurt, that's all. We did sneak around behind her back. I'm sure she didn't mean to ignore you. Beatrice thinks a lot of you.'

He's sticking up for her, of course he is. She's his twin.

A stab of guilt pierces the scaffolding I've constructed around my heart. *How must it be for you, Ben, stuck in the middle of the two most important women in your life?* I think. Maybe he's right. Beatrice is my friend, she wouldn't ignore me on purpose, she was busy sorting out her website, that's all. *It takes nothing to say good morning, to be polite.* I shake my head, dispelling this disloyal thought. I've been shagging her twin brother behind her back, she's got a right to be a little pissed off with me. And she'll get used to it, in time.

I take his hand and squeeze it. 'I'm sorry,' I whisper. 'I don't want to argue.'

'So, you're okay with taking things a bit slower,' he lowers his voice, 'on the sex front, for now? You still want us to be together?'

'Of course I do,' I say with relief, and suddenly the room seems brighter, the laughter less abrasive. 'And I'll apologize to Beatrice as well. She's got a right to be pissed off with me.'

'She's not pissed off with you. Look, it's probably best to leave it.' He sounds annoyed. 'Let's get the bill and go into town.' He reaches into his pocket, retrieves a battered wallet and taking out two crumpled notes he throws them on to the table. It's barely enough to cover his half of the bill, let alone mine. Not that I expect him to pay for me. He's smiling at me, his tone lighter, but it seems fake somehow, giving me the impression that he's hiding something.

Chapter Fourteen

Rain batters against the French doors and Beatrice cups her hands around her face to block out the light from her studio so that she can see into the garden. *Where is he?* The sky is cluttered with fast-moving, angry clouds and she longs for the hot temperatures of yesterday. How she wishes it could always be summer. Thunder rolls across the sky in a low roar, followed by the inevitable flash momentarily lighting up the garden. Beatrice jumps back from the window; she's always had a fear of being struck by lightning, imagining its electric fingers reaching through the glass to electrocute her.

She shivers, pulls her cardigan around her body. It's nearly midnight. Where is Ben? She doesn't feel safe until he's home, hates the fact the house is empty apart from her. She's at her happiest when the house is full of people, with Ben at her side. She fights the urge to call his mobile, not wanting to appear needy, even though she knows she is. She paces the room instead, trying to dispel the energy from her legs, her arms, her hands that are twitching to reach for the phone. Her eyes fall on to the velvet box next to her mobile. The lid is open exposing the sapphire bracelet nestled against the satin fabric, the piece that she's most proud of creating. She's promised to post it to her client in the morning. She's been paid handsomely for the bracelet, although it's not about the money, it's about the recognition of her talent.

Beatrice never thought she would end up as an artist. She wanted to be a lawyer when she began her degree at university all those years ago, the degree she never finished because everything went horribly wrong and she was forced to run away from it all.

It was the first August of the new millennium when she met him. Most of the students had gone home for the holidays, but she had hung around Exeter with her friend Laila, both not wanting to give up their flat, or to go back home to their families, enjoying their first taste of playing at being grown-up. They had gone to the local pub, the Seven Stars, which all the students frequented in term time because the beer was cheap. Spiller's 'Groovejet (If This Ain't Love)' was on the jukebox and even now, all these years later, she can't listen to that song without remembering how she felt when she first noticed him. He was leaning against the bar, chatting to his friend with a pint in hand, seemingly unaware of her reaction. Of how, for those few long seconds, she couldn't breathe, as if she knew that she had found her soul mate. As if she knew that they were destined to be together before they even uttered a word to each other. And when they did speak they couldn't stop, she was amazed by how much they had in common. He too was a student at the university, although he was doing a different course. When she found out he was on the same campus as her she couldn't believe she hadn't noticed him before.

Beatrice hardly ever allows herself to think of that time; it was thirteen years ago now and so much has happened since, so much wasted time, so many regrets. Her heart was broken and she had no choice but to leave, not only the university but the country as well. A few years later she heard through Laila that he had a new girlfriend, and it was as if her heart was being ripped out of her chest all over again.

She jumps as the front door bangs, bringing with it hushed voices, a giggle that echoes around the house. Beatrice rushes out into the hallway to see Ben with his arms around Abi's waist. Their hair is wet and plastered to their heads, Abi's hanging in cute tendrils, a limp umbrella dripping water falls from her hand and on to the doormat. She's looking up at Ben with her beautiful open face and Beatrice is surprised to see her expression is full of adoration. She never expected Abi to fall for him, not this quickly. They are both laughing and the sight of them together brings back unwanted memories. Memories that she tries hard to keep buried. She only wishes she could find someone to fall in love with and then the past could be erased as easily as a pencil drawing.

'All right, Bea.' Ben flashes her his lopsided smile, but Abi doesn't even glance in her direction. Standing by the old school radiator, Beatrice is suddenly awkward in her own home. There's something different about Abi tonight, she realizes, an aloofness that wasn't evident in her persona before. It's true that Abi has always been slightly jittery, with a shyness, a vulnerability that endeared her to Beatrice, but she was always so eager to please, so polite. When Abi told her, that day in her bedroom, that she reminded her of Lucy, she had been flattered, had felt that maybe this was the beginning of a long friendship that both of them so obviously needed.

'Have you had a good night?' she says in an effort to stem her jealousy. It's not their fault that she's single.

'Yes, thanks,' replies Abi shortly, still looking up at Ben, her arms encircling his waist. Beatrice is taken aback by her abruptness. *Was it all an act, Abi, your eagerness to be my friend? Was it only so you could get into my brother's pants?* Perhaps Ben's told her about yesterday, how upset she became in the park when she thought they were sleeping together. Would he be so disloyal? It wasn't the fact he was sleeping with Abi that had bothered her so much. Not really. She just doesn't want them to get too serious. Even she can see it's going too fast, that one of them is going to end up getting hurt, and Abi is so vulnerable. Putting a halt to their intimacy might slow things down, give each of them a chance to get some perspective on their relationship. Sex gets in the way. It's easier when you take it out of the equation, she thinks.

Abi uncoils herself from Ben and, clutching his hand, leads him up the stairs. 'Goodnight, Beatrice,' she calls over her shoulder, and there is something about the way she says it, the way she leads her brother up the stairs, that makes Beatrice think that she's taunting her, letting her know that she won't let Beatrice win.

It's not a fucking game, Abi. This is my life.

Ben has a stupid lovestruck grin on his face as he follows Abi up the stone staircase. Beatrice knows she must look like a disapproving landlady, standing at the bottom, wrapped in her thick woolly cardigan, arms folded across her chest, but surely Ben wouldn't go against her wishes? Surely he wouldn't be so cruel as to still have sex with Abi after everything she said yesterday? Not when he knows she has the ability to pull the plug on it all.

Beatrice sighs and flicks the switch to turn the light off in the studio. She must trust that Ben will do the right thing. She can't keep tabs on him as if she's his overprotective mother.

Her eyes pause on the velvet box on her desk, and she makes a mental note not to forget to post it to her client first thing. Another giggle emanates from the landing, causing her to forget all about the bracelet, and, closing the door on it, she follows her brother and his girlfriend up the stairs.

Chapter Fifteen

She's trapped on the top floor of the house, banging on the attic window and I know she's screaming although the sound is muffled by the glass, by the flames roaring around her. Her eyes are huge, terrified, and I run towards the house, trying to break down the front door, ignoring the fire licking the paint and causing it to warp, but the smoke knocks me back and I'm crying, exhausted, and she's getting smaller and smaller so that I can hardly see her. She's vanishing in front of my very eyes, and before I know it Callum's grabbing me around the waist, pulling me away from Beatrice's house, telling me there is nothing I can do.

'She's gone, Abi. She's gone. You have to let her go.'

'But I can't,' I scream, and I carry on screaming until my blood runs cold and my throat hurts. Suddenly Luke's face is in front of mine, his usual good-looking features contorted with anger so that he's ugly, scary, and he's turning on me, telling me it's all my fault. The house disappears and instead my old Audi is on its side in the ditch and Lucy's in Luke's arms and he's cradling her, crying, as he did that terrible, terrible night. And then it's not Lucy's face that stares up at me any more with her eyes open, unseeing. It's Beatrice's.

I awake with a start, my pillow wet with sweat, the sheets damp and twisted in knots at my feet, the duvet a heap on the floor. My heart bangs against my ribs as I sit up in bed, gasping for air. How I wish Ben was lying next to me, to soothe me, to remind me it was only a nightmare. *It was only a nightmare*, I tell myself as my heart slows, knowing that the events in my dreams might be different every time, but the outcome is always the same. As is the reality.

My twin sister is dead, Luke hates me and I will always blame myself. I will never be able to let Lucy go.

I'm rounding the stairs that lead to the basement kitchen when their raised voices stop me in my tracks. 'It's gone. It was on my desk last night and this morning it's vanished,' says Beatrice.

'Are you suggesting that someone has stolen it?' Ben's voice is unusually acerbic, his Scottish accent more pronounced. I've never heard them argue before and my heart skitters.

'It was there last night,' she repeats, her voice rising. 'That's all I'm saying. And now it isn't.'

'Maybe you put it somewhere else?'

'Why would I do that?' Her voice is clipped, cold.

I hover on the stairs, not sure whether to retreat or to continue into the kitchen. Hidden by the curved wall, I try to imagine the expressions on their faces.

'I don't know, Beatrice. But don't go accusing people until you're sure.'

'Accusing people? Who have I fucking accused, Ben? Nobody.'

His voice is calm as he answers. 'You say it's gone missing and your tone is accusatory. So come on, who do you think has taken it?'

I freeze, waiting. Her voice, with its hint of a Scottish accent but so much softer than Ben's, is barely audible over the whirl of the washing machine. 'Cass was in London last night and Pam was at her boyfriend's house. So there's only one person who could have taken it, unless of course you were with her all night? Were you? Were you with her all night, Ben?'

She means me.

Blood rushes to my head, making me dizzy so that I have to hold on to the wall for support. I can't guess at Ben's expression, and I don't wait for his answer as I scurry back up the stairs, tripping up them in my eagerness to get away and grazing my shin in the process. I don't stop to examine my leg but keep running until I get to my room. I close the door and lean against it, my breath coming in short, sharp gasps, the graze stinging, tiny dots of blood bubbling up on my skin. Did Beatrice

151

imply that I'm a thief? Or is my paranoia, my sickness rearing its delusional head?

I glance at my bedside table; my antidepressants aren't in their usual place. Maybe I forgot to take one last night? I crawl around on the floor on my hands and knees, in case the packet has fallen or slipped down behind the bedside table or my chest of drawers. And then I see the familiar cardboard packet poking out from under my bed. With relief I retrieve it, pulling the silver foil from within its cardboard mouth, like a dentist extracting a filling, but when I look there are no pills left. How could I have been so stupid? I check the date; my last prescription was almost three months ago, but there still should be a strip left. I shake the packet but the foils that fall on to the carpet are empty, their oblong blisters deflated. Panic rises in me, the darkness closing in. Did I take the Prozac before I went to bed? Why can't I remember? Things have been so hectic; moving in here, my relationship with Ben, that I can't remember when I last took one.

Ben had come to bed with me last night, although we lay fully clothed on top of the duvet, talking quietly. Then I must have fallen asleep because when I woke in the night, Ben had gone back to his room and I was still dressed in the jeans and jumper I had worn to the pub. My mouth was dry and sticky so I padded downstairs to the kitchen to get some water. Had I taken the tablet when I came back up? I don't think so. Janice told me it was dangerous to stop taking the medication and that

I needed to be weaned off them gradually, when the time was right. It's still early, surely I can make an emergency appointment with my GP or Janice? *It will be okay,* I tell myself. *There's no need to panic. Surely missing one pill won't hurt, I've done it before.* But what if I've missed more than one?

I sit on the floor against the bed, its iron frame digging uncomfortably into my back, but I don't care, welcoming the pain. I pull my shaky knees up to my chest and a sob escapes my lips. How could I have thought that those blasted pills would make everything okay? Now Lucy's gone I will always feel this way, as if I'm on the brink of a precipice and one false move could send me toppling over.

I've managed to avoid her all day.

I've spent the morning ringing around my contacts and I'm relieved when Miranda, my old boss, sounds pleased to hear from me, even telling me she might have a commission for me. 'Patricia Lipton has agreed to be interviewed for our arts pages, I know how you love her novels,' she tells me. It will mean travelling to the Isle of Wight as Patricia hates telephone interviews, but that might be what I need: to get away from Beatrice for a bit, to clear my head.

I manage to get an emergency appointment with my GP for more antidepressants. Afterwards I pop into town to buy a duvet cover that will match my new walls. I'm shouldering my way through the door around tea-time, carrier bag in one hand and umbrella in the other, when I hear her voice carry down the hallway in a breezy hello and I see her emerging from her studio. Even though the temperature is cool, she's wearing one of her cotton dresses, her feet are bare and she has a silver anklet that drapes elegantly over her tattoo.

'Oh, it's you. I thought it was Ben.' She sounds disappointed. 'Been shopping? I didn't think you had any money?' She glances pointedly at the carrier bag I'm clutching.

My face heats up at her directness. 'I . . . it was in the sale. It's a duvet cover. I need a new one, after the bird . . .'

'Right.' Her eyes are cold as they sweep over me. I push the front door closed and dump my bags and umbrella at my feet while I shake off my parka, hanging it on the coat stand.

She's still standing there, slim arms folded across her body, assessing me, and I squirm under her scrutinizing gaze. 'Those dresses I let you borrow,' she says. 'Have you finished with them?'

'Yes, thank you. It's not so hot now so I don't need them any more. Do you want me to get them?'

'Please.' She inclines her head towards the stairs and I walk up them, becoming more dejected with each step. I can hear the sound of her bare feet against the stone, sense her breath on the back of my neck as she follows closely behind.

I open the wardrobe to retrieve her clothes, leaving one dress on the hanger. The one that I bought at the vintage shop. The only one that belongs to me. I see Beatrice's eyes flicker to it but she doesn't say anything about it.

'Here.' I hand her the clothes and she drapes them over her forearm. 'Thanks for letting me borrow them. I've still got the green Alice Temperley, it needs washing but I'll do it.'

She shrugs but makes no move to leave. 'Do you have anything else that's mine, Abi?' Her voice is cold. I wasn't mistaken earlier, she knows I've stolen something from her.

'Like?' I meet her gaze.

'A sapphire bracelet, for example.'

I remember admiring the bracelet the day after I moved in, where it sat on her desk in her studio. 'Why would I have it?'

She sighs. 'I don't want to play games. If you have it then please return it. I've been paid for it already, it's for a new client and I don't want to let him down. It's a present for his wife.'

'Can't you make him another one?' This is obviously the wrong answer as her cheeks redden and her eyes narrow so that they are two slits in her face and she actually draws breath.

'I can't believe you,' she hisses. 'I've been a good friend to you. I invited you to live here, *rent free*, when I hardly knew you. I tried to help you deal with your grief over

Lucy, and this is how you repay me. I know you've taken it, Abi. I don't know why, but I know it's you.'

I open my mouth to protest but she slams out of the room before I can utter another word.

I'm stretched out on top of my new duvet cover, too afraid to venture downstairs in case Beatrice has told Pam and Cass about the bracelet. I know they are all sitting around the kitchen table eating a delicious meal (most probably prepared by Eva) and I can't bear to see their disappointed stares or hear their accusatory words. It doesn't matter what I say, she's made up her mind that I've stolen her precious bracelet. How I hate confrontation.

But hiding away makes you look guilty, I think. *How have I managed to get myself into this situation? Have I made the same mistake as I did with Alicia?*

The creak of my bedroom door makes me look up and I see Ben standing there, his usual lopsided smile on his face. 'Can I come in? I've missed you today.' He looks tired, the smudge of dark circles under his eyes noticeable despite his tan. I nod miserably, and then, as he takes a seat next to me on the too-soft mattress, I burst into tears. 'Hey, what's the matter?' he says, pulling me to him. I bury my head in his chest, comforted by the familiar scent of the fabric softener of his crisp white shirt mixed with a musty office smell. Tearfully I explain about what I heard this morning and Beatrice's coldness towards me tonight.

'I can't believe she spoke to you like that,' he says angrily when I've finished. 'She can't go around accusing people. Honestly, I don't know what's gotten into her.'

'You don't think I stole her bracelet, do you, Ben?'

He takes my chin in his hand and turns my face towards his and gently wipes away a tear. 'Of course not. She's over-reacting as always. She's probably moved it and has forgotten where she's put it. She's always doing that type of thing, don't worry.'

I lean against him, relieved. As long as Ben's on my side I can face anything. He asks me if I've eaten and when I explain I've been too embarrassed to face the others he takes me by the hand and leads me down to the kitchen. As I pass the large ornate mirror on the landing I catch a glimpse of my puffy eyes, my swollen clown's mouth. I've never been an attractive crier.

Beatrice and Pam are sitting at the table when we come in and they both glance at us, quickly looking away again. So Beatrice has told Pam about the bracelet, just as I thought she would.

'Is there any dinner left?' asks Ben. He's still holding my hand and I grip it like it's a life raft.

'Eva made a fish pie. There's some left in the oven,' says Beatrice, ignoring me. Their plates are empty and so are their wine glasses, plus the two bottles in the middle of the table. Ben lets go of my hand and walks to the Aga and I take a seat opposite Beatrice.

'Beatrice . . .' I begin. There's so much I want to say, but I know I'm not very good at confronting things. I'm

157

interrupted by Ben placing a plateful of fish pie in front of me but I know if I take a mouthful I will vomit. He sits next to me, handing me cutlery and a wine glass with a reassuring look in his eyes. I find it endearing that he's taking control, that he's looking after me.

'I see you've downed all the wine.' His voice is devoid of its usual warmth as he addresses his sister.

Pam looks uncomfortable and, making some excuse about having to call her boyfriend, hurries from the kitchen. The pitter patter of rain on glass, the occasional gust of wind rattling the windowpanes, are the only sounds to be heard. I pick at my food but Ben shovels his down with gusto, not put off by the tense atmosphere in the room that makes me claustrophobic. I yearn to run up to the sanctuary of my bedroom. I take a small forkful of pie before putting my cutlery down.

Beatrice looks from me to Ben as I stare miserably at my hands. I'm surprised when I see, from my peripheral vision, her hand reach across the table towards me. I keep mine folded in my lap.

'I'm so sorry, Abi,' she says solemnly. 'I should never have accused you of stealing from me.'

'So you've found the bracelet?' Ben's voice is sharp.

She shakes her head and I almost feel sorry for her. 'No, no, I haven't. But it doesn't matter, not in the grand scheme of things. As you said, Abi. I can make another one for my client. No big deal.'

Ben glances at me and I see it, doubt clouding his hazel eyes, but he remains silent.

'I'm sorry I sounded so flippant earlier. But I didn't take it, Beatrice. I'm not a thief.'

I think of all the people I've taken from: Lucy, Alicia, and yes, even Beatrice. Maybe I am a thief after all.

When I reach my bedroom there is a missed call and a voicemail on my mobile phone. I listen to the message from Miranda while pacing the length of the room. From my window I see Beatrice heading out of the garden gate. Where is she off to at this time of night? I push thoughts of Beatrice from my mind and try to concentrate on what Miranda is telling me. The Patricia Lipton interview is mine if I'm still interested. She's arranged for a night stay in a hotel and I leave the day after tomorrow. Adrenalin and purpose surge through me, and I know that Nia was right when she urged me not to give up my job. Getting away from this house, even for a couple of days, would be the best thing for me. For my sanity.

Chapter Sixteen

Beatrice marches down the street without an umbrella, not caring that the wind is whipping at her red mackintosh or that the rain splashes against her bare legs, not even noticing how soaked her leopard-print pumps are. The sky is dark, moonless, she shouldn't be out this time of night on her own, but it's Bath. She feels safer out here in the wind and rain than she does in her own house at the moment.

She shelters in the doorway of the café in the high street and lights a cigarette. She's started smoking more since Abi moved in. Her fingers tremble as she puts the cigarette to her lips and inhales deeply, savouring the sickly taste of the tobacco as it burns the back of her throat. She's still reeling from the argument with Abi and at the way she was cast as the bad guy at dinner tonight; her heart races when she recalls it. How can they treat her this way? After everything she's done. For both of them.

She had made an effort to be polite when she asked Abi to return her clothes this afternoon. True, she wanted them back, but it had been two weeks, surely Abi could have bought some summer clothes by now? And anyhow, she didn't want to see Abi wearing her dresses. Not after everything. Even so, she had been shocked when Abi angrily pulled her precious dresses from their respective hangers and almost threw them at her as if they were nothing more than rags. Then her facetious remark about making another bracelet, like it didn't matter about the first one, it was nothing that Beatrice's reputation was on the line, her hard work down the drain.

It had made Beatrice want to smack her smug face.

She takes another drag of her cigarette. *Maybe I was wrong to accuse Abi of stealing the bracelet,* she thinks as she exhales smoke into the damp night air. She tried to apologize at dinner, but it infuriated her to see how Abi had obviously gone running to Ben, making out that she, Abi, was the victim in all this. She had the gall to sit there, clutching Ben's hand, her face contorted with worry, playing the innocent little girl act while Ben sat next to her, big and protective and on her side.

Are you trying to turn Ben against me?

She had noticed the maroon tea-dress hanging in Abi's wardrobe this afternoon as well as the brand-new, still in the box, Dunlop Green Flash trainers on the shelf. Beatrice wonders if it has occurred to Abi how similar the two of them look. The same heart-shaped faces, ski-slope noses, fair hair, slim frame?

Are you trying to replace me, Abi? Is that what this is all about? Is that why you bought identical trainers? The type of dress I'd wear? This thought makes her shiver and she wraps her coat further around her body.

There would have been a time when Beatrice would have felt secure in the knowledge that she was Ben's number one girl, his priority. But now she's not so sure. It's true that she might have had an ulterior motive when she asked Abi to move in initially, but this is the last thing she thought would happen.

A streetlamp hums and flickers, its orange halo illuminating the fine rain that continues to fall. She takes another drag of her cigarette then stubs it out against the wall, flicking the stub behind her.

Whatever game you're playing, Abi, she decides resolutely as she thrusts her hands deep into her pockets and heads back into the rain, towards home, *I won't let you win. I've got too much to lose.*

Chapter Seventeen

The Mini, red and disconcertingly shiny, is parked just across from where I disembarked from the ferry, and the slightly built Asian man with a pretty, almost feminine face, ushers me towards it, unaware of my discomfort, my *fear*.

'Have you driven a Mini before, Miss Cavendish?' he says, clutching his clipboard to his chest. Regardless of his diminutive stature I have to trot to keep up with him. I shake my head. I'm finding it difficult to swallow. When we get to the vehicle he makes notes with a scratchy ballpoint pen on to a car-shaped diagram as to its current condition, and I hope it will still be scratch free when I return it tomorrow. He opens the door and leans inside to demonstrate how to start the engine, where the controls and indicators are, and how to use the built-in sat nav. And then he drops the key fob into the palm of my trembling hand and leaves me standing there, unsure if I have the nerve to get behind the wheel after all this time.

In London it was easy not to drive, what with a tube station a short walk from our house. Even in Bath I can take the bus whenever I need to go into town, or to visit my parents. It's a waste of money running a car, I say to Mum and Dad when they express concern about the fact I've hardly driven since the accident. My Audi was a write-off, but my insurance company had given me a couple of grand for the car and everyone had insisted I needed to buy another one, that I needed to 'get back on the horse' as it were. But then I met Alicia, followed by my attempted suicide, my breakdown. And when I was well enough to leave the psychiatric hospital to live with my parents, there was no need for a car. That's what I told myself, anyway. But the truth of it is that I'm scared. The last time I got behind a wheel I ended up killing my own twin sister. What if I ended up endangering the life of someone else?

Swallowing down the bile that's rising in my throat, I slide into the driver's seat and touch the wheel gingerly. Surely I can't do much damage in a Mini? A young mother pushing a pram crosses the road in front of where I'm parked, and I shudder as I imagine ploughing into her, the bonnet of the car lifting the pram high into the air, the screams of the baby . . . I fight the urge to retch. *I don't know if I can do this.*

I wait as the young mother manoeuvres her pram

safely on to the pavement before I have the courage to push the key fob into the dashboard, and I press the ignition button with a timorous hand. I sit there for a while, the car purring away, nauseous at the thought of driving through the streets of Cowes. I turn my head. The glisten of the late afternoon sun bounces off the sea in the distance, the white triangular sail of a boat bobs up and down. I take a deep breath, inhaling the scent of salt in the air, and I close my eyes, reminding myself of the mantra that Janice taught me, becoming calmer as I concentrate on breathing in and out. In and out.

Then I hear Lucy's soft voice in my ear, so clearly it's as though she's sitting in the front passenger seat next to me. *It wasn't your fault. You can do this, Abi.* I press my foot down on the clutch, push the gearstick into first and gently tap the accelerator, amazed as the car begins to crawl slowly away from the kerb and on to the road.

And I can't stop the smile spreading across my face as I hear Lucy whooping and cheering beside me as I drive, *actually drive*, towards Cowes.

The bed and breakfast that Miranda has booked for me has a view of the marina and a landlady who reminds me of my late grandmother. She fusses around me when I arrive, asking if she can make me a cooked breakfast in the morning and if I wish for my one solitary holdall to be taken up to the bedroom. I politely turn down any offers of help and escape to the sanctuary of my room, which is small but pleasant in a shabby-chic kind of way. I quickly unpack my wash bag and hang up the trousers I will be wearing for the interview tomorrow in the white painted wardrobe, a frisson of nerves mixed with excitement that I've been given this chance to interview Patricia Lipton. The room is chilly even though the sun is out. I unravel my cardigan, briefly putting it to my nose to inhale the comforting scent of home. Beatrice's home. I wrap it around me and head out in the vague direction of the marina, the breeze whipping my hair back, the smell of fish and chips in the air, the melancholy call of seagulls, and I'm reminded of Lucy and of my childhood at seaside places reminiscent of this, of me chasing her – always chasing her, although I could never quite catch her – dressed in our red swimsuits with the frills around the bottom, her yellow ponytail swinging as she ran, our laughter ringing out as we clutched our plastic windmills in our chubby hands, faces smeared with ice cream, and Mum and Dad trailing behind us with proud smiles as strangers stopped to comment on how pretty we were, how *identical*. Too identical, as it turns out.

I carry on walking, past the marina with its cluster of sailboats in white and blue, through the cobbled pavements of the town centre, on to the promenade with pensioners reclining on wooden benches looking out to sea, until I get to the beach. I pick my way over the shingles, amazed how quiet it is for July. There are a few families making the most of the last of the day's sunshine and a scattering of couples sitting holding hands or lolling against the wall. I make my way to the water's edge in my flip-flops and my jeans turned up at the ankle, enjoying the warm sea lapping at my toes. My thirtieth birthday is at the beginning of next month. Every time I think of it I get a stabbing pain under my ribs, the sense of loss, of going through life alone instead of sharing these milestones with Lucy. I'm getting older while my twin sister will forever be twenty-eight.

As I turn and glance back towards the road, I freeze. She's sitting on the wall, her long legs crossed at the ankle, her pale bob skimming her tanned shoulders, slim fingers fanned out to shield her eyes from the sunshine. At first I'm convinced it's Lucy, until I notice the dark markings of a flower weaving its way around her ankle. I squint to get a better look. Has she caught the train to Southampton and boarded the ferry to follow me here? I close my eyes and shake my head, hoping that when I open them again she would have evaporated like the optical illusion I'm hoping she is, because surely I must be imagining her sitting there. It's my illness, my paranoia. But when I open my eyes she's still there. There's nothing for it, I think, but to confront her, to ask her what the hell she's playing at. But as soon as I take a step forward she gets up, dusting down her summer dress, and hops off the wall with the agility of a cat, disappearing into the clusters of people on the street, leaving me staring after her, terrified that I'm losing my mind.

I spend most of the night tossing and turning in the double bed, as if my body is aware that it's meant for two. My head is full of all of them: Lucy, Nia, Callum, Luke, Ben, Beatrice, Cass, Jodie and Pam. Their faces are interchangeable as they race through my thoughts; a television recording on fast forward. Would Beatrice follow me here, and if so, why? I eventually fall asleep to the shriek of gulls as the sun filters through the slats in the wooden shutters.

But I can't shake the uneasiness that envelops me as I shower and dress. I pull on my smart black trousers that I've hardly had the need to wear since Lucy died. Now they gape slightly at the waist. The sun is high in the sky, but I throw on my denim jacket over my cotton blouse to be on the safe side. Then I pack the rest of my meagre items in the holdall and go down for breakfast.

The dining room has the same view of the marina as my bedroom. I'm surprisingly hungry and enjoy the sausage, bacon and eggs the landlady has made for me, nodding politely as she talks about the local sights.

The drive to Patricia's house is a pleasant one along slow coastal roads, and, thanks to the built-in sat nav, I don't get lost. My knees still tremble at being behind the wheel, but I am reassured by the car's compactness, the fact that I'm not carrying any passengers who I can inadvertently kill. I'm even confident enough to turn the radio on. Katy Perry is singing about fireworks as I drive past couples holding hands as they meander along the front, and children skipping in sunhats, eating ice creams. Then I turn into an unadopted side road that's little more than a track, the rough terrain causing the Mini to shudder and lurch over potholes until I get to wrought-iron gates that stand open, revealing a pretty Edwardian country house. I park next to a black VW Golf, wondering if the photographer is already here as I step out on to the gravel and crunch my way to the arch-shaped wooden front door, heart banging in my chest. I'm worried I will mess up and look stupid in front of an intelligent woman like Patricia. A woman who has written countless best-sellers, most of which I've read. She's one of my idols, and the thought of meeting her, of talking to her about her life, makes me forget everything else for a few minutes.

Patricia answers, tall and elegant and not looking her sixty-eight years. I introduce myself as she shakes my hand, aware that mine is clammy, and she ushers me into a large drawing room the same size as Beatrice's, except whereas Bea's is crammed full of brightly coloured sofas and eclectic artefacts, Patricia's reminds me of a sepia photograph with all its cream and brown hues. For all its beauty, the room has a lived-in look about it: a stack of books on the coffee table, dog hairs on the sofa, a cat's scratching post by the patio doors. I perch on the sofa while she takes a seat in an elegant armchair opposite me, next to a brick fireplace. The room has a view of a large back garden with an orchard in the distance, and I slowly begin to relax. I decline the offer of tea and we sit down.

'The photographer is setting up in the garden,' she says and although I'm a little intimidated by her, I realize I like her already, that she's not a disappointment. I pull out my notepad from my bag.

We spend nearly an hour talking about her childhood, how she came to be published and what inspires her to write her sagas, and as we talk I find that my confidence is coming back with every squiggle of shorthand I write on the page. I'm about to finish up with some tips for hopeful writers when the patio doors open, letting in a waft of the fresh summer air, the smell of hollyhocks, and I look up, shock searing through me so that my pen and notepad fall to the seagrass carpet. At first I think this must be another optical illusion. But no, it is him. He has a camera slung around his neck, his usual nonplussed expression on his face as he walks over the threshold, as tall and lanky as Ben. I haven't seen him since that day in hospital, a few months after Lucy died, but his beauty still makes the breath catch in my throat. He hasn't noticed me.

'We're ready for you, Mrs Lipton, if you're finished in here,' Callum says in his familiar South London drawl. I stand up and our eyes meet. He hasn't changed a bit, he's still as scruffy as a student in the same black leather jacket that he wore when we were together, faded jeans, beat-up retro trainers. His hair is shorter now, a few new lines around his face, his eyes the deep shade of royal blue that haunted me in my dreams and my nightmares for months after we split up.

'Abi . . .' His voice is gentle, our eyes locked. I'm unable to tear my gaze away from him and it's as though I'm transported back in time, that the last eighteen months have all been a horrible mistake.

I force myself to look away from him, and continue to talk to Patricia, determined not to let the fact that I'm in the same room as Callum stop me from being professional. I thank Patricia for her time, trying to keep my voice level and, ignoring Callum completely, I gather up my notepad and pen and hurriedly stuff them in my bag. Patricia walks me to the front door. If she's noticed the tension between me and her photographer she does a good job of pretending otherwise.

I wait until I'm safely in the car, and Patricia has gone back into the house, before falling apart. I lean over the steering wheel, gasping for breath, heart hammering. I'm shaking all over. *Concentrate on your breathing*, I tell myself. I can't drive in this state, I have to calm down. But seeing Callum again after all this time has given me such a shock I feel physically sick.

Eventually my legs stop trembling and my heart slows. What is Callum doing here? He must have engineered it, it can't be a coincidence. I look towards the house. There is no sign of him, thankfully. I need to get out of here, I don't want to talk to him.

I push the key fob into the ignition and start up the car. I'm putting the gearstick into reverse when I hear Callum's shouts and I see him striding across the gravel, camera slung around his neck. 'Abi, wait!' he cries as he reaches the car. I wind my window down.

'I've got nothing to say to you.' I can't look at him, I force myself to stare out of the windscreen instead. I have a view of a field of cows.

171

'Please, Abi. I was hoping you'd be here. Will you meet me for a drink in half an hour?'

'I didn't know you still worked for Miranda,' I say stiffly, still looking at the cows.

'I don't. I'm freelance. But Mike on Picture Desk called me about this job—'

'There's no point,' I cut him off. 'I've got nothing to say to you.' My voice is cold, steely. I rev the engine pointedly.

'Please.' The note of despair I hear in his voice makes me turn towards him and I meet his gaze full on. It still hurts to look at him. To remember . . .

I swallow, my throat is scratchy and raw. I give the briefest of nods.

His face brightens. 'There's a pub on the main road. It's called the White Hart. Can we meet there in half an hour?'

'I'll think about it. You should get back. It's not professional to keep Patricia waiting,' I say before winding the window up, shutting him out. I can see him from my rear-view mirror as I pull away, gradually getting smaller and smaller until I round the corner and he's out of sight.

Against my better judgement I'm sitting at a round table in the pub's dark, gloomy snug with mahogany wood panelling on the walls, sipping a Coke. Am I doing the right thing? Wouldn't it be wiser to let the past stay that way, rather than sit here and rehash it, apportioning blame?

I fire off a quick text to Nia, explaining the situation and asking what I should do. She replies within minutes, encouraging me to meet him. *Don't you want answers?* I text back that she's right, I do want answers. I'm at last ready to hear what he's got to say, however painful. I've just dropped my mobile into my bag when I spot Callum walking in. He saunters to the bar, probably ordering his usual pint of Stella, and then he joins me by the square leaded window with the faded red curtains.

'Do you want to sit outside?'

I shake my head. 'It's fine in here.' I want to snap at him, tell him that this isn't a date. I don't want to join everyone else at benches in the beer garden, I want to get this over and done with.

'So, how have you been?' His legs are so long that his knees are almost under his chin as he perches on a velvet-topped stool. He places his heavy Canon digital camera on to the table next to his pint.

'What do you think?'

He sighs. I'm not going to make this easy for him. 'Nia said you've moved out of London,' he tries again. 'She didn't say where.'

'I told her not to.'

There's a pause as he takes a swig of his lager, I can tell he's trying to think what to say next. I remain silent, sullen. He puts his pint down, surveys me. 'You're looking well.' And I know he's remembering the last time we saw each other. I can remember it too, the shock in his usually laughing eyes as I lay curled up on my side, legs pulled

173

up to my tummy on that narrow bed in that sterile green room with nothing but a sheet over me, a drip in my arm and bandages on my wrists, and I recall how a tear crept out of his eye and snaked its way along his nose; he thought I hadn't noticed as he quickly wiped it away. *Proper men don't cry, do they, Callum?*

The sun streams through the window, illuminating the dust motes floating above our table, before it disappears behind a cloud again, the room gloomy once more.

'You know . . .' He doesn't look at me, instead he picks up a beer mat, his long fingers working away at the cardboard edges. 'It's not such a coincidence that I'm here today. Mike told me you were interviewing Patricia Lipton. I wanted to see you, but I was still surprised you actually came. I know you haven't been working . . .'

'I've done the odd piece for Miranda since I moved out of London,' I say, defensively.

He holds up his hands. 'Look, I don't want to argue with you. I wanted to see you, to see if you were okay.'

'To assuage your guilt.'

He hangs his head and I know it's a low blow. How can I blame him when it's my fault too? 'Does Luke still hate me?' I say in a small voice.

He lifts his head and a jolt of desire rips through me. I know, in spite of everything that happened, he will always be special to me, my first love.

'I don't know, we don't talk about it. I've hardly seen him since he moved out.'

I remember how it was still raining when the ambulance arrived. Luke was cradling her in his arms. He followed the stretcher on to the ambulance as if it was his God-given right, leaving me slumped by the tree, too scared to move while a paramedic checked me over. Lucy never made it as far as the hospital and I wasn't with her when she died. We entered the world together but she left it without me by her side. Extensive head injuries, they said, while the rest of us escaped the car crash with sprains, cuts and bruises.

'He said he'd never forgive me,' I mutter.

'He didn't mean it, Abi. He was devastated. His girl-friend had recently died.'

I feel a burst of indignation. 'He took over, I'll never forgive him for that. It was his fault I wasn't there when she died.' I press my fingers into my palms and concentrate on the pain my nails are causing my flesh, rather than the tears that threaten.

'We all loved her.' He says it quietly and I know that, at last, I'm ready to hear the truth. I need to know what happened that night. For the last eighteen months I've tried to block it out, avoiding the issue even if Janice encouraged me to face it, to talk to Callum. But I didn't want to revisit that awful night, to remember that my last words to Lucy had been said in anger.

'That night . . . You said you thought Lucy was me, but that wasn't the case at all, was it, Callum?' He chews his lip and I know he's considering whether to be honest with me, whether it might send me over the edge again.

I place my hand on his. 'I need to know the truth now. I was hiding from it before, but it's better to face up to it. I'm not angry with her. I've never been angry with her. But please tell me the truth. Were you in love with Lucy?'

He shakes his head. 'Oh, Abi. Of course I wasn't in love with her. Not in the way you think. Your crazy jealousy always gnawed at our relationship. Lucy was my friend, that's all.'

A flare of anger flickers inside me, but just as quickly it's gone. He's right, I know he's right. I can't lie to myself about it any longer. But I take my hand away from his and cup my glass.

'I know I was jealous—' I begin.

'I liked that you were jealous,' interrupts Callum. 'At first, anyway. You were possessive, but it made me feel as though you loved me. But after a while it got tiring.'

I lift my eyes to look at him. 'You can't blame me for being jealous. Before you met me, you went out with Lucy.'

'And how many times did I have to tell you that it was for two weeks, Abi? Two bloody weeks, months before I met you. You know that we only went on a couple of dates, but it came to nothing. After that she met Luke. We didn't have much in common. Whereas with you . . .' He lets his voice trail off. He doesn't have to say it. We were together for four years, we shared everything. We had a passion for the same music, the same films, and each other.

176

'The night of the Halloween party. You kissed her, Callum.'

He sighs. 'I thought she was you,' he says gently. 'You were both dressed as witches. It was dark. You were identical twins, Abi. I kissed her thinking she was you. I told you all this at the time.' I can hear a touch of exasperation in his voice and I think back to our relationship, to all of the times when he had to reassure me that he didn't fancy one of my friends, or didn't still harbour feelings for Lucy, that I was the one he wanted to be with. I can see how it must have been tiring. It must have been exhausting.

When I saw Callum kissing my sister that night, I pulled them apart with a ferociousness, a strength, I never knew I possessed and stormed out of the party with both of them following behind me, protesting their innocence. But I hadn't believed them. I hadn't *wanted* to believe them, I was so consumed with jealousy. Luke had been right when he made that statement to the police saying my judgement was impaired when my car went off the road. I had been screaming at Lucy. I can't bear to think how I accused her of fancying my boyfriend. Even Luke had told me I was talking nonsense, but I had been on a roll. All my insecurities bubbled over and spewed out of me. The last thing I remember before I lost control of the car was Nia telling me to calm down. Calm down, she had said. If I had remained calm, we might never have crashed. If Callum hadn't kissed my sister, my last words to her wouldn't have been vicious ones and she probably wouldn't have died. So many ifs. We were so close, the five of us, we did everything together, and in one night everything changed for ever.

'I'm so sorry,' I say in a small voice. *My jealousy cost you your life, Lucy.* A tear snakes down my cheek and I don't bother to brush it away.

Callum grabs my hand in both of his. 'Abi, you finished with me and refused to speak to me after the accident. I know you blamed me, but it was a stupid mistake that I wish I could take back.' He lowers his voice. 'I would do anything to take it back.'

I sniff. 'I know, I wanted someone else to take it out on, but really I blamed myself. I still blame myself.'

'Abi, you can't blame yourself. It was an accident.'

I shake my head. I will never believe it wasn't my fault, regardless of what anyone else says. 'After the accident, my head was a mess. The truth was, I suppose I was always a little jealous of Lucy. I always felt she was everything that I wasn't. She was cleverer, nicer, easier to be with. I always joked with her that she was my better half. She denied it, of course, but she was.'

'Listen, Abs, I can't imagine what it's like to be a twin, or how it must feel now. But you have to know, I never thought Lucy was your better half. Lucy was Lucy. And you are you. And I loved *you*. Do you believe me? About that night? It's important to me that you do.'

'I believe you,' I say truthfully. We sit in silence for a while and then he asks about my life now. I tell him about moving to Bath, about meeting Beatrice, and Ben.

'You know, they're twins too. It seems destined somehow, that I was meant to meet them, although . . .' He raises an eyebrow to prompt me to continue. 'Beatrice is very over-protective of Ben. She seemed to want to be my friend at first, but since Ben and I got together . . .' I glance at him to gauge his reaction; if it bothers him that I'm with someone else, he doesn't let it show. 'Well, Beatrice has distanced herself from me. And then I thought I saw her yesterday.'

'Here? On the Isle of Wight?'

'Yes.' I reveal everything, about Janice, my post-traumatic stress disorder, my paranoia, but I can't bring myself to tell him about the bracelet. 'So I know, deep down, that it couldn't have been her. It makes no sense.'

Callum nods, gently squeezing my hand. 'Don't let jealousy or paranoia cloud your judgement or ruin what you have with Ben.' His next words hang in the air, unspoken. *Like you did with us.*

Chapter Eighteen

They fall through the door, laughing and windswept. Beatrice can smell the sea salt on his hair and she thinks how she's missed this, their easiness with each other. It's dusk, her favourite time of day in the summer. The house is quiet with no sign of Pam or Cass and she's relieved that she's able to have him all to herself for a while longer.

'Thanks for today, Bea.' He pushes the door closed with the sole of his trainer and throws his car keys in the direction of the hallway table where they clatter into a ceramic dish. 'You always know how to cheer me up.'

'We deserved a treat.' She reaches up and squeezes his upper arm affectionately, marvelling at his strong, toned muscles. 'Now go and put the kettle on, I need to pop upstairs.'

'You're very bossy,' he jokes as he strides down the

hallway. She waits until he's rounding the steps that lead to the kitchen, then she kicks off her sandals and dumps her canvas bag with its bucket and spade, suncream and Evian, and races up the two flights of stairs before she has a chance to change her mind. She knows he will come looking for her soon.

Abi's room is immaculate. The new duvet cover that Beatrice suspects is from the White Company – *I thought you had no money, Abi?* – has been pulled tight across the bed, the walls are now painted a pretty lavender and the smell of Jodie has been replaced by something floral, familiar. Four books are stacked neatly on her night stand, next to a silver framed photograph of Abi and Lucy, smiling, tanned, their arms around each other's necks. It's the photo from the newspaper cutting, but in colour instead of black and white. Beatrice picks it up and examines it, trying to see the variations in their faces, but it's like a game of spot the difference. Lucy's eyebrows are more arched, as if she's had them threaded, a pink gloss staining her lips, her hair neater, straighter, and it's obvious that Lucy took more care in her appearance, was more feminine, but apart from these small concessions to fashion, to beauty, they are mirror images of one another. Beatrice finds their likeliness uncanny.

She replaces the photograph and then her eye catches the large plastic daisy on top of a curvaceous perfume bottle that sits in the middle of a cluster of face creams and body lotions, and a chill runs down her back.

Daisy by Marc Jacobs. It's the same scent that she wears.

Why would you do that, Abi? Why would you deliberately buy the same perfume as me?

Beatrice picks up the book on the top of the pile, it's a hardback with a ripped plastic cover, possibly a charity shop find or, as she discovers from flipping over the front page and noticing the inky stamp mark, from Bath Central Library. Patricia Lipton, the author's name, rings a faint bell. She turns it over to read the synopsis on the back, some boring story about a workhouse that Catherine Cookson would be proud of. Beatrice replaces it. It's not her type of thing at all. She opens the drawer, her heart lurching when she notices a blister pack of pills. Surely they aren't contraception pills? The pack has no indentations, no pills have been removed.

'What are you doing?' His voice is sharp, causing her to spring away from the drawer, dropping the pills on the floor.

'I . . . um . . .' she turns to see Ben in the doorway, his eyes narrowed. It only takes a few strides before Ben's standing before her. He bends down to pick up the packet, his eyebrows drawn together.

'I can't believe you're going through her things. What are you playing at? And what are these?' He turns them over in his hands. 'Fluoxetine. Put them back,' he snaps.

She takes them from him. 'Are these antidepressants?'

He nods, his jaw clenched.

'Then shouldn't she have taken them with her? I'm

obviously no doctor, Ben, but surely she can't miss a dose?'

'It's not right being in her room without her knowledge,' he says. He wanders to the window, pulling aside the curtains that Abi still hasn't got around to replacing and that are at odds with the rest of the bedroom, and peers out the window. Beatrice goes to stand behind him, her fingers still wrapped around the packet of antidepressants. Over his shoulder she notices the lamplights on the street below fluttering into life.

'I'm sorry. I thought . . . the bracelet, you know.'

He sighs. 'Can't you just let it go?'

She pulls his arm. 'Look at me, Ben.' He turns to face her, his eyes downcast. 'I think she stole that bracelet. I don't know why. Maybe she's jealous, maybe she wants to sabotage my new business. Maybe she wanted it for herself, or needed some money. I don't know. I'm sorry, I realize you're fond of her, but . . .'

'I love her, Bea.' His voice is unusually soft and the sound of it makes Beatrice reel. For a moment she thinks she might be sick. He tilts his eyes up to meet hers, searching her face as if waiting for her reaction, and there is something behind his expression, a smugness, as if he's used those words on purpose, to provoke her, to hurt her.

'Even though she may be a thief?' She knows it's a low blow, but she can't resist.

'I don't think she is. But if she did take your bracelet, as you claim, she needs our help.'

His words shame her.

'You're right.' She walks towards Abi's bedside cabinet and puts the packet of antidepressants back in the drawer where she found them. She's about to close it when something sparkles, catching her eye. Nestled in the corner, almost hidden by the scented drawer-liner dotted with rosebuds, is an earring.

'Ben, look at this.' And she can't help a sense of satisfaction as she places the earring triumphantly in the palm of his hand where it sits, unaware of its significance, delicate and daisy-shaped and yellow as the sun.

Chapter Nineteen

Somebody has been in my bedroom. It's barely perceptible but I can tell by the curtains that are pulled back a fraction too much; the wrinkled indentation on my duvet cover where someone has been sitting on my bed; the drawer to my night stand that has been left ajar; the Patricia Lipton novel that has been replaced upside down.

I dump my bag next to the bed and hurry to the wardrobe. Throwing open the doors, I stand on my tiptoes to reach for the box containing Lucy's letters, hidden on the shelf above my meagre selection of clothes. Relief surges through me as my hands grasp it, but when I bring it down I can tell straight away that someone has been rifling through them. The letters, that I had taken such pains to bind with an elastic band, are now loose so that they swim across from one end to the other like unfettered fish as I carry the box to the bed. Feverishly, I count the letters and my heart drops. This time there is no mistake; three of the letters are missing.

I take a deep breath to fight the nausea, thinking of Beatrice, painfully aware why she's done this.

I'm about to replace the lid when I notice something shiny shoved in one of the envelopes. Is it a photograph? Puzzled, I pull it out while at the same time thinking that I never keep photos in with Lucy's letters. I freeze in shock, letting the box slip off my lap and fall on to the carpet, spilling letters everywhere.

A chill runs down my spine.

The photograph is one I've never seen before. It's a six-by-four inch black and white, head-and-shoulders shot. By the mid-length fair hair I suspect the picture is of me. Except I can't tell for sure because someone has deliberately, and by the look of it, quite violently, scratched the face off.

I know I have to bide my time before mentioning the letters, and the photograph, to Ben. I get my chance a few days later.

We're sprawled out on the stripy sun-loungers that are a permanent feature on the terrace since the heatwave. At our feet are empty glasses, half-eaten packets of crisps, an ashtray and a bottle of sunscreen that Ben earlier slathered over his freckled nose. His face is turned up to the cloudy sky, his eyes closed, although the sun isn't strong enough to provide any real warmth and I'm covered up in jeans and a cardigan.

The Sisters

Both of us have skirted around the issue of Beatrice and the missing bracelet since I returned from the Isle of Wight. I've hardly seen her, it's almost as if she's been going out of her way to avoid me, and when we do bump into each other at breakfast, or pass each other on the stairs, our conversation is anodyne, courteous. In spite of everything, the cold-shouldering, the petulance over my relationship with her brother, her accusations, her stealing Lucy's precious letters, the dead bird, the creepy photograph, I am sad that it's come to this. In my weaker moments, I want to rush up to her, to apologize for everything that's gone wrong and to resume our friendship. But I know that can never happen, not while I'm dating Ben. I was mistaken, thinking I could have them both. I've been too greedy.

I clear my throat, suddenly nervous about how to broach the subject with Ben, but I'm desperate to get those letters back, and short of returning the favour and going through Beatrice's room, I'm at a loss as to what to do. The game I've been forced to play has reached stalemate.

Ben turns over on to his elbow, squinting up at me. 'Are you okay?'

'There's something I need to tell you.'

'Uh oh, is this serious?' he jokes. But he adjusts his lounger into an upright position, like mine, and stubs out his cigarette.

'When I was in the Isle of Wight . . .' I begin.

'You met up with your ex-boyfriend,' he finishes. His

187

smile slips from his face and for a moment, a millisecond really, I glimpse another side to him. A side I haven't seen before; hard probing eyes, set jawline; almost a completely different person. But, as quickly, it disappears and he's Ben again. Warm, familiar, safe.

I can't speak for a few seconds, I'm so surprised. 'That's not what I was going to tell you,' I manage eventually.

'It's none of my business,' he mutters, lowering his eyes. I want to reach out and touch him, tell him that he has nothing to be jealous about, but something stops me. 'How did you know anyway?'

He shrugs. 'Beatrice.'

'How the hell does Beatrice know?'

He frowns as if the idea never occurred to him. 'I don't know, I assume you told her.'

I exhale in frustration. He's blind, oblivious to the fact that Beatrice is barely speaking to me, that we're involved in some bizarre power struggle over him.

It was you, wasn't it, darling Bea? Sitting on the wall that day, I think, silently fuming. *You did follow me to the Isle of Wight. But why? To cause trouble?*

'Why are you so angry?' He swings his long legs over the edge of the lounger so that he's facing me. 'If anything, I should be angry with you.'

'I thought you said it was none of your business,' I snap.

'You're my girlfriend.'

'So you wish I'd told you?'

He blinks. 'Yes, I wish you'd told me.'

The Sisters

I clench my fists at my sides. 'Beatrice is a stirrer.' I feel an explosion of anger in my chest, the words spilling out of my mouth uncontrollably. 'She hates that I'm your girlfriend. She wants you all to herself. She stole some letters that Lucy had written to me. They're all I have left of her, Beatrice must realize how important they are to me. I know she's been through my room. I know she put the dead bird on my bed to freak me out – you said yourself her cat is too fat and lazy to chase anything, let alone kill it. Do you know I found a photograph? It was a photo of me, I can tell because I'm wearing that white T-shirt of mine, with Blondie on the front. I don't even know when the photo was taken. Or by whom.' I pause for dramatic effect. 'It had white scratch marks where my face should have been. Don't you think that's a bit threatening?'

He freezes, a look of horror on his face. It almost makes me want to laugh. But instead I say, 'She's trying to scare me. Maybe she's hoping that I will move out, I don't know. But it's sick.'

He's silent, processing what I've told him. Eventually he says calmly, 'If she's been through your room it's because she thinks you've stolen her bracelet.' He says this without raising his voice. 'But I can't believe she would plant a nasty photograph in your things. Bea isn't vicious.'

I hesitate. 'She's been moving my antidepressants,' I blurt out. 'They never seem to be in the same place. And one time the packet was empty, as if someone had taken

189

great pains to pop all the pills out of their blisters. I had to get an emergency supply. You know how dangerous it is to miss a dose, don't you?'

He nods, but I see it. Disbelief. It passes over his face like a cloud over sunshine and I'm suddenly furious.

'Do you know what I think?' I don't wait for him to answer. 'I don't think her bracelet is missing at all. I think she's making it up to point the finger at me. To put you off me. And she's obviously winning – you're on her side. Twins stick together, don't they? I should know that more than most,' I laugh, although I don't find it funny. 'What was I thinking, getting involved with the two of you?' Tears sting my eyes. I blink them back.

'Abi,' his voice is soothing, patient. It's the voice of the doctors that treated me when I was on the psychiatric ward. 'Of course I'm not on her side. Please don't put me in the middle. I love you both.'

It's the first time that Ben's said he loves me. I can't help it, a tear escapes and runs down my cheek. He reaches across and takes my hand. 'Come here,' he says, and I join him on his lounger, my legs snaking between his, my head on his chest. He strokes my hair back from my face, his other arm clamping me to him protectively and my anger vanishes along with my paranoia as I remember Callum's warning. I can't let my jealousy, my illness, ruin what I've got with Ben.

'I'll talk to her, I'll sort it all out. Please don't worry. Everything will be all right.'

I desperately want to believe him.

*

Later that night, as I'm walking up the stairs carrying a mug of tea and a plate of Eva's chocolate cake, I hear raised voices coming from Beatrice's bedroom. I pause, straining my ears, pleased that the walls are thinner than they appear. I can hear the low rumble of Ben's Scottish drawl, but it's indistinct so I can't quite catch what he's saying although I'm sure he mentioned my name. Then Beatrice's higher-pitched tones, shrill with indignation. 'Of course I haven't got her precious letters.' I can't hear Ben's reply but I know he will be defending me. He loves me. I can't help smiling to myself as I push open my bedroom door with my foot.

Beatrice is already sitting at the wooden table when I come down for breakfast the next morning. She's flicking idly through a newspaper, her slim fingers curved around her porcelain mug. She's wearing a pink silk dressing gown, her face devoid of make-up, and I think how tired, how wan she looks. I switch on the kettle and stand at the worktop waiting for it to boil, my gaze firmly fixed on the window. A woman walks past, all I can see are her calves encased in sheer denier tights and nude heels. It sounds as if she's talking on a mobile phone, some nebulous conversation that gets louder and clearer as she passes and then fades, along with the sound of her footsteps.

Beatrice doesn't say a word until I'm sitting opposite her with my cup of tea. 'Morning,' she says, without looking up from her newspaper.

I mumble a greeting and take a sip of my tea. There is so much I want to ask her. How did she know I was meeting up with Callum? Had she followed me to the Isle of Wight intent on making trouble for me and Ben? Is she afraid I might take Ben away from her? Why is she trying to frighten me? I suspect it's her, yet it still freaks me out. But I don't know where to start, it all sounds so far-fetched, so ludicrous, even to me.

We are both silent for a while but the tension between us is palpable and I squirm in my seat. Where are the others? I know Ben's gone to work today, but I haven't seen Pam or Cass emerge from their bedrooms yet.

'Beatrice,' I say. My voice sounds strained in the quiet room and the mug in my hand trembles at the thought of confronting her, but I have to clear the air between us. I know where I stand with Ben now. He loves me and there is nothing Beatrice can do about it, despite her best efforts. 'Can I ask you something?'

She lifts her head and I notice for the first time her puffy eyes, like she's been crying. 'Go ahead.' She sounds unconcerned, bored.

'When I was on the Isle of Wight I thought I saw you, at the beach. Were you there? Is that how you knew I met up with Callum?'

She stares at me, her eyes widening, and she shakes her head, emitting a bark of laughter that makes me uneasy, scared. 'So this is the role you've cast for me is it, Abi? The jealous and possessive twin sister? What about the jealous and possessive girlfriend?'

'I'm not jealous, or possessive.' I think of Lucy, of Callum, and I know this is a lie.

'Oh, Abi.' She takes a deep breath, her eyes holding mine as if she's trying to read my thoughts. 'Who are you?' she says eventually, and there is a kind of wonderment in her voice as if she is unsure of who I am. Sweat prickles my armpits.

'What do you mean?' My hand trembles so that hot liquid jumps out of the mug I'm holding and splashes on to the table. I put the mug down.

Beatrice is still staring at me, as if she's baffled by me. 'Oh, come on, Abi. You can stop the innocent act now. Ben's not here, it's only the two of us.'

I blink at her, confused.

She sighs. 'Have it your way. I didn't even know you went to the Isle of Wight. Why would I? You've hardly spoken to me for weeks.' She pushes back her chair and folds her newspaper under her arm. 'I feel sorry for you, Abi.' She pauses as if considering if she should say what comes into her mind next, as if she's worried that it might implicate her in some way. 'But please, help yourself too. Take your medication.' And with that she pads out of the room, her bare feet squeaking against the Bath stone, leaving me sitting at the table, alone.

I spend most of the day in my bedroom with my laptop, only venturing down to the kitchen to refill my coffee cup or to grab a sandwich. I bump into Eva in the kitchen making some sort of pie, her delicate hands busily kneading the dough, while Pam languishes by the Aga, chattering away so quickly in her broad accent that I doubt Eva is able to understand a word of what she's saying. Neither of them acknowledge me as I prepare my lunch.

Miranda, pleased with my Patricia Lipton feature, has commissioned me to do a telephone interview with a well-known comedian. It turns out the comedian is only funny on television, his answers are monosyllabic and he moans about having a cold, which I infer is a euphemism for a hangover. Desperate to get away from the house, after I've finished interviewing him I put my laptop in my bag and walk to the little coffee shop in the high street, where I rattle off a thousand words and email it to Miranda.

Later, as the clouds obscure the sunshine, turning everything grey, I close my laptop and head back. I've had two cups of strong coffee and I'm shaky and bilious as I turn into the street. I slow down as I see them coming through the gate of number nineteen, Beatrice with one arm linked through Ben's and the other clasping Cass's hand, Pam and her boyfriend trailing behind. They turn left in the direction of the tennis courts and I watch their retreating backs, the squeal of laughter floating towards me, Beatrice's head thrown back in glee, the proverbial Queen Bee, and I think that she's winning. I can't go back there. I'm no longer able to spend nights with Ben because of the sex ban, I'm no longer welcome to join in when Beatrice organizes some jaunt. She's trying to push me out, she's reminding me that they are all *her* friends, not mine. None of them are mine.

I turn back towards the high street, hoisting my bag firmly over my shoulder, and I keep walking, away from *that* house, away from them.

It's a two-minute stroll from the bus stop, down a hill and past the canal with its many pretty barges and pubs overlooking the water. Rain, wispy and insubstantial, but the kind that can drench you in minutes, begins to fall.

My parents live in a terraced cottage in the village of Bathampton. It's the type of cottage you read about in children's books, with stone mullioned windows and roses around the door, the sort where a wolf is waiting to trick you, dressed in your grandmother's clothes. But I know there are no wolves waiting to ensnare me here; I've left those at home. My mum answers the door, a surprised expression on her kind, familiar face, and as soon as I see her I burst into tears.

'Abi?' Her voice is sharp with alarm as she ushers me over the threshold and into their small square hallway. Dad comes rushing out of the sitting room and they both crowd around me, asking in urgent, panicked voices if I'm okay, asking if I've tried to harm myself. I tell them, through tears and snot, that of course I haven't tried to kill myself and they laugh with relief, pushing me firmly by the shoulders into the armchair by the television. Their favourite programme, *Emmerdale*, has been paused so that a woman with black hair, her mouth open as if about to shout an insult, is frozen on the screen. Their pug, Belle, a deliberate misnomer even though we think she's gorgeous, jumps on to my lap and begins nuzzling my armpit. I cuddle her to me, taking in her familiar malodorous doggy smell. She's been in the family for nearly fifteen years and as I cling to her neck I often think how she must miss Lucy too. Although it's the end of July, the wood burner is on and the room is stifling, but my parents can't abide the cold; they always planned to emigrate when they retired, but they've decided against that now. Because of me. Dad sits on the adjoining sofa, not speaking, but watching me and Belle, waiting for me to talk. Mum returns with a cup of tea – her cure for everything – which she thrusts into my hands. 'Ooh, you must be freezing, you're only wearing a little T-shirt. I can see goosebumps on your arms,' she says and rushes upstairs to retrieve a cardigan. It's good to be here, to be looked after, and as I settle back in my seat with the dog on my lap, I wonder why I resisted moving back here. I glance up at the photographs that adorn the fire-place, my eyes halting on the graduation shot of Lucy. There are hardly any of us on our own, but this one, larger than the rest, domineering, taking precedence over the smaller six-by-four-inch frames, is the exception. Dr Lucy Cavendish.

Mum comes back with a chunky beige cardigan that she wraps around my shoulders. 'The spare room is made up, if you want to stay the night, love?' she says as she perches next to my dad.

'What's going on, Abi?' says Dad. They both wait and I open my mouth to tell them everything: how I've fallen in love with Ben, how I felt safe in his arms at night, that he kept the nightmares, the guilt, at bay, how he made me feel worthy again, but after several weeks of great sex he's suddenly decided it's against his possessive sister's house rules to continue sleeping with me; about Beatrice and how she reminds me of Lucy in so many ways, except she has a controlling side to her nature, a side that Lucy never had, and that she's angry, perhaps jealous of my relationship with Ben; that she's leaving nasty things in my room to scare me into moving out, and that she's succeeding, that I'm constantly terrified of what else she will do or say, that she's already turned the rest of the house against me and now I'm worried that slowly, insidiously, she will turn Ben against me too – after all, there is only room for one woman in his life and surely that has to be his twin sister? Because, as you know, Mum and Dad, there is no greater bond than that of a twin.

But how can I say any of this? Especially to them? So I close my mouth and sip my tea and tell them what they want to hear, that I've had a bad day, that I've been working too hard and that I'm tired. 'Honestly, it's nothing to worry about,' I say. And if it wasn't for the quick look they exchange when they think I'm unaware, I would have thought I had convinced them.

I'm drifting off to sleep in the spare room under the eaves, in the double bed, snuggled under a Cath Kidston duvet cover, when my mobile vibrates on the pine bedside table next to me.

It's gone midnight but I lean on my elbow to see who's calling. Ben's name flashes up. I answer it.

'Abi? Where are you? I've been so worried.' Even though his voice is urgent, panicked, I can't help but think he hasn't been *that* worried, considering this is the first time he's tried to ring me.

'I'm at my parents' house.'

'Aren't you coming home?'

I lay back on the pillows, watching the light from the moon dance on the ceiling. 'Not tonight, no.'

He falls silent. In the background I can hear the Rolling Stones' 'Paint It Black', the familiar cacophony of voices, the clinking of glasses that tell me a party is in full swing. 'Beatrice thought it would be nice to hold a small soiree.' He says this last word with a self-conscious laugh. 'I hoped you would be here.'

'I didn't know about it.'

'Well, it was sort of impromptu.' He sounds tipsy.

'I needed to get away for a bit.'

'Away from me?' His voice is unusually thin and reedy.

'Not from you.' I close my eyes, imagining the party that's going on without me, imagining who she invited.

'Abi . . .' he says, I can hear him breathing through the phone. 'I know you and Beatrice haven't been getting on that well. But she's sorry, I know she is. She should be more understanding.'

More understanding of the mentally unstable, paranoid

girlfriend, you mean, Ben? But I don't say it. I haven't got the energy for an argument.

'I will be back tomorrow.'

His voice brightens. 'That's great, because we need to talk about what we're going to do for your birthday next Saturday. We can do anything you want. It's a big one.'

My birthday. My head pounds at the thought of spending another birthday without Lucy. 'To be honest, Ben, I'd love it if the two of us could spend it together. Maybe go somewhere on our own?'

'You don't want a party? You're going to be thirty. Beatrice thought—'

'No,' I say sharply. 'I definitely don't want a party.'

'Whatever you want. I'll organize something special, just the two of us. My birthday treat to you. We could go to London?'

'No, not London.' I can't possibly face London at the moment.

'What about somewhere on the coast then? Lyme Regis or Weymouth?'

I agree that Lyme Regis would be nice and he assures me that he will sort it out, that he knows exactly the place, that it will be a surprise. As I hang up I'm more optimistic than I've been all day, and I fall asleep to the thought of spending the weekend with Ben, cuddled up in our hotel room, walks along the front, acting as a normal couple in love with nothing to worry about; no sex bans, no house rules. And best of all, no Beatrice.

Chapter Twenty

It never crossed my mind that I would reach thirty and Lucy would not. But when I wake up in the room that I still think of as Jodie's I'm painfully aware that I'm doing this without her, that regardless of my dread, August third has come around, and I'm turning thirty alone. Will it ever get any better, or am I destined to spend every birthday buckling under the weight of her absence?

Our parents always spoilt us on our birthdays, making sure to throw us a party no matter how tight things were financially. Mum, who was born in the depths of winter, continually informed us how lucky we were to celebrate our birthday in the summer, even though most years the sun was an elusive guest while overcast skies and thundery rain gatecrashed our parties. Not that this put her off. If the rain was particularly bad, she would retrieve the awning from the garage and get Dad to erect it over the patio, insisting that we sit outside to make the most of the summer irrespective of the droplets of rain that ran off the awning and down our necks. She would invite the whole estate as well as our classmates. And Lucy and I would giggle at the sheer silliness of it all, as Mum bustled around us, making sure everyone had jelly and ice cream along with waterproofs and wellies. 'You'll be thankful for these memories one day,' she would happily chide us when she noticed our conspiratorial giggles, carrying out cheese-and-pineapple sticks protruding painfully from a foil-wrapped orange. But she was right. I look back on each and every one of the birthdays that we shared as children with such nostalgia, such longing, that it becomes an intense, gut-wrenching pain.

I suppose it isn't so strange that, as the years inevitably roll on without her, I will become more absorbed in my childhood, in the past, in a time when we were happy.

The doorbell rings and I spring out of bed, wrapping my dressing gown around myself, and hurry down the stairs. But before I can get to the front door Beatrice is closing it, a huge bouquet of white lilies and roses in her arms. Lilies are my favourite flower. Roses were Lucy's.

'Happy birthday.' Beatrice smiles at me. 'These have just arrived for you.' She hands them to me and I almost drop them, they are so heavy. I press my nose against the petals of a velvety rose. Who would have splashed out on such an opulent bouquet? 'Come with me, I'm sure I've got the perfect vase in the kitchen.' I follow as she pads off down the hallway, her pink silk dressing gown billowing out behind her.

Since returning from my parents' house I've noticed that Beatrice has gone out of her way to be nice, including me in an excursion to an art gallery, which I politely declined, and a party at Niall's house, which I readily accepted, and as the week has progressed it's almost as it used to be between us, and I suspect Ben had a word with her after I left. Whatever he said seems to have worked. We've reached some kind of impasse. Neither of us have mentioned the letters, the photograph or the bracelet. And even though I toss and turn at night at the thought of those lost letters, of the eerie photo of me with no face, nervous of what might come next, I have no choice but to bide my time, for now.

Everyone is in the kitchen when we come down, and as I round the last step they all start singing Happy Birthday energetically. Ben stands at the Aga, poised over a frying pan that sizzles and crackles. After the singing he bounds over to me, wrapping his arms around me, almost crushing the flowers as he plants a big kiss on my forehead. 'Happy birthday,' he says. 'Who are the flowers from?'

'I'm not sure yet, I haven't read the card,' I say, slightly overwhelmed. It's as though I've spent the last few weeks in the servant quarters, only now being allowed to mix with the gentry. Pam shoves a card and a bottle of expensive champagne at me, while Cass hovers by my side with a cup of tea.

'Here, let me have those,' says Beatrice, noticing I've got no spare hands with which to take the tea. She lifts the flowers from my arms and lays them on the worktop as she bends down to search in the cupboard underneath the sink for a vase.

Ben steers me to the table, tells me he's cooking breakfast, bacon sandwiches as a special treat. His enthusiasm is so endearing that I can't bring myself to tell him I'm not a fan of bacon. Pam and Cass take a seat opposite me while Pam chatters away about when she was thirty 'many moons ago', as if it isn't obvious, by her many lines and grey parting, that it was nearly two decades ago when she was my age.

Cass shyly pushes a wrapped gift across the table. 'It's not much,' she blushes. I thank her and open it, unable to hide my surprise when I see it's a large black-and-white print. It's of me – but it could be Lucy, or Beatrice – a close-up so that only my face and the top of my shoulders are showing in a white T-shirt. I'm deep in thought, the wind blowing some strands of hair across my cheek, the background out of focus so that I can't tell where or when it was taken. Callum is a great photographer but this is in a different league entirely. 'Cass, it's amazing,' I say, genuinely touched. The others crowd around me to see it, exclaiming at its loveliness. Suddenly my blood runs cold. There is something sickeningly familiar about this photograph – the pose, the blonde hair, the white T-shirt – and it slowly occurs to me where I've seen it before. The photograph is a larger version of the one I found in my bedroom, the one where my face had been scratched away, leaving a large white spooky void.

'Can I have a copy?' Ben grins as he returns to the Aga, spatula in hand, oblivious to my discomfort. My heart is racing, my head swims. Am I about to have a panic attack? I turn to look at Beatrice, to see how she's reacting to all this, but she's leaning against the worktop, a smile on her lips, the bouquet of flowers arranged beautifully in a vase behind her.

Ben serves up bacon sandwiches and as I look around the table, at Beatrice perched next to me happily recounting her and Ben's thirtieth birthday a couple of years ago, at Cass smiling shyly at her over her coffee cup, at Pam gurning and flashing her gold tooth, it's as if I'm in some surreal play. Did Cass leave that photograph in my bedroom? Was she acting on Beatrice's behalf? Was it meant as a warning? A threat?

'So,' says Beatrice, turning to me. Her plate is empty. 'What have you got planned for today?'

I open my mouth to say that Ben has promised to take me to Lyme Regis for the night when he interrupts me. 'It's a surprise, remember?' he says. A look I can't read passes between them and I take a bite of my bacon sandwich although it feels like cardboard in my mouth. All I can think about is that damn photograph.

'Oh, I nearly forgot my gift,' she says, handing me a small parcel prettily wrapped in embossed butterfly paper.

'Oh, thanks,' I mutter, aware that I must sound ungrateful, but I'm terrified of what I'm going to discover inside. I open it with trepidation. The box is small, navy blue, recognizable as the kind that Beatrice uses to package up her jewellery before selling it. My mouth goes dry. I lift the lid and gasp. Sitting between the crevices of dark velvet is a bracelet. At first I think it's the bracelet that has allegedly gone missing. It's very similar, sparkly silver, but instead of being inset with sapphires this one shimmers with small round yellow stones.

'Peridot,' she says watching my reaction. 'The birth-stone for a Leo.'

'I always thought my birthstone was a ruby.' I'm amazed at her thoughtfulness. I gently touch the bracelet, then slide it on my wrist. It's a perfect fit.

'Not for an August-born Leo. I've done my research. Do you like it?' And by the childlike eagerness in her voice I realize that it's important to her that I do and it confuses me. What's going on? Is this another of her tricks to play with my mind?

'I love it,' I say, trying to sound normal. Deep down I am touched, but I don't trust her motives. Not any more. She smiles in answer then gets up and empties her dirty plate.

'Oh, don't forget this—' She hands me a tiny envelope that's next to the vase. 'It came with the flowers. Don't you want to know who they're from?'

I take it from her and slide the card from the envelope, frowning as I read the words. They're so unexpected, so shocking, that the ink swims in front of my eyes. And I cry out, the card falling from my hand and on to the stone tiles, only semi-aware that Ben is picking it up, that the others are all watching my reaction as he reads out the card.

Happy Birthday, Abi. Have a great thirtieth. Wish I could be with you.

Love Lucy xx

There is a deathly silence as they all digest what's been written, as the realization dawns on them that I've been sent flowers by my dead twin sister.

I can barely breathe. Beatrice breaks the silence first. 'Could she . . . could she have ordered them before she died?'

'Of course not,' I moan, covering my face with my hands, fighting the urge to vomit my recently ingested breakfast. 'How would she have known I'd be living here? Anyway, there's no way Lucy would have been that organized. She died nearly two years ago.'

Ben massages my shoulders comfortingly. 'It's okay, Abi. It's someone's sick idea of a prank.'

'And the photograph.' I grab it from the table and wave it at Cass's startled face. 'This is identical to the one I found in my bedroom.' I explain about the scratched-off face, but they all gawp at me as if I'm making the whole thing up.

'You're upset, understandably,' says Beatrice. 'I'll get rid of the flowers.' I can hear her footsteps behind me, hear the squelch as the flowers are lifted out of the vase, the gurgle of water sluicing through the plughole, the wet stems dripping on to the cold tiles. She says she will put them in the recycling box and her voice is brisk, conciliatory, helpful. I turn to see Cass and Pam hovering by the stairs, unsure of what to do or say. They hurry out of the room after Beatrice as she holds the dripping flowers away from her as if they are poisoned.

'I'm so sorry.' Ben sinks into Beatrice's recently vacated seat. 'Please don't let it ruin your birthday.'

I shake my head. 'Can't you see?' I groan. 'Someone is out to get me.' I'm aware of how paranoid I sound.

He takes my hand and kisses it in answer. 'That's not true.'

'Then how do you explain all this?' I wail. 'It's got to be someone from Bath,' I say, ripping up the photograph that Cass had given me for my birthday. It's a reminder of all the horrible things that have happened since I've moved in. From the corner of my eye I can see Ben staring at me in shock, but he doesn't say anything. 'Nobody from my old life, apart from Nia, knows this address.'

He raises an eyebrow.

'Don't be ridiculous,' I snap. 'I've known Nia since I was eighteen.'

'What about Callum?'

I pull my hand from his. 'Callum would never do this.' I think of Luke and I discount him quickly. As much as he might hate me for the accident, he would never stoop this low or use Lucy to get at me. It's got to be someone who never knew her. Someone who lives in this house.

'Where did the flowers come from? Which shop?'

Ben's head shoots up. He reaches for the card that he slung on the table. 'It doesn't say. And neither does the envelope.'

I think of Beatrice, standing by the front door this morning with the flowers already in her arms. I never saw a delivery person. She could have rung the doorbell herself and waited in the hallway for me to come down. I close my eyes, biting my lip so that I draw blood. I thought we had a truce. Surely Beatrice wouldn't be that cruel?

I remind myself that I hardly know Beatrice at all.

I try not to let it ruin the rest of my birthday, telling myself it's exactly what the culprit would want. But I watch Beatrice carefully, noting she's chirpier than she has been in weeks as she bustles around the house, singing under her breath. I want to believe it's because we've put our differences behind us and not some other, more disturbing reason.

I'm in my room packing a small overnight bag when Nia calls to wish me happy birthday. I can hear the echo of a tannoy announcer in the background and Nia explains she's at the train station. When I enquire as to her whereabouts she manages to avoid the question, instead asking about my plans and I tell her about Ben's birthday surprise, that I'm hoping the hotel will be in Lyme Regis as I've never been. I decide to keep quiet about how we're unable to spend nights together because he doesn't want to be 'disrespectful to Beatrice's house rules' – words which irk me because they remind me how much of a control freak and how possessive his sister is. For reasons that aren't clear even to me, I find that I don't tell her about the flowers or the photograph.

'You're going away tonight?' She sounds puzzled.

'Well, hopefully this afternoon, although Ben hasn't said.'

'It's, well . . .' She falls silent and for a minute I think we've been cut off, but her voice comes back on the line, faint and indistinct, telling me she hopes I have a lovely time, that she will come and visit soon. The phone goes dead, making me wonder why she's acting so mysteriously.

By mid-morning Ben still hasn't revealed where he's taking me. I tell him I'm going to my parents' for lunch. He seems relieved that I'm going out, ushering me to the door, telling me not to come back before teatime. The hours I spend with my parents are long, excruciating as we all do our best to pretend we haven't noticed Lucy's absence, that only one of us is turning thirty today. We sit around chatting, with plates of birthday cake on our laps that none of us have got the stomach for. By teatime I tell them I need to get back as Ben is taking me to Lyme Regis.

'When are we going to meet this new boyfriend of yours?' says Mum as she hugs me goodbye. I laugh and tell her soon, and I put my arms around her, surprised as always by her thin frame, by how tiny she has become since Lucy died, and I'm worried that if I hug her too hard I will crush her.

As I arrive back at Beatrice's house, the sun disappears and I pause, my hand on the wrought-iron gate, and turn my face up to the greying skies, closing my eyes as I remember those birthday parties in the rain, and I sense it – exactly as I did that day in the car on the Isle of Wight – that she's with me, and as the first drops of rain fall, I take it as a sign that she's acknowledging those wet parties of our childhood. 'Happy Birthday, Luce,' I whisper.

'Abi?' I open my eyes to see Ben standing in the doorway, frowning. 'What are you doing? It's pissing down.' It's then I notice the balloons bobbing, like decapitated heads, tied to the gate, the daisy-shaped fairy lights above the front door, the lanterns in the garden lighting the pathway. I tentatively push open the gate, brushing past the balloons with Happy 30th printed all over them, and I'm suddenly cold to the bone. The romantic night I envisioned with Ben in Lyme Regis fades before my eyes.

'We're not going away tonight, are we?'

A shadow of doubt passes across his face. Wordlessly he holds his hand out to help me over the step. He leans into me and I can smell his familiar aftershave, as his lips brush my ear. 'I'm sorry, Abi. Please look surprised.' And before my brain can even process what he means he's leading me down the hallway and up the stairs to the colourful drawing room. He's simultaneously opening the door while pushing me into a roomful of people who all chorus 'Surprise'. Someone pops a party banger, another thrusts a glass of champagne into my hand, and I can do nothing but blink in astonishment as I take in Beatrice, smiling widely as she stands in front of Monty, Niall, Maria and Grace, with Cass at her elbow as if she's a toddler hanging on to her mother's skirt. I can see Pam snogging her boyfriend (a different one, lanky with a ponytail) by the fireplace and Nia hovering awkwardly beside them. 'Nia?' I'm so shocked I almost drop my glass. She edges past the others looking shame-faced.

'I'm sorry I couldn't tell you,' she says when she reaches me. She pulls me into her arms and I swallow back tears. 'Is this okay?' she whispers into my ear and I manage to nod, to squeak that of course it's okay, when really a hard lump of disappointment lodges in my throat, and even though I'm delighted that my oldest friend is here with me to celebrate my birthday, a party is the last thing I want. A party only highlights that Lucy isn't here.

Later, when everyone is dancing to 'Groove Is In The Heart', I spot Ben through the melee, laughing with Beatrice and Nia. I go up to him and take his arm, asking if we can talk in private. Not waiting for an answer, I lead him through the living room and out on to the terrace. The sky has turned violet-grey, the threat of rain still hanging in the air. I see Monty in deep conversation with Pam and her new bloke in the corner, Niall is perched on one of the wet sun-loungers with some people I don't recognize, sharing a spliff. Ben follows me to the railings and leans back against them. The distant screech of a seagull makes me shudder, I'm always surprised by how many seagulls there are in Bath.

'Are you okay?' he says distractedly. He's watching the smokers on the sun-loungers. 'I hope they're not going to burn their fags out on that wood. It's teak. Those loungers were bloody expensive.' I want to tell him I couldn't give a toss about the sun-loungers. He reaches into the back pocket of his jeans to retrieve his cigarettes, tapping one out of its packet and into the palm of his hand, and offers it to me. When I shake my head he places it between his lips and lights it. I've noticed how twitchy he is when he doesn't have a fag in his hand. 'Are you enjoying the party?'

'Not particularly.' I'm pleased when I see the hurt in his eyes. 'What happened to the romantic weekend break you promised me?'

He takes a deep drag of his cigarette before answering. 'It was only an idea. But Beatrice said a party would be better.'

I bite back my anger. 'This was Beatrice's idea?'

He looks confused, as if worried he might say the wrong thing. 'Well, yes. I wanted to take you away somewhere. But Beatrice said she'd already arranged a party, had already asked Nia. She'd spent a lot of money on the catering and the wine.'

My whole body tenses. 'And you didn't think to tell her that I specifically told you that I didn't want a fucking party?' I snarl. I carefully enunciate each word to make my point.

He's taken aback. 'I did . . . But she, quite rightly, pointed out that you love parties. That you'd be happy to see Nia. I thought . . .' He looks at me helplessly and I know it's not his fault. I'm well aware of how manipulative Beatrice can be. Although I wish that, for once, he would put me first instead of always worrying about offending his precious sister. I take a deep breath but I'm unable, or unwilling, to stop the harangue that emerges. 'Why can't you see what she's doing?' I cry. 'She doesn't give a shit about me, this was her way of preventing us spending the weekend together. Without her. She's got you wrapped around her little finger, Ben. Why can't you see that?'

I turn to storm off but he grabs my upper arm, forcing me back roughly as if I'm a dog on a retractable lead, his fingers digging into my skin. His face is pinched, white and inches from mine. 'She did this for you, Abi,' he spits. 'She organized all this for you, even finding out the number of your oldest friend so she could invite her too. And all you can do is bitch about her.'

'Get. Off. Me,' I hiss between clenched teeth. He releases his grip, shock registering on his face at his actions.

'I'm sorry, Abi. I'm so sorry.'

'Fuck off, Ben.' I push my way through the crowd, tears blurring my vision, faintly aware of Nia breaking away from Beatrice to follow me as I run from the room.

Chapter Twenty-One

Beatrice has a clear view of them through the open doorway, Abi in her usual jeans and T-shirt, face pinched in agitation, Ben stooped so that his face is level with hers, his eyes narrowed in anger, the spittle flying from his mouth. Beatrice recognizes the expression on his face, the anger. She knows how Ben hates to lose control.

Next to her she senses Nia stiffen. 'Are they having a row?' Nia shouts over the music, concern etched across her pretty face. 'I thought this might happen. Abi was hoping for a romantic weekend alone with Ben, not a party.' Beatrice shrugs in an effort to appear nonchalant when inside her heart is pounding with glee. She's unable to drag her eyes away from the scene unfolding on the balcony.

Ben is trying to stop Abi from leaving, but she pulls away from him and stumbles into the living room, her eyes wet, her face pale, pushing her way through the alcohol-fuelled crowd towards the door to the landing. 'I'd better go after her,' says Nia, handing her glass to Beatrice. She takes the glass wordlessly and watches as Nia darts after Abi.

She waits. One beat, two beats. And then she goes to him.

His face is set, impassive as she approaches. 'Here,' she hands him Nia's untouched glass of champagne. 'You look as though you could do with this.' He takes it without a word, knocking back the contents in one gulp. *You poor darling,* she thinks. *Being with Abi has brought it all back to you, hasn't it? The past. What we've done.* Because she can see that now. She can finally understand why he was attracted to Abi in the first place. A gust of wind blows her thin cotton dress around her thighs and she wishes she was wearing a cardigan.

'You were right when you warned me that she's damaged,' he says eventually. 'I didn't understand how much. I do now.'

She pulls him to her in answer, wrapping her arms around him, wishing she could make the hurt go away. When he's in pain, so is she. She rests her head on his chest, comforted by the steady beat of his heart which reverberates through his shirt. 'She's jealous of me,' she says. 'Because I'm your twin and she knows how special that is.'

He pulls away from her, rubs his hand across his chin. 'I know.'

'All this stuff she's saying, Ben. About the letters, and the bird and that photograph. She thinks I'm trying to ruin your relationship. But you know it's rubbish, don't you? She's ill, Ben. I don't think she's taking her medication – it was in her drawer when she was on the Isle of Wight. She should have taken it with her. She stole my earring, you saw it for yourself. There's something else too.'

'What?' he asks wearily.

'I think she saw me, that day when she was on the beach. She mentioned it in the kitchen, I didn't know what to say . . .'

'Okay, Bea,' he snaps, and then he notices her stung expression and his voice is softer as he adds, 'Look, she told me she thinks you're moving her antidepressants.'

Beatrice takes a deep breath. 'For goodness' sake, Ben. You don't believe her, do you?

'Of course not,' he says, too quickly.

'I think she's dangerous, Ben. She's seriously screwed up. She bought a dress exactly the same as the sort I always wear, she's got the same perfume. And the same trainers. I can't help but think she's trying to be me. To replace me . . .'

Ben laughs. 'That's ridiculous.'

'Is it?' She stares at him, deliberating whether to say it. 'Surely you've noticed?'

He crosses his arms. It's a defensive gesture. His biceps are strong and tanned. He's wearing another new shirt. Designer, no doubt. 'Noticed what?'

She opens her mouth to say it, but she can't find the right words. It could all sound so terribly wrong.

He sighs then puts a cigarette in his mouth and lights it. 'Look, Bea,' he says after a few puffs. 'Abi needs our support and understanding, you know that. She's had such a hard time. Losing your twin – can you imagine?'

She stares at him for one long incredulous moment. 'I can imagine exactly how that feels.' His expression softens. 'But it's no excuse for her behaviour.'

He's silent for a moment, assessing her through a fug of smoke, and she knows he's searching around in his mind for a solution. Solid, dependable Ben. A typical man, desperate to fix things, make good a bad situation. 'Do you think we should ask her to move out?' he says eventually.

Beatrice's heart quickens. She's thought it on numerous occasions, of course. But she never imagined that Ben would agree. She chooses her words carefully. 'It might be for the best. There has been a lot of tension in the house since she moved in.'

He turns away from her to look out over the garden, flicking his cigarette butt over the balcony, then grips the iron railings as if he's been hit with the sudden onset of vertigo. Beatrice rubs his back, the way she used to when they were younger. It's still light, the grey clouds heavy, the grass glistens with raindrops, the air smells washed, refreshed. From inside the house someone has put on 'Psycho Killer' by the Talking Heads and people are yelling along with the words.

'Beatrice?'

She turns to see Nia standing in the doorway. She's wearing a red-and-white polka-dot dress that clings to her curves and compliments her dark Celtic looks. Beatrice removes her hand from Ben's back as Nia joins them, wrapping her arms around herself at the sudden change in temperature. She has intelligent brown eyes and a no-nonsense demeanour that Beatrice admires. 'Abi wants to be on her own,' says Nia in her sing-song Welsh accent. 'I knew this day was going to be hard for her.'

'We shouldn't have thrown her a party, it was thoughtless,' says Beatrice. Ben protests as soon as the words are out of her mouth, assuring her that her intentions were good, that she didn't know how Abi was going to react, although she notices that Nia doesn't say anything, she stands there regarding the two of them as if she's trying to work them out, as if something about them bothers her.

'Should I call an end to the party, tell everyone to go home?' asks Beatrice, wrinkling her nose and surveying the clusters of people laughing, drinking and dancing.

Nia glances at her watch. 'It's still early. Maybe Abi will join the party later, I think she's disappointed.' She turns to address Ben. 'When I spoke to Abi earlier today she was adamant she was going away with you, Ben.'

Ben lights up another cigarette. He smokes too much, it worries Beatrice. His eyes are bloodshot and she's sure that while Abi remains living here, the tension, the worry

218

of it, is going to make him ill. Not for the first time, she regrets asking Abi to move in.

'I think we got our wires crossed,' says Ben, his eyes flicking towards Beatrice.

You can say that again, she thinks, surveying her brother.

Ben flicks his cigarette butt over the edge of the balcony and steps away from the railings, handing Beatrice his empty glass. 'I'm going to speak to Abi, I need to tell her I'm sorry.' Beatrice opens her mouth to protest, to ask him if he's still going to suggest that Abi moves out, but realizes anything she says will be futile, so she swallows her words, watching him weave his way through the throng of people, smiling and nodding politely to those who call out a greeting, until he disappears from her sight.

'It must be hard for you,' Nia says suddenly, by her elbow. The sky has darkened so that Nia's face is in shadow and difficult to read. They are the only ones left on the balcony. The heavy beat of a dance tune wafts towards them.

'What do you mean?'

'Ben being your twin. Trying not to be over-protective.'

'I love him,' she says. 'I don't want him to get hurt.'

'And you don't think Abi is right for him?'

Beatrice thinks about her next words carefully, not wanting to offend Nia. 'Abi moved in here as my friend. I never wanted her to become Ben's girlfriend, and not because I dislike Abi, it's, well, she's been through so much. And since she's moved in and taken up with Ben . . .' she sighs. 'There has been nothing but trouble.'

'What do you mean?'

'Look,' she says, turning to face Nia. 'There's been a lot of weird shit happening.' And she launches into all of it, finishing up with the dress and the trainers.

Nia groans. 'Not again.'

Beatrice shivers. 'This has happened before?'

'Well, not exactly, but . . .' She hesitates.

'What do you mean?'

'Beatrice, as soon as I saw you I thought you resembled her,' she says in a rush.

Beatrice frowns. 'Lucy?'

Nia shakes her head. 'Not only Lucy, but Alicia.'

She has a sudden sense of foreboding as she asks, 'Who's Alicia?'

Nia fidgets, wrapping her arms even further around her body as if to hide herself. Beatrice can tell Nia is clamming up, knows she probably regrets what she's already said. 'I can't talk about that, you will have to ask Abi. It's not fair for me to say anything.'

Beatrice swells with indignation. 'I know that she tried to kill herself. I know more than you think, Nia. This is my house. I need to know who I'm living with, for fuck's sake. Is Abi dangerous?'

Nia swivels around. 'Of course she's not. She's better now, she seems better, especially now she's on the anti-depressants.' But her voice wobbles and she sounds unsure.

'But she's not always taking her bloody antidepressants. Don't you understand?' Beatrice snaps. She's as taut as an over-stretched elastic band. She has a hunch that whatever happened with Alicia didn't end well. She remembers the intensity in Abi's eyes, the neediness that emanated from her when they first met, and she knows, deep down, that she fed off Abi's vulnerability, that she liked that Abi was so desperate to be her friend. It made her feel wanted, special. 'Please, I need to know.' There's a silence and Beatrice holds her breath, aware that any sudden movement might change the course of things, that Nia might decide against confiding in her.

Nia is silent for a while and Beatrice is convinced the moment has been lost, until Nia says in a voice slightly louder than a whisper, 'I'm only telling you this because I care about Abi and I'm worried.'

And Beatrice listens, her heart in her throat, as Nia tells her how Abi became obsessed with their new neighbour in the weeks after Lucy died, how she befriended her, convinced that they were soul mates, how she began to stalk her. 'She would turn up at places where she knew Alicia was going to be. She got jealous when Alicia went out with other friends. I think Alicia thought Abi was too intense, too needy. I understood, of course, I've known Abi for years. But Alicia didn't have that history with her, couldn't make allowances for her grief. In the end, after a few months of this, Alicia told Abi that she wanted her to stay away and Abi, well . . . she reacted badly.'

'What did Abi do?' The blood pounds in Beatrice's ears. 'Nia, you need to tell me.'

Nia groans through her fingers, muttering that she's betraying Abi's trust. Anger surges through Beatrice. She wants to scream at this girl, and at herself, for putting both her and Ben at risk by inviting a stranger into their home. She doesn't care about loyalty or trust, at this moment she needs to know the truth. She makes an effort to sound calm when she speaks, belying her fear, 'What did Abi do when Alicia terminated their friendship, Nia?'

And, in a small voice that's almost lost in the thump of the music coming from the drawing room, Nia says, 'She attacked her.'

Chapter Twenty-Two

I lie on my bed with my eyes closed. I can hear the sounds
of the party – the rhythmic thump of dance music, the
clink of glasses, the low hum of various conversations
– being played out beneath me, occasionally broken by
a sudden burst of laughter, a door slamming, feet on
stairs. I can't face any of it.

As the light begins to fade, Ben pushes the door open
with an anguished expression on his face and he hurries
to my bedside. He kneels beside me as if in prayer, assuring
me that he's sorry, that he loves me, that he wishes he
could be the boyfriend I want him to be. Wordlessly I
move up to allow him to squeeze next to me on the
narrow single bed and we lie this way for a while, in
silence. When he takes my hand, I let him.

'You know,' he says eventually, into the darkness. 'I

don't understand what's happened between you and Bea. You used to be so fond of each other.'

'I can't understand it either,' I admit, thinking of all that's happened.

'She thinks you're paranoid and jealous.'

'I probably am.' I'm close to tears. 'But I think she's possessive and controlling. Look, the dead bird can be explained away. Maybe. But the photograph? It was menacing, surely you get that?'

He nods, but doesn't interrupt me.

'I was so happy about the thought of going away, spending time just the two of us. To get away from this house. Away from Beatrice's bloody rules. Does that make me possessive?'

He reaches over and hugs me in answer.

'And the flowers, who would do something so cruel? Some of my letters have gone missing too. It's all weird stuff, Ben. Surely it can't be in my head? You saw the flowers.'

He clears his throat and fidgets, clearly uncomfortable about what he's going to say next. 'I found a number for the flower shop, an independent little place near Pulteney Bridge. I rang them and they remember a woman placing the order, she came into the shop.'

My heart pounds and I wait.

'Abi,' his voice is full of concern. 'They described you.'

My blood runs cold and I think of Lucy, remembering the note that came with the flowers. *Love Lucy.* How could it be possible when she's dead?

And then I think of Beatrice. The florist described me but they could also be talking about her. Tall, slim, blonde . . .

Before I have the chance to answer, Beatrice bursts into the room saying she needs to talk to me urgently. Nia is close behind her. Ben looks from me to his sister, as if terrified about what Beatrice is about to reveal. She clicks on the main light, illuminating how pale, how anxious, both she and Nia look. Ben and I sit up simultaneously. 'What's going on?' he says.

Nia perches at the foot of the bed, looking wretched. 'I'm so sorry, Abi. We're all worried about you, I had to tell her.'

I don't know what she's talking about. 'Tell her what?'

She looks at me imploringly with her huge brown eyes. Eyes that have always reminded me of a basset hound. 'About Alicia.'

The room swims and, with a sickening thud of clarity, I'm aware that I can't trust my oldest friend. That I'm forever going to be tied with the mental illness tag, that I'm never going to be believed because Abi's a sandwich short of a picnic, she's been in a mental facility, didn't you know? How can you believe anything she says? She's paranoid, delusional. It's as if I'm in a nightmare, where I'm trying to explain myself, trying to tell everyone that I'm perfectly sane, that it was a stupid mistake, a one-off, I'm not dangerous, I'm not a nutter, but no sound comes out of my mouth.

My eyes fill with tears.

'I'm so sorry, but Beatrice says you're not taking your medication and I'm worried for you, Abi.' She stares at me with her forthright expression. 'I'm worried for you,' she repeats, tears appearing in her eyes.

'Why does everyone keep saying that?' I say, finding my voice at last. 'And I am taking my antidepressants.'

Beatrice makes a disbelieving sound and wrinkles up her nose. She's still standing by the doorway as if she's afraid to come near me. I want to tell her that I know she's been in my bedroom, that she's been moving my antidepressants, playing with my mind. But by the way they are all staring at me, as if I'm a complete nutcase, I know they wouldn't believe me anyway.

I take Ben's hand and stare at him imploringly. 'The thing with Alicia – yes, it's true.'

'What happened?' he asks.

'I got a bit obsessed with her.' I flinch when I notice Ben's incredulous expression, and I know how bonkers, how screwed up I must sound. I close my eyes, like a child who believes nobody else can see them if they shut their eyes tightly. 'Basically I stalked her, and when she told me to fuck off, as she had every right to do, I . . . well, I went for her.'

'You did *what*?'

I open my eyes. Ben looks appalled.

'I hit her,' I clarify.

'She had to be pulled off her,' states Beatrice, gleefully it seems.

'Did . . . did she go to the police?' asks Ben.

'The police were called, but she didn't press charges. I gave her a black eye. I felt terrible about it and I . . . I . . .' I let the implication of my suicide attempt hang in the air. 'I was admitted to hospital a few days later.'

Ben leans forwards and folds me in his arms. I'm trembling, tears running down my face. He strokes my hair, tells me it's all going to be okay. Then he barks for the others to get out of the room, to leave us alone. I'm surprised to hear him acting so authoritarian, for actually shouting at his precious sister. I realize that he's sticking up for me. That he's on my side after all.

When the others have filed out, Nia mouthing apologies over her shoulder as she leaves, Ben takes me to his room, tells me he doesn't want to leave me on my own tonight, that Nia can have my bed. 'I regret not taking you away somewhere,' he murmurs into my hair, as I curl up in his arms. 'I regret so many things.' And then he kisses me, urgently, in the way we did when we first met, before all his talk of Beatrice's rules and respect, and as he starts to peel the clothes away from my body I ask him if he's sure, and he tells me he is, that he is going to put me first from now on. And as we slowly begin to make love I can't help but think that this is what makes me different to Beatrice, that sex with Ben belongs only to me.

When I wake up the next morning the sun is streaming through the curtains and I have a sense of renewal, of hope. The birthday I've been dreading is over, I've had an amazing night with Ben. Maybe it's because of the enforced hiatus, or the drama of last night, but the sex was better than it's ever been.

And I'm not entirely sure why, but I get the sense that the events of last night have altered things between us, made us closer. Ben has had a sudden insight into my confused, obsessive, paranoid mind, and it seems he likes what he sees.

Beatrice and I don't talk about what happened. We're cordial with each other at breakfast. She's perched next to Nia, eating toast at the large oak table, her hair is damp as if she's recently emerged from the shower and she's wearing a yellow shirt that clashes with her hair yet still manages to look good on her. It hurts to see them sitting next to one another. My best friend and my enemy. *Is this another person you're trying to turn against me, Beatrice? Someone I've known nearly half my life.*

When she sees me she mutters something about having a lot to do and, snatching a triangle of toast from her plate, hurries from the room. I'm aware of Nia's eyes following me as I go to a cupboard to retrieve a mug to put under the coffee machine.

'I'm so sorry, Abi,' she blurts out as soon as I sit down opposite her. Irrespective of the fresh white blouse she's wearing she looks as if she's hardly slept. 'I was worried about you, but I shouldn't have told Beatrice about Alicia. It wasn't my place.'

I tell her that she's right, she shouldn't have said

anything, but I acknowledge how persuasive Beatrice can be, an animal ready to pounce on her prey, how she won't give up until she's got it firmly between her teeth. 'I probably should have told them about Alicia anyway,' I concede, sipping my coffee. Nothing can dampen my mood this morning, or wipe the memory of my night with Ben.

'So you're not angry with me?' She smiles weakly, hopefully.

'Not any more.' I reach out and take her hand, giving it a gentle squeeze. 'I know you only told her because you were worried about me. I do trust you, Nia.'

She slumps back against the chair with obvious relief.

'And it's lovely to have you here,' I say. 'What do you think of the house? Of the twins?'

She tells me how amazing the house is, how I've landed on my feet, that it's such a coincidence, that I should find myself in a house with twins, after everything. 'And they look so alike, don't they? Facially, I mean. He's the male equivalent of her,' she finishes.

'Except for their eyes,' I say, thinking of Ben's hazel eyes in comparison to Beatrice's almond-shaped honey-coloured ones.

'Is that why you were first drawn to her, Abi? Be honest. Was it because she resembles Lucy? And you?'

I shrug. 'I suppose. She caught my eye because of her similarity to Lucy. But her bubbly personality is like Lucy's too. Although not this nasty side . . . that was something I wasn't expecting.'

'Are you disappointed not to have gone to Lyme Regis?' she asks.

'I was, but it's all worked out for the best. Something changed last night. Ben, well, he . . . we . . .' I laugh as Nia squeals in disbelief. We sit in silence for a couple of seconds and then Nia adds warily, 'I do feel sorry for her though. I know she's over-protective, but I still don't fully understand what you've got against her, Abi. Why did you rush off last night? Was it because you were disappointed about not going away? Or was there another reason?'

And then I explain everything.

She frowns as I talk, her eyes creasing up so that I can see the beginnings of crow's feet, another reminder of how we are both ageing when Lucy isn't. She stays silent but her face pales as I describe the dead bird on my bed, the malicious photograph, the flowers claiming to be from Lucy, and when I finally finish, slightly out of breath and dry-mouthed, she leans back in her chair, her face grave. 'That's fucked up. Why didn't you tell me all of this before?'

'I didn't get the chance, and I was worried that you would think I'm being paranoid, what with my history.'

She considers this for a moment. 'It sounds as though Beatrice is being very manipulative. I'm worried for you. The photograph, the flowers – there's real malice in those things. Abi . . .' She pauses as Cass skips down the steps into the kitchen. Beatrice's ally. Beatrice's spy. We watch in silence as Cass busies herself with the coffee machine, completely ignoring us, in a world of her own. When she takes her mug and scuttles from the kitchen, Nia speaks again. This time her voice is more insistent, threaded with fear. 'I don't think it's safe for you to stay here, Abi. You need to move out.'

Chapter Twenty-Three

'They're in the kitchen, having some sort of pow-wow,' says Cass, handing Beatrice a cup of coffee. 'I couldn't hear what they were talking about. When I came in they fell silent.'

'Thanks,' says Beatrice, taking the mug and sipping it slowly. She's nauseous, jittery, she has too much nervous energy flowing through her veins. She pushes Sebby off her lap as she stands up from the sofa and he jumps to the floor with a disgruntled mew at having his sleep rudely disturbed. She pads over to the French doors, goosebumps on her arms as she cups her hands around her mug. It rained overnight, the sun-loungers are wet and littered with empty beer cans and cigarette butts. The detritus from Abi's party is still evident on the carpet, the coffee table and the mantelpiece: fag ends, wine stains, crisp packets, empty and half-filled glasses of bubbly. The room smells of stale body odour and bad breath. Eva will be in later to make everything look as new again; she knows how Ben can't stand mess, that it makes him stressed.

Cass comes up behind her and places a hand on her shoulder. 'Are you okay, Bea?' she asks softly, and Beatrice shakes her head, biting her lip to stop herself from crying. How can she explain to Cass this grief that she feels? As if she's losing Ben all over again. She thought she was doing a nice thing – a kind thing – for Abi by throwing her a party. She thought it might make up for all the bad things that have happened, that it would get Ben on side. But no, Abi still manages to find a way to throw it back in her face, to turn everything on its head so that she's the bad guy. Even hearing that his darling girlfriend is an obsessive stalker who attacked her own neighbour hasn't put Ben off her. *What will it take, Ben? For you to see her true colours?*

'She's a bunny boiler,' she says, her voice sounding raw, hoarse, in the silent room. 'Don't you think, Cass? I think she's fucking dangerous. I want her out of this house.'

Cass squeezes her shoulder. 'Don't worry,' she says softly, reassuringly. 'I think she will be gone very soon.'

Chapter Twenty-Four

The tension around my birthday somehow dissipates and the rest of August goes by harmoniously enough. Nia rings me most days, urging me to come to London to live with her, but I tell her I can't move out. At least not yet, and not without Ben.

I refuse to let Beatrice win.

Beatrice is holed up in her studio, setting stones into silver rings or necklaces; Ben takes on a short contract with a big technical firm along the M4 corridor and I receive more and more commissions from Miranda. On the occasions we are all home, we spend evenings together eating Eva's homemade cottage pies or casseroles while sharing a bottle or two of wine. Sometimes Beatrice throws an impromptu party, and I'm not surprised when she declares happily one day that she and Niall have started dating. She seems joyful, reminiscent of how she was when we first met. If she's noticed that I'm sneaking into Ben's room every night, she doesn't comment on it, and it's as if she's no longer interested, no longer cares what the two of us get up to. On the surface, at least, we are getting along fine, but I don't trust her completely. I find I'm still wary, still waiting for her next move.

Before I know it, a couple of weeks have passed since my birthday. It seems as though the three of us have found a way to make it work and I'm more hopeful. I say this to Ben one Sunday as we walk around Prior Park Landscape Gardens. The sun is high, the sky a pale blue. Ben tucks my arm in his as we wander along the Palladian Bridge, showing me the names and dates and messages from lovers and friends that have been scratched into its Bath stone columns, marvelling at the inscriptions from over a hundred years ago.

'I'm glad,' he says. 'It's important to me that my two best girls get on.' And I feel it, a trace of jealousy. I know I can't have him all to myself; after all, who better than I to understand their bond? But sometimes their relationship reminds me even more of what I've lost. We walk along in silence, both deep in thought, our shadows stretched out in front of us, elongated versions of ourselves, and I'm curious as to what's going on in his mind, because every now and again he's like a television that has abruptly been switched off so that I'm no longer able to see what he's thinking.

As we move off the bridge towards the lake he says,

'My contract has come to an end, but another company has offered me a job, in Scotland. The money's good, I can't turn it down.'

In front of us a mother is grappling with a screaming toddler, trying to hoist him over her shoulder towards the café with the promise of cake. I smile at her sympathetically. 'How long for?'

'It's a week contract, possibly two.' I can't bear the thought of being away from him for that long; he's the anchor to my boat and I worry that I will float out to sea, directionless, without him.

'Do you need to take the contract?' I say. 'What with the trust fund . . .'

He stiffens. I've offended him, wounded his male pride.

'I'm from a working-class background. It doesn't seem right not to earn my own money,' he snaps.

I remember Eva telling me about his rich grandparents, their rambling house on the outskirts of Edinburgh. It doesn't sound as if it was a very working-class background to me. But I bite my tongue because I can understand how he would want to earn a living and not rely on family inheritance. Since I've been working, I've been giving money to Beatrice for rent, in spite of her protestations. It doesn't seem right not to pay my way. I know how Ben feels.

By now we've reached the café – or rather a hut with wooden tables set out in front of it, overlooking the lake. The tables are mostly taken up with young families; children run about with ice creams, making the most of the last remnants of summer. We manage to find a small table semi-hidden by an over-enthusiastic bush, with a view of the lake. I take a seat while Ben goes to the hut to buy us coffee.

He returns clutching two takeaway cups with plastic lids and hands one to me as he manoeuvres his long legs over the bench seat opposite. Over his shoulder I watch as a flock of seagulls descend on the lake, foraging for a snack and scaring away a couple of ducks.

'Will you be okay? In the house with Beatrice and the others? Without me?' he asks. I'm pleased that he's worried about me.

'Everything seems to have settled down, and I'm getting on OK with Beatrice again. It makes life a lot easier.' He nods and takes a sip of his coffee. 'All that weird stuff that happened, Ben. It was awful, it was as though I was losing my grip on reality.'

'I can imagine.'

I shake my head, trying to chase the unwanted memories away. It's all in the past, I remind myself, I need to forget it.

Ben has been in Scotland for the past ten days, leaving me wafting around the house, unsettled, like a spirit with nobody to haunt. I miss him the most at night, so I sleep in his bed, inhaling the smell of him that lingers on the sheets, imagining him here with me.

On the Friday that Ben is due home I'm sitting at the kitchen table with my laptop. Pam is at the sink washing out brushes; her hair has gone from tarmac black to a blood orange – a home dye job that went wrong apparently, although it has now 'grown on her'. She's wearing baggy paint-splattered overalls and is chattering away, totally oblivious to the fact that I'm trying to write an article I promised Miranda. I log on to Facebook, distracted by Pam's incessant chatter, knowing I won't get any work done while she's in the room. As I do every week or so, I go on to Lucy's Facebook page that I've still kept running, not quite able to contact them to disable it, taking comfort from the past posts on her timeline, the photographs she uploaded before she died, the funny messages on her wall that we sent to one another. Her profile photograph is of the two of us, taken at some party; grinning inanely, hair damp with sweat, a crowd of people dancing behind us, slightly out of focus. I smile at the memory, remembering when Nia took the photo at the opening of a new club in Covent Garden. With beads of perspiration on our foreheads, our hair pushed back from our eyes, our lips bare, even I have to scrutinize the photograph to remember which of the smiling, fun-loving girls is me.

The letters in the box upstairs are the only private things I have left of her. Yes, I can access her Facebook page, click on the videos that I have of her, but it's the letters that mean the most, because in them she poured out her thoughts and feelings. When I read them, I can hear her voice, I can imagine that she's talking to me. Letter-writing was something we shared, something personal, between the two of us and not for her three hundred Facebook friends. And when I think that three of those precious letters have been taken by Beatrice and hidden God knows where, a flicker of anger burns inside me so intense it takes me a while to calm down and regain my composure. I'm biding my time, but I will get those letters back.

Pam is still chattering away but her words wash over my head. There is something new on Lucy's timeline, her status has changed. My heart starts to race and I rapidly blink to make sure I've read it correctly. But there is no mistake. The three words float in front of my vision so that I'm dizzy.

I've been replaced.

My fingers tremble as they hover over the keyboard. I can see by the date that it was written yesterday. My mouth goes dry. Has her account been hacked? Maybe it's some idiot mucking about, but why write such a thing? What does it mean?

'Are you okay, love?' says Pam, noticing my shocked expression.

I can't bring myself to tell her because, as much as I'm fond of Pam, admire her reassuring presence, her confidence, not even minding that she's slightly self-obsessed, I doubt she would understand. When I received those flowers on my birthday she had appeared nonplussed, almost dismissive, assuring me there was probably a logical explanation. As if there could be.

So I plaster a tight smile on my face and tell her I'm

fine, and she seems to believe it as she gathers up her paintbrushes, humming as she trots up the stairs to the next floor.

Why would you write that, Lucy? I think, before checking myself, tears stinging my eyes as it sinks in that, of course, Lucy didn't write it. How could she? *She's dead. She's fucking dead!* I take deep breaths, try to concentrate on my breathing. I slam the lid of my MacBook, telling myself that it's a mistake, that it doesn't mean anything. That it's not at all weird, eerie, *sick* that a message has appeared on my sister's wall nearly two years after she died.

When I check again later, the message has disappeared, leaving me doubting whether it was ever there in the first place.

It's dark when Ben's little Fiat finally turns into the street. I watch from my bedroom window as he pulls up outside the house. I run downstairs, throwing open the front door as he's stepping on to the pavement. He's dressed in a moss green corduroy jacket that I haven't seen before, and a woolly beanie hat pulled down over his head, hiding his hair. Although it's only the end of August the weather has taken a turn for the worse so it seems more autumnal. I've missed him so much. I rush towards him but something about his demeanour makes me hesitate by the wrought-iron gate. He looks tired, the tan he acquired over the summer has faded and his shoulders are slumped. I call out to him and he glances up; his smile, when he realizes it's me, transforms his face. I open the gate and fall into his arms and he drops his suitcase on to the pavement to hug me. 'Oh, I've missed you,' he says into my hair as he squeezes me tightly, urgently. 'It's been a hideous few weeks.' I nod sympathetically, remembering his late-night phone calls bemoaning his boss, the ridiculous long hours, 'the shambolic company' that he's working for.

He picks up his suitcase and we go into the house. 'Where's Bea?' he asks. 'How have the two of you been getting on?' I assure him that Beatrice has been great, that the four of us have muddled along together quite nicely for the last ten days. And even though Cass is still an enigma to me, I'm used to her quiet ways now, her slinking about the house like a cat; the only person she seems comfortable with is Beatrice. As we go into the kitchen, he asks me if I've seen much of Niall and I can tell by his faux air of nonchalance that he is trying to quash his feelings of jealousy, that it bothers him to know he's not the only man in his sister's life any more.

As I reheat some of Eva's chicken casserole for his dinner I tell him that Beatrice isn't home, that she's gone to some art gallery with Niall. His face falls and I pretend not to notice, disliking the way it makes me feel. I put the plate of food in front of him and go to the larder to retrieve a bottle of wine. 'Something tells me you need this,' I say as I pour him a glass of Chablis. He smiles gratefully, his eyes shaded with fatigue. I pull out a chair opposite him and pour myself a glass too. It's on the tip of my tongue to tell him about the cryptic message on Lucy's Facebook page, but he looks so tired, so fed-up that I can't bring myself to worry him.

Later, when we're in his bedroom, I go to his Bang and Olufsen music system and I'm about to turn it on when Ben shouts at me, causing me to jump.

'Don't touch that,' he snaps, coming to me and pushing my hand away. 'It's expensive.'

I experience a stab of hurt but remind myself that he's had a long journey, a stressful ten days at a job he hated. He's just tired, frustrated. It's become obvious that he's a little pedantic about certain things; he hates me washing or ironing his precious designer shirts, or touching any of his expensive gadgets. And that's fine. It's one of his quirks. It doesn't mean anything. So I step away and get into bed. When he joins me I go to remove his boxer shorts. 'Not tonight, Abi,' he says, shuffling his body to the other side of the mattress. 'My mind is all over the place. I need to sleep.' He turns over so that I have no choice but to stare at his back, at the mole in the shape of a four-leaf clover on his right shoulder, and his words send a chill through me.

I leave Ben sleeping the next morning and take the bus into town.

It's a crisp day, the sky a vivid blue that borders on violet, and the clouds float past a little too fast, suggesting rain is on its way. I wrap my chiffon scarf higher up my neck as I get off at Bath Spa bus station and head towards

Milsom Street. I've seen a pair of ankle boots that I want
to try on; now that I'm earning more money, I can afford
to buy them. I'm walking with my head down, hands
thrust into the pockets of my parka, my mind full of Ben
and what could be troubling him, and I don't see the
woman heading towards me until I almost bump into
her.

'Sorry,' I say, looking up. Jodie is standing in front of
me, dressed in a puffa jacket and grey skinny jeans, a
smile on her usual sulky mouth. 'Jodie, how are you?'
She's carrying a leather rucksack on her back that looks
like a large beetle.

She stares at me and I can see that she's trying to place
me, working out where she knows me from, and then
her eyes light up as it finally dawns on her who I am.
'Abi, isn't it? How's it going, living with the freaky twins?'

I'm irritated at her disloyalty. 'They're not freaky.'

She laughs but it sounds hollow, insincere. A woman
tries to step past us on the narrow pavement and tuts. I
apologize and move aside, Jodie follows suit. The faint
spittle of rain kisses my cheek. Even though I don't warm
to Jodie, I ask her if she's got time for a quick coffee, that
I would like to ask her some questions. She ponders my
offer, and I can see her weighing up what to do. I can tell
that part of her would love a good gossip about the 'freaky
twins' as she calls them, but the other part is wary about
getting involved, about saying something that could get
back to them. In the end she agrees and we head into a
coffee shop near the Roman Baths.

We grab the only empty table left upstairs, sinking into the chairs in relief. Jodie removes her backpack and shrugs off her Michelin Man coat. By now the rain is thrashing against the windows in a fury, the café is packed and the shared breath of strangers and steam from hot drinks has caused condensation to smear the windows.

'It always seems to rain in Bath,' says Jodie, surveying the downpour. 'Anyway,' she takes a sip of her caramel latte, cursing that it's too hot. 'What did you want to talk to me about?'

'Look,' I say, leaning forward conspiratorially. 'Do you remember what you said to me? That day in your bedroom? You warned me to "watch my back".'

She shrugs. 'Yeah. So what?'

'What did you mean?'

She narrows her blue eyes. 'Why do you want to know? Has something happened?'

'You're still friends with Cass, right?'

'Yes,' she says haltingly. 'What's all this about?'

'But you fell out with Beatrice?' I ask, ignoring her question.

She sighs and she looks young to me then; she can't be much more than twenty. 'When everyone first meets Beatrice they fall under her spell. She's beautiful, funny, talented, smart.' She could be talking about Lucy. I nod encouragingly, sensing that there's more she wants to say. I'm right. 'But she picks people up and drops them when she's bored of them. Have you not found that out by now?' I can sense in her an unspoken hurt at being left out in the cold.

'I'm not sure,' I admit. 'My feelings for Beatrice are complicated.'

'Are you in love with her?'

I almost spit out my coffee in shock. 'Of course not. Why do you say that?'

'Oh, everyone falls in love with Beatrice. Cass is absolutely smitten.'

'Cass?'

'She's gay. Didn't you know? She's totally in love with Bea, follows her everywhere, won't hear a bad word about her.'

Now it all makes sense. How could I have been so blind?

She takes a noisy slurp of her coffee. She's wearing a baggy black T-shirt of a band I don't recognize and, as I assess her from across the table, I think that she has a pinched kind of face as if she's always cross, even when she's smiling. 'I fell out with Cass when I left. But we're friends again now. She can't help her infatuation, can she?'

'Do you think Beatrice is that way inclined?'

'They did have a thing a while back. They thought nobody knew, but I did.' Something tells me that not much gets past Jodie. I feel a twinge of . . . what? Excitement at the thought of the two of them together? Regret that it was never me? 'But Beatrice is messed up. She told Cass that some guy broke her heart when she was at university, that she's never gotten over it. And the way she is with Ben, so possessive, it's weird.'

'What do you mean?' I'm still reeling about the lesbian revelation.

'Come on,' she scoffs. 'I don't know exactly what's going on there, but something isn't quite right. She has a hold over him, I know that much.'

I sit up straighter, expectantly. I long to tell her what's been happening since I moved in, how I believe that Beatrice is probably behind it, that it's all stopped now she's met Niall – until yesterday. But I keep my mouth shut. I don't trust that Jodie won't go blabbing to Cass. 'What makes you say that?'

And then she tells me.

A couple of weeks before she moved out she overhead them talking – 'I wasn't eavesdropping,' she insists, although I suspect she probably was. She was coming down the stairs when she heard raised voices from the drawing room. Ben was agitated, she could hear him pacing. Beatrice was stretched out on the sofa. She could see her bare legs, crossed at the knee, and her hands clamped around a glass of wine, through the half-opened door. 'He was shouting at her, telling her that nobody could ever find out, that she had to promise not to say anything to "her". I've no idea who the "her" was. He alluded to some crime, something from their past. I was scared, Ben sounded out of his mind with worry. And Beatrice . . . Well, she just sat there, almost teasing him, as if she enjoyed having this secret with him. I got the sense that he was a lot more worried about it getting out than she was.' Jodie pauses, making sure she's got my undivided attention. She has. 'But the weirdest thing was, I'm sure he called her Daisy. If it wasn't for the fact I recognized her voice, saw those legs and that tattoo around her ankle, I would have assumed he was talking to someone else.'

'Daisy?' I frown, remembering. 'That was their mother's name.'

Jodie shrugs. 'I dunno. Anyway, I must have made a noise on the stairs because Ben threw the door open and caught me listening, his face . . .' She gives a theatrical shudder. 'He was furious. He snarled at me, insisting I tell him what I'd overheard. He didn't believe me when I played the innocent. After that, Beatrice made it difficult for me to stay.'

'In what way?'

'Oh, I expect you've had the cold-shoulder treatment. I imagine you know what that's like.'

I smile tightly, suddenly feeling an affinity with Jodie because she's right: I know exactly what that's like.

When I get back the house is empty. I run up to my room and start up my laptop, logging on to Facebook and go straight to Lucy's page.

There are no new words on her timeline but there is a link to a photograph. I click on to it and gasp as her face comes into focus, filling up the screen. It's the black-and-white, head-and-shoulders shot of Beatrice wearing her own jewellery. The photo that Cass took for the website. I remember the words from yesterday, *I've been replaced*. I never knew what that meant before but now, alongside the photograph, I understand. I laugh, relieved. I'm not going mad. My illness hasn't returned.

Somebody has been playing with my mind on and off since I moved in. Now I know who.

It's always the quiet ones.

Chapter Twenty-Five

Beatrice swears under her breath as the garnet she's trying to set into a silver ring clatters on to the oak desk. Her fingers are too thick, ungainly. She flexes them, clicking her knuckles and causing Cass, who is lying on the leather sofa with her legs draped over the arm, to look up from her book. 'Are you okay?'

'I keep dropping this bloody stone,' she snaps, picking it up and trying again. Her stomach aches with the beginnings of PMT. She's got more work than she can handle now that her website has gone live, and it is overwhelming her.

'Do you want me to help?' asks Cass. Beatrice shakes her head, wishing she would go away. Cass has become very clingy of late, and she suspects it has something to do with her new relationship with Niall. Not that she can actually call it a relationship. Even though he's ludicrously good looking she's beginning to find him boring; they haven't got much of a connection. She knows he's dead wood, that she's going to have to cast him adrift.

The sky turns grey, darkening the room. Without taking her eyes from her book, Cass automatically reaches behind her to switch on the lamp. *She is beautiful*, Beatrice thinks as she surveys her friend, with her small button nose, her elongated, intense dark eyes, her platinum blonde crop. *And she would do anything for me.*

She places the ring on to her desk with the stone next to it where it glints red and orange in the lamplight. She's not in the right frame of mind to concentrate on this today. Ben is back. She hasn't seen him for nearly two weeks and she was out with Niall when he returned last night. She had rushed home but was surprised to hear from Pam that he was in bed. She had gone to his bedroom, pushing his door ajar gently to see if he was still awake, and had been shocked to see Abi sleeping next to him, her head on his chest.

He might tell her otherwise, but she can sense it. Her grip on him is loosening.

She's really missed Ben. It's the longest they have spent apart in years. She understands why he had to rush off and why he had to stay there as long as he did, but it irks her that he hasn't come to see her yet, that he went straight to Abi first. This is all her fault. She was distracted by Niall, had allowed herself to believe that she might have actually found someone worth losing Ben for. But she has now seen past Niall's pretty insubstantial face to the nothingness beneath it. How can she ever begin to connect with someone else when she's always comparing every relationship she has to the one with her twin? How can she ever better their bond?

'Hi.'

She turns to see Ben standing in the doorway, his hair stuck up in peaks, a tired smile on his face.

She rushes over to him and throws her arms around him. 'I've missed you. Are you okay?'

'I'm exhausted, it's been an emotional ten days,' he says. Then he notices Cass on the sofa. She's sitting up now, book on her lap, eyeing them inquisitively. He doesn't have to say it, she knows what he's thinking, that they can't talk here in front of Cass. She gently pushes him out the door, calling to Cass that they will see her later.

'Let's go for a walk,' she mouths once they are in the hallway. He nods. They pull on raincoats and Beatrice grabs an umbrella as they hurry out the door and head towards Alexandra Park.

'Where's Abi?' she asks, linking her arm through his. A weak sun filters through the clouds and she wishes she was wearing trousers instead of a dress. Her feet are cold in her leopard-print pumps.

He shrugs. 'I haven't seen her yet this morning.'

Beatrice is tempted to tell him she knows Abi is sharing his bed, but she doesn't want it to escalate into an argument. He's a man who has needs. Could she prevent him from having sex, from getting close to someone else? It was naïve of her to think she could. Since Abi's birthday, Beatrice has tried to make an effort to keep things on an even keel, for Ben's sake.

Instead she listens as he tells her about London, how strange it was for him, being there after all these years. That tiny house, so dark and dingy, smelling of boiled cabbage and Paul's dirty socks. The life he was so desperate to escape from. She squeezes his hand in sympathy when he describes all that went on there.

'So Paul still lives there?' she asks when he's finished.

He nods. 'Yep, and he still hates me. But he's jealous. I've got the life he wants.'

They fall silent. The only sounds to be heard are the squeak of their footsteps on wet tarmac and the faraway yap of a dog. It begins to rain again and Beatrice stops to put up her blue spotty umbrella. Ben takes it from her as he usually does, just as she knew he would, and holds it up over the both of them.

'Have you told Abi about London?' she asks.

'She thinks I went to Scotland for work. I can't tell her, Bea, you know that.'

She chews the inside of her mouth as they reach the top of the street, turning left into the park. So many lies, she thinks.

Due to the cold, wet day, it's deserted; it's how Beatrice prefers it. She shivers in her thin scarlet mackintosh and Ben stops to put his arm around her.

'Are you cold? Do you want to go home?'

She shakes her head, she wants to keep him talking,

she wants to hear about Abi, because it's obvious to her that their relationship can never work, not when he's keeping so much from her. *I know all your secrets Ben. I know them all yet I still love you, am still here for you. Always.*

She searches her mind for the right words to bring Abi back into the conversation. 'I think Abi has missed you a lot.' Ben steers them toward a large oak tree as the rain gets heavier.

'I missed her too. I missed you both.' He still has his arm slung over her shoulder and she snuggles her head into the crook of his armpit. They stand and watch the rain running off the leaves and plopping on to the grass that is turning muddy. Neither is inclined to move on. 'She says the two of you are getting on better,' he says. He's still holding the umbrella over the both of them.

'I'm doing it for you, Ben. I know she means a lot to you, but I still think she's cuckoo.'

His body tenses up. Eventually, 'What makes you say that?'

'The flowers. The bracelet. The letters. I think she's lying about all of it. You know,' she turns to look up at him, trying to keep her face expressionless although she's brimming over with excitement at her findings. 'I read this study on the internet about twins, mainly identical twins. And this professor who's done all this research said that sometimes the surviving twin takes on the personality of the dead twin.'

He fidgets, closes the umbrella, drops his arm from around her shoulders. 'What are you trying to tell me?'

She pauses, unsure if she should continue. But she needs to protect him. She knows Abi is bad news, that Ben's going to end up getting hurt. 'You said the florist described the woman who bought the flowers for Abi's birthday, right? They described Abi, or Lucy. Was Abi doing it thinking she was Lucy? Did she, for that moment, forget her own identity?'

Ben stares at her for a couple of seconds and then bursts out laughing. 'You are joking? You're saying Abi thinks she's Lucy? That's fucked up.'

'Abi's fucked up.'

'Not this again, Bea. I don't want to hear it.'

'And the other stuff. The bracelet, the letters that she says I've taken. I think it's all for attention, to drive a wedge between the two of us.'

'You've said this before. I don't believe it.'

She folds her arms, suddenly furious. 'So you think I stole her letters?'

He runs a hand over his face, exasperated. His hair is wet from the rain and water drips from the end of his nose. 'I don't know. You think she stole your bracelet, so maybe you did it to get back at her?'

Angry tears spring in her eyes. 'You think I'm a thief? That I would be that petty?'

He doesn't look at her; instead he bows his head, kicking a pile of wet leaves with the toe of his boot.

'We found that earring in her bedroom. She stole it

from me and we've never confronted her. *I* never confronted her. Because you told me not to. So do you think she stole my bracelet?'

His head shoots up so that he's staring right at her, his eyes unusually hard, his jaw set tight. 'I don't fucking need this right now,' he snaps, his face turning red. 'It's been a hellish few weeks and all you can do is bleat on about Abi.' Spittle flies from his mouth and she takes a step back from him, so unused to seeing him angry but she knows he has a temper, she's seen it once before. 'This is all doing my head in.' He roughly shoves the umbrella at her so that one of the prongs pokes her in the chest and she gasps. Then he turns the collar of his jacket up, thrusts his hands into his pockets and, with his head bent, stalks off into the downpour, away from her.

She doesn't try to stop him, or catch up with him. A sob escapes her throat as she watches his retreating back and she sinks on to the sodden grass, not caring about the wet mud that smears on to the back of her bare legs. Her worst fear has come true . . . Abi has won.

Chapter Twenty-Six

I close my laptop and sit very still on my bed, listening to the rain throwing itself against the sash windows, contemplating my next move. Then I creep out of my room. From my viewpoint on the landing I can see into both Beatrice's and Ben's bedrooms. They are empty. I lean over the balustrade and look down on to the next floor where the sitting room is, straining my ears. Sound carries in this house, yet I can't hear the low hum of the television or the mumble of chatter, the clinking of wine glasses or the familiar clatter of cutlery or banging of cupboards that tells me someone is in the kitchen. Eva isn't due to come in until Monday and I'm certain that Cass and Pam went out together earlier. As far as I'm aware, they aren't back yet. Neither are Ben or Beatrice.

The house is empty.

I hesitate, my heart thumping against my chest, and then,

with a sudden resolve, I go to the narrow, winding staircase that leads up to the attic rooms. With trepidation I take a step, and when I'm sure nobody is about to jump out of the shadows to berate me, I continue my way to the top, the wooden stairs creaking underfoot. The first door I come to is a bedroom, square and compact with a single bed pushed up against a window, and a pine wardrobe next to it. By the paintings hanging on the wall I take it to be Pam's room. I'm about to walk on past when a brightly coloured oil painting catches my eye. It's of two girls running hand in hand through what looks to be a cornfield. I can just make out the backs of their blonde heads, their wheat-coloured hair blowing out behind them as golden as the corn, their red dresses and the blue sky the only other colours in the painting. They are holding hands, they look the same age, they look like twins.

Why has she painted twins? Did she do it before I moved in? I can't remember seeing the painting in May when I first looked around the house. Is it a coincidence that the girls in the painting resemble me and Lucy?

I force myself to leave the room. I can't be distracted, there isn't much time.

Cass has the bigger of the two attic rooms. It's pretty, with sloping ceilings and framed black-and-white prints hanging on pale green walls. The double bed is unmade, the duvet bunched up at the foot of the bed revealing crumpled sheets. I look around the room wildly, unsure where to start. I walk around the bed, spotting another door, different from all the rest, heavy, a firedoor. I push

it open, expecting to see a wardrobe or en suite. Instead
it's a darkroom. A strong acidic smell hangs in the air.
Above the sink, photographs are pinned up on a make-
shift washing line with wooden pegs. I blink in the darkness, grappling along the wall for a light switch. I find
it and click it on and the room is flooded by a dull red
glow. I quickly glance behind me to make sure I am alone
before walking further into the room. I pick up a contact
sheet with its rows of miniature photographs and I gasp
as my eyes scan every one. They are all of Beatrice. Some
look as though she's been taken unaware, some are obviously posed for.

I'm thinking how obsessed Cass must be with Beatrice
when the door slams behind me, trapping me in the little
room.

The walls begin to close in on me. For a few seconds
I can't do anything, I'm frozen to the spot. Then the
adrenaline kicks in and I run to the door and wrench it
open, relieved that I'm not locked in. I prop the door
open with my foot while leafing through the pile of
photographs on the worktop. I pause when I notice that
one stands out from the rest. I pull it down from its peg
to get a better look. It's a side profile of Beatrice's face,
and next to it a side profile of mine, superimposed
together so that it makes up a whole, disjointed face.
The result is unsettling. The print is sticky in my hand.
I'm not sure what to do with it or even if it proves
anything. I've only got half-thought-out theories as to
why Cass would do this to me anyway.

I leave the room, letting the door swing shut behind me, the photograph still in my hand. As I dart down the stairs I'm startled to see Ben lumbering up the main staircase, his hair slick with rain, the bottom of his jeans wet and heavy. His features are set in a scowl so that he looks drawn, troubled, until he sees me, and then he regains his normal good-natured repose.

He takes in the photograph that I'm clutching to my chest and my location. 'What are you doing?' His expression darkens again.

I pause and it crosses my mind to lie to him. Except I've got a photograph in my hand and it's obvious I'm coming from the attic. I wait for him to reach the landing before handing it to him. 'I found this in Cass's bedroom.'

He takes it from me and glances at it. 'Bit freaky,' he says half-heartedly, handing it back to me. 'Why were you in her room?'

So I tell him about the sinister message that appeared on Lucy's timeline and the photograph and my suspicions that Cass is behind it. 'I bumped into Jodie, she told me that Cass is in love with Beatrice and they had a fling. Maybe Cass is jealous.'

I expect Ben to understand, even sympathize, but he's staring at me, his jaw tensed. 'You met up with Jodie?' he says in an unnaturally quiet voice. His face is white. 'She's a silly little liar. Why would you believe anything she said? You know nothing about her.'

'I . . . I bumped into her . . .'

'And you believe that Cass and my sister had, what? A lesbian fling? That's an outrageous lie.'

I remain silent, fiddling self-consciously with the photograph.

'Let me see your computer. I want to have a look at this message and photo for myself.' He pushes past me and marches into my room.

I follow. 'They've been wiped off,' I say, as he grabs my laptop from the bed.

'Of course they have.' He gives a sarcastic laugh and drops the laptop so that it lands softly on the mattress. 'Because they were never there, were they, Abi?'

His words are a slap in the face. 'They were,' I insist. 'I'm not lying.'

Ben slumps on to my bed, his head in his hands. 'I don't know who to believe any more,' he murmurs through his fingers. He looks up at me with red-rimmed eyes. 'I've recently had an argument with Beatrice. She thinks that you have some mental disorder. She thinks you're confusing reality with fantasy and that you have a split personality, that you sometimes think you're Lucy and do these weird things. And I stuck up for you.'

I freeze at his words, turning cold all over. My legs give way beneath me and I slump to the floor. 'You think I've got some personality disorder?'

He shakes his head. 'I'm not saying I believe it. But Beatrice certainly does.'

I think of the paranoia, the survivor's guilt, the post-traumatic stress disorder, of all the things I've been diagnosed with since Lucy died. Could Beatrice be right? I think of the flowers addressed to myself but from Lucy, the florist describing me. 'That's unfair of Beatrice,' I snap. 'The florist described me, but it could be her description too, remember?' The accusation hangs in the air between us, something bad, rancid, like a fart.

I think of the Facebook stuff when I'm the only one who has Lucy's password, her log-in details. Unless her account has been hacked, it would be impossible for someone else to write those things on her wall. Especially Cass. Even the photograph I'm still holding doesn't mean anything. Okay, Cass is in love with Beatrice. They may or may not have had a sexual relationship, Cass might have been a bit jealous when I moved in, but I'm with Ben. She knows that. I'm no threat. So why would she do it?

And that leaves his sister, his twin . . .

'Beatrice is doing this to me,' I insist, getting to my knees. Ben puts his head in his hands and groans. 'Don't you see, Ben? Can't you see what she's doing?' I can hear the desperation in my voice but Ben shakes his head. 'Why don't you believe me? Why do you always think she's right?'

'Here we go again,' he mutters, partly under his breath. His head shoots up and I notice how exhausted he looks.

'Here we go again?' I mimic, standing up, my heart thumping. 'Is that what you think? That I'm bleating on and on . . .'

He stands up too, so that we're facing each other. His

hands are clenched by his sides. 'We keep having the same fucking argument, Abi.'

'Because you don't believe me,' I cry.

'Don't shout at me,' he says calmly.

I want to hit him, I want to pummel my fists into his chest, I want to shake him until he sees that I'm not making this up. Instead I hurl the photograph at him, but because it's light, almost weightless, it drifts to the floor. Then I sink on to the carpet and burst into helpless tears. I can't stand it any more. I can't bear him thinking I'm always the one who's being unreasonable, or paranoid. 'I can't do this any more,' I cry. 'I've had enough.'

For a moment Ben is silent and then I feel his arms about me.

'Abi, don't say that.'

'Then tell me you believe me. Tell me you think Beatrice is talking nonsense.'

He hesitates and I pull away from him. 'I'm moving out,' I say into my hands. 'I can go and live with my parents again.'

He's kneeling next to me but I shift away so that my back is to him. 'Abi, I don't want you to do that,' he says. 'You have to understand how hard it is for me. She's my sister . . .'

'And I'm your girlfriend.'

I wipe my eyes with my sleeve, filled with resignation. We keep going around in circles, but nothing will ever change. I know that our relationship is over, it's almost a relief. Beatrice has won.

'Abi, look at me,' his voice is urgent, panicked. I turn reluctantly towards him. 'Let's move out. Together. It's obvious it's never going to work, the three of us living under one roof. And I'm too old to still be living with my sister.' He gives a rueful smile.

Yesterday I would have been delighted to hear this. But it's too late. I shake my head, pleased to note the hurt in his eyes.

'You don't believe me,' I say. 'So what's the point?'

'Oh, Abi. I do believe you. Please . . . I love you. I want to be with you.'

My resolve is weakening. Sensing it, Ben pulls me into his arms and we sit there, on the champagne-coloured carpet with its moth-shaped stain, gently rocking in sync with one another. Then he says quietly into my hair, 'I've got enough cash now. We can rent somewhere soon. What do you think?'

I pull away so that I can see his expression, to make sure he's serious. 'You would do that? Even if I am a bit wacko?' I attempt to laugh through my tears.

'I want you, Abi. We can't be together here. This thing with you and Beatrice, it's never going to stop, is it? Always blaming each other, this power struggle you have.' I open my mouth to protest but he shoots me a warning look. 'Come on, it's obvious. And I'm flattered. But I have to make a choice. And I choose you.'

And as he bends to kiss me I think, *I've won. He's chosen me over her.* So why do I not feel as triumphant, as delighted, as I should?

*

As the three of us sit around the kitchen table later that evening, avoiding eye contact, Ben tells Beatrice of the choice he's made. She's silent for a while, chewing the inside of her lip, but I notice that her face pales, her eyes shine too brightly. She hangs her head in resignation after making one last sad attempt to change his mind, looking as though she might throw up. I sit silently sipping my tea, gripped by guilt as she hangs her head, her perfect bob falling around her beautiful face. She lifts her head with a sigh and narrows her eyes, and it's as if she's weighing up something in her mind. 'Are you sure about this, Ben?' she says softly, not looking in my direction. 'Does Abi make you happy?'

He takes my hand and tells her that yes, I do make him happy, that I'm what he wants, what he's been waiting for.

'So this is the end?' she sighs and her shoulders slump. 'I've only ever wanted you to be happy, Ben. Please believe that.'

She pushes back her chair and walks silently out of the room. We both stare at the coffee cup, the one with the bird on the front, her favourite, noticing the pink lipstick stain on the rim, and I feel a tinge of unease. Why didn't she put up more of a fight? Has she accepted defeat so readily? Will she really let him go?

Chapter Twenty-Seven

I wander through the house trying to imprint it on my memory. I touch the daisy-shaped lights that are wound around the banister, run my hand along the tastefully painted walls, enjoy the warmth from the underfloor heating through the limestone tiles under my feet, lounge on the squashy velvet sofa in the drawing room, stand on the terrace overlooking the garden below, swing my legs over the arm of the tatty antique armchair in the kitchen, as Beatrice and Cass did the first morning after I moved in. I bask in its beauty. *I will miss this house*, I think. Because for a while I was happy here, for a while the house held within its walls the promise of a life I was desperate to be part of. A life that was so different, so much more glamorous than the one I had been trying to escape from.

*

One morning two days later, I'm sitting at the kitchen table with my laptop, ostensibly typing up an interview for Miranda, but really surfing the net for places that Ben and I can rent together. The house is eerily quiet apart from the clunking sound of the old school radiators as the boiler cools down. Ben is at work, and the others have gone to see a friend of Beatrice's who is opening an artists' studio in Frome. I wasn't invited to join them.

I'm scrolling through the details of a flat in Walcot Street when a loud ding dong reverberates around the quiet house, causing me to jump. *It's someone at the front door,* I tell myself as my heart begins its familiar war dance and I tear myself away from the computer, and the fashionable flat in Walcot Street, to answer it. A crumpled-looking woman with short, greying hair and ruddy cheeks hovers on the step. She's older, perhaps in her late fifties, early sixties at a push. 'Hello,' she says in a thick Scottish accent. Her eyes crinkle as she smiles. She's barely five foot tall and plump, wearing a faded blue mackintosh and sturdy brown boots under a long skirt. She's holding a large handbag in the crook of her arm. Behind her the street is quiet, the sun balloons in the china blue sky. The air smells fresh after a recent shower. 'I'm looking for Ben.' Her eyes dart hopefully behind me into the hallway.

'Ben?' Why is she looking for Ben? 'He's at work, he won't be home until tonight.'

'Oh,' her face falls in disappointment. 'Of course he is, I didn't think about that. I'll come back later.'

'I'm sorry,' I say, apologizing because she looks so crest-fallen. 'Can I tell him who called?' I can't let this woman walk away without knowing who she is. She glances about her, as if she expects he will walk down the street at any moment.

'I'm his mum, lovey. Don't worry, I'll catch him later. I'm staying with his brother in Bristol for the week, so there will be other opportunities. I tried to ring him, but he never answers his phone and I'm worried, you see. After his father's death . . .' She pauses, her chin wobbling, then she makes an effort to compose herself. '. . . I saw Ben only last week. There was an argument . . . I want . . .' She stops and her eyes widen in panic, as if she's said too much. 'Never mind, I'll come over again tonight – will you tell him that, lovey? Will you tell him I'll come back this evening, around eight?'

I'm gawping at her in astonishment. Blood pounds in my ears. 'His mum?' I can hardly believe what I've heard. 'You're Ben's mum?' I repeat, in case I've thought those words rather than said them out loud.

Her face clouds over and I can see the confusion in her watery blue eyes. She doesn't resemble Ben, or Beatrice. 'Yes, I'm his mother. Who are you?'

'I'm his girlfriend. Abi.'

'Ah,' her face lights up and she looks at me properly now, as if seeing me for the first time. 'Yes, he mentioned you when he came to visit me last week. Ah, and what a bonny lass you are.'

'You saw him last week?' I hold on to the doorframe for support. 'In Scotland?'

She laughs. 'I know I've still got the accent, but no. We don't live in Scotland any more, we've lived in London for the past ten years. Streatham. He came to stay with me there.' She lowers her voice. 'I expect he told you about his dad dying. He'd been ill for a long time, but still, it was a shock.' Her eyes glisten. 'I think Ben has taken it hard, no matter what Paul says.' A beep of a horn makes her turn around, and that's when I notice the red Mondeo purring alongside the kerb further down the street. 'That's Martin, my other son. I better go. I'll see you later, lovey.' She rubs my upper arm affectionately. 'I'm Morag, by the way. It's so lovely to meet you.' Then she's out of the gate and scurrying towards the waiting car, and I watch, in shock, as she folds herself into the passenger seat, handbag on her lap, and as the car moves off I sink on to the cold stone step, my head reeling. How can that be Ben's mum when his parents were killed in a car crash over thirty years ago?

I pour myself a glass of wine from the half-empty bottle in the fridge, even though it's only eleven o'clock. Edgy and unnerved, I down it in one gulp. Then I ring Ben. He picks up the phone straight away, an edge of panic to his voice. I never usually phone him when he's working. I blurt out everything while doing laps around the kitchen table, hoping he can explain it away, but already knowing that's impossible. What other explanation could there be?

He's silent for too long, before spluttering, 'What did she look like?'

'She's in her late fifties I think, she has a Scottish accent, similar to yours, Ben. And she said she saw you last week, in London. You said you were in Scotland last week so I don't understand.'

'I was in Scotland last week.'

His impatient tone doesn't deter me as it might once have done. 'And she also mentioned a brother of yours, living in Bristol. What's going on? Do you and Beatrice have a brother?'

'Of course we don't,' he snaps. 'Look, Abi, I'm at work, I can't talk about this here. I'm coming home.'

'You can't leave. What will your boss say?' My voice is shrill and echoey in the quiet kitchen. He sounds so angry, so shocked that I'm beginning to think this must be a trick, that whoever wrote on Lucy's Facebook page and sent me the flowers on my birthday, has also sent me a middle-aged woman pretending to be Ben's mum. Am I losing my grip on reality, just as Beatrice said? Are the messages from my dead sister and visits from Ben's dead mum all in my imagination? The woman, Morag, looks nothing like Ben, Beatrice or the young mother called Daisy in the photograph in the drawing room. And if Morag is their mum, who the hell is the woman in the picture? And why would they lie about her? 'She said she will come back tonight. She mentioned a Martin waiting in the car. She said her name was Morag. That's an unusual name, Ben.'

'I don't know her, for fuck's sake,' he hisses. 'Don't you believe me?'

'I don't know what to think . . .' But he's already hung up. I throw my mobile on to the antique armchair and pour myself another glass of wine, but after one sip I gag and rush over to the Belfast sink. I take gulps of air and lean over the sink until the nausea passes, then I slump on to the armchair, my legs shaking. My phone vibrates under my bottom and I pull it out from underneath me, hoping that it's Ben ringing to apologize, to explain away this woman who claims she's his mum. But it's Nia. I quickly recount what has happened and promise that I will call her back tonight. I can't face talking to anyone other than Ben at the moment.

Less than an hour later I hear Ben's Fiat pull up outside the house. I'm sitting at the bottom of the stairs as he rushes in, his face pale, his tie askew. He jolts when he sees me, and his eyes soften. 'Oh, Abi.' He joins me on the step and wraps his arms around me, hugging me to him, murmuring into my hair that everything is going to be all right. Usually I love being in his arms, take comfort in being soothed by him. It makes me feel safe. But not now. Now it irritates me that he's assuming, yet again, that the problem is mine. I pull away from him.

'What's going on, Ben? And don't try and tell me I imagined that bloody woman, because I didn't. She was there,' I point in the direction of the door. 'In the flesh. And she said she was your mother.'

He wrinkles his nose, smelling the alcohol on my breath. 'Have you been drinking?'

'I've had a couple of sips of wine. And no,' I say when

his expression suggests that my drinking might be the reason I'm seeing his dead mother, 'I hadn't been drinking before she arrived.'

'I don't understand it, Abi. It makes no sense.' He shakes his head, looking anguished. 'Why would someone pretend to be my mum?'

I sigh. 'I don't know, Ben. You tell me.'

He shrugs and runs his hands through his hair. 'Are you sure this happened, Abi? Could you have been mistaken? Maybe she didn't say she was my mum. Maybe she said something else.'

Anger builds, but I try to keep my voice calm, even as I say, 'I know I've had problems with my mental health in the past. I know I attempted suicide. My illness means I can be paranoid, maybe I even sabotage my life out of guilt at times, I don't know. But I've never been delusional, Ben. I've never imagined talking to someone, having a conversation with someone standing in front of me, only for it to be a figment of my imagination.' I grab his hand. It's clammy. 'You have to believe me.'

'I don't know, Abi. It's all so strange.'

'She said she was going to come back this evening, about eight o'clock. Let's see what she says then.' I glance at him, trying to read his expression, to see if he's lying. I remember Jodie's words. The freaky twins, she called them. She believes they are hiding something. Is this it?

'That's true,' he mumbles. I notice the beads of sweat on his forehead, his clammy palms, the shirt collar that he keeps fingering away from his throat as if it's choking him and I realize he's fretting. I only wish I knew what he was fretting about.

I don't believe this woman is a figment of my imagination. I know I saw her, talked to her. She told me she was Ben's mum. She didn't seem the type of person who would play such a mean trick in order to mess with my head. She looked like a mum; a lovely, rosy-cheeked, kind mum. She had a Scottish accent, she seemed genuine.

But as eight o'clock approaches, I'm on tenterhooks.

Beatrice, Pam and Cass are still not back from Frome, so Ben and I roam about the house, each pretending we aren't listening out for that knock on the door. We have our dinner together – a lasagne that Eva popped in earlier to make – and a glass of wine. We don't listen to any music, or turn the television on.

Eight o'clock comes and goes. Nine o'clock, ten o'clock and nothing. By eleven Beatrice comes home with Pam and Cass, shattering the silence as they kick off their shoes and hang up their coats, laughing as they do so. I hear them clatter down the stairs into the kitchen, chattering over each other, discussing some artist I've never heard of.

'She's not coming back, is she?' I say as we get ready for bed at midnight. Ben is standing in the middle of the room with his boxer shorts on, reminding me that we haven't had sex since he got back from Scotland.

'Of course she's not,' he mutters, and I see it, the look on his face. He's almost grey, *ashen*, with what? Disappointment in me?

I pull the nightdress over my head, loathing his side-ways looks of concern, with the words he refuses to say. At best he thinks I'm deluded. Mentally unstable. At worst he thinks I'm making it up. Either way, he doesn't believe me.

'You know,' I say, gathering up my jeans and jumper. 'I'm going to sleep alone tonight.'

'No,' he says coming over to me. 'You can't go. I'm sorry, I do believe you. I don't understand it, that's all.' He takes my clothes from me, places them on the chair, ushers me into bed and climbs in beside me. 'I love you so much,' he says into my neck, and as he takes my nightdress off he makes me forget the anger and the hurt as he kisses my questions away.

Ben rings work to say he's sick the next day, and I know he's waiting to see if this mystery woman, this Morag, turns up again. It gives me hope that he might believe me after all. He makes me promise not to tell Beatrice, as she will only worry. When he's out washing his precious car, I ring Nia, apologize for not calling back last night. I tell her everything.

She listens without interrupting. In the background I can hear the hubbub of her office; the ring of phones, the indistinct natter of her colleagues, the faint sound of Radio One. I imagine her funky, open-plan office in Covent Garden with the glass partitions and the fashion photographs adorning the walls, and I'm suddenly envious. I close my eyes, wishing that I could turn the clock back, that my life had never changed so irrevocably, that we are all living in our Balham terrace and the only thing I have to ring Nia about is to discuss which new club we are going to try out tonight.

'Do you think I'm going mad, Nia? Do you think I could have imagined it?'

'You're not going mad, Abi. I don't want to hear you say that again.' She says it so forcefully, so matter-of-factly, that I long to believe her. 'I can't tell you how sorry I am for what happened when I came to visit. But I never thought you were going mad. I was worried that if you stopped taking your antidepressants you would . . . you would . . .'

She doesn't have to finish her sentence for me to know exactly what she's trying to say, that the memories of finding me in that bathtub haven't left her. Will probably never leave her, and I feel terrible about that.

'Oh, Nia,' I whisper.

'Anyway. Let's not dwell.' I want to laugh. That is Nia's mantra in life and not for the first time I wish I was as confident as her. 'You know, Abi, I think he does believe you and that's why he's home today. That's why he's out washing his car right now. He's expecting her to come back and he wants to be there when she does.'

I move to my bedroom window, mobile clamped to my ear. On the street below, Ben sweeps a large soapy sponge across the bonnet of his car, but he seems distracted, his head snapping around every time he hears the far-off sound of an engine. He drops the sponge into a bucket, causing soap suds to splash on to the pavement, and walks around to the back of the car to open the boot. *What are you doing, Ben?* I hear a car chug into the road. My stomach tightens. It's the red Mondeo from yesterday. It parks outside a house further up the street, engine still running. Ben hears the car and steps away from his Fiat. For a couple of seconds he hovers on the pavement in his short-sleeved Fred Perry, as if undecided. When he glances up at my window, I instinctively move out of sight. I don't think he's seen me. When I look again I see him swinging his long legs into the passenger seat of the Mondeo.

'The Mondeo has turned up,' I whisper into the phone, not sure why I'm lowering my voice when there is nobody else in the house. 'Ben's got into it.' I hold on to the windowsill, my head spinning as the car pulls away from the kerb. The last thing I see, as it drives past the house and disappears from view, is Ben's pale face at the window, looking up at me. His eyes briefly meet mine and then he's gone. 'Oh God, he's seen me.' I'm finding it hard to swallow, my mouth is so dry. 'What's going on, Nia?'

'For some reason Ben's lying to you, Abi. He's gone willingly with whoever is driving that car, so he obviously knows the woman who called yesterday, in spite of what he tells you.'

I groan and think about the woman, this Morag, and something occurs to me for the first time. 'Why didn't she ask for Beatrice?'

'What do you mean?'

'Yesterday, she knocked on the door and asked to see Ben. If she is their mother, why didn't she ask to see Beatrice, her daughter?'

'I don't know, but listen. You have to go and look in his car.'

'What? I can't do that.'

'Don't you want to find out why he's lying?'

I swallow but my throat is dry. From the window I can see that the boot of Ben's Fiat is still open and sticking up in the air. I tell myself I'm doing him a favour by going to his car and closing the boot. I haven't got keys, but at least if I close the boot nobody will know that the car isn't locked.

'Okay,' I say.

'Go, go, go,' she says, sounding like a sergeant major. I run down the stairs and into the street, looking both ways to make sure nobody is watching me before daring to approach his car, mobile still to my ear. 'Are you there?' she says. 'Are you at the car?'

'Yes.' I ping the windscreen wipers back against the windscreen and walk around to the boot.

'You have to have a good look inside the car, for clues,' barks Nia, channelling her inner Miss Marple.

'For goodness' sake, Nia,' I snap. This is wrong, snooping around his car. I don't want to think badly of Ben, I love him and I can't bear the thought that he might be lying to me, that he would rather let me think I'm going crazy than tell me the truth.

Nia, sensing my ambivalence, says quietly, 'I can

imagine this is horrible for you, Abi. But something isn't right here. And you know it.'

'Jodie thinks so,' I admit, tears springing to my eyes. I fill her in on what Jodie told me.

'He's hiding something, they both are.'

I nod, although I know Nia can't see me. A tear drips down my face and I tell her I will call her back soon. She's disappointed, but makes me promise to call if I find anything out that explains Ben's strange behaviour. I assure her I will.

'And, Abi . . .' She pauses, as if debating whether to be honest with me.

'What is it? You can tell me, Nia. You're the only one I trust at this moment.' It's not until I say it that it hits me how true it is.

'Okay. When I came to stay with you last month, I thought something seemed off with the two of them. I couldn't put my finger on it, I still can't. I know you were worried about Beatrice . . . but there was something about Ben . . .' she hesitates. 'I can't put my finger on it. But it was enough to make me concerned about leaving you with them. Please be careful.' Her words unnerve me, but I tell her that I'm fine and end the call. My fingers are trembling as I place my mobile in the back pocket of my jeans. I poke my head over the parcel shelf to see into the main body of the car, but it's remarkably tidy. Ben's neatness almost borders on OCD, he won't even let me eat in the car. What was I hoping to find?

And I realize then that I have no choice but to trust

him. I'm sure he will tell me what's going on when he gets back, there must be a simple explanation for it all. There has to be. Because I can't bear the thought of losing Ben, he's been my life raft these last few months, keeping me afloat. He's the reason I can get up in the morning, that I can face the day without Lucy. I can't bear to think about what it means for us, for me, if he's been lying.

I'm reaching up to close the boot when I notice something out of the corner of my eye. At first I think it's a speck of flint, or fabric poking out from under the matting where the spare wheel is kept, but on further inspection I can see that it is pink and paper-thin, contrasting sharply with the black interior. I give it a tug. It's stiff like the corner of a piece of paper. Blood rushes to my head as I feel desperately around for the latch, but before I even manage to wrench it open I have an idea of what it is. But I still gasp in shock. I still stumble backwards as if I've been punched. Because nestled on top of the spare wheel, lifting and falling gently in the breeze, are three pink envelopes, dog-eared with age, my name and university address scribbled on them in Lucy's familiar scrawl. And next to them, curled up in the spare wheel is a silver bracelet, its rich blue sapphires glinting in the late afternoon sun.

Chapter Twenty-Eight

There is a chill in the air as Beatrice steps off the bus. The sun is hiding behind a large ash-grey cloud, taking with it the little warmth that is left of the day. She wraps her chunky knitted cardigan around her body, a burst of wind whipping at the silk of her tea-dress so that her bare knees are exposed, her toes retracting in her pumps. She falters at the estate agent's window to peruse the flats available to rent. Why does she continue to do this, to torture herself?

He's leaving me. He's really leaving me.

It's been days since he told her, but only now is she beginning to believe it. She's lost him, the last of her family. The one thing she has dreaded for years is actually happening, and as the realization dawns on her, something unexpected shifts inside her. Relief. She has been so desperate to cling on to him, terrified of losing him, but now she's experiencing a certain kind of freedom that she hasn't felt in years.

'Wait up.' She turns to see Cass running towards her, the camera that hangs around her neck bouncing against her chest. 'Are you okay, Bea?' she pants, worry etched into her lovely elfin face. Loyal, beautiful Cass.

Beatrice bites the inside of her lip to stop herself from crying, from telling Cass everything. All these years she's kept their secret, even though it has been eating her up inside, as if she's a pumpkin with its flesh hollowed out so that eventually it sags and decays, withering into mush. She needs someone to fill her up again, to replace her insides, to make her glow. She's already shed one skin, one persona. She thought Beatrice Price would be something different entirely, but at the end of the day she's still the same person, except maybe she's not, maybe she's worse than the person she was trying to escape from.

Cass is still staring at her quizzically, her head to one side. She's so young, so fresh, so guileless. She knows Cass would never hurt her, but would she still care about her if she knew the truth? Would anyone?

'I'm sorry, Cass. I didn't mean to walk off, I'm in my own world.'

Cass smiles in relief and links her arm through Beatrice's. 'Are you upset about Ben?'

Beatrice nods and they walk the rest of the way in silence. As they turn the corner into their street Cass asks if they should have a game of tennis before it gets dark. 'Why not,' Beatrice says, knowing that this is Cass's way of trying to cheer her up, of taking her mind off Ben and his imminent departure.

When they reach the gate to the house, Beatrice pauses. Abi is rushing out the front door grappling with a large holdall. Her face is deathly pale, her eyes red and alarm bells begin to ring in Beatrice's head. 'Abi?' She pushes open the gate with a creak. Abi stops on the pathway when she notices them, her face anguished, almost fearful. 'Where are you going? Are you okay?' *Have you finally lost it, Abi?*

Abi blinks at them, her face changing from fear to anger, her big green eyes wild, and Beatrice instinctively pulls away from Cass. Lowering her voice, she urges her to go into the house. Cass glances from one to the other wordlessly, but does as she's told; always compliant, thinks Beatrice, always so trusting.

Abi drops the bag on to the black-and-white-tiled pathway where it lands with a smacking sound. With her dishevelled hair and wild eyes she looks as though she belongs in some mental facility and Beatrice's heart begins to beat a little bit faster, nervous that Abi might attack her as she did Alicia. *I knew you were fucked up, Abi. How can you not be, after everything that's happened to you?* She grips the gate, ready to swing it shut if Abi makes a lunge for her.

'I'm going to stay with Nia for a bit,' says Abi. Beatrice remains silent, worried about saying the wrong thing, not wanting to provoke Abi when she's obviously lost it. 'Your mother turned up here yesterday, I doubt

Ben's told you. It seems Ben is very good at hiding things.' She laughs. It's the laughter of a person who is teetering towards hysteria and the sound of it unnerves Beatrice.

'What are you talking about? My mother is dead.'

Abi stares at her and Beatrice squirms under her scrutinizing gaze, all the while trying to figure out what to do. Should she call Ben? She can't let Abi wander off alone when she's having some kind of breakdown. 'Where's Ben, Abi? Shall I ask him to come home from work?'

'Oh my God,' she says, the blood draining from her face. 'You don't know, do you? And all this time I thought it was you.'

'Thought what was me? Abi, you're scaring me.'

'Join the club,' says Abi, wrenching her bag from the floor and over her shoulder in a fireman's lift. 'I've been scared for months, Beatrice. *Fucking* months.' She stalks towards her and Beatrice instinctively backs out of the gate. 'I thought I was losing my mind – and trust me, it wouldn't be that hard. But that's what he wants, isn't it? He wants me to think I'm going mad. I don't understand why.'

'Who?' A coldness washes over Beatrice and goosebumps pop up on her legs. 'Who are you talking about?'

'Ben,' she hisses. 'Your precious brother.' She stops when she reaches Beatrice and her eyes soften. 'I'm sorry I thought it was you. But you were so possessive of him, so jealous. And I can understand it. I'm a twinless twin now. But I can still understand.' She looks so sad that tears spring into Beatrice's eyes.

A twinless twin. Beatrice knows exactly how that feels. A tear escapes and trickles down her nose. 'Are you leaving Ben?' she sniffs. She still doesn't understand what Abi is trying to tell her. *What do you know, Abi? What do you know about my mum?*

Abi seems to consider this, her eyes never leaving Beatrice's. 'I want to know why he lied to me. But I need to get away, can you tell him that? Tell him I need some time by myself, but I will be back.' She reaches over to give Beatrice a hug, but the holdall gets in the way, swinging into Beatrice so that the hug is awkward. 'We could have been good friends I think, if it wasn't for Ben. But that's my fault.'

She pulls away, hoisting the holdall more firmly on to her shoulder, and walks out the gate, her fine blonde hair blowing around her face. As she rounds the corner out of sight the heavens open, drenching Beatrice in seconds. She rushes into the hallway, slamming the front door behind her and sinking on to the bottom step.

Oh, Ben, she thinks as Abi's words swarm around in her mind like the pieces of a jigsaw puzzle that are jostling to be put in the right order so that the whole picture can become clearer. *What have you done?*

Chapter Twenty-Nine

I lean my head against the window as the train pulls out of the station and watch as the mellow brick of the city recedes behind the rain-spattered glass; a watercolour with the paint running. Everything has changed, nobody who lives in that house is who I thought they were. *Even you, Ben. Even you.* I disguise a sob by taking a sip of the bitter coffee that I managed to grab at the station, thankful that there is nobody sitting next to me, the carriage is nearly empty. It seems not many people want to head into Waterloo at 5.13 p.m. on a wet Wednesday afternoon.

My coat is so saturated that the rain has seeped through to the back of my top. I shuffle out of the parka and discard it on the seat next to me. My head is pounding and I want to throw up, my whole body is trembling from a mixture of cold and shock.

When I discovered Ben's stash, I couldn't take in what I was seeing, what it meant. My first thought was that Beatrice had put the things there in a bid to frame Ben, to split us up, but deep down I know she wouldn't do that, even if she doesn't want us to be together. She loves Ben too much to make him out to be the bad guy. I snatched the letters, clasping them to my chest as if Lucy's words could penetrate my heart, relieved that at least I had them back, but I left the bracelet where it lay in the ridge of the spare wheel, not daring to touch it, and replaced the boot's floor. Then I slammed the door shut and rushed into the house, my mind whirling. I called Nia straight away, sobbing down the phone, barely comprehensible.

'You need to get out of the house, Abi, and quickly, before he comes back.' I shiver now when I think of her words. She urged me to get out of Bath and to come and stay with her. I managed to grab my never-been-worn maroon vintage tea-dress as well as the green Alice Temperley of Beatrice's that I've never gotten around to giving back to her, and all of Lucy's letters and photographs, the things that are too precious to be left behind.

I wasn't expecting to see Beatrice as I was coming out of the house, and it occurs to me now that I never told her about finding the bracelet or letters, that, instead, I just ranted at her about what a liar her brother is. I could tell by her open, puzzled face that she had no idea what I was talking about. I think I know her well enough by now to be able to read her expressions, to gauge her feelings, but maybe not. I'm obviously not a very good judge of character; I fell in love with Ben and I thought Beatrice was trying to terrorize me. The good twin and the bad twin. Could I have mixed them up?

The sky darkens and the lights flicker on in the carriage. They are too bright, intensifying the pounding in my head. It hurts to look at them so I keep my eyes firmly shut as I try to remember everything that has happened in the months since I moved in. My head is fuzzy, I'm finding it hard to formulate anything constructive in my mind. What I do know though, what has become obvious, is that Ben led me to believe Beatrice took Lucy's letters and that she did so because she thought I had stolen her bracelet. And all the time he knew this to be untrue because he had them hidden in his car. A fresh wave of nausea engulfs me.

At some point I doze off, because when I open my eyes again the carriage is half full and a bald man wearing a North Face waterproof is hovering by the seat next to me, silently pressurizing me to move my coat. I drape it over my lap, the dampness filtrating into my jeans. It's too dark to look beyond the window, all I can see are the passengers in the carriage reflected back at me, and my face, *her face*; too pale, eyes dark, haunted.

Nia is waiting for me at Waterloo station by WHSmith as arranged, nervously jigging about in her too-large navy duffle coat so that she looks about twelve years old. As I edge through the crowd, it strikes me that this is the first time I've been back to London since I was discharged from the psychiatric ward over eighteen months ago. Her face lights up when she sees me and she rushes over, pulling me into a hug.

'Oh, Abi, thank goodness,' she says. I always forget how dinky Nia is, she barely reaches my shoulders. 'Are you okay? You don't look well,' she says as she takes my arm and leads me towards the tube.

I nod, assuring her I'm still in shock, but I'm disorientated by all the people, the noise, the smells. This used to be my life, yet it feels so alien to me now.

The tube is packed even though it's gone seven and we have to stand as the train hurtles along the Northern line, veering around bends at a terrifying speed; a miasma of damp clothes and bad breath hangs in the air, even though a window is open. My face is too close to some stranger's armpit. I'm concentrating hard on not becoming panicky and claustrophobic, while Nia, sensing my discomfort, chatters on about her day in the office, a pitch that she had to do to land a new client. Eventually the train stops at East Finchley and we stumble off, but before I can even get my breath back we are whisked along the platform, up the numerous steps and around winding corridors until we reach the street. I take in lungfuls of fresh air, the rain on my tongue.

'Muswell Hill is about a fifteen-minute walk from here, so let's catch the bus,' says Nia as she takes my hand and leads me to the bus stop. My holdall is digging into my shoulder and my mouth is dry, but I summon up the energy to drag myself on to the bus and then five minutes later to drag myself off of it and down two leafy streets to Nia's flat. It's on the top floor of a Victorian red-brick house. 'It's only a one-bedroom, but I have a sofa bed in the living room,' she says as she turns the key in the front door. It reminds me of the flat I had in Bath before I moved in with Beatrice and Ben. There are even two bicycles pushed up against the wall in the communal hallway and letters and flyers littering the welcome mat. She picks them up and flicks through them before shoving them through the letter box of the downstairs flat. 'They're never in,' she tells me. I follow her up two flights of stairs to the top floor. Her flat is small and cosy, with a living room that leads directly on to an open-plan kitchen separated by a kind of breakfast bar. I dump my bag and flop exhausted on to the brown linen sofa while Nia puts the kettle on. She takes my holdall into her bedroom, telling me I can have her bed tonight. I want to cry with gratitude.

'Here,' she hands me a cup of tea and joins me on the sofa. 'You look done in.'

'Thanks, Nia,' I whisper. I can sense the beginnings of a sore throat. I take a sip and rest my head against the back of the sofa. 'So, how is it, living in North London?'

'It's okay,' she smiles as she cradles her cup. 'I miss you though. I miss our Balham days. It's lovely here, but . . .' She lets the rest of her sentence hang between us and I understand, perhaps for the first time, that her life too has drastically changed since Lucy died.

I glance around the living room, at the magnolia woodchip walls, at the drab curtains at the window, at the melamine kitchen cupboards that someone has attempted to paint red, at the fat armchair with its multicoloured patchwork throw that I bet Nia's mum knitted, and the place reminds me of a well-worn but comfortable dressing gown. A bit shabby, but cosy, warm, real. It's a far cry from Beatrice and Ben's huge, five-storeyed Georgian town house with its artwork and artefacts and pretensions.

And as the rain hammers ferociously on to the roof and rattles the rotting window frames, as I snuggle down on to the unfashionable sofa, drinking tea from a chipped mug with Nia by my side, my oldest friend, the person who I trust implicitly, I know where I would rather be.

Ben has tried to ring me eleven times and he's left two voice messages. I perch on the edge of Nia's bed with the phone pressed to my ear and listen as his familiar Scottish voice pleads with me to contact him, that he's worried about me, that he can explain everything if only I would ring him. I so want to believe him, but I'm not convinced that he won't spout more lies. How can there ever be a reasonable explanation as to why he hid my letters and Beatrice's bracelet in the boot of his car, and sat back and watched as we accused each other? What about the other stuff? The bird, the photograph, the sinister Facebook messages, the flowers . . .? And this woman – Morag. Is she his mother? And if she is, why did he tell me she was dead? I want to gag when I think of it all, the lies, the manipulation.

I lie awake most of the night listening to the wind shaking the little attic window and staring at the brown edges of a water stain on the ceiling. When I do eventually fall asleep I dream of Ben who morphs into Beatrice who morphs into Lucy. When I wake up I'm more exhausted than I was before I went to bed.

The next morning Nia stands over a frying pan, sizzling on the hob. She always was the first one up, the most organized out of all of us. Seeing her standing there, in her familiar flannel pyjamas and sheepskin slippers, I have a flashback to the past, to the house we all shared in Balham. I half expect Lucy to emerge from the bathroom with a distracted look on her face as she hurries to find her keys, her phone, her overlarge satchel, late for the doctors' practice as usual.

Nia turns to see me standing there. 'Are you okay?' she says. She places two plates of bacon and eggs on the breakfast bar with the expertise of a waitress, thanks to the three years working at Sam's Café in Cardiff to fund university. 'I know you probably haven't got much appetite, but try and eat something,' she says as she slides on to one of the leather-topped bar stools. 'You're looking too thin.'

I've missed her forthrightness. What you see is what you get with Nia, no mind games, no saying one thing when she means another. For perhaps the first time, I appreciate how easy she is to live with, and how I took that for granted.

'Aren't you supposed to be at work?'

Her cheeks turn pink and she looks shamefaced. 'I rang in sick. I didn't want to leave you on your own. You've had a shock.'

'Nia, you didn't have to. But thanks.' I sit next to her and, for her benefit, try to swallow the eggs that taste of rubber. 'Ben keeps trying to ring me,' I say as I push the food around my plate.

'What are you going to do?' Her brown eyes are full of concern.

I sigh and put down my knife and fork. I've hardly touched my food, but Nia does a great job of pretending not to notice. 'I honestly can't get my head around all of this.'

'I can imagine,' she says, taking a swig of coffee.

'Why would he do all this? Why would he hide the letters, the bracelet? Does that mean he sent the flowers too? Oh God, Nia.' My heart races. 'And who is Morag? How can she be Ben's mum?'

Nia shakes her head. 'I don't understand it either.'

'I've been such an idiot. I moved in with them when I hardly knew them, got involved in their lives, fell in love.'

'You were vulnerable and they preyed on that,' she says, her eyes narrowing in anger. 'It actually makes me fucking angry.' She slams her mug down and regards me thoughtfully. 'You know, I can't help but think that Ben must be some kind of sociopath. Maybe he gets his kicks out of scaring vulnerable women.'

Did I really get Ben so wrong? Caring, dependable,

funny, sexy. How can he be a sociopath? I can't believe that he would do this to me. The version of Ben that I have in my head is shifting, moulding into someone else entirely different, yet I can't quite believe in this new, warped Ben.

'Have I made a terrible mistake, Nia? There must be an explanation for all that stuff in his boot . . .' I push my plate away, my stomach is in knots.

'Abi,' she says with a warning tone. 'How can there be a mistake?'

'Maybe someone else put those things there to turn me against him? There are other people in the house. What about Cass? I found that weird photograph of us, I think she's in love with Beatrice.'

'If that's the case, then surely she wouldn't want to split you and Ben up?'

'Maybe she sees how upset Beatrice is because Ben is moving out to be with me, and she wants to stop it from happening, so this is her attempt to split us up?' I jump up from my stool and begin pacing the room, hope giving me a renewed energy. 'That sounds plausible, doesn't it?'

Nia shrugs as she tucks into her breakfast. 'Not especially, no,' she mumbles through a mouthful of egg. 'Firstly, your letters disappeared months ago and so did the bracelet. Why would she have taken them so long ago? She couldn't have known then that Ben was thinking about moving in with you?'

The hope seeps out of me.

'Also,' she continues relentlessly, not realizing that every word she speaks is as if I'm being stabbed in the chest, 'what's all this about his mother? He's obviously lying to you about that. He got in a car with them yesterday, remember?'

I clutch my chest. 'What if they kidnapped him?'

'Abi.' She glares at me. 'He got in the car willingly. You saw him.'

I cover my face with my hands and groan, sinking on to the sofa. 'He must be a sociopath, because you know what?' I lift my head to look at her. 'I thought he loved me. Especially at the end, he told me that we should get our own place. Move away from that house. He was willing to leave Beatrice, his own possessive twin sister, for me.'

Nia is silent as she consumes the rest of her bacon, but I can see the cogs in her brain ticking over, I know her so well. When she's finished she places her knife and fork together neatly on the plate and comes and sits next to me on the sofa, handing me my mug of coffee. I take a sip but it's lukewarm.

'I know twins have a special bond. But isn't it a bit weird that they still live together when they are well into their thirties?'

I frown and bend over to put the mug on the thread-bare carpet. 'I lived with Lucy.'

'Yes,' she says. 'But you were the same sex, you were best friends as well.'

'So are they, I suppose.'

'I think they've got a weird relationship.'

I turn to look at her. 'What do you mean?'

'I don't know. She's so possessive of him. It's almost as though . . .' She shakes her head.

'What, Nia? What are you trying to tell me?'

She shakes her head. 'Ignore me . . . I'm an only child, I don't understand what it's like to have a sibling, let alone a twin.'

'You think she's got some sort of hold over him?' I've thought it before, of course, especially since meeting up with Jodie.

Nia nods, although I'm not entirely sure that was what she was going to say.

While Nia is in the shower I can't help but check my phone. Three more missed calls from Ben, and another message begging me to call him. My fingers waver over his name, haunted by the sound of despair in his voice. One press of a button and I will be speaking to him, he will give me a simple explanation that explains everything and I can go home and we can get on with our lives. I hesitate, and before I can help myself, I press down on his name. The phone barely rings before he picks it up. He sounds breathless, panicked. 'Abi? Abi? Is that you?'

'Yes . . .' I say quietly. I close my eyes at the sound of his voice.

'Thank God, I've been so worried. So has Beatrice. She said she thought you were having some kind of breakdown. Where are you?'

Some kind of breakdown. Suddenly I know what he's

going to say, what excuse he will use. *It's so easy to explain everything away by blaming me, huh, Ben? Everything is always my fault, my imagination, my crazy, fucked-up, paranoid mind. Not this time, Ben. You can't use that excuse on me ever again.*

'Abi? Abi? Are you still there?'

I put the phone down.

Chapter Thirty

I spend two days holed up in Nia's flat. Ben doesn't give up trying to call me, even though I never answer. At first his voicemail messages are cajoling, pleading, begging, eventually becoming urgent, angry, asking why I refuse to speak to him, why I've left him, how can I do this to him?

How could you do this to me, Ben?

At first I'm afraid that he will ring my parents to hassle them, cause them even more worry, so I call them to explain where I am, but it's not until I replace the receiver that I remember that Ben has never met my parents, he doesn't even know where they live. He hardly knows anything about me, and it turns out I know even less about him. We lived in a cocoon – me and him in that trust-funded Georgian house with his twin sister and her weird friends. We weren't living in the real world at all.

On Friday lunchtime the intercom to the flat buzzes.

I'm folding up the sofa bed and I wonder idly if Nia has come home for lunch and forgotten her keys. I move to the window and push aside the dingy curtain to make sure. The buzzer sounds again, more urgent this time. From the little window up in the eaves I can just make out the corner of somebody's muscular shoulder on the pathway below, sandy hair that brushes the collar of a tanned leather jacket, and I know it's definitely not Nia.

My mouth goes dry. Is it Ben? Has he managed to find Nia's address and track me down? Then I remember that Ben hasn't got a leather jacket. I hover, unsure of what to do. When the buzzer is pressed again I go to the hallway and push the button to answer. 'Hello,' I say with trepidation.

'Abi?' says a voice I recognize. A voice from the past.

'Yes . . .'

'It's Luke.' The magnolia woodchip walls creep in on me. How does he know I'm here?

'What . . . what do you want?' I can't believe I'm speaking to him, that he's outside Nia's flat. I haven't seen him since the court case; the blame flashing in his stormy blue eyes has haunted me ever since.

'Please, we need to talk.' This could be a trick, I think as my hand hovers over the intercom. If I let him in, we would be alone in this little flat, me and him with his grief and his accusations.

Luke would never hurt you.

I hear Lucy's voice, so soft, so clear, ringing out in the cramped hallway. But it could also be my own.

I let him up and open the door and wait, hearing the tread of his feet on the stairs, my heart racing. I see him before he sees me; the familiar floppy dirty blond hair, the worn leather jacket, but gone is his once happy-go-lucky demeanour, now he stoops as though he has the weight of her death on his shoulders. Do I look that way too? Now he is standing before me and his face pales. He's seeing a ghost.

'Lucy.' It's barely a whisper, carried on the end of a sigh. Tears sting my eyes and I blink them away.

'Hi, Luke.'

'I'm sorry,' he says, and rushes over to me, pulling me into an embrace. I'm so shocked I can't move for a couple of seconds, it's not the reaction I was expecting. Then I rest my head on his shoulder and close my eyes, taking in the familiar smell of his leather jacket, the comfort of his strong arms around me. He's as tall as Callum. As Ben. When he pulls away, he has a shy smile on his lips and his eyes are red. He clears his throat self-consciously. 'Can I come in?'

I lead him into the kitchen and switch the kettle on. The colour is starting to come back into his cheeks but he stands and stares at me as if he can't quite believe I'm here, although I know he's not seeing me. He's seeing Lucy.

'It's a shock, I know,' I say as I reach up to the cupboards for two chipped mugs. 'I experience it every time I look in the mirror.'

'You're the spitting image of her.'

'We were identical twins, Luke.' I laugh and it breaks the tension between us.

'I still miss her so much.' His voice wobbles and for one moment I'm concerned he's going to break down, but he visibly composes himself and slides on to one of the stools at the breakfast bar.

'Me too.' I hand him a coffee, black with no sugar.

'You still remember how I have my coffee,' he says as he takes the mug from me, and I notice that his hands are trembling.

'Of course, I spent years making it for you.' Something about the way he sits there, with his rangy figure encased in that familiar jacket, the way his fair hair flops over his forehead, reminds me of someone. And it hits me. He reminds me of Ben. Why didn't I ever think it before? Luke doesn't have the freckles, his skin has more of a golden hue, but the shape of the chin and the high cheekbones are similar. Have I been subconsciously attracted to a man like Ben because I know Lucy would have been? 'How did you know I was here?'

'Nia.' He glances at me. 'Don't be cross with her, I've been badgering her for ages. Since you met up with Callum. He rang me after he saw you. He said you think I hate you.' He looks sad as he reaches across the breakfast bar to take my hand. 'I couldn't let you think that,' he says softly.

'I deserve it. Those things I said to Lucy. The way I treated her. It was my fault.' A tear trickles down my nose and plops on to the breakfast bar. I'm embarrassed, crying in front of Luke after all this time. I scrunch up my eyes, trying to block out the memory of the shock and disappointment that I witnessed on my sister's face as I screamed at her that night, accusing her of fancying my boyfriend. And when I stormed off she ran after me, desperately trying to get me to hear her side of the story, promising that she would never do anything to hurt me, ever. Yet I didn't want to listen, I never gave her a chance to explain. And now it's too late. I will never get to hear her voice again. 'I would do anything to have five minutes with her. To tell her how sorry I am. She died thinking that I hated her,' I say, tears seeping from my closed eyelids. 'And it breaks my heart.'

'Abi,' he says softly and he squeezes my hand gently, reassuringly. 'She knew you didn't hate her, you have to believe that. It was obvious to anyone how much the two of you loved each other. She thought the world of you, Abi. And she knew you felt the same.'

I open my eyes and drag my sleeve across my wet face. He pulls a tissue from his pocket and hands it to me. 'It's clean, I promise.' I laugh through my tears.

'I'm so sorry, Abi,' he says, suddenly serious again. 'I feel terrible that I blamed you for the accident. I was angry and I was devastated at losing her. I wanted to lash out at someone and you were the easy target. But I should've been there for you.' His voice catches. 'Lucy would have been so disappointed in me.'

I shake my head. 'No . . . Luke, she wouldn't, it's me she would have been disappointed in. I killed her.'

'Stop it, I don't want you to say that.' He grips my hand more firmly to emphasize his point. 'I said some awful things . . . I'm so sorry. I was just so . . .'

'I know,' I sniff.

'But it wasn't your fault. It was an accident, I know that now. Deep down I always have.'

I smile. His words have made me feel lighter inside. I've missed him. He was with Lucy for years, he was like a brother to me. 'I couldn't bear the thought of you hating me,' I say eventually.

'I could never hate you,' he takes his hand from mine. 'I've been selfish, I should have been there for you. Lucy would have wanted me to look after you.'

'She would have wanted me to look after you too,' I say through the lump in my throat. 'She loved you so much.' How could I have ever been jealous? How could I have thought that night that she wanted to kiss Callum when she loved Luke as much as she did?

'Seeing you . . . your face. It's as though I'm seeing Lucy again. I was worried it would hurt too much. ' He flashes me a wobbly smile. 'But now I know it's a gift. Through you I get to see her. Is that weird?'

I shake my head tearfully. 'No, it's not weird, Luke.' I understand exactly what he's trying to say. I remember the words Mum said to me in the hospital after my failed suicide attempt, when I asked her how she could bear to carry on living without her other daughter. And through her tears she said, 'Because Lucy lives on through you, Abi. When I look at you, I also see her. When I hear

301

your voice, I also hear hers. So she can never be truly gone, don't you see? If you die, my sweetheart, then there is nothing left of her in this world.'

'Can we sit on the sofa? My arse is killing me on this stool,' he says and I laugh in agreement, relieved that we've cleared the air after all this time.

Lucy would be proud of us.

We jump down from the stools. 'Come here, you,' says Luke, his voice thick with emotion and he wraps me in a big brotherly hug. 'Promise me we won't lose touch again?' He kisses the top of my head and I imagine, I hope, that wherever Lucy is, she knows how much we love her. Will always love her.

'I promise,' I say as we pull apart.

We take our coffees and sit on Nia's squidgy sofa with the faded arms and catch up on the last two years. Luke tells me he's been promoted at the media company where he's worked for a year.

'I've thrown myself into my job since she died,' he says. 'It kept me sane.' He carried on sharing the flat with Callum for a while, but now he lives on his own in Islington. 'Callum's been very worried about you. He says you're living in Bath now, near your parents.'

'Yes . . .' I hesitate. How much should I tell him? I'm finding it hard to admit that my life has taken another wrong turn. That nothing has gone right since Lucy died. Then I remember something that Beatrice told me when I first moved in, about being at Exeter University.

'Actually, I live with a girl who used to go to your

university. I don't know if you were both there together, but you're about the same age.'

His eyes light up. He hasn't changed that much, he still likes any excuse to relive his student days.

'What's her name?'

'Beatrice Price. She's got a twin brother. Ben. Although I think he went to a university in Edinburgh. Do you know her?'

He shakes his head and frowns. 'The name doesn't ring a bell. But it was a long time ago. What year was she there?'

'About 2000 or 2001 I think.'

'What course?'

I try to remember. 'Not sure, to be honest. She's a jewellery designer now. Oh, wait. I have a photo, she's very attractive, maybe it will jog your memory.' He smiles sadly and I inwardly berate myself for having said something so insensitive. 'Let me go and get my phone.' My mobile is charging in Nia's bedroom. As I unplug it my heart sinks when I see another missed call from Ben.

'Here,' I say when I return to the sofa. I sit next to Luke, holding the phone up so we both have a view of the screen. 'We took some selfies on the day I moved in with her.' I find the photo straight away, it's one of the last ones I took. Beatrice is pouting and I'm sticking my tongue out, our arms thrown around each other's shoulders. We look as though we are great friends, I think. Like sisters. It's a shame how it all turned out.

'Oh my God,' he says, taking the phone from me to

get a better look. I think he's going to make some joke about how silly I look, but he doesn't. Instead he says, 'I went out with her at university.'

I freeze. 'What? But you don't remember her name?' He scrolls through a few more photographs that I took that day, of Beatrice and me in various daft poses outside her house.

'She's not called Beatrice, that's why. Well, she wasn't when I knew her. She was called Daisy. Daisy McDow.'

The room swims. I recall Jodie telling me about Ben calling Beatrice by the name Daisy. Luke hands the phone back to me and I continue to stare at her photograph, at her beautiful heart-shaped face, at her almond-shaped eyes the colour of Acacia honey. *Who are you?*

'She never mentioned having a brother, let alone a twin,' he continues, his eyebrows pinched together, remembering. 'And I went out with her for a few months. It was quite serious for a while.'

I can't believe she wouldn't have mentioned her brother, her twin. They're so close. 'Are you sure she didn't tell you about Ben?'

He nods. 'Definitely, I would have remembered if she'd had a twin brother. I met her mum once as well and no mention of a twin.'

Blood pounds in my ears. 'You met her mum? But she died when Beatrice was a baby.'

He frowns. 'No, she didn't.' He shifts his weight from one leg to the other and his leather jacket creaks.

'Can you describe the woman?'

304

He pulls a face. 'Blimey, Abi, I can hardly remember. It was nearly fourteen years ago.'

'Please, this is important.' I lean closer to him. 'Was she short? A bit frumpy?'

'No, she definitely wasn't short. She was very tall and slim and quite glamorous. Posh, I would say.'

'Posh?'

'She had money, I could tell by the way she carried herself, the way she spoke, the clothes she wore. Put it this way, she didn't look the way most of the other mums did, that's for sure.'

My mind is racing. What does all this mean?

'You know,' he continues. 'I was crazy about her for a while. But she was a bit odd.'

'In what way?'

He shrugs. 'Quite intense, I suppose.'

I ask him if he's sure it's the same girl, urge him to look at the photos again, but he nods, telling me that he's not mistaken, it is definitely her, definitely Daisy McDow. 'She's not someone I'd forget in a hurry,' he says, his expression darkening.

'What happened between you?'

He fidgets and I can tell talking about his past, before Lucy, is making him uncomfortable. He swallows. 'I finished with her. It was getting too serious. I was only nineteen. I didn't want that sort of relationship.'

I remember the evening in Beatrice's drawing room when she confided in me about a boyfriend at university breaking her heart, causing her to leave and go travelling,

305

how devastated she felt on her return to learn he had met someone else. Was that someone else Lucy?

'Did she leave university after you broke up with her?' I say, although I dread his answer.

He frowns, remembering. 'She must have, because I never saw her again.'

'Oh, Luke, she told me about you, said she was devastated after you finished it. I don't think she's ever gotten over you.'

He turns to look at me, guilt etched all over his handsome face. 'She seemed pretty upset when it ended but . . .' He frowns. 'We were only together a few months.'

'And then you met Lucy?'

'Not until a couple of years later, but yes, then I fell in love with Lucy.'

I look at the photograph of me with Bea. Our fair heads close together, the same shape faces, the same wide mouths. Bea closely resembles Lucy, I've always thought so. But I've never thought too deeply about how much we look alike, which is ridiculous, considering Lucy and I were identical twins.

'Don't you think Beatrice – Daisy – looks like Lucy?' I say, my eyes still on the photograph.

He shrugs. 'I suppose I've got a type. Some men do. What has this got to do with anything, Abi?' asks Luke.

I remember Beatrice's pained expression that night on her sofa when she recounted her lost love. 'I'm not sure,' I say. 'But she's been lying to me for months. They both have. I just don't understand why.'

I'm busy stuffing the rest of my clothes in my holdall when Nia gets back. She wafts into the bedroom, bringing with her the scent of rain.

'Oh, you're angry with me,' she says, her face crumpling as she notices my packed bag on her bed. 'I thought it would be good for you to see Luke again.'

'It's not that, Nia,' I say as I roll up my jumper and cram it into the bag, pulling the cord tight. 'It was great to see Luke. But I need to go home and face Ben.' In a gabbled rush I tell her everything Luke told me about Beatrice. 'I want to find out why they've both been lying to me. And then I'm going to move out of there.'

'Luke went out with Beatrice at uni? What a small world.'

'Why has she changed her name, Nia? Why did she never mention to Luke about having a twin brother? Why are they lying about their parents?'

'I don't know, but what I do know,' she says, barely able to contain her excitement as she rummages around in her bag, 'is this—'

She pulls out a yellow Post-it note with the enthusiasm of a little girl showing her mum what she made at school. She thrusts it at me. I take the Post-it note and on it, scribbled in Nia's familiar scrawl, is an address in Streatham, South London.

'What is it?'

'It's the address for a Morag Jones.'

My head pounds and I slump on to the bed, my

shoulders sagging. 'How do you know it's the right address? Ben's surname is Price.'

'I've done some digging, called in a few favours. It's the only Morag registered in London with a Ben living at the same address. You did say she lived in Streatham, right?'

'Yes, but it could be a coincidence.'

'Well, come on then. Let's go over there and see. What have we got to lose?'

'But . . .' I sigh. 'Morag was in Bath two days ago. She's probably not even in London now.'

'I know that,' she says patiently, as if talking to one of her minions at work. 'But somebody might be there. And they might tell us everything we need to know.'

'I don't know . . . I . . .'

'Come on, Abi. You're a journalist, for crying out loud! You search for the truth for a living.' She grabs my hand and pulls me from the bed. She's surprisingly strong for someone so tiny. 'It's not even five yet. We can probably be there before it gets dark.'

And despite my reservations I can't help a frisson of excitement as I shoulder on my parka and follow Nia out on to the windy street, because, at last, I might finally get some answers.

Chapter Thirty-One

Beatrice stands at the window and watches as Ben ferrets around in the boot of his car. *What are you doing, Ben?* She could never understand why such a tall man wants to own such a small car. Maybe he likes the idea of overpowering it. Maybe it makes him feel masculine, sitting in the driver's seat so that his head is nearly touching the ceiling, the seat pushed as far back as it will go in order to give his long legs enough room to reach the pedals. She flinches as he slams the door shut and kicks the bumper with the toe of his Chelsea boot. Then he bangs the wrought-iron gate behind him as he stomps into the house, slamming the front door with such force she's half expecting to hear the shattering of broken glass.

Ben's behaviour is beginning to worry Beatrice. He hasn't gone to work in the two days since Abi left, he's barely speaking to her and she gets the impression that somehow he blames her for Abi's abrupt departure. Her heart sinks as she hears his feet clomping up the stairs, and she braces herself as he throws open her bedroom door so that the back of it crashes into the wall behind, making her wince.

'Beatrice,' he barks and she reluctantly moves away from the window. His sandy hair is greasy, his polo shirt is creased and he looks as if he hasn't washed or showered in days. She hates what he's doing to himself, what he's going through. If only she could make everything better.

He strides over to her. 'You have to tell me again. What exactly did Abi say to you when she left?'

She sighs. 'Ben, we've been through this. I've told you everything I can remember.' He groans and covers his face with his hands. She goes to him, wraps her arms around his back, his top is damp with sweat. 'Please don't do this to yourself.'

'I can't bear it,' he says through his fingers. His body is trembling. *Oh, Ben.*

'She said you lied to her, I've told you this. But she didn't say what you've lied about. Does she know, Ben? Does she know our secret?'

He pulls away from her and begins pacing the room. 'Morag turned up here.'

'What?' Beatrice stares at him in horror. 'You didn't say.'

'I didn't want to worry you.' He stops and turns to

her. 'Do you think that's what Abi meant, about me lying?'

She frowns, trying to remember. 'She did say something about my mum but I thought she was being . . . well, a bit weird. Is that what she meant? She thinks Morag is my mum?'

'Of course,' he snaps. 'She thinks she's *my* mum.'

'She is your mum, Ben.' He glares at her so that she shrinks, *shrivels up*, under his scrutiny.

His next words are spoken slowly, coldly. 'You know that's not true.'

Guilt worms its way into Beatrice's heart. When Abi left she looked so freaked out with her wide eyes and her pale face. She always had been on the wrong side of skinny but with her baggy jumper and her oversized parka she had looked positively waiflike and Beatrice had jumped to the conclusion that Abi had finally lost her marbles; it was the most logical explanation, knowing her past history. But she had been talking sense after all. 'You know,' she says. 'She's been acting so oddly, Ben. Stealing my bracelet and that earring. Not taking her medication. I know she thinks I sent her those flowers on her birthday, but I didn't.' She pauses, watching Ben carefully. 'You have to believe me when I say that.'

Ben is staring at her, but by his glazed expression she can see that he's looking right through her and that he hasn't heard a word she's said. She wants to shake him.

'How can she fucking leave?' he mutters, almost to

311

himself. 'Why won't she answer my phone calls? I need to speak to her now. Nobody walks out on me.'

Beatrice bites her lip, refraining from telling him that, of course, it was always going to end this way. They've kept too much from Abi. Their past was always going to come knocking on their door. 'She knows you're lying to her about something, Ben. She said she's been scared for months, that you want her to think that she's going mad – what did she mean by that?'

'I don't know.'

'Can't you tell her the truth? She knows about Morag now.'

'Tell her the truth?' He's finally listening, she thinks as his head snaps up, but his expression is contorted, his face unusually ugly. 'Tell her what exactly?' he snarls. 'About what happened at university? Oh yes, I'm sure she'll come running to me with open arms then.' His fists are clenched at his sides, his knuckles white. 'I can't lose her,' he mutters. 'I can't, Beatrice. I've never loved anyone as much as I love her.'

'Not even me?' She hates herself for voicing her fears. Why has he always made her feel so weak?

His eyes are cold, his jaw set tightly as though he's making an enormous effort to keep a lid on his anger. And his next words are like a knife to her ribs as he says with a quiet menace, 'Sometimes I wish I'd never met you.'

Chapter Thirty-Two

The address on Nia's Post-it note leads us to a narrow tree-lined street in Streatham Hill where all the houses look the same; red-brick, three-storey Victorian terraces with large bay windows. The sky has turned an inky blue and lights in living rooms are being switched on all along the street, emitting a warm amber glow from the windows as we pass, making me wish I was settled in front of a television somewhere with a cup of tea instead of pounding the streets in the cold, being blown about by the wind.

We stop outside number fifty-three. The house isn't as smart as its neighbours with their box hedges and diamond-shaped black-and-white tiled pathways. The red door needs a paint, the windowpanes are rotting, an old, stained mattress is propped up in the garden behind a couple of overflowing dustbins, and a bike missing its rear wheel has been left to rust in the overgrown grass.

Claire Douglas

'Do you think this is the right address?' I say, frowning over Nia's shoulder to view the Post-it note she's still clutching. A sudden gust of wind buffets against us, propelling us into the small front garden and causing one of the bins to topple over so that it spews its debris into our path. The Post-it note flutters out of Nia's hand and we both watch in dismay as it joins a swarm of leaves that have been tossed into the air, the yellow paper conspicuous against the burnt orange as they swirl around each other and dance down the street.

'I bloody hope so now,' says Nia, staring after the note helplessly. She links her arm through mine and we step gingerly over the empty baked-bin tins and soggy newspaper that is strewn across the path. Nia raps loudly at the front door with her knuckles. My mouth is dry as we listen out for telltale signs that someone is home and I bite back my disappointment when we don't hear any.

'It might not be the right Morag,' I say. 'And even if it is, she could still be in Bath.'

Nia unlinks her arm from mine and moves towards the door, cupping her hands around her face to peer in through the rectangular pane of glass. 'I think I can hear someone, there's a light on, I can smell something cooking,' she says, her hands muffling her words. 'I can see . . . oh!' she stumbles forward as the door is wrenched open, causing her to trip over the threshold. A short plump woman is standing staring at us in bewilderment and my heart beats faster as I realize it's her.

'What's going on?' She looks down at Nia sprawled

314

on the floor. 'What are you playing at? And what have you done to my bins? I don't want any trouble.'

Nia stands up blushing and apologizing. I move forward so that the light from the hallway illuminates me. When she recognizes me, all the colour drains from her face.

'What . . . what are you doing here?' And I know that Ben has warned her, that any information I was hoping to retrieve from her isn't going to be forthcoming and I berate myself for allowing my shock to prevent me questioning her more thoroughly the other day.

'Mrs Jones. Morag,' I begin, but she puts her hands up and backs away from me as if I'm about to mug her.

'Please, I don't know how you found me, but I can't talk to you.' She goes to shut the door on us but I wedge my foot in the small crack, to prevent her from closing it.

'Has Ben told you not to?'

'I shouldn't have turned up the other day. I'm sorry. It's none of my business.' I'm shocked by the desperation on her face. The fear. 'Please move your foot. You need to go away.'

'But I'm his girlfriend, I'm Abi.' Tears sting my eyes. 'I just want to understand what's going on.'

'It's not my business,' she repeats, and reluctantly I move my foot so that she can slam the door on us. It bangs with resounding finality.

We both stare at the door in dismay. Eventually Nia says into the darkness, 'I think you need to go home and demand that Beatrice and Ben tell you everything. And then move out of there. Do you want me to come with you?'

I shake my head. 'The thing is, Ben's too clever. He will turn it around on me, make out it's my fault, that I'm being paranoid.' We are so close to finding out the truth and now I might never know what they've been hiding from me. Who have I been living with for the past four months? But Nia is right about one thing: I need to end it with Ben. Our relationship is over.

The thought of leaving Ben makes my heart ache. I still love him, or maybe it's the idea of him. After all, how can I love a man who deliberately manipulated me for months? I was in love with the carefree, privileged life that both he and Beatrice represented. I wanted to fall into their world, like Alice in Wonderland, in a bid to escape my own. But they've lied to me from the moment I walked into their lives.

'Let's go,' Nia says, tucking her arm in mine again. We are about to turn and walk away when the front door creaks open, flooding the pathway with light once more. I expect to see Morag standing in the doorway, so am surprised when a man in his early twenties leans against the doorframe, backlit by the glow from the hallway. He has closely cropped hair and a silvery scar in his right eyebrow. He's wearing a charcoal hoodie and jeans slung so low on his hips I'm amazed they don't fall down.

'Abi?' he calls.

'Who wants to know?' says Nia.

He's wearing grubby white socks as he steps over the threshold, pulling the door shut behind him. There is a faint drizzle in the air and he tugs his hood over his head.

'I'm Abi,' I say from behind Nia. Has he come to see us off the premises?

'I'm Paul, Ben's brother. Well, adopted brother.' He holds out a hand for us to shake. His nails are bitten down to the quick, but we take his proffered hand, not wanting to offend him. 'I shouldn't be talking to you, Mum will kill me. Let's walk to the end of the street, I don't want her to see us.'

In silence we follow him further down the street. He stops in front of a house covered with scaffolding. It looks empty. He perches on the low brick wall, digging his hands deep into his pockets and retrieving a feeble roll-up. He sticks it between his lips and lights it. We watch him, wondering what he's going to say.

'What's going on? Are Ben and Beatrice adopted? Did they grow up here?' I fire questions at him without waiting for him to answer.

He assesses me through narrowed eyes and takes a deep drag of his cigarette. 'Well, I'll say this much,' he chuckles, his gaze lingering on my hair. 'Ben definitely has a type.' He exhales slowly. 'You really have no idea, do you? But then I don't suppose that bastard would have told you anything.' The venom in his voice shocks me. 'Yes,' he says before I can open my mouth. 'They're adopted. But Ben didn't grow up here. We grew up in

317

Glasgow. We moved here about ten years ago.' He has a strange accent. Scottish mixed with a bit of Mockney.

'So the twins are adopted?' I clarify, in order to be sure. 'And Morag is their adopted mother?' Now it makes sense, but why did Ben have to hide it from me? Are they embarrassed about their upbringing? And how can they afford their beautiful house if it wasn't some trust fund from their rich grandparents, as I've been led to believe? Where else would they have got all that cash?

Paul shakes his head. 'Morag is Ben's adoptive mother.'

'But not Beatrice's,' says Nia quietly by my elbow. I swivel on my heels to gawp at her, thinking she must have got it wrong.

'I don't understand,' I say, glaring first at her and then at Paul. 'Are you saying they didn't grow up together?'

His grin is sinister in the growing darkness and, shrouded by shadows and with his hood pulled over his head, he looks as if he's some type of Grim Reaper. 'No, they didn't grow up together. They didn't even know the other existed until they were nineteen. They were separated as babies, each going to a different family. Beatrice ended up with some toffs in Edinburgh apparently.'

I frown at him. 'They didn't grow up together?' I repeat, gripping on to the wall for support. The bricks are cold and rough under my fingertips. My mind is swimming with fragmented memories, snippets of the different things that they, and Eva, have told me since I moved in. Now that I think about it, I can't remember them ever saying they grew up together. I assumed that they had. Why would I have ever thought otherwise?

Beside me I hear Nia exhale. 'There's more to this, isn't there?' she says. Why do I get the sense that she knows something that I don't?

'Oh yes.' He takes another drag, slowly blowing the smoke out through his nostrils, and I think how he looks nothing like Ben, but then he wouldn't, I suppose, considering they have no shared genes.

'Why are you telling us this when your mum refuses to?' says Nia, eyeing him with disdain.

'Because Ben's a nasty little prick,' he says, flicking the remainder of his cigarette over the wall. 'We haven't seen him in years, then when he finds out Dad's on his last legs he's here, playing the dutiful eldest son, hoping to get a piece of the pie—'

'You mean money?' I interject, glancing down the street to their eyesore of a house.

Paul follows my gaze. 'The house might look a state now, but my dad had money all right. He was a tight-fisted git, he never gave us anything. Said we'd get it all when he died. Ben was worried he'd get written out of the will, so he turns up here to nurse him. Then Dad forgets everything that wanker has put this family through and leaves him some of his hard-earned cash.'

'How much?' I say, thinking of their trust fund. It makes no sense if his dad only died a few weeks ago. And surely it wouldn't be enough to fund the kind of lifestyle that Beatrice and Ben seem to be enjoying.

'Oh, about twenty grand each.' He grins, taking another drag. 'Where there's money, there's Ben. He can't resist, even though his toffee-nosed twin sister is sitting on a small fortune.'

'You sound as though you hate him,' I say, amazed. 'He's your brother.'

'Adopted brother. He's a cruel bastard, Abi. Can't you see it?'

I think of Ben, of his warm hazel eyes, his strong arms that held me, protected me. I think of the times he stuck up for Beatrice, his twin, even when I was adamant she was in the wrong, I think of the times when he caressed me, loved me. 'No,' I answer shortly. 'I don't believe you.'

He shakes his head and gives a short, bitter laugh. 'He can be very charming. He's never had any problem getting the pretty girls to fall for him. But I know him.' He glares at me. 'I know him, Abi. He's cold, he's calculating and he's cruel. And he will stop at nothing to make sure he gets what he wants. It's usually money, but sometimes it's a woman too.'

I think of the way he manipulated both me and Beatrice, and my heart sinks as I begin to suspect that Paul could be telling the truth.

Nia grips my hand and I know it's to prevent me from interrupting. 'Tell us about him,' she says gently.

'Mum and Dad didn't think they could have kids,' he says in a low voice. 'So they adopted Ben as a baby. About two years later out popped Martin and a couple of years after that I came along. Totally unexpected. We're her real kids, but Ben was always the favourite. I think he felt threatened by us, because he knew he was adopted – Mum never hid it from him. He particularly hated me; being the youngest, I suppose. He was eight when I was born. Even as a toddler I remember him kicking me under the table, or pinching me when nobody was watching. He would play mind games too: hide my toys, make out that I had lost them so I would get into trouble. One time I found some of my cars hidden in his wardrobe; he had peeled all the stickers off of them.'

'That was just sibling stuff, surely?' I say scornfully.

Paul ignores me. 'One time, when I was six years old and walking home from school, I got set upon by a load of teenagers. I looked up to see Ben a little way in the distance. I thought he would come and help me, but he stood there and watched as they kicked the shit out of me. He had a calm, detached look on his face the whole time. I was six years old, for fuck's sake. Another time I got home from school and my pet goldfish had been flushed down the loo. He told Mum he'd watched me do it, and she believed him. I'd never hurt a pet. When Martin was seventeen he was totally in love with this girl from college, she was beautiful, sweet, kind. Ben stole her away, because he could. The poor girl didn't stand a chance. Ben was always the good-looking one. He dumped her a fortnight later. He didn't give a shit about her, all he wanted was to get one over on Martin. Ben's never loved anything in his whole life. There are so many things that fucker did to me, and to Martin. Nasty, manipulative stuff.'

'And what did your parents do about it?' I ask, sick to my stomach.

'Oh, he always managed to talk his way out of it.'

But not this, I think angrily. He will never be able to talk his way out of what he's done to me.

'I was so relieved when he left home,' Paul continues. 'Couldn't wait to see the back of him.'

A chill descends down my spine and I pull my coat tighter around me. The wind has picked up and it's nearly dark. I look into the sky, expecting to see stars, but I remember we're in London, the night sky is hardly ever clear, unlike Bath. Before I found that stuff in Ben's car I would never have believed that he could be nasty and manipulative. But now I see that I fell in love with a monster. 'So where does Beatrice fit into all this?'

'That's where it gets interesting,' says Paul. 'He meets Beatrice, his twin sister, for the first time at university. They were drawn to each other – that's what I heard him telling Mum, anyway, as though that excuses everything. They only went and started a relationship, not knowing they were related.'

Bile washes up my throat and I think I'm going to be sick. 'A relationship?'

'That's right. They were lovers before they found out they were twins. Can you believe it? My brother shagged his own twin sister. When they found out they were related, they freaked out. Didn't see each other again for years. Then she inherits all this money from her adopted father and Ben manages to worm his way back into her life. I remember seeing him reading the obituary in the newspaper, so he knew she had come into money. Within weeks he had made contact with her again. Three months later, he moved to Bath to live with her.'

I feel a rush of vertigo. Paul's pale face, with his gleeful yellow-toothed smile, swims in front of me, and I can't help it. I vomit into the neighbour's box hedge.

Nia rubs my back and holds my hair away from my face. 'You had no idea?' Paul says when I've recovered. My whole body is trembling. The smile has slipped off his face now and he looks concerned for me. 'I'm sorry, but you deserve to know the truth.'

I stand up, staring at him through my blurred vision.

'He was desperate that you weren't to find out,' he says, his voice more serious now. He jumps off the wall and stands before us. He's as tall as Ben, but thinner. I imagine him as a cute six-year-old kid being beaten up by thugs while his older brother did nothing to protect him and I fight the urge to vomit all over again. How could I have not seen Ben for the person he really is? Why was I so gullible? So desperate?

'Abi,' he says intently. 'Ben went for my mum, the other day. She's terrified of him now.'

Nia's voice is sharp. 'What do you mean?'

I grab hold of Nia for support, my legs still weak. I don't know if I have the strength to listen to any more horrible revelations about the man I thought I loved, thought I knew.

'She went to stay with Martin in Bristol last week. The soft mare thought that Ben might actually be mourning for Dad. When she couldn't get hold of him, she was worried. So she went to Beatrice's house to look for him. He wasn't there, so she went back a couple of days later with Martin . . .'

That must have been the day I saw him go off in the Mondeo, I think. I can still taste acid in my mouth and I hope I'm not going to be sick again.

'He was furious with her for coming to the house twice,' Paul continues relentlessly. 'Martin said when they got to his flat, Ben went mental. Ranted at both of them, before flying at Mum, pushing her to the floor. He actually raised his fist, was going to hit her, Martin was sure of it. Martin wrestled him out of the house and we haven't seen Ben since. I came out here to warn you, Abi.' His voice takes on an urgent tone. 'He's not only a manipulative liar, but when he's backed into a corner, he can be dangerous.'

Chapter Thirty-Three

He's like a caged animal, brimming with barely concealed menace, unable to settle as he prowls around the house. Beatrice has never seen this side of him in all the years that she's known him, both then and now, and it scares her. She's unable to find the right thing to say, or do, to make everything better, and she knows she's lost her power over him, she's not the one he loves the most any more. Her twin intuition has failed her; maybe it was never there in the first place. Maybe it only works when you've grown up with your twin. She envies Abi. She may have lost Lucy, but they shared a childhood, they were proper twins, and that's something she never got to experience with Ben.

It's nearly ten o'clock and she is alone in the house with him. Pam and Cass are staying over in Frome with Trudy. They invited her along, but she declined because she was worried about leaving him. Since their argument and the cruel way he spoke to her, she wishes she had gone out with them after all. She knows that Ben will always have the capacity to hurt her because she loves him – has always loved him, more than he has ever loved her.

She can hear him in his bedroom, slamming about the place; a toddler having a tantrum because his playmate has had to go home. She considers going to him but doesn't know if she can bear to hear any more of his insults, to witness his complete lack of consideration for her. Abi, Abi, Abi. How did she become so easily replaced? She should have noticed, should have realized that Abi is her brother's obsession, just as he is hers.

Through the walls she hears his mobile trill, followed by his deep muffled voice speaking urgently to someone and she can't help herself, she throws open her door and rushes into his bedroom. Her first thought is how cold and dark the room is, before she notices that the doors to his balcony are propped open by the stone Egyptian cat he's so fond of, his curtains billowing in the wind.

'It's freezing in here,' she says. He's sitting on his bed in the darkness with his head bent, staring at the phone in his hands, and he looks so vulnerable, so sad, that she's compelled to go to him regardless of how nasty he's been.

'That was Abi. She's on her way home.'

An unexpected surge of relief takes hold of her. 'That's great news, isn't it?'

He tosses the mobile on to the carpet. 'She's only coming back to get her stuff, and because I told her I was away with work.'

Her stomach drops. 'Why did you lie to her?'

'So that she would come back. If I can talk to her, explain, I can make her see . . .' His voice trails off and he stares at the phone in his hands. When he looks up at her again she takes a step back from the bleakness in his eyes. 'She knows.'

Beatrice gulps. 'Knows what?'

'Everything,' he says, in a monotone that is beginning to alarm her.

It is as though Beatrice's windpipe is narrowing. She tries to keep the panic from her voice. 'How can she know everything, Ben? It's impossible.'

'I've tried to stop her finding out,' he continues, still in the same eerily calm voice. 'It was my worst fear. You were the only thing I couldn't control, Bea. I was scared you were going to tell her.' He turns again to the window, as if searching for answers in the stormy night.

'Me?' she laughs nervously. 'Why would I tell her?'

He turns to look at her again, kneeling on the floor in front of him now, but she can't read his expression, his face is concealed by shadows. The only light in the room comes from the full moon outside. 'You never had anything to lose, did you? Except me.'

'I didn't tell her, I promise.'

He carries on as if she hasn't spoken. 'I know you're in love with me and I think it's fucking disgusting. I hate what we did, I hate having to look at you, to be reminded. And then I meet her, so beautiful, so precious, so vulnerable, and there you are with your jealousy and put-downs, always reminding me that I have to play along if I want to live in your fucking house, have your fucking money, otherwise you might spill the beans.' His voice is gradually rising, spit forms in the corners of his mouth.

She can't help herself. She laughs bitterly. 'You're joking, surely? Ben, don't you see? You've chosen a woman who looks exactly. Like. Me.'

He frowns as if it's occurring to him now.

'And I wouldn't have spilled the beans, I wouldn't . . .' She trails off, anger spent as she contemplates their situation.

He shakes his head although he doesn't take his eyes off her. 'I couldn't take the risk. Especially when the two of you seemed so friendly. I had to keep you both apart.'

Then it hits her why Abi really left, what she was talking about the other day when she walked out. 'You did it all, didn't you? You stole my bracelet and her letters, you wanted her to believe that I had it in for her, that I was jealous of your relationship. And you wanted me to believe she was jealous of ours. Is that why you wanted to go to the Isle of Wight that day? I didn't know that's where Abi was, but you did. She saw me on the wall – did you plan that, Ben? Was it another mindfuck? Did you plant that photograph too? And send the flowers? What about that dead bird on her bed? I had my doubts

Sebby would do such a thing, but I thought I was wrong. Oh my God, Ben that's . . . that's so sick.'

He laughs. But it's a laugh devoid of humour and it scares her more than anything else has tonight.

'It wasn't hard to do. You made it even easier with your possessiveness.'

It hurts to hear the venomous way he's talking to her. Does he hate her that much? 'You're right, I am possessive – because I love you. I'm in love with you, I can't help it. I've tried to see you as my twin brother, but I can't, I can't . . .' she sobs, her whole body convulsing at finally being able to say the ugly truth. 'I want you so, so much. And I know you love me too. That's why you chose her, don't you see? Because you actually want *me* but you can't have me so you chose the next best thing, someone who looks like me, someone—'

'Shut up,' he says.

She stands up so that she's towering over him, tears and snot running down her face. 'Don't you think I feel fucking guilty too, Ben? Don't you think I worry about what will happen to me? It's against the law, what we've done. But I don't care any more. I love you and I want to be with you—'

'I said SHUT UP,' he screams, jumping up and grabbing her by the wrists, shaking her. 'Shut your fucking disgusting mouth.'

'Stop it. Ben, stop it, you're hurting me,' she pleads, a ricochet of fear making her tremble. 'Please, I want to be able to move on too. I don't want to love you this way.'

329

'You'll never let me go, will you?' He says through clenched teeth. He yanks her away from the bed towards the balcony. When he next speaks his voice is once again calm, detached – terrifying. 'I'm sorry, Beatrice, but I have to do this. I have to end this ridiculous situation and then there will be no more secrets. No more lies.' And it occurs to her, for the first time ever, that he could cause her physical harm.

She screams for him to stop as he drags her on to the Juliet balcony, pleads with him as he pushes her hard against the metal railings, and she kicks out at him, tries to strike him in the shins, but he's so tall, so strong and she's unable to stop the blow to the head that makes her cry out, causing her eyes to lose focus; she's unable to prevent his hands from clamping her throat; and as he presses his fingers around her windpipe she finds she's unable to make any sound at all.

Chapter Thirty-Four

It's raining as I step out of the taxi and pay the driver. I stand at the wrought-iron gate and watch as it creeps away into the dark night. I pull the hood of my parka over my head and look up at Beatrice's house. I've always thought of it as her house and now I know why. It never belonged to Ben. It still makes me queasy when I think of the secret they were so desperate to hide. Incest, the ultimate taboo, and I've been living alongside it, unaware, for months. Paul had assured me that it was all a long time ago, before they even knew they were related, but how can I be sure? How can any girlfriend Ben has in the future ever be sure? They had a sexual relationship before they discovered they weren't merely brother and sister but twins. Not surprising they are so messed up and that Ben went to such great lengths to ensure I never found out.

The sash windows look dark, opaque, and the shutters are open. When I rang Ben earlier he told me he was away with work and that Beatrice was in Frome with Pam and Cass, visiting friends. His voice was distant on the phone, no more pleas for me to return, no more declarations of love. He didn't even react when I told him I knew what he'd done, the secret he was trying to protect. It was as if the fight had gone out of him. As if he no longer cared about losing me.

After I put the phone down on Ben, I told Nia I was returning to the house. She urged me to wait until Monday, so she could come with me. 'I'm on weekend duty,' she explained, wringing her hands. But I assured her I'd be fine, that Ben was away so I wouldn't have to face him. My plan now is to grab the rest of my stuff and then take a taxi to Mum and Dad's.

I turn my key in the lock and let myself into the dark hallway, dumping my bag on the doormat and shouldering off my wet coat. I flick the switch, blinking as my eyes adjust to the light, nausea rising when I see Beatrice's leopard-print pumps sitting neatly beside Ben's black Chelsea boots. I never want to see either of them again. I tear my eyes away from their footwear and shiver. I'm cold to the bone. I've been sitting in my damp clothes for the two-hour journey from London and my jeans are sticking to my legs. I peel them off and wriggle out of my long-sleeved top so that I'm standing in the hall in my underwear. I bend down to rummage through my holdall for something, anything, to put on when I hear it.

A bang. Coming from above my head. Ben's room.

I stand up, my heart racing, and listen. Was I mistaken? Nothing. Then I hear a miaow and see Sebby padding down the stairs and my whole body relaxes. It's only the damn cat. I bend over my holdall again and pull out the first thing that comes to hand. Ironic, I think, as the silky material runs through my fingers. Beatrice's green Alice Temperley dress. I throw it over my head, inhaling her scent as I do so. Parma violets. And I remember how Ben had stared at me that night in the drawing room when I first wore this dress, how he urged me not to let his sister turn me into her clone. How Maria had stopped me in the street, thinking that I was Beatrice. And it hits me: Ben was attracted to me because I look like his sister.

I stare at myself in the gilt-framed mirror above the radiator.

'Oh my God,' I say to my reflection, and I'm filled with revulsion. *He fancied me, he wanted me, because I resemble her, the one woman he couldn't have.* I recall the sex: it was mind-blowing. Was it because he was thinking of her when he was with me? The room spins and I hold on to the pink radiator, wondering if I'm going to faint.

Another bang, louder this time, and my heart jumps into my throat. Someone's upstairs. I freeze and for a second I contemplate grabbing my bag and running out into the wet night. But Ben is not here, and it might be Cass or Pam, or even Beatrice. I've been living here for four months. What am I afraid of?

I hear Paul's voice, low and urgent. A warning. *When he's backed into a corner, he can be dangerous.*

Ben is *not* here, I remind myself. He told me he was away with work. I tell myself not to be so pathetic and, once I've locked and bolted the front door and thrown the keys into the china bowl, I grab my holdall and head up the stairs to my bedroom.

I'm nearly at the top step when I see him. He's standing on the landing, outside the drawing room, casting a long dark shadow over me. I freeze and drop my bag in shock. I can hear it bumping down the stairs, spilling its contents all over the stone steps and floor. 'Beatrice?' he says. His voice is almost unrecognisable. He sounds confused and even in the half-light I can see his face is deathly pale.

'It's me, Abi,' I say and he frowns, appraising me in Beatrice's dress. I make an effort to keep my voice light. 'I thought you were away. With work.' *It's only Ben*, I think. *He's still the man who said he loved me, who shared my bed. Surely he wouldn't hurt me?*

He stares at me, shaking his head, as if trying to dislodge an unpleasant thought or image from his mind.

'Abi,' he says, with a dismissive sniff. 'Of course.' He seems distracted, slightly confused.

'Do you want me to leave?' I say, hopefully, grabbing the banister, a glass petal from the fairy lights digging into the palm of my hand. I don't even notice the pain.

To my dismay he shakes his head and rubs his hand through his sandy hair. 'No, don't leave. I'm sorry, I lied to you. I wanted you to come home and I knew you wouldn't if you thought I was here.'

He's right about that.

I turn to look behind me. At the door I've locked and bolted, at my bag, which has landed at the bottom of the stairs, at my mobile phone which has fallen out of the pocket, and for a split second I consider making a run for it. I tell myself I'm being ridiculous. Paul has unnerved me, that's all. I'm sure Ben isn't as bad as he's made out. Maybe Paul's jealous of Ben, felt in his shadow, I know how that can feel, after all. But then I think of all the horrible things Ben has done to me since I moved in. How he manipulated me, scared me, played with my already-fragile mind, and I know his actions are that of a twisted man. A fresh wave of revulsion washes over me.

But I have to play the game. 'Maybe we should talk?' I say, knowing there is nothing he could say that would excuse what he's done, all the lies he's told.

For a second he looks hopeful, switching to disbelieving. 'You want to?'

'Of course,' I say. 'Why don't I meet you in the kitchen? I need to get a cardigan from my room, I'm freezing.'

He stands aside to let me pass him on the landing, his face relaxing with relief. 'I'll put the kettle on,' he says, flashing me his usual lopsided, charming smile.

Whereas once it would have made my stomach flutter with lust, now it turns me cold. Somehow I have to make him believe that everything is normal, until I figure out what I'm going to do.

335

'I'll be five minutes,' I say, trying to smile back, although it comes out more as a grimace.

My skin crawls as he brushes his lips against my cheek and I watch as he descends the stairs, as he bends over to pick up the detritus that has fallen out of my bag. He places my mobile phone on the table next to the keys and I'm shocked that he can act as though nothing has happened, as if he wasn't the one responsible for the flowers, the photograph, the nasty Facebook stuff. He's a very talented actor, I think as I watch him. It's as if he has no conscience, feels no guilt.

When he's out of sight, I dart past the drawing room and up the next flight of stairs to the bedrooms. *I'll grab the rest of my stuff and get out of here,* I think, trying to contain my rising panic. It will be fine as long as I keep calm. As long as Ben thinks everything is normal between us. I click on the landing light. I'm less jittery now that I'm no longer in the dark.

The door to Ben's bedroom is ajar, giving me a view of his balcony. I can see that he's left his French windows wide open, the white curtains flapping in the wind like two ghosts, letting in the rain, which has caused a dark stain on the carpet.

I'm about to turn away and head for my room, when I freeze. There's a foot. A bare foot and leg, just visible from behind the French doors, illuminated by the full moon. I know it's Beatrice's by the tattoo of a daisy that weaves its way around her ankle, and with a sickening thud in the pit of my stomach I'm suddenly aware that the dark stain on the carpet isn't rain, it's blood. A chill runs through me.

I run through his room and on to the balcony. Beatrice is slumped against the wrought-iron railings, her head at an odd angle, angry red welts around her neck, her tea-dress soaked through from the rain. For one terrifying moment I think that she's dead, that he's killed her. I lift her wrist, trying to detect a pulse; relief washes over me when I find one. I bend over her, shaking her, as my dress plasters itself to my body in the torrential downpour. *Wake up, Beatrice, please wake up.* But she's out cold. With horror I notice the gash on her head, the rain causing rivulets of blood to run down her face. *Oh, Ben, what have you done?* And in that instant I know that Paul was telling the truth – that Ben is frighteningly dangerous. He's capable of so much more than planting threatening photos and cryptic messages. He's capable of violence, of murder.

'Please, Beatrice,' I cry, pulling at her arms, slapping her cheeks, trying to revive her. 'Please, wake up. We have to get out of here.' The rain is pounding hard against my back as I shake her desperately. 'Please, Beatrice. Wake up. WAKE UP!' I need to get her away before Ben becomes impatient as to why I'm taking so long. *Come on, oh please, come on!*

'What's going on?'

Terror shoots through me at the sound of his voice. I look up. Ben is standing in the doorway staring down at us. His eyes are narrowed, assessing the two of us crouched on the balcony – both with nearly identical sodden dresses, both with strands of dripping blonde hair whipped across our cheeks.

'What have you done?' I whisper, incredulous, hugging Beatrice to me. There is blood on my hands, on my dress. 'She's your sister – your twin sister.'

I'm light-headed with fear as it dawns on me how trapped we are, out on this tiny balcony in a storm, with no one in earshot, no one who even knows we're here.

'This is all your fault, Bea,' he says coolly. His voice is hard, his eyes blank and unseeing. His whole face is contorted, ugly with a glimpse of the monster that lives inside. I've seen that look before, that day on the terrace when he found out I'd met up with Callum. Flickers of the evil that lies behind his charming façade – I was too blind to notice.

'Ben, I'm Abi. Not Bea. This is Bea – you have to let me help her.'

'You thought you could control me,' he continues, seemingly not hearing my voice. 'You thought you could tell me what to do – the pair of you. The fucking pair of you! But you were the worst, Bea. You thought you could take it all away, the money, the house, with your veiled threats when I wouldn't do as you wanted. Well, I won't let you. I won't fucking let you,' he hisses. And I know that he's looking at me, but he's seeing Beatrice.

He's lost it, he can't see me – or rather, he only sees Bea, even when he's looking at me – and suddenly everything becomes frighteningly clear. He's going to kill me.

338

I want to rage, to fight, to save myself and Bea, but I'm also overcome with a sense of calm, because, at last, I'm going to be with Lucy. It's inevitable somehow that her death would be so closely followed by my own. Like our births. And then I think of my poor parents. They've already lost one child. They can't lose another.

'Ben, please . . .' I try. There is no point screaming. My voice will be lost in the wind and rain. 'Please,' I try again. I need to make him see reason. He can't do this. Confusion and doubt flit across his face and I can feel his hesitation. 'I'm Abi. I came back . . .' My voice trembles. I'm too terrified even to cry. 'Please . . .'

'Shut up, shut up,' he mutters, shaking his head. And then he lunges towards me, grabbing my wrists, his fingers digging into my scars as he drags me away from Beatrice, so that my knees scrape against the ground. He pulls me to my feet. 'You're a bitch too,' he says, and he slaps me across the face, hard. I can taste blood. I'm too shocked to react, my cheek is throbbing. 'You must think I'm stupid, all that crap about wanting to talk.' His hands are around my throat now, his fingers squeezing my windpipe and I know that I'm not going to be able to get out of this. I am going to die here tonight.

Lucy, help me. Please help me. I don't know what to do. Dark spots swim before my eyes, I'm light-headed.

Kick him in the balls. I can hear her voice in my ear, sharp, insistent. *Kick him in the fucking balls, Abi.* I do as she says. I lift my knee and ram it hard into his groin. He grunts, and I do it again, following the knee with a

339

stamp to his right foot. It works, he stumbles backwards into his bedroom and then I see it, the stone Egyptian cat he uses for a doorstop. I bend over and pick it up and as he comes at me again, his face red with fury, I swing it upwards with all my might, aiming for the side of his head. Because of his height I ram it into his shoulder instead, but it's enough to throw him off balance, causing him to fall back against the French doors, his head snapping against the glass with a crack. His eyes widen in shock before he sinks to the floor, a shatter of glass falling around him. I can see the glisten of blood by his ear.

I stand over him, my heart hammering, the stone cat poised in my hand. But he doesn't move, his eyes are closed. Have I killed him and if so how would I explain all this to the police? I drop the Egyptian cat and bend over Beatrice, shaking her again, this time with more force. She's stirring, moaning.

'Get up!' I whisper with a sob in my throat, not wanting to alert Ben if he is still alive. 'Come on, please, Bea, please get up!'

She groans and touches her head where her hair is matted with blood. 'I can't,' she gasps. 'I can't.'

'Come on, before he wakes up,' I urge, still whispering. 'We need to get out of here, please, Bea . . .' I try to suppress my panic, knowing I have to keep my head if we're to have any chance of getting out alive.

With all my strength I manage to pull her to her feet, but she's groggy, dazed, and slumps heavily against me. Ben moans, his eyes flickering behind their lids. I haven't killed him, I've only succeeded in stunning him, we need to hurry. We need to get out of here. Beatrice tries to move her feet and I put my arm under her armpit and half drag, half carry her over the threshold, out of his bedroom.

Come on, Bea. Come on!

We are nearly through the door when I feel a scratch of fingernails on the back of my calf and then the horror of his hand closing around my ankle. I turn to see him stretched out across the floor towards me, hunger and madness in his eyes.

'Get off me,' I scream, trying to pull away, but his grip is firm, his teeth clenched with concentration as he reaches the other hand towards me as well. I'm trying to keep hold of Beatrice and trying to shake him off at the same time. I'm frantic, desperate, annoyed with myself for dropping that stone cat. I kick backwards, the heel of my trainer striking his nose. He releases my ankle. 'You fucking bitch,' he screams, holding his nose, which is spurting with blood.

'Quick!' I tumble through the door with Bea, who looks white with fear. 'Run!'

Still gripping each other, we hobble as quickly as we can down the first flight of stairs. My heart is beating so fast it's as though it's going to explode out of my chest. As we round the next staircase, I see him bending over the banister above.

'Abi, Bea, I'm sorry,' he calls. 'Come back.' He has blood on the collar of his polo shirt and smeared under his nose, his hair is standing on end and he has a dark sweat patch under each arm. He looks deranged.

In my eagerness to get away from him we nearly fall down the last few remaining steps. I grab my phone from the hall table where Ben put it earlier, ready to call the police. My hands are trembling so much I can hardly unlock the door and I'm still wrestling with the mortice lock as Ben begins his descent.

'Wait!' he yells.

The fucking lock won't work. I can't get out. Ben's getting closer, Beatrice is sagging against me and we're stuck. He's going to catch up with us, and this time I know he won't let us get away.

'Come on!' I scream at her. 'Stand up. Help me.' I can see it takes a lot of effort for her to pull the lock back while I turn the key and between us we manage to wrestle the door open.

'You can't go,' cries Ben, jumping down the last four steps. He's nearly reached us.

'Leave us alone,' I scream.

He makes another lunge towards us, managing to grab Beatrice and pulling her to him, stretching her out between us like a tug of war. 'Please . . .' he says into her hair. 'I'm so sorry. You can't go, Bea. I need you. Daisy. My Daisy.'

We're nearly free, and I can't leave Beatrice with him. She's sagging towards him as though she's a rag doll, or a sunflower touched by the first rays of the day.

He touches the side of her head where the gash is and I'm amazed to see tears in his eyes. It's as if the evil spirit that made him do those awful things upstairs has left him, giving us the Ben we thought we knew and loved. But as I watch him caress her, apologizing and kissing her head, I wonder if it's another piece of manipulation. Another way of getting what he wants.

'I'm so sorry, Daisy. I'm so sorry that I hurt you.'

I can see her resolve weakening, her grip on my wrist loosening. *What's the matter with you?* I want to scream at her. *He tried to kill you, for fuck's sake.* My fingers are hovering over 999.

But she straightens up, away from him, the sunflower reaching towards the sky.

'You need to be on your own,' she says to him gently. She lets go of my hand but only to reach up and touch his face tenderly. She loves him. She truly loves him. 'I know you didn't mean it. I know you're under a lot of stress. But too much has happened.'

His face contorts, the evil spirit entering his body again, and he grabs her upper arm. 'You can't leave . . .' He's interrupted by the creak of a gate two doors down and a stocky man in his late forties, walking his greyhound, strides past. He raises his hand in greeting when he sees us, unaware of what's going on. But his presence is enough to distract Ben and he releases his grip on Beatrice. She slumps against me and I take the opportunity to drag her out of the front door, slamming it in Ben's face, knowing he won't come after us. Not now.

It's over.

Chapter Thirty-Five

We stand on the pavement, the rain beating down on our heads, both breathless and shaking. My arm is still linked through hers. 'Should we take you to the hospital? Get your head looked at?'

'I'm fine, Abi,' says Beatrice wearily.

Her eyes keep darting to the royal blue front door of the house. Is he going to come after us again? With a gasp of fear I start pulling her down the street, away from the house, and with trembling fingers I call my dad and ask him to come and get us.

'He'll be here in five minutes,' I say, hanging up. She's still staring towards the door. 'He won't come after us . . .' I try to make my voice confident, assured.

'I know,' she sighs. 'I know he won't, Abi, it's not that. It's . . . he's there on his own. I can't just leave him. He's in such a state. What if he does something stupid . . . what if he tries to harm himself?'

I stare at her incredulously. She's shivering in her little tea-dress, her hair is matted with blood and she's soaked through, and all she can think about is her psycho of a brother.

'He nearly killed you!' I choke the words out as if his hands are still clasped around my throat.

'He wouldn't have killed me,' she says calmly. 'He loves me.'

'Look at your neck, Beatrice. He was going to kill you. He smacked you across the head. You have a wound. How can you even say all that? Don't you want to press charges?' At this suggestion, she shakes her head, tears springing to her eyes.

'He's my brother, my twin.'

There is no arguing with her, I need to get her away from this house. I tug on her arm gently. 'Please, Bea. Come home with me. My parents have said you can stay as long as you want.'

Reluctantly she allows me to guide her towards the end of the street.

Dad leaves us alone in the kitchen with a worried, sideways glance. Mum fusses around Beatrice, wrapping her up in a huge fluffy dressing gown, as if she's a child. She accepts my mum's kindness, still in shock and I can tell that she's numb, that this evening's events are still sinking in.

'I've made up the spare room for you,' says Mum, placing a steaming mug of tea in front of Beatrice where she sits at the small round table. She mouths to me over Beatrice's head that they are off to bed to give us some space. I smile at her gratefully. I'm too worried about leaving Beatrice on her own to go and get changed into a pair of spare pyjamas, so instead I sling one of Mum's cardigans over my wet dress. Luckily, the house, as usual, is as warm as the tropics.

I take Beatrice's hand in mine. It is cold and dry. 'Bea, please drink some tea. You need something hot and sweet for the shock.' Her face is pale, her neck pink and raw from where his hands have been.

She turns her red-rimmed eyes to me. 'He wouldn't have killed me, you do know that, don't you? He was angry, confused. It's all been so stressful for him, coming to terms with what we've done.'

'Bea,' I say gently. 'His brother Paul has told me everything. I know about your past, about the two of you. I thought Luke was the one who broke your heart at university, but it wasn't him, was it? It was Ben.'

She nods slowly and takes a sip of her tea. 'It was stupid of me, letting him move into my house. But I was so happy when he got back in touch, asking to meet. Nearly eight years had passed since . . . since we parted and I thought I was ready to have him back in my life, as a brother. After we met up a few times I asked him to move in. I'd recently bought my house in Bear Flat and I suppose I thought it was a way for us to be together – not as husband and wife, like I thought, hoped, when we first met, but as the twins that we are.'

'Oh, Beatrice.' I can't imagine the shock, the horror, the disgust, at finding out the man you think is your soul mate, the one you've chosen to spend the rest of your life with, is not only your brother, but your twin.

'I'm sorry I accused you of stealing my bracelet,' she says. 'And I wanted to tell you about me and Ben so many times.'

'I'm sorry too. For everything.' I touch the necklace at my throat, remembering how I felt when she gave it to me that day at the Open Studio, how happy I was to have something that Beatrice had made with her own talented hands. 'But I need to be honest: I took your yellow earring. It was silly of me, I felt compelled to take it, not that it's any excuse. I wanted something . . .' I hesitate, finding it hard to explain myself. 'I wanted something of yours.' I cringe at the desperation in my voice. Maybe that was why I was so attracted to Ben. 'But it was Ben who took the sapphire bracelet and my letters, to keep us at loggerheads. I found them in the boot of his car, the day I left.'

'I guessed that, later,' she says. She's still shivering. 'Ben was terrified I was going to tell you about our past. He wanted to keep you and me apart, wanted to cause trouble between us so that I wouldn't feel guilty about keeping our secret from you. I think he thought if we became too close I would find it hard to continue lying to you, and if I told you the truth his greatest fear would become a reality. He would lose you, and his right to a normal life.' She smiles sadly. 'Thank you for being honest about the earring.'

'While we're being honest with each other, can I ask you something?' She nods, still cupping her hot drink, the sleeves of her dressing gown pulled over her hands. 'Was it you I saw on the Isle of Wight that day?'

She looks shamefaced. 'I honestly didn't know at the time that you were there too. Ben asked if I fancied a trip to the seaside and I was so pleased that he wanted to spend some time with me, so pathetically grateful, that I said yes.'

'You mean he followed me to Cowes?' My mind swims at the thought.

She nods, cradling her mug. 'It was only when I saw you on the beach that it became obvious what was going on. Ben had gone to get an ice cream.'

I stare at her, perplexed. 'Didn't you think it was strange? That he wanted to follow me?'

'When I confronted him about it he said he was worried about you. That you'd been acting crazy – which at the time I thought you had – and he wanted to make sure you were okay. I believed him, I thought he was being a caring boyfriend.'

'Did he follow me to Patricia Lipton's house? Did he see me meet up with Callum?'

She frowns, shaking her head. 'No, I'm not sure how he found out about Callum.'

I'm silent for a moment, shocked at the lengths Ben went to. 'Things would have been okay, if I hadn't got involved with Ben,' I say with a sniff.

A tear slides down her face. 'I was jealous of you,' she admits. 'After he and I got back in touch, you were the first girl that he fell for. I know that I can't have Ben in that way, but honestly . . . those feelings that I had for him at university haven't completely gone away.' I try to hide my discomfort. 'For him it's very different. He sees me purely as a sister now.' Her lips wobble as she tries to force a smile.

I reach across the table to squeeze her hand but remembering what I found out about them earlier my guts twist, and I take my hand away again and place it back in my lap.

'I don't think he does,' I admit. 'Don't you see, Bea? The resemblance between us? He chose me because I look like you, because somewhere deep down he is still attracted to you. And the ridiculous thing is that I was attracted to you because you resemble Lucy. It's all so fucked up.'

She makes a choking sound that might be a laugh. 'I realized from the moment I saw your photo in the newspaper how alike we looked.' So she had known about me before we met. I hadn't imagined the recognition in her eyes. 'But I didn't think any more about it,' she continues. 'I assumed Ben had moved on, that he didn't see me in that way any more . . .'

Claire Douglas

Slowly she begins to tell me about growing up in Edinburgh as the only child of the affluent devoutly Catholic McDows, Annabel and Edward. They told her she was adopted when she was very young and she knew that her biological parents had died in a car accident when she was a baby. The only information she had about them was their names, Helen and William Price, and that one photograph that the McDows let her keep, the one that now sits on the mantelpiece in her living room.

'My birth parents called me Beatrice Daisy Price, but the McDows dropped the Beatrice. They thought Daisy McDow sounded better. I changed it back to Beatrice Price when I found out about Ben.'

Her adoptive parents never told her she had a twin brother. In those days the authorities found it hard to place siblings together, so separated them as babies, and Ben was adopted by Morag and Eric Jones in Glasgow. They'd decided to keep his Christian name.

Beatrice couldn't wait to leave Scotland and go to university in England. She liked the idea of Exeter, as it was near the coast, and chose to take a degree in law, like her adopted father. There she met Luke; he was exactly her type – blond, blue-eyed and tall – and they had fun together for a while, but at the end of the first year, as they were breaking up for the holidays and talking about maybe going travelling during the summer, he finished with her, saying he wasn't ready for anything serious. She was disappointed but not devastated, deciding

350

to stay around Exeter with one of her friends. It was only a week later that she met Ben for the first time in a pub. He was on her campus, doing a BSc in Computer Studies, but their paths had never crossed before. 'As soon as I saw him, it hit me,' she says softly with tears in her eyes. 'It was mutual attraction at first sight.'

Their affair was intense, immediate. I glance at my hands as she tells me this bit; the thought of them being in love, having sex, is still hard to hear. It turns my stomach to know they were lovers.

They were inseparable that summer, deciding to move in together once the new term began. 'I knew he was my soul mate, he said I was his. Neither of us had ever felt that way before. We had so much in common, our birth-days were on the same day and when he told me he was adopted too, I couldn't believe it. For once I had met someone who truly understood me.'

'How long were you together?'

She swallows, a faraway look in her eye. 'Three months.'

It was when her parents came to visit, at the start of the new term in October, that Beatrice found out the truth. She was so excited at the thought of Ben meeting her mum and dad that as soon as their elegant feet stepped out of their Bentley she thrust her new boyfriend at them.

'Mum looked horrified when she saw him,' she recalls. 'I know now that she was seeing what we had failed to – our obvious likeness; our heart-shaped faces, upturned freckled noses and full mouths. And she knew that I had been separated from my twin brother, but had never shared this with me because she didn't want me to be upset by it. She had her suspicions but it was the photograph that did it. I had asked her to bring it with her, you see. I wanted to show Ben. He told me his parents had also died when he was a baby and that he had a photograph that he kept in a box in his wardrobe at home in Glasgow. I should have guessed, the information we both had was identical, although I knew my parents' real names when he didn't. Maybe I didn't want to see the signs.'

'Ben recognized the photograph?'

'Straight away. It was the one he had at home. After that Mum had to tell me what she knew, about the twin brother who I had been separated from as a baby.' She pales, remembering. 'Abi, it was horrific. Ben and I were stunned, of course, then disgusted, but in spite of all that we still loved each other. You can't switch those feelings off.

'My parents were terrified we would stay together, even though we knew the truth. I think Mum could tell that I wasn't ready to give Ben up that easily. There was this huge row, and my parents told me I had to leave university that very day. Ben was crying, then he was furious, ranting at them, calling them liars, saying they were trying to keep us apart.'

After everything that's happened tonight, I can imagine Ben's rage.

Beatrice gulps, wipes her eyes and continues: 'Anyway, my parents literally dragged me to the car. I don't think they knew what to do, they were repulsed by the whole thing. Ben told me afterwards that he went home and told Morag everything, and she confirmed what we already knew. He finally saw that my parents weren't lying, and stayed away from me, growing more and more disgusted at what we had done. Don't get me wrong, I was disgusted too. But I found it hard to get over him, we had such a connection. So I went travelling, tried to get on with my life. I knew I couldn't have him. How could I? And I was doing okay, I got a job working in a jeweller's, my dad died leaving me a trust fund, so I moved to Bath. Bought the house, began doing it up, met Eva who said she would clean for me . . . I got on with things. Until I got a letter out of the blue, about six years ago, from Ben. And my life turned upside down again,' she sighs, remembering. 'I was in a right state, I didn't know what to do. His letter had unearthed all the old feelings I thought I'd buried. Anyway, we met up for a coffee, got on well. He wanted us to be together again, this time as brother and sister. As twins. I wanted that too, you have to believe me, Abi. I never thought I'd fall in love with him again . . .' She lets out a sob. 'I'm so sorry . . .'

'Oh, Beatrice.' We sit in silence; there is nothing else to say.

I remember Paul's words, how Ben is driven by money. How Paul had seen Ben reading the obituary for Beatrice's adopted father. He knew how rich her dad was. He knew that he would have left her a lot of money. Was that the real reason he got back in touch? It sounds as though he had a different upbringing to Beatrice. Now he has the finer things in life and that's something he would hate to relinquish. But I can't bring myself to voice my suspicions to Beatrice; she wants to believe that he loves her, that they have a strong twin bond.

She closes her eyes. 'Then you came along, Abi. And it all went wrong.' When she opens her eyes again they are full of tears.

'Does anyone else know? Pam? Cass?'

She shakes her head. 'I've never told anyone. I was too ashamed. Ben never wanted to talk about it either,' she says. 'He was repulsed by what happened between us at uni. I knew he had a temper, I knew he could lie about things, even be manipulative at times. But what he's done, how he hurt me . . . and you . . .' She groans, a tear trickling down her cheek.

I push back my chair and go over to her. She falls into my arms and I hold her as her body convulses with sobs.

I wake up early the next morning after a restless few hours' sleep full of nightmares where Ben is chasing us. I grab the quilt around my body and pad into the spare bedroom, hoping to see Beatrice sound asleep, but the bed is neatly made and the room is empty. It's as if she's never been here.

She's gone back to him.

All this time I thought she was controlling him, but I

was wrong. He was the one pulling the strings in their relationship. She will never leave him.

Oh, Beatrice.

The sun is trying to shine, but is half-submerged behind a black cloud. The pavements smell fresh, washed, after last night's storm. I stand on the doorstep and ring the old-fashioned brass doorbell. Dad is sitting in the car, watching the house as though he's a policeman on stakeout. I've not admitted to him what took place here last night; Dad would be the first one to contact the authorities if he knew. I've only told him I need to get my stuff because I'm moving out. I'm grateful for Dad's reassuring presence, but my heart pounds against my ribcage as I wait, terrified that Ben will answer. I never want to set eyes on him again.

I'm relieved when it's Beatrice who pokes her head around the door, looking shamefaced. She's pale but beautiful in one of her many tea-dresses. She opens the door wider when she realizes that it's me.

'Bea, I can't believe you've gone back to him,' I hiss. I want to cry, knowing that she's forgiven him, and she'll go on forgiving him. For ever.

She bites her lip and I can see that she's fighting back tears. 'He's sorry, Abi. He wants to apologize.' From behind her I can see Ben hovering in the hallway and my palms begin to sweat. He comes over to us, wrapping his arm around Beatrice's waist.

His hair is washed, neatly combed and he's had a

shave. He smiles and it's like looking at a different person to the one who terrorized us last night.

'Please come in, Abi. Ben won't hurt you.'

'As if I can believe that,' I snap. 'Have you forgotten yesterday, Bea?' Despite my bravado my legs are trembling and I don't move from the doorstep. I don't look at Ben.

Ben leans forward over Bea's shoulder. 'Abi, please, I'm so sorry. I don't know what came over me yesterday. I didn't mean to hurt you. I wouldn't have hurt you, you have to believe that. You have to . . .'

I look at him. He's all chastised smiles and puppy-dog eyes. But I can see through his act now. I've glimpsed the monster underneath.

'Save it,' I say, holding up my hand. 'I'm not interested. I only came here to check that Bea is okay, and to get my things. My dad is sitting over there,' I turn and point to my dad's waiting car, purring by the side of the road. 'You wouldn't want to mess with my dad. He was in the army years ago.'

Ben hangs his head, muttering of course he understands, that he wouldn't dream of hurting me, that he wants my forgiveness and understanding for last night.

'I can never forgive myself. What I did to Bea . . . and you . . .'

'The truth of it is, you want Bea, but you can't have her, so you chose me instead. Her carbon copy.' It's all I can do to get the words out; I'm trying to swallow the hurt I still feel at being lied to, manipulated, used.

He runs his hand through his thick hair. 'That's not

true,' he says, but he doesn't sound convincing. 'I did love you, Abi.'

I roll my eyes. 'You're a liar, Ben. If you loved me, why did you do the things you did?'

'I didn't mean to hurt you, or Beatrice,' he says. 'I don't know what came over me. I am sorry, Abi. I know you don't believe me, but I am.'

He's right, I don't believe him. I can't believe a word that comes out of his twisted, lying, manipulative mouth.

'I'm assuming you wrote the Facebook messages? Planted the photograph that Cass took innocently, and then scratched my face off? The flowers? I must say, it was clever of you to pretend you rang the florist and to say that they described me. You knew I'd jump to conclusions and accuse Beatrice.'

'I had to make sure you never found out about me and Bea,' he says. 'I did it all because I loved you, Abi.'

As I watch Ben, languishing in the doorway, with his arm around his sister, wearing his crisp Armani shirt and J Brand jeans, I know that there is more to it. He gets a kick out of playing with people, scaring them, messing with their heads.

'I suppose it's obvious,' I say. 'You being so good with computers. What did you do, Ben? Hack into her account?' I don't wait for an answer. 'And Callum? How did you know I met up with him?'

'I looked on your phone,' he says. 'Saw a message you sent to Nia. What's the point of going over it all now, Abi? Huh? What's done is done.'

I have a sudden urge to ram his head into the wall. 'What kind of person are you, Ben?'

He stares at me, his face darkening and I'm worried that I've gone too far

Beatrice rubs his arm. 'Abi,' she says. 'Ben is really sorry. He's been under a lot of stress . . .'

I roll my eyes, my stomach curdling at the thought of them together. 'You might have forgiven him, Bea. But I can't.'

He looks at me, all the warmth gone from his eyes. 'I can't make you forgive me, Abi. But I am sorry. For what it's worth.'

Which isn't much, I want to say. But I don't. With one last glance in my direction, Ben retreats into the hallway and I see him round the stairs into the basement kitchen. I know I'll never see him again.

'Your things are here, Abi,' says Beatrice in a small voice. I see a pile of boxes stacked by the radiator and imagine Beatrice and Ben clearing out my room, getting rid of all evidence that I ever lived here.

Beatrice helps me carry the boxes to the car. Dad jumps out when he sees us approaching. 'Everything all right?' he says to me. I smile weakly and nod, handing him a box which he puts in the boot.

I hover by the passenger door after we've loaded all the boxes. I'm concerned for her. 'Are you going to be okay, Bea?'

'Of course.' She smiles brightly and embraces me, I can smell the apple shampoo of her hair, the Parma Violet washing powder on her dress. 'Thanks for everything you did last night. I'll never forget it,' she says quietly.

Dad, realizing this is girl talk, folds himself back into the driver's seat.

'Chuck him out,' I urge. 'You don't need him, Bea.'

'You know that I do,' she says as she pulls away from me. 'Please promise me one thing, Abi. Please don't tell anyone about us.'

I look at my trainer-clad feet. 'Nia knows.'

'Nobody else?'

'I won't tell anyone else. I promise.' I lift my head to look at her. 'But I just don't understand why you're doing this.'

'I think you do,' she adds, her eyes bright. 'He's my twin, he's the other half of me, Abi. And he needs help. You know that, right? I want to help him get better.'

She turns to go, but I grab her arm. 'Beatrice, there's one thing I need to tell you. I haven't been totally honest with you. I . . . I was jealous too. Of your relationship. I tried to stir trouble a few times, I made out to Ben that you were hiding my antidepressants . . . I wanted him to . . . I don't know . . . defend me, believe me.'

'Shh, Abi. I understand.' She stands there in her leopard-print pumps, the soft cotton of her dress brushing her knees and with the sun casting its weak light over her face, the highlights in her fair hair. I draw a breath at the similarity to Lucy. It's as though I'm losing her all over again.

'Take care, Bea,' I sniff.

'You too, Abi,' she says sadly. 'You too.'

She bends down to scoop up her fat ginger cat, then turns away from me and walks back into the house.

Chapter Thirty-Six

I've been living in London for six months now and with every day that passes I become a little stronger, a little more hopeful about the future. Miranda offered me my old job back on the features desk and Nia suggested that we rent a bigger flat together in Muswell Hill. Neither of us says it, of course, but each telepathically agrees that staying north of the river is less painful somehow; not so many memories of our old way of life.

Living with Nia is gloriously uncomplicated after everything.

I've only heard from Bea once. A month ago she emailed me to tell me she has sold the town house in Bath and that she and Ben have moved away, somewhere nobody knows them. She never gave a forwarding address. Reading between the lines, I suspect they've renewed their relationship and are living as a couple. Nothing would surprise me any more.

I still see Lucy in the most unexpected places. Sometimes she's in front of me on the bus, the same swishy blonde bob and long, elegant neck, until she turns around and it is as if she's wearing a mask, some other person's face is superimposed in place of hers. Other times she's at a party that Nia and I are attending, or eating popcorn in the row in front of us at the cinema. Last week I thought I saw her behind the till in Sainsbury's, except she was young – too young. Lucy in her teenage years.

And each time I see her I make sure I walk in the opposite direction. Because she's not Lucy. I know that now. As I know how dangerous my mind can be, how little I can trust my own judgement. After all, I got it so wrong with Bea.

Today, a sunny breezy Tuesday in early March, I'm meandering through Hyde Park in my lunch hour, killing time while waiting to interview some up-and-coming actor at the Ritz. I'm wearing the tea-dress that I bought last year in the vintage shop in Bath, with a long grey cardigan. I'm feeling happy, confident, when I see her. She's sitting on a wooden bench reading a book, a Burberry mac is wrapped around her slim body, her legs, encased in black skinny jeans, are crossed at the knee. She has wire-framed glasses pushed back on to her blonde hair, and she frowns in concentration, her eyes flicking back and forth across the page. Despite the promises I've made to myself, I can't help but stare at her wistfully, imagining sitting next to her, and striking up a conversation. Instead I hoist my bag firmly on to my shoulder and go to walk past her.

As if aware that I'm watching her, she lifts her head and fixes her big green eyes on me, and my heart stutters in my chest as if I've been punched. She resembles Lucy more than anyone I've ever seen, apart from myself; more than Beatrice, more than Alicia. She smiles such a warm inviting smile that it stops me in my tracks, my resolve weakening.

'Hi,' I say shyly, standing before her. 'Can I join you?'

She places the book she's reading face down on her lap. 'Of course.' She has an accent. Possibly Scandinavian. If she's alone in this country she might need a friend. It gives me a little thrill.

'I'm Ingrid,' she says, extending a delicate hand with a playful giggle. Her laugh is high and tinkly, it's just like Lucy's. And I'm sold.

I take her hand and perch next to her, so close that I can smell the coconut scent of her hair and I know that I've finally found her. She's the one. I took my eye off the ball before, I allowed myself to become distracted. But not this time. This time everything will work out. I'll make sure of it.

'I'm Abi,' I say, pulling the tea-dress firmly over my knees. 'But you can call me Bee.'

Acknowledgements

I would like to thank the following people for making this book possible:

To HarperCollins and *Marie Claire* magazine for holding the debut novel competition; the fantastic team at Harper, in particular my editors Martha Ashby and Kimberley Young for their great advice, guidance and enthusiasm; to my wonderful agent, Juliet at The Agency Group (I feel incredibly lucky to be on Team Mushens!); to my talented writer friend, Fiona Mitchell, for encouraging me to enter the competition; to my mother, Linda, father, Ken, step parents, Laura and John, brother, David, and sister, Sam, for all their unwavering support throughout the years; to my two beautiful children, Claudia and Isaac (who won't be allowed to read this book for a long, long time) and last, but definitely not least, I'd like to thank my lovely husband, Ty, for his patience, understanding and belief in me (and for being a comma guru!).

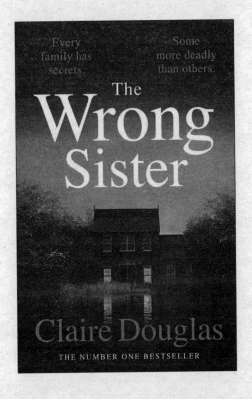